By L. Rockwood

Defiant Revival

Published by DREAMSPINNER PRESS
www.dreamspinnerpress.com

Defiant
REVIVAL

L. ROCKWOOD

Published by

DREAMSPINNER PRESS

5032 Capital Circle SW, Suite 2, PMB# 279, Tallahassee, FL 32305-7886 USA
www.dreamspinnerpress.com

Defiant Revival
© 2016 L. Rockwood.

Cover Art
© 2016 AngstyG.
www.angstyg.com
Cover content is for illustrative purposes only and any person depicted on the cover is a model.

ISBN: 978-1-63477-849-7
Digital ISBN: 978-1-63477-850-3
Library of Congress Control Number: 2016913756
First Edition October 2016
v. 1.0

Printed in the United States of America
∞
This paper meets the requirements of
ANSI/NISO Z39.48-1992 (Permanence of Paper).

For Rae, my favorite person.
Without you this novel would be
nothing but adverbs and dick jokes.

CHAPTER 1

May 2nd, 989

IT WAS mercilessly hot the day they met, as it had been every day for months. I was surprised to hear that Billiam actually saw a puffy cloud float by. In these years of endless war and seasonless days, they had evolved into a sign of good luck. Like luck, they were fleeting, rare, and ultimately disappointing. The vegetation had been withered from the drought and continually burnt by attack. It seemed no one alerted the air to all the dryness beneath it, for the sticky humidity hung all about. Was the moisture of the earth simply waiting above it until the earth was once again a suitable place to reside? Or was it the corpses piling in the valley that required the company of thick, stinking air? Whatever the reason was, it had been like that.

The days of slimy sweat and dry throats had been many, and the travelers outside the city walls grew ever fewer. There was nothing different about the day Billiam exited the gates of city Drummond from the hundreds of days before nor the seven suffocating months to follow. What I found surprising was that he had never done anything without style that I could recall. In this vein, why did he start the future on such a bland and thoughtless afternoon?

I suppose I can forgive him, as there were extenuating circumstances and little to no variety in the weather. This was simply the first available day that he thought he knew what he was doing enough to venture out. Three days later, there actually was a short rain, and all the carts leaving got stuck in the muck and blood outside the gates. That would have made for a far more interesting exit if you ask me. Regardless, on this completely ordinary day, Billiam left the walls of Drummond and had a meeting that changed the entire world. If you are going to do something to affect so many others, urgency can be more important than an entertaining story.

The city of Drummond was the heart in the enveloping rib cages of the Casperland peninsula. The lungs would be the large forests surrounding the shores of the Casperland nation. The city of Casper lived at the peninsula's tail, and obviously was intended to be the more successful of the brother cities, given the nation's name and such. A few villages sat along the western shore. Nothing was stupid enough to get beaten across the rocks of the east. Three towns and a village or five hung around the middle valleys of Casperland, between the competing cities. With other lands becoming a much larger part of the nation's economy, Drummond's accessible location and secure, canyon port eventually brought about its growth into the capital it is known as today. This geography lesson is tedious but necessary to show there was something to Casperland outside of Drummond. It shows there was life and community and opportunity outside those gates in the past.

Access past Drummond grew increasingly exclusive and monitored following the devastating bombing of Casper by the fearsome nation of Knox, over a decade prior. All travel outside of the city had become completely marginalized into government transportation of goods to the two remaining villages and one fishing hamlet allowed to live on in Casperland.

Before things were made this stringent, merchants could make pilgrimages, and some lucky or stupid families could try to visit loved ones. By the time Billiam finally walked out, however, all exits and entrances of Drummond had to be governmentally approved and were still at the traveler's own risk. In order for citizens to leave, they could try to get an expatrias permit, the processing of which never took less than six months, not that I've ever heard of any being approved. Taking one of the transport jobs could get you out of the city, but with no privacy as your guards and cohorts would monitor you the whole time.

The best way, and the way dear Billiam opted for, was through the Westend sewer. Cardinal Aldrious hadn't bothered to have people investigate or monitor any of the sewer systems, as he would never demean himself to think of wading through excrement. Due to this pretense, the guards were not aware that the sewer tunnel had a dry path to an overflow, which emptied into a small lagoon. This runoff was a safe, short distance from the gates, with no wading through human waste necessary, and a relatively easy exit for those of us who knew about it.

It was nearly midday when the subterranean section of Billiam's journey met its end. At last, he was able to remove the itchy burlap prison that had entrapped his visage the last hour. In order to make sure anyone else who might be taking a stroll through the sewers could not identify him, he had taken the guise of an anonymous peasant. The dirty shawl bent the shape of his bowler hat slightly, but nothing could distort the noble features and brilliant mustache underneath.

Billiam was a long wisp of a man, his lankiness making his strength deceptive. He was a well-trained swordsman and archer as well as an immaculate tailor. His thin face was brought to a perfect end with a strong goateed jaw. Unlike what I presume other heroes to think, he saw no value in saving the world if he couldn't look good while doing it. After smoothing his tailcoat, straightening his skinny black tie, and sneaking a quick peer in the reflection of a puddle nearby, his adventure was able to continue.

He had only a quarter hour jaunt through the wastes left until he reached his destination—Drummond's mass grave, bitterly referred to as Peace Valley. The rotting corpses—citizens and foreigners, criminals and the hopelessly ill, enemies to the crown both real and imagined—these were the cost of the "peace" granted us by the cardinal. The beastly creatures controlled by Cardinal Aldrious and his sect, the Mortanions, had to be sustained somehow. The sacrifice of one's corpse served as a royal pardon.

Said creatures were wicked winged beasts known only as reapers. They were generally five feet long with double that for a wingspan; rotten lizards with bodies covered in sparkling, black scales and dusty feathers smothering their appendages. Their gaping mouths housed at least three rows of crimson teeth. It is unknown whether their teeth actually are red or are perpetually stained with human blood; however, it is unlikely anyone who finds out would live to tell us. Their handlers, low-ranking Mortanion brothers referred to as goons, were the only people who regularly patrolled the wastes. They were few but could summon reapers to attack when they saw a trespasser. The beasts would lunge at travelers on their own, but a simple umbrella with a painted red eye was enough to deter them. Thus the purpose of the goons was to summon an attack on said umbrellas.

Billiam's parasol was made of a sheet of black silk with a piece of fine red ribbon stitched in around the top and clutched tightly in his left hand. As he approached the cliffs, the odor of sun-dried flesh from the valley finally reached his nose. Pulling his handkerchief out of his pocket, he began to scan the valley of corpses. It took only moments for him to spy his target.

A huge black and ratty umbrella poked out from the shade of the cliff on which he stood, just a few paces to the right. An eye was scrawled in what was likely blood, though it was an oxidized brown barely resembling the prior crimson. The pole jutted out from a large deteriorating baby carriage fitted with the hairy legs of a man on either side. The frame of a spritely, wild-looking woman could be seen crawling and rummaging through the bodies next to the carriage's feet.

This creature was, without a doubt, the famous enchantress Chammerline DuBois the XII, who since her exile had adopted her childhood nickname, Shemmy. This eccentric master of a dying craft was the only hope for his kingdom, the only hope for his heart, and happened to be weighing two obese forearms in either hand.

He needed to implore her; she needed to know her importance. He feared her wildness but hoped reason could still be won, and thus he beckoned to her, "Hello to you, my lovely girl!"

"What you sayin'?" A raspy but high-pitched voice, heavily accented by the slang of the slums, rang up to him.

"I said, a hearty hello to you, my lovely girl!" Although he was shaken by the importance of this interaction, he knew he could still be the most charming man she'd ever meet. She could not resist nor detest him, could she?

"I assure you, mate, I ain't lovely, and I haven't a need for no hullos," she yelled up with a dismissive wave, never turning her face to him.

Billiam sensed too much charm was used, dialed it back, and proceeded instead with his honest approach. "Oh don't worry, miss, I could give a damn whether you are lovely or not; I was simply trying to be pleasant. I am a dandy and shan't be getting excitement from you either way."

Billiam could make out a beet-red blush that appeared all across her face in an instant, forcing her wild eyes to make contact with his at last. She hurriedly gasped out, "Shush yer mouf! That is not a fing you want goons hearin', and I dun need the damn attention." It was meant to sound angry and dismissive, but they both heard only excitement.

He began to realize the secret he used to gain her trust by showing vulnerability, was actually something she was quite keen on. The practice of homosexuality had become formally outlawed following the discovery of the Promise of Aegis and the kingdom's conversion to the orthodox MortiAegis religion forty years ago. Although it was never an entirely accepted way of life, there were never laws against it prior. Dandy was a common term for homosexual men, and there were also female fans of their shows of affection. Cabarets of such acts could be sought out in certain neighborhoods before Drummond's conversion. The current rouge upon Shemmy's face provided Billiam with assurance he would definitely get through to her.

Relaxed and now confident in his approach, he calmly replied, "You are quite right, but now you shouldn't fear talking to me, as we are both criminals in the eyes of the crown. Neither of us are about to cry to the goons, are we, Shemmy?"

"Aye, so yer a fan, Mr. Dandy? I won't bother arguin' no innocence, then. Get to the point, eh?"

"I was hoping to employ you, if you are so inclined. Should we, perhaps, go somewhere a bit less vulnerable before we get to the particulars?" He smiled down at her and noticed the gleam of her grin back up at him beneath her knotted mess of hair.

"I s'pose yer right, Mr. Dandy." She had finally decided on the plump appendage she clutched in her left hand and set it in her legged carriage, tossing the reject down, back to the grave. "Come along now, Gam," she instructed while facing her carriage, before turning to Billiam and singing up with a wicked smile, "let's go back to my place, dear." She swayed her arm in an inviting motion, beckoning her visitor down.

"Oh wonderful, and you can call me Billiam. Also… must I really go down there? Is there not any other way around?" The smell of rotting flesh was enough to permanently scar his psyche. The idea of seeing it up close or, most awful of all, having to feel it gave him the need to be sick.

"No, Mr. Dandy Billiam. Come on down!" She yelled as if commanding a circus show, full of bravado. "You'll see a rusted chain 'bout twelve paces to yer right. Climb that and you'll get only 'bout halfway down, but there's a great, big fatty to cushion yer fall." She laughed as she swept her mop of hair out of her eyes. Her face was dirty and smudged with dried blood, but her eyes gleamed a sparkling sienna. Billiam was surprised to see she actually was lovely, although probably sadistic as well.

Swallowing hard, both stomach and pride, he nodded down to her and began his twelve-pace march, the last steps of his favorite suit. He grabbed the chain and shimmied down the cliff, one pointed loafer at a time. Said loafers met a comfortable stoop at the same time his hands were grasping an inch above the chain's end. He spotted the purple-tinted soft landing Shemmy had mentioned. All he could think of was falling through its skin as if it were a rotten tomato. If that happened, every fiber in his clothing, every piece of hair on his head and body, were sure to be compromised. To the left of the fat corpse was a spot free of flesh or feces. It was a sharp-looking patch of rock and at least a five-foot jump but appeared quite clean. Billiam realized it was madness and pure egomania to choose broken bones over soiled suits, but his immaculate aesthetic was far too important for him to be able to humble it.

Kicking hard against the cliff, he let himself go, spinning as far to the left as possible. He could hear Shemmy's cackling below him as he fell helplessly toward the jagged rocks. Unfortunately it was farther than he had thought. He had no choice but to prepare to roll, holding his hat and tucking in his head, landing shoulder first on a torso. His calves got their fall caught by the rocks, slicing one trouser leg from ankle to knee. Almost completely defeated, he used his last bit of strength to roll onto the ground off of the torso. He pulled his legs close to his chest and wiped dust off of his limbs until his eyes forced themselves shut.

A jostling motion was the first thing Billiam perceived as he began to rouse. The next sensation was the pittering sound of bare feet slapping against soft ground. His eyes refused to open, and his head throbbed. His back felt comforted, almost embraced, yet his legs were being blown about in a breeze. The musky odor of death that completely filled his nose when everything first went dark still lingered yet had become much fainter. He pried his right eye open slightly to see a wooded path moving around him before it fell back shut.

If my eyes will not obey, perhaps my mouth shall, he thought to himself. Gasping out a coarse breath, he muttered, "'Emmy…? I'm alive… yes?"

"'Course ya are, Dandy, no thanks to yourself. I told ya to land on the fatty, not swan dive for a jagged fuckin' rock," she replied, sounding irritated and to be a few paces ahead.

"I… it was too… too disgust… I couldn't…." The words coming out of his mouth snapped him awake with the memory of the horror that befell him, or rather, that he fell on. "My shoulder! My trousers!" he screamed, while frantically brushing at his shoulder with one hand and grabbing at his leg with the other. The top of the hand going for the shoulder grazed against a cheap, tacky-feeling fabric before the hand moving toward the pants could feel the passing air around it.

Billiam immediately leapt a few paces forward and onto his feet. "You put me in your corpse carriage?" he shouted, spinning around toward his abductor.

"You was out cold. I ain't in the habit of waitin' for nightfall in the middle of Peace Valley, and we got something to discuss I 'spose, so I could'nae leave ya. I hate to admit it, but I dun get sought out too often of late. I'm intrigued, so I got ya in Gam, I did. You did'nae fit well. 'Tis a babe's pram after all."

As mortified as he was, Billiam knew she had saved him. "Right, thank you, miss. I should be fine to walk from here. How long have we been traveling?"

"Erm… I'd say something around ten minutes or so. We got about two more 'til we at me shack." She scratched her head, feigning innocence and smiling to Billiam as he marched backward ahead of her.

"What were you saying about nightfall? Was I out for even a full minute before you hoisted me atop your appendages? I am, of course, grateful for my rescue, but I think it may have been a bit hasty." Billiam grit his teeth, thinking of how long it might be until he could rip off his suit and burn it. I do not agree with becoming so attached to trivial possessions such as clothing, but I will admit that no coat since has achieved that level of dashing on him.

"Oi, so yer a neatnik, ey? Ya dun like the dead? Explains yer stupid stunt. I ain't the patient sort, so if ya want my help, ya better don't pass out." Irritated but thoroughly amused by this stranger, she sighed dramatically before pointing ahead of her. "Turn around, Dandy, home sweet home right there."

He smiled as he swung his leg around, but the grin was fleeting. This home, as she called it, was barely standing. Sheets of rusted metal tied to each other with large vines struggled beneath a mud-covered thatch roof. Holes were crudely cut through the walls to produce mock windows. A wooden door, vaguely attached to the metal siding with rusty hinges, swung slightly in the wind. To the right of the door, a disembodied arm held up its hand, wielding a muck-covered paintbrush. It robotically slathered the slime against the side of the shack, staining the metal green before drying to an off-white.

Noticing where her companion's gaze had landed, Shemmy chimed in, "I thought a sprucing up would'nae hurt, and I was'nae even expectin' company!"

"I am disturbed but also quite impressed by your productivity, Miss DuBois. Painting your own house without being present, now that is something! Kudos!" He really was impressed. Having spent his formative years as a royal page, efficiency and clever solutions gave him a delight like nothing else.

"You mean it, I can tell!" She jumped with glee as she cheered, "See, neatnik, the dead can be neat too! Now scoot yerself in. I'd like to know wot someone as prim as yerself could possibly want wif the likes of me. Gam, you rest yerself out 'ere now." As she said that to her carriage, she swayed her arm down, drawing a shape with her finger. Gam the pram knelt to the ground and ceased its animation. Gesturing out to the arm and drawing a symbol over to her left side, she called, "O'er there now, please." Billiam watched in horror and splendor as the arm clawed with its fingers to drag itself and started painting the other side of her shack.

Once they entered the shanty, Billiam sat down on one of the cut-off trunks surrounding a large fallen log that seemed to be her dining table. "I know I have truly come to the right person! You are a master," he exclaimed. Gazing around the small hovel he saw a bowl of water, kept frozen all on its own, with some slices of meat preserved atop it. On her makeshift bed, (a term I use loosely to refer to a heap of strange blankets and cushions) sat two more disembodied hands. These ones were cut off at the wrists and busy at work knitting something from a pile of twine. A mud-and-blood-covered squirrel ran through a wheel on a concrete slab counter at her behest, starting a rushing of water and powering a single hydroelectric lightbulb hanging from the ceiling. "Just fascinating!"

"Aye, yes, I'm an enchantress. That's why you sought me. No need to marvel now. If you did'nae know it, you would'nae be here. What, pray tell, do you want, Billy?" He bristled at the nickname, which produced a snicker from Shemmy.

She leaned against the counter behind her, reached up, and grabbed a dusty mead bottle. Fiddling blindly again, she produced two crude vessels made of wood. While pouring the thick liquid in the glasses, she laid her gaze heavy upon him. He knew it was now or never, that he must plead his case.

He sat up, adjusted his tie, and cleared his throat a bit. He then took a big swig of the syrupy liquor, gulping it down before he could fear the dirt and grime he must've swallowed along with it. "How much do you know of the state of politics in the capital, Chammerline?"

Grimacing, she replied, "Fine, I won't call ya Billy, and you won't utter that bourgeois name at me again, fair?" Once her guest nodded, she continued, "I have been banished from the capital for witchery, I'd say, 'bout six years now. 'Twas a year after the king and queen got butchered, poor sods. They had themselves a young prince—little pretty thing named Micah, right? Well he succeeded them, with the assistance of the cardinal, who was to advise 'til 'is twentieth. That should be soon, aye?"

"You are better informed than I could've guessed; however, Prince Micah fell gravely ill over four years ago. They believe it was a slow-acting poison, leaving the boy comatose. Thus the cardinal has been exclusively ruling the nation. It's lucky you were booted when you were, as exile is not something we witness anymore, only sacrifice." Billiam blinked slowly, leaning back before opening his eyes to gauge his hostess's reaction.

Her face had twisted to a frown under her matted, raven hair. Pieces completely tangled into braids and holding bones or feathers framed her face as she gulped at her mead. "I was, by blood, a noble lady, as they say, before my start in enchanting, so I knew the family. They mighta had a lot, but they had just as much misery. Their daughter, the slow one, we shared a tutor when we was young."

Shemmy furrowed her brow, which was no longer covered in any hair. Her eyebrows had been burnt off, common with enchanters who have beckoned flames for otherworldly powers. In the place of her eyebrows, six small dots about half a centimeter apart were tattooed in black. This was an ancient practice of enchanters and shaman from the days before religious civilization, when the spiritual arts were accepted and celebrated. The fact that she knew of this and wore it was proof enough of her affluent upbringing and education. She allowed herself to become wild and dirty, which fit the crazed persona she created, but she was far more than that.

"Prince Micah's twentieth birthday is on July seventeen, precisely two and a half months from today. The truth, however, is that he perished a year ago." Billiam paused for a moment to choke down his feelings. Shemmy stared at him, bug-eyed and motionless as he continued, "Since the prince has died before his twentieth, the crown should've been passed to his dim half sister Margaret and her equally diminished husband, Damon, Earl of Chricton. The cardinal has kept him preserved in ice to hide this fact from Princess Margaret and the people. My group and I only know of his death because I have retained friends in the castle. Keeping up the guise that the prince is still alive though ill will allow the cardinal to stage Micah's surrender of the crown to him. We cannot allow this to happen!" Overcome, Billiam grabbed Shemmy's hands into his own; his tears fell, and he could not stop them.

"You need to revive the prince and thwart the evil cardinal? Ya wanna save the kingdom and all her people from continued damnation?" she asked in a singsong tone, without hesitation or emotion.

"Precisely! The prince must be resurrected so that change can finally flourish."

"Lovely! You seem quite sure about this. 'Tis a shame it's bleeding impossible. Humans cannae be brought back to life." She shook her head and smiled, though sadly.

"No! It must be possible! I see all you have done here; I heard of the man you resurrected. I know you have done it! Please, Shemmy, I need him!"

"Aye, you care for him personally, then?" She was the one to reach for his hand this time, holding it softly. He barely looked up at her, his face distorted by tears as he nodded solemnly. "Then you would'nae want for him what became of that man. True, he was alive. Yes, he was breathing, his blood pumping, wif my commands all his parts able to move. That ain't life though; he could'nae do nuffin' on his own except breathe and bleed and shit. The spark o' life ain't sumfin' we humans 'ave been able to recreate in centuries. Ya dun want your prince to simply be a breathing poop machine. Worse than death, dat is." She gave his hand a firm squeeze, then let it go, feeling assured this topic could now be put to rest.

Instead, energy returned to Billiam. "Of course I know that, but you were working without these—" Possessed with a sudden excitement, he dug into the inner lining of his coat to produce two sparkling, foot-long needles before exclaiming, "The ancient enchanting needles of the first peoples! We researched your experiment immensely to find whatever components were missing. These were two of them." When he pointed them out toward her, she feverishly grabbed at them, but he yanked them away before she even got a single touch. "We went through a lot to get these. We found one fully preserved, and then a woman of my group traveled to the edges of Gamola to find the only man who was able to recreate its twin. So, you cannot have them unless you are using them to bring back Micah!" Feeling triumphant, he swung the needles back in his coat and awaited her response.

"I'm impressed, Mr. Dandy. You researched well. In the ancient days, they did'nae crudely draw their hexes wif their hands. A 'chanter would knit the energy around 'um directly into their target. But that's not—"

"Not all?" he interjected. "Why of course it's not. You need the blessing of a faerie pool: sacred water of the dreaded lands man can hardly find and never survive, right? I have a map, and I have faelocks in my organization as well, who have taught me the tricks of entry. I just need you." The grin on his face was so large it threatened to outstretch and knock over the flimsy, metal walls.

Shemmy closed her eyes and pondered hard. "I guess, well, yeah, we prolly could do it, then? That does nae mean I'm agreeing, juss means it's a possibility."

"Really? That's wonderful! So if you did agree, we'd have to travel to the faerie pool, bless the needles and—"

"No, silly man! The needles dun need blessing, the boy does. I dunno how keen I am on abducting a dead royal and trekking him into extremely hostile territory." She scratched her head, not knowing whether to feel excited or frustrated.

"Hmm, I see, so the prince would have to come with us. Actually, I would feel much better knowing he's with me."

Shemmy suddenly became giddy and blurted out, "Awlright, then tell me the real story if you expect me to do this! Saving the world's all well and good, but I can tell your passion ain't there, least not entirely. He's your lover, then, isn't he?" She grabbed her knees up to her chest and smiled excitedly.

Billiam felt his face getting hot with embarrassment before letting out an irritated sigh. "Fine, well we weren't really lovers, technically. Our relationship was much more than that, and also more innocent. I am in love with him; I have been as long as I can remember." He waved his hand, as though this should be something she already knew. It was so clear to him and all those around him it had simply become a matter of fact. "Since the cardinal threw me out of the castle five years ago, and I have not been able to see him in so long, now possibly ever again, that love is practically boiling away at me. It's a burning feeling of despair I will not be able to escape unless I try everything in my power to revive him. I must finally be with him, and I believe in my heart it will happen."

He looked up at Shemmy to see she was practically drooling. Billiam just shrugged and continued his tale. "I grew up in Micah's service and spent my entire young life at his side. My father, Ackerman Grimhart, was captain of the Order of Logos, the scholar knights who used to be right hand to the royal family. He had been a page and dear friend to the king, and thus it was decided when I was aged two

I would become page to the infant prince. I was akin to a servant, but more so his attendant and furthermore companion. He was my best and only friend, and I his. The climate in the castle changed a lot as the war began raging. We were nine and eleven when Casper was finally bombed out. Micah and I were scarcely allowed to leave the castle, and at times not even his room. We were each other's only comfort, and after his parents were assassinated, I vowed to become his strength.

"I knew at that time in what way I loved him, and to my surprise, he professed it to me first. Our young love never got acted upon physically besides the comforting hugs I gave him. I held him through the night the first weeks after his parents passed, but I was then banned from the prince's bedchamber at night. The cardinal had deemed it improper at our ages. The very day he told me I was his true love was the day all knights, all those belonging to the Order of Logos, and myself, were banished from the castle. I was gripped hard on the shoulders by one of the MortiAegis monks and ripped from Micah, who had been embracing me. He was screaming and cursing, throwing a child's tantrum. I wanted to do the same, but I still believed in my vow to be his strength. I yelled to him I would be back, it would all be okay, and that I loved him too. Another monk slammed his door, and that's the last time I saw him directly. I do not want to have lied to him."

Shemmy's eyes watered, and her face glowed brightly. "So sad!" she gasped. "The love of two boys ripped away before it could even begin! Oh no, no, no! I must bring back your prince to you!" She shot up to her feet, ran to Billiam, and swung her arms around his neck from behind. She hung off him like a strange, love-crazed monkey.

"Wait... you didn't care to do it if it meant a chance to stop the reign of terror by the cardinal and this endless war, but you will gladly for a chance that I can realize my love with Micah? Had I known you were so crazy for the love between men, I would have rethought my entire approach. I could've worn something skimpy and poofish, or even brought a friend." He smirked as Shemmy's arms went limp and she flopped down to the ground.

"Dear Spirit, I am glad you did'nae. If you had, I prolly would agree juss so you could have yer love. However, I won't do it for free. Dat would be stupid."

"Of course, we will pay you handsomely, and the prince is sure to grant you pardon on your exile."

"Money? Pfft. What need I have for dat? I dunno what payment I would want though…." She scratched at her matted hair, while still lying on the ground where she fell. Grinning wickedly, she looked up to him and asked, "It's prolly treason to ask to watch you pumping the prince's backside, eh?"

Billiam's only possible response to her vulgarity was to immediately drop his face in his palms. "Should you be successful, I can't imagine the prince objecting to you witnessing a single kiss between us." Billiam was tired of being subjected to that embarrassing blush once again, as his cheeks warmed up at the thought of said kiss. "To subject him to anything else for your amusement is a depravity I will not allow!" Seriousness erased all bashfulness from his face as he yearned to protect Micah, although he was neither there nor alive.

"Yes, yes, yer right, prudency and all that load. I will settle for a kiss, then. However, I must ask for something else. Wifout me, it's hopeless, right?"

Billiam nodded and outstretched his hand to pull her off the ground where she had remained splayed. She propped up partially and climbed back onto her stump.

"Think, think, think…. Wot do I want? Hmm…." She closed her eyes for half a minute before opening them wide, finally inspired. "I've got it! I want a loft wif a lab attached in ol' Drummond and a lifetime supply of Leonard Lemonington's sweet, cinnamon cream puffs! Also I require a kitten dat's colorpoint, hopefully chunky, and definitely cross-eyed. All dat's nonnegotiable."

Billiam smiled and shook his new ally's hand. "My Order's budget can definitely afford the cost of rent on a grand loft and accommodate any of your cream puff and pastry needs. Luckiest of all, my darling seal-point cat named Buttercup is positively fat with kittens at the moment. The presumed father runs into light posts on the daily, his cross-eyedness has blinded him so."

"Oh perfect! Oh so exciting! Making history, saving the kingdom, getting sweets and a kitty cat! Today is blessed by the earth spirits, no doubt it is." She smiled and wriggled like a giddy child. Billiam could hardly believe it had worked, that she really would do this. Her brashness melted away before his eyes, and he saw the kind, exuberant lass she truly was. "Now let's get you that Micah's virginity!"

She jumped and cackled, dancing around her hovel while scooping up various objects in her arms. Billiam, mortified once more, was now free of so much excitement that he could start to fear introducing her to his people. She was a blasted madwoman and a shameless pervert; delightful, yes, but she was deranged.

"I must ask that you not speak about sexual acts involving our prince around any of the people I will be introducing you to. It will most likely shock them, as it's not something they think about daily like I do." He grinned devilishly as he said the last part. He would have never openly uttered that in front of anyone, especially someone he just met. He feared she could be rubbing off on him already.

"Also, you shouldn't bring too much. We have plenty of necessities for you at our lodge. I will help carry anything you might truly require, of course." With that, their journey as a team truly began. A rather dull battle cry from Billiam, but it would suffice in getting them on their way back to Drummond by nightfall. Chammerline would thus be inducted into what was once the mighty Order of Logos, whether myself and the current members could tolerate her or not.

CHAPTER 2

May 2nd, 989

"I CAN'T believe you didn't tell me about the hill path around the valley," Billiam scoffed and looked down longingly at his wretched suit. *You could have been spared*, he thought to himself. Shemmy just giggled as Billiam threw the burlap shawl at her face.

"Well, it took longer. I ain't one to wait for nothing, especially not some poof's suit," she sang, sticking out her tongue.

"It only took an hour more, at most. The difference in smell alone would be worth a day's travel." They reached the sewer entrance with little time to spare before darkness overtook the wastes as a result of bypassing the Valley of Peace.

Having but one peasant's shroud, it was obvious the banished enemy of the crown ought to be the one hidden. Billiam grabbed away the bag full of Shemmy's strange-smelling belongings so she could pull the shawl over herself. He adjusted the cover over most of her face; it was a rather distinguishable one after all. Tucking the bag under his shoulder, putting his page skills to good use, he encircled her arm with his own. "Shall we then, my lady?"

"Gah, must you be so polite? It's awkward to feel like a noble again," she groaned and became bashful, bouncing on her feet a bit. "Awlright, Drummond, let's see how you've been treatin' yerself."

They entered into the dark and dingy tunnel, walking on the foot-wide concrete path against the wall. The foul-smelling liquid lay below them only a short distance. Keeping himself in front, he placed Shemmy's arms around his waist. This was done only because the tunnel had very little visibility to begin with, and coupled with her shawl, she was essentially blind. Having him helpless ahead of her, she could not control her giggling. Her mind knew no limits to perversion, and a dirty thought constantly danced through her brain.

Thankfully there were no other hangabouts in the sewer that evening, and they made their way easily through their half-mile single-file trek. The only difficulties were about a dozen inappropriate pinches given to Billiam, and later, when he tripped her so that she fell within inches of the muck. I'm sure it was an accident.

Their danger to each other ended as they reached the ladder that would bring them to a safe entry point in the rundown edges of Westend. He picked up Shemmy easily by her shoulders and swung the giggling fool around him so that she could go up the ladder first. This was half for her safety, and half for his dignity.

"All right, Shemmy, please knock three times on that manhole, pause for thirty seconds, and knock twice more," he instructed.

"Heh, manhole... gladly," she replied. *Rap, rap, rap.* She banged with her knuckles. Humming a short tune as she waited, she executed her final knocks: *Rap, rap.*

The metal plate removed itself before she could fully withdraw her hand. A pretty young woman's face appeared in the bright space where the manhole cover had been. Brown frizzy curls bounced around her cheeks, and she smiled as she dropped down her hand to pull Shemmy up.

"Hullo, Miss!" the lass squealed, hoisting the enchantress up and out to the street. Shemmy was small framed, but then again so was she, thus the force tumbled them both over. "I'm so glad you came, and early too! I'm Jessica, but you call me Jess, okay? I feared I'd be sleeping on this manhole tonight." She was giggling as she helped Shemmy and herself up.

Billiam managed to wriggle out on his own, not that either of the ladies had any intention of helping him. He quickly slid the manhole cover over, closing the heavy metal as delicately as possible to avoid garnering excess attention. Jessica was none too cautious as she excitedly examined her new friend.

Billiam went to gather the belongings she had with her to make it seem as though this alley truly was her home. As he started to pull down her quilt tent, Jess laid her hand on his shoulder. "Just wait, you. This really is someone's living space. That old crow Maggie let me borrow it and her stuff. Silly me, and I thought you knew everything." She smirked while waggling her finger at him, prompting Shemmy to join in as well. Before he could rebut or even sigh at her, she stopped her teasing demeanor. She smiled sweetly and assured him, "We can leave it all right here. Maggie is at the lodge, and to make it a fair trade I was letting her use my room. I am a bit scared to see the state of my linens, but I am so excited you made it back!"

Grabbing both their hands, she pulled them along at her skipping pace, down the alley and through the streets. Jessica was extremely high-spirited and friendly, almost without exception. She had soft caramel-colored skin that always smelled of warm sugar and vanilla. Her round face was bursting with joy, studded with faint freckles across her nose and long-lashed green eyes. That day she was sporting a cute yellow sundress that bounced around her body. She stood only five feet tall, with a very important quarter inch she always reminded me of. Shemmy outstood her by about three inches, with Billiam over a foot above Shemmy, making them a very unbalanced-looking trio.

Jessica skipped along so quickly, the shawl began to slide off Shemmy's head. Billiam stretched his arm out across the two girls and they halted. "I am very excited too," he told Jess happily, "but we really shouldn't go revealing our guest yet." Walking around the front of them, he covered Shemmy's beaming face once again with the burlap veil. "We need to slow down, but you can keep holding her hand. We don't want her to slam into a pole, well… at least we ought not."

"Ha! Geez, Pa. Take away all our fun," teased Shemmy, as she and Jess both stuck out their tongues to our thoroughly exhausted hero. "I like you!" she exclaimed while she clung to Jessica. They were obedient enough to slow down slightly, though neither of them wanted to offer a hand to Billiam any longer, so the poor dear walked solo. He must have been terribly disappointed.

The sunset was in its full colorful glory by the time they reached the lodge. The street's oil lamps were being lit around them, illuminating the sign above the door. Shemmy was surprised to see it really was an inn, aptly named "The Philosopher's Rest." She thought she was being escorted to some clandestine rebel clubhouse, so she was relieved to see something much more genial.

"Ooo, it 'ave a tavern in it?" she asked Jessica.

"Of course it does, silly goose. A lodge without a bar ain't a lodge at all. Now, let's not just stare at the entrance. You have so many people to meet!" Jessica swung open the door, skipping and waving as she ran inside.

The smell of warm bread and roasted meats rushed into Shemmy's nose. She had been so long removed from cooked meals and surrounded by the smell of death that she had forgotten how much she missed the warm embrace of a food's aroma before devouring it. Walking into the large wooden room was as overwhelming as it was comforting. The bright lighting and communal atmosphere felt like a long-awaited reunion; however, one step in and she felt she couldn't proceed. It must've been some strange, succulent dream that couldn't possibly go any further.

"It may not be the royal castle, but this is our home. Welcome to the current hub of the mighty Order of Logos, protectors of the realm and the quest for knowledge. We also have brilliant meat pies!" Billiam told her with a smile. By wrapping his arm around her shoulder, he gently forced her awake and into the room, walking them both straight over to the bar. "Now, shall we get you a drink before bombarding you with introductions?" Turning to the barmaid, he implored sweetly, "Might we have two warm ales, my dear?"

"Of course, of course, Billiam!" The girl turned around instantly, sliding her upper body along the bar to just barely reach Billiam for a hug. The familiar face turned to Shemmy and greeted her politely. "It's a pleasure to finally meet you, Miss. We've all been hoping to for such a long time."

"What? Jessica, I already met ya! How'd ya get back there so fast? Where'd yer other outfit go? I liked it better." Feeling utterly confused, Shemmy turned to Billiam. He was laughing loudly, prompting her to frown.

"You met my sister, dear. She is far fonder of wearing little dresses than I am. I get cold easily," she explained, smiling and tugging on her pale sweater. "My name is Katrina. We are twins, of course." She handed Shemmy her ale first, then turned to Billiam to give him his and make some small talk.

Shemmy sipped her beverage and studied this new friend, entranced. Shemmy could not recall if she had met such identical twins before. Kat was just as small and cute as her sister. Her honey-brown hair was the same mess of curls as Jessica's, but she wore part of hers tied up, making it look a little less wild. Her eyes still sparkled green, and she had the same warm energy, but Shemmy conceded she definitely was a different girl. Jessica was exuberant and outgoing; Katrina seemed so calm and gentle.

After downing half her ale and taking turns ogling either one of the twins, Shemmy and I finally had our meeting.

"Welcome home, sir." I am of a polite nature, and as Billiam was acting leader of our humble group, naturally I wanted to greet my superior first. After, I turned to the wild sprite he brought with him and quietly said, "I am pleased to meet you, Miss," with a small bow.

She looked at me slack-jawed and mystified. "Yer tall" was all she could mutter out.

"Yes, yes I am," I replied, and I had figured that was enough introduction for me. I have never been one for frivolity or meaningless chatter. To me, Shemmy was merely a means to our end. I felt no need to familiarize with her; tools are to be used, not befriended. Sadly, Billiam was not going to let me get off that easy, and he grabbed my arm as I turned to walk away.

"Shemmy, this is my second-in-command. Her name is Leke. Please treat her with the utmost respect. She is a faelock, thus she is quite tall, and her sense of humor is a bit lacking, but she is also my dearest friend," Billiam informed her, his jibe mixed with love.

I waited until now to introduce myself, as I knew my introduction to Shemmy would arrive in this part of the timeline. I saw no point in making a show of myself twice. I am Leke, your narrator through this record of our toils. I am Billiam's greatest friend and confidante, and he is mine. I was a private in the Order of Logos before it was disbanded and was personally trained by Captain Ackerman Grimhart. I have been charged with compiling this log, and I'm doing my best to ensure it is not dreadfully boring. I will not claim nor deny omniscience; however, I do have a keen memory and an objective stance on all our players, for the most part. I agree that I was not the worst choice for this task.

"You must be a pureblood, den? I 'ave never met one of you!" Her squealing and excitement had already begun aching my head.

"You still haven't met one; you are to have met two. My brother is there by the stairs, waiting his turn, I suppose." I pointed over to him, hoping to be free of her interest at last.

"Oh wow! Leke, you told a joke! That's wonderful," said Katrina sweetly, which prompted both Billiam and Shemmy to start snickering like idiots.

"I may not have the sense of humor you all have, but I do have a knack for puns and rather enjoy sarcasm. Now, Zan, please come over already." I slunk my head down and turned away before Billiam could grab me again.

I presume, as Shemmy herself mentioned, faelocks are not common and do probably deserve some explanation. In our realm throughout history we have had three species of sentient, intelligent beings. Firstly there are the humans who have sprawled all over the globe of Corseca, populating like wild. Next there are the faeries: small and savage, winged creatures that can commune with the forces of nature in ways the humans could never begin to comprehend. They live in few places in the world, preferring to have no interaction with humans and sealing off their woods with tricks of the eye and traps. They range from an inch to a foot in height, glow with light pink- or blue-tinted skin, and speak telepathically with one another.

The third species would be the ogres, who are all extinct now. They were gigantic bundles of muscle, credited with the building of mountains, smashing canyons down with their fists, and filling the rivers with their tears. This, of course, is utter shit, yet their strength and size would be nothing short of unbelievable if it were seen today. It is approximated they grew to be at least three stories tall and weighed over ten tons. Despite their build they were not brutes. They were kind and intelligent beings who were perpetually docile. Their peaceful nature impressed the faeries, and somehow, which I think would be horrifying to witness, they ended up mating with the ogres. As far as we know, they were of only one sex. There is no record of them ever procreating with one another, rather they had extremely long lifespans.

The ogres were hunted and wiped out by man centuries ago, due to being either poached for their large organs or out of religious vehemence. According to MortiAegism, both ogres and faeries were wicked interlopers, deserving of death. The faeries were much harder to kill, hence them not being victims of genocide as well. The ogres, on the other hand, abhorred the violence and would simply submit. Obviously, they could not have been that wise if they cared not for their own survival, but they are gone, and there is no need to think of them further. Their part in all this was the spawn that had been made with faeries. This new species became known as the faelocks.

We faelocks range from seven to nine feet tall. Our skin is usually gray or silver, but with a regular human flesh tone of varying shades showing through. We look much like humans that have been pulled tight and long, like taffy. Our necks are always at least a foot long and far more flexible than man's; our arms and legs are overstretched as well. Some of us have extra elbow and knee joints to accommodate for the added length; where this gene comes from is not known, and neither my brother nor I were lucky enough to inherit it. Faelocks are not known to be telepathic but are very empathic and perceptive. We seem to have received that from the faeries along with our extreme speed and dexterity. We do not perform the magic tricks faeries and enchanters do, instead we can clearly see through them and interfere with them. We have a small talent for harnessing and releasing bursts of energy but can do nothing truly wondrous. From our ogre ancestors, we received our resolve, calmness, and inhuman physical strength. They also burdened us with our unique approach to relationships. I will explain that further to Katrina when my brother gets himself in an awkward situation, and I'd like to avoid redundancy.

Although faelocks share traits of the creatures that produced them, they are far too dissimilar to either to not be entirely their own species. Thusly, the faeries never accepted them in their dark, wooded communities. The ogres were physically strong but spiritually weak, and as they died out, the faelocks felt no loyalty to them. They ended up migrating to the lands of humans and adopting their ways of life.

As Shemmy referenced, some faelocks mated with humans, creating a much more balanced creature of half mother and half father than the faeries and ogres had. They are known as halflocks and look simply more human than faelock or less human than other humans, however you prefer to look at it. My brother Zan and I had two faelocks for parents and thus are considered purebloods.

Back to the timeline, I had made my few steps away and over to my associate Malcolm by the time Zan finally got his lanky body off his seated position on the steps. He walked over to Shemmy, obviously paining himself to walk slower than his long legspan allowed. His hair was cut quite short; only peeks of his navy blue strands could be seen from under his bowler cap. We had the same grayish-yellow skin that gave us an unpleasant green tinge in direct sunlight.

He bowed to Shemmy without pulling off his cap and gave her one of his disgustingly fake smiles he thought were so human. "'Ello, Shemmy! My name's Zan, an' it's a pleasure to meet ya!"

Liar, I thought to myself with a smirk. He lied about the pleasure, and he lied about his poor grammar and poor manners. Lying as frequently as he did was uncommon among faelocks, but it was a constant for him. He adopted this behavior as a result of being bewitched by a burning need to be liked and accepted by humans. He had possessed this desperation for as long as I could remember.

He kindly squinted his lavender eyes through his silver-framed spectacles as he shook hands with Shemmy. Conversely to before, he faked a lack of smile as he congratulated Billiam on his return, albeit solemnly. Billiam completely ignored his presence. Shemmy was shocked, as she had not seen him react coldly to anyone thus far.

We Knights of Logos dressed all about the same. We no longer got to be trussed up in chain mail or silks, but our black suits fought to retain some of our nobility. We had plain black bowler caps on our heads, with a small L insignia hidden in the bands. The uniform consisted of a white dress shirt, black slacks, and whatever cut of black coat you fancied. Some of us wore ties, and I liked to wear my black cotton handkerchief knotted around my neck loosely. My brother opted against it and would at times leave his shirt unbuttoned at the top. He could be a little tawdry, and today seemed to be one of those days.

Zan quickly fled to the kitchen, after which Billiam rose from his seat and placed his hand on Shemmy's shoulder. "I will save parading everyone in front of you until tomorrow, as we will be going over our next moves. I am now off to scald my skin with boiling water and throw my suit in the fire," he informed her with a grin, though we could all sense he was entirely serious. He turned to Katrina and asked, "You and your mother will see to it she gets a comfortable room and anything she needs?"

"Of course!" chimed in Jessica from behind him. "I can't wait to wash this filthy head of hair, and I know Momma will be up to the challenge of these blackened fingernails," she said while pinching at Shemmy's cheeks.

"Please dun make me too clean," Shemmy squeaked, looking at both twins with eyes full of fear. "It took me ages to get this dirty."

Billiam heard the girls laughing and screaming, "Ewwww!" as he ascended the stairs to his room on the third floor.

"We're putting you up in room twelve, Shemmy! You are the twelfth after all!" Jessica explained and plopped a large bowl in front of her. It was filled with half a chicken and mashed potatoes, all smothered in some dark and delicious gravy. Shemmy grabbed the chicken and started gnawing on it, while wiggling about happily in her chair.

"I thought you were staying in twelve since Maggie soiled your room?" Katrina asked her sister. "I still don't understand why you actually gave her your own room. You could've said any of the empties were yours."

"Maggie is quite shrewd for a human filled with more ale than blood, and she caught my lack of books the second I walked her into twelve. I don't need the room anyhow, as Leke has invited me to bunk with her. I shan't be passing up that offer, as I am too excited to sleep anyhow!"

"And you don't sleep if you are in her room?" Katrina was drying off Billiam's glass with her bar rag, and felt as if she was missing something. Shemmy laughed and choked on her potatoes a little. She had many a comment to add, but shoveling food into her mouth with her hands was all she could focus on.

For some reason, all of us in the lodge kept Katrina in the dark about any number of things. She was a smart and sensitive girl; it was not as if she was incapable of handling a secret. None of these omissions were malicious truths being hidden from her, yet none of us wanted to burden her. Perhaps it was because we all remained protective of her. She had been training to join the Order of Logos before falling ill when she was eleven. She suffered complications from pneumonia and was rendered feeble for five years. She devoted herself to her studies, instead of swordsmanship, and decided against joining the Order when she recovered. She was twenty-three years old at this time and completely healthy, yet none of us remembered to remove our kid gloves.

"Right, I'm going to leave before that one's mouth is no longer full. I'll check on your mother and see how preparations are going. I can help her to get a bath ready, as well," I called over to the gaggle of girls. I got up, leaving Malcolm to his research at the booth. He lifted his fingers as his silent farewell.

The second floor of the lodge was filled with the scents of lavender and lemon. This was result of the furious cleaning and laundering being performed by our house girl, Alex, and the twins' mother, Nairee.

"Nairee, you know she has been living in shit and corpses by choice for the last six years, right? You needn't put yourself out so," I reminded her while grabbing the mop away and finishing her round on the hallway.

She just smiled at me, closing her kind eyes. "It doesn't matter your guest, a hostess needs to be on point or what good is she?"

Nairee was born on the island of Gamola, the southernmost livable area on our globe. It is a wild nation, and they are the only people who have been able to continue their communication with spirits. They actively perform rituals and enchanting on a large scale. The population is small and undeveloped, making them a target for pirates and slave traders. Although the Gamolans would fight back fiercely with their talents, they could still be ravaged long enough with modern weapons to allow their enemies time to abduct their children and steal their resources.

Nairee was one of these unlucky children who was stolen and sold to a captain in Knox. When that captain was captured as a prisoner of war here in Casperland, the teenage Nairee escaped. The man had been training her as an assassin, and her first instinct had been to rescue him. After arriving in Drummond, she came to realize the things really worth fighting for. She joined Logos, met and fell in love with her husband Pierre, and eventually found her former owner. She got to kill him herself, though he was a pathetic wretch in a dungeon by that point. Things turned out pretty well for her, and although this is a grossly abbreviated story, it is a glimpse into her strong character.

Her cool brown skin was still smooth, despite the decades of battle and fifty years of life. She was a mother to all of us in the lodge, in one way or another. She was also one of the deadliest of us, having destroyed three battalions herself during the first and second invasions of Casper. She would never let war or age diminish her spirit. Having her command at the mopping post stolen, she simply went with Alex to pick up as they made Shemmy's bed in seconds.

"We should get a boiling-hot bath ready. Your daughters want to try to clean up that ragamuffin. Where do you keep the towels you care nothing for?" I called to her, grinning as I put her mop away in the closet.

"They are up above, in that same closet. The brown-colored ones will do fine. I suppose they will probably need my help, huh, Leke? I hope she doesn't have any fleas. All right then, child, I'll get the water started. Go up to my room and get me my strongest smelling salts and oils off my dresser. Definitely the tea tree, and ya probably ought to get some scouring pads from the kitchen too."

I nodded and accomplished all her prep work. This absolved me from any responsibility in the actual cleaning of Shemmy. They still relied on me to carry the clawing mess up the stairs, before dropping her in the washroom with the ladies and locking the door behind me. I was thus able to retire and slept soundly until Jess joined me, I'd gather to guess a full three hours later. She had a few bald spots and reeked of tea tree but seemed extremely proud of herself.

In regards to the current form of the Order of Logos and our plan to save the kingdom, I ought to dole out some more facts. Post his forced retirement, Captain Grimhart purchased this inn from its elderly and childless owner. It was chosen for its more private location in the poorest part of town and its generous amount of rooms. Most lodgings in Drummond had five to ten rooms, while this habitation boasted over double that with a wholly unnecessary twenty-six guest rooms. This excess made it possible for Grimhart to house all his remaining loyal knights while having plenty of spare rooms to rent to real guests. That extra income was nice, but not nearly as beneficial as having a legitimate business to justify the gaggle of knights still hanging about together. Thus "The Salty Wench" transformed into "The Philosopher's Rest," and the Order of Logos received an extension on their lease on life.

Captain Ackerman still resided in the attic-turned-suite on the fourth floor. He fell into convalescence following a stroke shortly after

Micah's own descent into illness. Henceforth, the captain's only son Billiam became our commander under close guidance by his elders, Nairee and Pierre.

The three elders' plan had been the assassination of the cardinal and reclamation of the castle. It was right as they started to make their move toward Cardinal Aldrious that the prince fell ill. It also happened to be immediately after a diplomatic visit by the queens of Alafor, our neighbors to the north, that Micah entered his coma. The cardinal naturally blamed the queens, yet they had been here to negotiate joining forces, which would have been beneficial to both sides. There was no proof or visible motive for the Alafor to attack the prince, but Aldrious worked his nation into a frenzy. He began plans to invade Alafor and cut trading immediately, but no attacks were ever actually launched.

Following Ackerman's stroke, Billiam assumed his role as captain. He knew that their strategy must change. He was sure the cardinal suspected the coming attempt on him, and that is why he proved his willingness to hurt the prince. It also explained the absence of hostility toward Alafor, as they were merely a scapegoat. Billiam convinced his people they shouldn't be after the cardinal nor the castle, they should be behind their prince instead. Thus our route to the current plan was forged.

Research was done on healing Micah via enchanting yet was adapted to his resurrection following his death. Besides the resurrection of Micah, there was much to be done. We needed to make allies outside of Drummond, as the atmosphere was sure to become intolerably hostile once the prince went missing.

We worked steadily and swiftly so we'd have means and men to return to Drummond before the prince's twentieth. The hope is that the people will lose faith in Aldrious and turn from religious fanaticism enough to welcome back their king. The people themselves would remove the cardinal; at least that was Billiam's idea. Planning was practically complete and execution of the plan would be upon us. The only part that would need to be adjusted was the extraction time of Micah. Now that we knew Micah had to be present in the faerie woods, it had to be rescheduled immediately; however, it seemed the change would actually be beneficial.

CHAPTER 3

May 3rd, 989

NOON ARRIVED by the time Jessica finally baited Shemmy out of bed. She came armed with a plate of buttermilk flapjacks heaped five high, smothered in lingonberry jam and whipped butter. She fanned the smell above Shemmy's head until she dreamily began to follow the floating breakfast downstairs.

The drowsy girl in a white nightgown who arrived in the dining area was barely recognizable. I realize I refer to her as a girl quite often, but Shemmy was twenty-eight years old when we met her, older than most of us. This is the fault of her immaturity, no doubt. Despite that, in her newly clean state she looked very young and lost. Her skin was actually three shades lighter than we had seen the day before. Her raven hair was no longer filthy but frizzed up all around her head. It would take longer for it to recover than her dirty skin had, yet there was no way she would let it. The collection of dreadlocks along her face was left intact, though all but one bone was removed. The last one that refused to be rescued was a finger bone poking from the bottom of the braid on the left side of her face.

Shemmy took in her surroundings while chomping mechanically at her pancakes, this time forced to use a fork and knife by Nairee. Curling her bare, permanently stained feet in the legs of the stool, she scanned the room, noticing the faces she had met last night and some she hadn't yet. As exciting as this complete and immediate change of life had been, she was starting to feel overwhelmed. She thought of how she really needed to stop rushing into things, no matter how terribly boring caution was.

Billiam sat down behind her at the next table with the chairback facing him and surprised her by brushing her hair. He pulled it a bit, but she could tell he really was trying to be gentle.

"Nairee is bringing us coffee with cream and real bars of chocolate melted right in!" he whispered over her shoulder. "Spirit, I cannot believe how good you smell, but you still have way too much of this mop. I hope we have time to get you to a barber. If not I can hack some off with my dagger while we are on the road." He pinched her cheek hard as he said it. He then set the brush down, got up, and moved to her table to sit beside her.

His excitement helped her to feel reassured about her uprooting. "Oi, good. You were scarin' me there for a moment, wif how nice you was being." She pulled on her nightgown with disdain and asked him, "I do get to wear real clothes again, right?"

"Hmm, I suppose we could allow that," he teased. "Though you slept so long, everyone is more than ready for our meeting. You are stuck in your gown until it's over."

"Here's your coffee, children," Nairee said kindly, setting the mugs of steaming sweetness in front of them. "You ready for me to gather everyone, then? I'll set us all up around this table. No need to move our guest of honor." She smiled at Shemmy and gave the oak table a good knock. The large round table was one of four in the tavern's dining area and could comfortably fit ten. There were twelve of us all together, counting Alex, though Nairee could make it work fine. Alex had no pivotal part in our mission, but she could not bear leaving her girl out.

I came down the stairs, carrying the elder Grimhart in my arms. My brother followed me, holding his wheeled chair in one hand and a quilt in the other. Ackerman was having a good day and was able to talk slowly, so he insisted on being present for the meeting. He would, of course, still let his progeny lead. He simply wanted to make sure that Billiam got all his bases covered before the captain could put his approval on letting the plan proceed.

Ackerman had grown thin and light, a shadow of the beastly warrior he once was. White hair covered his sixty-year-old body, and sleep collected in his eyes. I gently wiped it away when we arrived at the ground floor while my brother set up his chair for him. I wheeled him over to be at the right of Billiam, and as Shemmy was already at his left, I sat myself next to Ackerman.

The table was rounded out by the twins next to Shemmy, followed by their mother and their father, Pierre. My brother sat beside me, and a young man named Roland, Zan's battle partner and protégé of sorts, was next. To his right sat Alex and then Malcolm next to Pierre, completing the group. This circle was the Order of Logos and the only hope for revolution. We were a bit ragtag to look at, but all skilled in our own right and excited to be given our personally tailored commands.

Billiam stood up and pushed in his chair, remaining behind it so he could view the whole group. "Good afternoon, everyone!" he greeted us nervously.

"It's afta'noon?" Shemmy was a bit bewildered as she slurped down the last bit of her coffee.

"Yes it is, sleepyhead," Billiam teased her, but immediately straightened up. He knew his father would not approve of the informality. "All right, first off, I am delighted to inform you all that it looks like there will be an opening for us to acquire Micah tomorrow. I know this is quite sudden, but it gives us almost two and a half months to complete our goals by the prince's birthday. This is still not an overly comfortable amount of time but should be sufficient.

"I have split us into four teams. The first team, A, will go to Alafor, where relations will need to be repaired so that the prince can find safe haven there after his resurrection. The next, team F, will be responsible for going to the faerie wood of Failingveil to revive the prince, before meeting with A in Alafor, as it is the closest quasi-friendly kingdom to Casperland. Team G will go to Gamola to offer aide and encourage them to fight with us, with the promise of forging a permanent alliance once the throne is reclaimed. Team D will maintain the lodge as long as possible before going west to see if there is any help in the isolated land of Khur. Team D will be the only team not participating in the extraction of the prince, as it would obviously make their stay here far too dangerous.

"On to the extraction: Team G will be outfitted with the guise of wine merchants with a delivery for the cardinal. He will be at parliament the whole day tomorrow as the third deployment of troops to Knox is to be negotiated. We have one of our friends in the castle, a slave girl named Marla, who is eager to help. The cardinal is rather fond of her, and she has been given mostly free rein of the grounds. She will receive the shipment and guide them to the wine cellar and through the castle, to the prince. Instead of wine, the bottles will be filled with a knockout gas Pierre concocted. Team G and Marla will be outfitted with discreet breathing devices so they do not fall prey to their own trick. The goal will be to incapacitate guards and monks, as creating casualties is of no benefit to us. After the prince is back, those men will hopefully be among our allies.

"Team F will be piloting a modified hot-air balloon we have acquired. It is outfitted with two mechanical wings that can be manipulated with a pulley system to get us to our intended location. It will also have a very clever cloaking spell cast on it, which Nairee learned from the Gamolans. It lasts only twenty minutes. Team A will ride with them and drop from the hot-air balloon into the courtyard outside Micah's room exactly three minutes after team G enters the castle. Team A will help with any crowd control as team G exits into the courtyard, carrying the prince. Leke will be on team A, and she will carry the prince up the rope to the balloon, passing him off to team F. Once F has Micah, Leke will jump and the rope will be cut so their retreat can begin immediately. The goal is to get past the Valley of Peace before the cloaking spell wears off.

"A and G will cooperate to get out of the castle through the servants' tunnels. Marla will guide you and carries a key to the sewer entrance below the castle. The teams will follow the sewer south and arrive at the Marken River. There you will see two boats guarded by one of our allies. Team G will have a skipper prepared, which will be able to weather the seas, whereas A will have to make do with a small canoe to cross the river. Team F will land in the cover of woods, near Shemmy's house, where a cart and two horses will be waiting. They can then proceed northeast to the faerie wood.

"The extraction and escape should take no longer than ten minutes. Marla will escape along with the teams and join G, as this is the only way to assure her safety. All of this information is included in the primers that Pierre wrote up. Any questions before I go over team assignments?"

Ackerman grunted before being able to mutter out, "Risky as hell, but should work... proud of you... son." His face glowed with more life than I'd seen in three years, but worry still collected in his brow.

"Will Marla be of use to us, besides being alive?" Malcolm asked coldly.

"Well she is not a soldier, but she is extremely loyal and will be quite charming with the Gamolans. You are also not on team G, Malcolm, so you needn't worry."

Malcolm nodded and continued scratching along on his notepad, as he had been during the entire presentation.

"I might be daft or somethin', but sounds to me like the same plan we discussed a hundred times over?" Roland muttered out through his fingers.

"It is similar yes, but even you should have been able to catch the creation of a fourth team. The Alafor team was double the size prior as we thought Failingveil would be taken care of already," Pierre lectured the boy, following it with a loud scoff.

"Well yeah, I mean, I know that. I just meant like we dun really need to hammer over it, don'cha think?"

"It is important Shemmy knows everything, and as teams are sure to have changed, you best pay attention to all of it," I added dryly.

"Yes, I agree Shemmy ought be fully prepared. She met us just a day ago. Is this even enough time? The plan hinges on her completely, no?" Katrina asked, looking first to Billiam but landing her gaze on me.

Sighing quietly, I answered, "This change of plan benefits us in two ways, despite the urgency it requires. Firstly, Failingveil is closer to Alafor than Drummond, so it'll be a more discreet trek for the living prince. Second, the journey and revival can now coincide, buying us all the more time to gain allies. If we wait and hold Shemmy's hand for a week, we are losing half our advantage. She is an expert, and it is not as though she can practice on someone without taking a week's excursion to the woods, not to mention someone's life." I noticed as I finished speaking Shemmy had leaned her torso over the table to grin at me like an idiot. I had apparently flattered her, which was not my intention, so I grimaced and leaned out of her sight.

"Fair" was all Kat replied as she nodded and smiled at Billiam. "I am fine to continue."

"Excellent. Thank you, Pierre and Leke. Those were my sentiments exactly. Anything else?" Billiam asked as he glanced down at the paper in his hand. All the notes thus far had been laid upon the table, but the new team assignments stayed in his clutches. Only he and Pierre had been involved in redrafting them, so I was just as eager as anyone else to hear it.

Zan smiled obsequiously and chimed in, "I can't have any questions until I know what I'm doing, so I think you are safe to proceed."

"Right," conceded Billiam. "Team G is naturally Pierre and Nairee as they are already familiar with Gamola and should be able to pull off the ruse flawlessly. Team A will be Leke and Malcolm, though I would like Jessica to go with you as well." The three of us stared at him in disbelief, not expecting Jessica to be involved in the mission so directly as she was not a trained fighter whatsoever. "She will be guarding the boats and join with you on the mission to Alafor. She will not be participating in the prince's extraction. I felt the two of you would need someone a bit more cheerful, as this is primarily a diplomatic mission. You are both so quiet and glum, she will balance out the team well."

"Oh, well I bet I'm the best boat sitter you will ever see!" Jessica chirped, excited to be included.

"Team F will be Shemmy and myself. Zan, you will be coming with us too. That will leave Roland and Katrina as our gatekeepers, team D. Alex will be taking my father to the loft we purchased in the heart of the slums, keeping him hidden."

Zan shot up as soon as he heard his name. "Nonsense! Why the hell am I with you and not Roland? And why in the world would you put Katrina in such a dangerous post?" Slapping his hands down on the table, he pointed an angry gaze at Billiam before walking over to Katrina and setting his hands on her shoulders. I realize I never mentioned that Katrina and my brother were betrothed. At the point of this meeting their romance was about three years old. She looked up at Zan, but didn't seem worried in the least about her assignment.

"Katrina is smart and is well trained in explosives by her father, as well as being the only one I trust to care for my cat. Have more faith in your lady. As to why you are stuck with me, Shemmy made it clear to me that when we reach the faerie spring, I will need to hold the prince for her as she revives him. We will need someone fearsome to protect us from the faeries while she performs the ritual. It may take quite a few minutes. I know that you will protect me with your life, since you are in love with me, and protect the prince since I am in love with him. You won't want me to feel the pain of losing him again. That is why I need you with me," Billiam replied, staring seriously at Zan. The whole table seemed enveloped by uneasiness, until Shemmy's outburst of laughter broke it.

Zan's gray skin turned completely porcelain white, and his eyes bulged as he jumped back from Katrina. "I have no idea what nonsense you are spouting, you egomaniacal faggot!" He spat out the words along with actual spit, overcompensating his rage to an extreme. "I will protect you and the prince out of my belief in him and duty to the crown. Cease your shameless self-flattery!" He still hadn't regained any color as he turned his back to the table, trembling with fear and anger.

Billiam waved dismissively and responded, "You asked."

Ackerman mustered up enough strength to outstretch his hand and swat it against his son's. This was to show his distaste for him causing a scene, but I could tell he was fairly amused.

Roland got up, grunting out, "Thanks for making everything fuckin' weird, guys." He pushed his long blond hair out of his face and walked over to his wounded friend. He broke dress code, as always, wearing a gray sweater over his dress shirt, and baggy black jeans instead of trousers. He had a collection of chains hanging off his pants, individual expression I suppose, the jingling of which created a nice diversion as he crossed the room. "We'll go out for a smoke, hm?" Pushing his friend along, he walked out quickly, trying to maintain whatever shred of cool they might have left.

Katrina had her head sunk down since Billiam first uttered that strange reason. She felt as though she was behind everyone most of the time, and here was another thing she didn't know. She thought to herself, *Why would Billiam say something so obviously untrue? Does Zan truly fancy a man? Am I not enough?* It made no sense to her. She pushed out her chair, coaching herself to remain calm. "Seems we are taking a break?" she queried, forcing a smile and trying hard to let no tears escape. "I'm parched," she continued while running over to the kitchen.

"Ten-minute break, everyone!" Billiam shouted. Turning to Shemmy, he whispered, "If I had a wet rag, would you be able to enchant the water to freeze around it?"

"Easy as lemon cake!" She had been pawing through her strange-feeling hair the entire meeting and had started to make some new braids.

"Wonderful, come with me." He walked with her the few paces to the bar and leaned over it. He emerged with two rags and soaked them with the water hose they had at their tap. With these in hand, he slapped on a stool, prompting Shemmy to sit beside him. Nairee and Pierre had come over to gather around Billiam's father as they quietly discussed particulars of the plan. Alex left to start dusting upstairs.

Katrina was a rather private girl, so as she cried over the sink, she left it running to avoid being heard. Jess came up behind her with a hug, and I put my hand on her shoulder. Between loud sobs, all she could say was, "I don't understand," about three or four times. After she calmed some, she tried speaking more. "We made love as recently as yesterday afternoon.... In the beginning it was him who.... He sought me, fought for me. Why would Billiam think that?" She turned around to fall against her sister's chest, and Jess played with her hair.

I felt a great need to comfort her as I had grown fond of the twins upon moving in with them when the inn was first started. "Katrina, you should know faelocks, like Zan and myself, have a different way of being attracted or falling in love than humans. We take after the ogres, who were practically asexual, and we put much more importance on our platonic relationships." She looked at me and stopped crying but seemed just as upset. "This leads us to become extremely attached and eventually attracted to people we admire. This was true of Billiam's parents, as his mother was a faelock and private in the Order. She looked up to Ackerman like no one else, and fell madly in love. Many faelocks fall for their heroes, no matter their gender, and that is why our species' population is frequently in decline." This last part caused Katrina to bawl again.

"You ain't helping, Leke!" Jess squealed.

"I'm not done," I said calmly, grabbing Katrina's shoulders and turning her toward me to hug her. "Billiam is half faelock, and he knows of the way we think and feel. That is why he has been so hopelessly in love with Micah since boyhood. Micah is his prince, and he always looked up to him despite his younger age. Billiam knows it is likely that either my brother or I might fall for him, being the acting captain. I love him as a second brother, but neither of us would be attracted to each other in an intimate way, so that leaves Zan. He probably just guessed and ended up hitting a sore spot. Whether Zan has any real feelings of that nature for Billiam, I cannot tell you. What I can tell you is he is mad for you and has been since the day you met."

I abhorred lying, but I also hated seeing Katrina in so much pain. I was partially telling the truth; the farce was simply feigning ignorance of what Zan's relationship with Billiam had truly been. We really are ensnared far more by feelings of adoration and honor than physical or lustful ideals. It was because of this that Jessica and I could maintain our carefree and secret relationship. I enjoyed her body and company and she mine, without any troublesome emotions like love mucking things up.

"Good save!" I saw Jess mouth to me.

Katrina picked her head up off my stomach and let a smile break through her stormy face. "Oh gosh, finally. It made no sense to me. I never knew that about faelocks! I am ashamed of Billiam for being so hasty; it seems so unlike him. Perhaps Zan does have a secret affection for him, but he truly does love me, and I'm the one he's with. That's what matters!" She backed away from me suddenly and frowned. "Physically he won't be for the next few months, though. He will be with Billiam. I can't just sit around here knowing he's there and might be falling in love with our captain!"

She turned to Jessica, grabbing her hands hard, and implored her, "Sister, switch me spots, please! I can't stay here with his memory all around, jealousy and worry biting at me constantly. It's already happening. If Billiam doesn't allow it, we can just pretend to be each other. Please, Jessica!"

"What? I have no explosive skills. What am I going to do without Leke protecting me?" Jess wanted to help her sister but felt very reluctant about this.

"You will have Roland! You can just leave Drummond sooner if there are even whispers of danger. Khur is not supposed to be a frightening place at all." She was now on her knees, pulling on Jessica's legs as she begged.

Jess looked at me mortified and then lovingly down at Katrina. "Roland ain't even remotely a replacement for Leke, and you know that. However, you are my sis and my best mate, so fine. I will be a stupid gatekeeper instead of an awesome boat watcher."

"I think you have those two things confused," I teased Jess, laughing as I knelt to help Katrina up. "You feel better, then? You'll get to talk everything out with Zan too. There's nothing to worry about."

"You're right, and I do. I hope you don't mind protecting me instead," she said, her face starting to look like its regular self again. The sadness had distorted it terribly.

"I'm sure I will have much less protecting to do this way." Both the girls giggled, and I got a small punch in the arm from Jess before we were ready to rejoin the group.

At the time Jess and I were consoling Katrina, Billiam and Shemmy were making themselves comfortable at the bar. He had reached over it and fumbled for a bottle of mead. Shemmy kneeled up on her stool, grabbing two glasses from the rack above her. They had begun sneaking in their quick drinks when Zan and Roland came back.

Roland sat back in his seat and plopped his leather boots on the table, before Nairee quickly smacked them down. Unfazed, the young rebel leaned back in his chair, appearing to have fallen asleep in an instant.

Roland was the bastard son of a prostitute named Amber Dallow, though Pierre and Nairee unofficially adopted him when his mother went missing. Roland was nine at the time and hadn't seen her since. He had no education prior to his adoption, so Nairee devoted herself to giving him knowledge on a variety of subjects while she nursed Katrina through her illness. Roland's mother gave him a gun when he was four, to help protect them from her dates. He continued using pistols as he grew up and had a natural talent that was fostered by Zan when he joined the reformed Order. He was an asset to our group, but he was only eighteen, and his lack of discipline was worrisome.

Roland was the only person I had seen my brother care to take under his wing.

Billiam felt a tap on his shoulder. As soon as he spun around, Zan's fist slammed square against his right cheek. His whole skull seemed to vibrate with the force. Recovering his wits and regaining his breath, he calmly said, "Well, I deserved that." He grabbed his face and put his other hand onto Shemmy's shoulder. "Be a dear and freeze one of those rags now please."

She nodded and drew a hex, freezing the water all around the rag. She set it over the right side of his face for him.

"I can't believe you would say something like that in front of everyone. I mean Katrina and your damn father were right there! Do you not think of anyone but yourself?" Zan was seething mad but equally embarrassed.

"I could've asked you that same thing over a hundred times, wouldn't you say, Zan? Besides, when else was I to say it? Who knows how things will turn up and if I'd get to humiliate you ever again? I hate the thought of your secrets being buried with either of us." Billiam had turned from him to gulp some of his mead. He was acting once again as if he barely noticed Zan's presence, even when speaking to him.

The tension was getting to Shemmy. She, like everyone except those two men and myself, had not a clue what Billiam could be referring to. It excited her, but all the drama that rose from it was bringing her down. "I say you boys oughta kiss and make up! Or get your aggression out wif a good wrassle, a nekkid one!" She grinned from ear to ear, and Billiam snorted out a laugh.

"Only in his dreams and my nightmares, Shemmy," he grunted before turning and bracing himself. The second punch landed in his left eye and forced him to fall back against the bar. Shemmy froze the next cloth with no prompting this time and handed it to the punching bag.

"Why do you think I'd be good for protecting you, if you apparently cannot stand me and I am content bashing your head in? You are being stupid, Billiam," Zan chided, while rubbing the knuckles on his right hand and finally sitting beside him at the bar. "You are being rather morbid too. Obviously if you do bring me with you, there is no way either of us will be meeting our graves."

"Zan, you know you owe me at least this much." Shemmy saw a pain fall over Billiam's face, but it was not physical. He edged over a bit in his chair, only getting an inch from Zan, but even that short distance made him feel more comfortable. "I need Leke to lead her own team, and you are the only other I have confidence in. I feel you will protect me just as fiercely and probably be less clouded by emotions than your sister. She loves me like family, an unshakeable bond. Your affection for me is far more practical, thus I feel you will have better judgment when it comes to the protection of myself and the prince." He looked at him seriously and grimaced before turning forward. "That is my reason. I just uttered the short version."

He held his hand out to Zan, who feigned a disgruntled face and shook it briefly. In truth, his heart was beating like a jackhammer, feeling things get better between them and having Billiam's hand in his own. It had been a year since he had touched him in any way.

"I dun get it," Shemmy groaned, hating to be left in the dark on a topic so juicy.

"You don't need to," said Zan with his large fake smile. His mood was immediately lifted by the small contact with Billiam. "You really should get your meeting back in order, sir. Also, no more of this!" he lectured, grabbing the bottle and both glasses in one swift motion. "No one wants to hear about a life-threatening mission from a drunkard."

"About that, you are telling the truth," Billiam replied, pulling the frozen rags from his eyes and staring at his reflection in the bar's shining, metal sink. "I don't think I'll have black eyes. Just a bit puffy, I'd say, with no permanent deformation, thank Spirit," he muttered after pulling himself away from his reflection. He looked much more disturbed by his proximity to Zan than by his swollen face.

"No matter how mad I may be, I wouldn't be stupid enough to damage a face like that beyond repair," Zan replied cheerfully.

Shemmy scratched her head as she followed the men toward the meeting table. She had thought that hearing them speak would shed light on whatever was going on between her soon-to-be travel companions. Conversely, their interaction provided her with more questions than answers. She could only hope Billiam's interactions with Micah would be much more satisfying.

The boys and Shemmy arrived back at the table just as the girls and myself had taken our seats. Zan jabbed Roland in the side to wake him up, encouraging an entirely unmanly yelp to leap out of him. He was about to be angry but could see his strange friend was feeling better. Instead, he returned the hard poke with a smile. "All sussed out, then?"

Zan nodded and grinned sheepishly across the table to Katrina. She forced a smile and returned the gesture.

Malcolm set down his pen and sat up straight in his chair. He hoarsely asked, "Are the juveniles done reliving primary school, now?" Ackerman scoffed loudly at this, causing a small coughing fit.

Malcolm was a portly fellow. He was scarcely as tall as Shemmy but made up for his diminished height in rotundity. His balloon of a body seemed a bit less silly when clad in his well-tailored suit than it had in the ill-fitting chain mail back in our heyday. His skin was a golden tan, and his eyes were hooded, traits he inherited from his ancestors who came to Drummond from Khur about a century prior. He was thirty-eight years of age and was completely cynical and utterly rational. I rather enjoyed that about him, actually.

"Right, I am quite done providing entertainment for this afternoon. Everyone else?" Billiam said, grinning and sending a look to each of the younger members at the table. "Well, I didn't quite plan my responses to inquiries as thoroughly as I did the presentation itself. Do forgive me.

"In the briefings Pierre will be handing out, there are specific tasks for each group. The main objective is to find people to stand behind our prince. We must get their sympathy, their love, and their loyalty. We will be strangers from a country whose current leader is feared and hated, so this will take tact and persistence. The key is to show how joining us will benefit them, not ourselves. We will be fully prepared for battle, but after the prince's extraction, the only group expected to have genuine violence thrust upon them is my own. It is important you know what you all mean to me and that you are not sacrificial lambs. That may sound weak for a leader to say, but we are the only real strength remaining in this nation, and that makes each of our lives invaluably precious. This being said, give your all, fulfill each task in the briefing as quickly and completely as possible, and take the utmost care of one another." Everyone yelled a small cheer and gave the salute of Logos to their leader, by holding their hand lengthways from their face and raising it swiftly above their heads into a fist. Shemmy was exempt from this, of course.

"Gear and weapons shall be prepared at nine tomorrow morning. Pack light, and to the specifics of your location, of course. You shouldn't wear your little dresses in Alafor, Jessica. You'll come back with frostbitten legs!" he teased with a smile.

"About that...." Jess rebutted before trailing off. She stared at the table, twirling her finger in her hair until Katrina nudged her hard with her shoulder. "Right, well, I don't wanna go. Katrina said she would. I gotta see those kittens when Buttercup pops. Someone needs to make sure the perfect, most stupid-looking one is saved for Shemmy. That, and I refuse to wear sweaters...." It wasn't the most convincing performance, as she was still not thrilled about having to stay behind.

"Oh, so Kat refuses her cat duty? That's a bit unexpected. I guess you and Shemmy really are fast friends, huh, Jess?" he asked, not believing her reasons at all, but also not caring enough to anger the girls.

"Katrina, are you sure?" Zan called, attempting to get up before she waved him down dismissively.

"You were worried about me staying here, weren't you? I will be fine; I'll have your sister with me. I've always wanted to see Alafor, and I obviously have a much more suited wardrobe!" she replied, sounding warm but looking distant.

Billiam was a bit baffled but felt he could stop the meeting now, regardless. "That sounds fine, girls, if you are so decided. Each team can meet with Pierre individually to get their briefing pamphlets and discuss any particulars. As I said, nine in the morning is when we will be equipping, and nine forty-five we move out. Until then, take care of whatever you need. It feels like short notice, but we've been waiting for this for five years, so it really isn't. In fact, it's about damn time!" We all cheered and saluted again. Shemmy attempted, but smacked herself lightly in the face and then gave up. "Make sure you all have some fun tonight! No oversleeping!" That last part came with a thunk on the head for Shemmy.

We all began to disperse, taking turns to stop by Pierre before going off on our own way. Shemmy got up, letting us all see how her gown had gotten stained with everything she had consumed. Nairee's face froze when she saw the mess that girl made of herself.

Once we'd all gotten our information, I went to speak with Billiam, and Roland joined us. Quietly Zan and Katrina walked outside together. Malcolm and Pierre wheeled Ackerman into the kitchen to get him some real food and sneak him some ale. Nairee and Jessica descended upon Shemmy, first pulling her upstairs to change, and shortly after taking her out to town to shop. A wash of normality fell back over the lodge. At the end of this day everything would change. The faces we had seen every day, we wouldn't see for months at the soonest, if we'd even see them all again.

That night, Nairee and Alex prepared us a grand feast. Zan and Roland attempted to make music with their flute and piano and were mostly successful. Katrina and Jessica poured drinks generously, but by nine all members of Logos were cut off. It would be unfortunate to wake up with a hangover when one's life was on the line. There were many citizens in the tavern that night who must've thought the patrons were just being exceptionally jolly.

As the commotion died down, I had a chance to approach Billiam privately. "Well, Captain, it is finally happening," I said, putting an arm around his shoulder. I am eight feet tall, and although Billiam only shot up to six foot six, our shoulders were about the same height, my neck taking up a lot of my length. "You are ready?" I asked, locking my gaze with his dark brown eyes.

"Aye, well I think everything is put together as well as can be. It all works on paper. I won't feel totally comfortable until it's done, and we land in the woods." Billiam was hardly able to stand still.

"I was talking about you, not the plan. I mentioned nothing to the girls about him. I think that Katrina is fine. I worry about you, and not just because of Zan, but because of Micah. I feel your emotions with you, you know. This resurrection ritual… there is no concrete evidence of it ever really working or how well. I need to know you will be okay, no matter the outcome," I continued, to which he fell into me, letting tears slide down my neck.

"Shemmy, she will buffer me from Zan fine. I worry not about my choice there. I know it surprised you, but I need one of the two of you with me. You are the only one I can trust to take over, should something happen to my group. I cannot stand being near him, but I know he is devoted to me and will fight like a one-man army to protect me. I will put my feelings aside if it benefits the safety of the prince.

"However, if Micah... if anything is critically wrong... I assure you, I will not be the least bit okay. I will be destroyed and will be able to lead no one." He hugged me tight, still crying, as I took caution to make it so that no one saw him in this state. "You will take care of everyone. You will take care of me? If I can't have him or the real him, you are in charge. No one can know this, but you must be ready. You will feel my pain and know to change the plan. I doubt I will be able to let myself live for more than a minute if we fail."

I held him for a moment before saying anything. "Of course, Billiam. I just needed to hear that you truly understand. Please do not lose your resolve unless it needs to be lost. I am not sure why, but I actually do think this will work. You will have your love at last; I feel it in my bones. Take that not as a premonition, but know I believe in you and in Micah. I have faith in that creature you brought as well, though you don't need to tell her that."

"Leke, thank you so much. You are my anchor, hard and cold, keeping me grounded always. I really... I need this to work. I need my life to finally be better." He wiped his face on my shirt, transforming himself back into our fearless leader. "Let's start a revolution, my dear friend!" he exclaimed, and for the others, this was the first audible part of our conversation. With that he was ready to stop hiding his face in my neck and start making his good nights.

Roland and Zan were taking the sleeping elder Grimhart upstairs, so I tended to another passenger. I grabbed Jessica off her swaying position on a bench and carried her to my room. While ascending the steps, I pressed my face up against her skin, getting my fill of her warm vanilla scent before we were to be apart.

CHAPTER 4

May 4th, 989

MORNING FELT far too soon, warm in my bed with Jessica curled into me. This was not the case for Billiam, who had slept approximately half an hour in five-minute intervals throughout the night. By the time the sun rose, he gave up that hopeless endeavor.

He kept feeling as though he needed to pretty himself, to become an immaculate visage. As quickly as this anxiety would wash over him, it passed and he grieved for it. He knew he was to see the prince, but the prince would not be able to see him. He was bubbling up inside so much so that his nervousness was what actually woke me, not daybreak.

As I mentioned, we faelocks are incredibly empathic. My strong bond with Billiam allows me to experience his emotions when they reach extremes, kind of like a knock at the door of my soul. When he knocks as loudly as this, I have to answer the door promptly, or he will never stop banging.

Slipping out from under the sleeping beauty, I snaked my long body onto the wooden floor. Climbing up the stairs from my room on the second to Billiam's on the third, I prepared myself for the wretch. I went to return the knocking, but his bedroom door was wide open. I saw him in the mirror, untying and retying his necktie twice before he saw me.

When he did finally see my reflection, the shock forced a little yelp out of him. "Leke, good morning! You look terrible."

"What do you expect? You woke me up," I grumbled, crossing his room to fall back onto his bed. "Give yourself hypertension and you might pass it on to me too."

He laughed, but it was to please me, not because he meant it. He sat next to me and frowned before tugging on my flannel pajama pant leg. "I do not ask you to share my feelings. I would rather you not be burdened by it. I cannot… I won't be able to relax. You should get used to not sleeping, until he… if he…."

That last thought actually caused me physical pain, so I punched him for it. "Stop it, Billiam. As much as I want you to be realistic, I don't want you to turn into a morose weakling. You are our confident, valiant leader. How disappointed will Micah be when he is revived and you are shocked to see him, blubbering like a baby? No! You must be ready for him, like you have been. It is destiny for him to be brought back to you, and that is how he must be greeted. It is with that confidence that you need to handle this whole mission, even before he can appreciate it."

He flopped backward, landing squarely on my stomach and knocking the wind out of me. He was obviously feeling better as that emotional pain in my chest was no longer seething. He was still forcing me to choke on his nervous butterflies, but the full-fledged terror was no more. "Leke, I cannot wait! I am sad you will not be there."

Rolling out from under him and into a seated position, I responded, "I am actually quite glad it will take you at least a week to get to Alafor after reviving the prince." He grew upset at this, so I grinned and continued, "You may not be acting like such a lovesick puppy dog at that point. You are going to be disgustingly happy; feeling it will be more than enough."

"You know me too well, friend." He was smiling as he got up, though he began pacing. "Pierre is already double-checking all the wine bottles. Malcolm will be procuring their disguises from that tailor woman any moment now. What do I do?"

"Does Nairee need any help prepping the balloon or readying the spell? Perhaps you should make Shemmy observe. I know it's not the same as enchanting, but if she can pick it up, it may prove quite useful," I suggested. I knew even the tasks he was speaking of, the ones the others were doing, were more last-minute checks than anything. We had gone over everything so many times, despite accelerating the date of execution. There was really nothing left to do but to actually do it—a logic that was lost on this anxious man at the moment.

"Brilliant, Leke! We need to be off to the balloon, then! Waking up Shemmy may take a while. You get yourself dressed, and I will start on raising the beast." He got up and bounced around like a gleeful child. He was so excited, he barely remembered his hat and thought nothing of putting on a coat.

Following orders, I left to prepare myself. Walking down the hallway to the stairs, I saw Zan poking his head through his doorframe. "Thank you for making him feel better," he mumbled, letting go of his chest and hobbling back to his bed.

Billiam had taken my thought of bringing Shemmy to watch the ritual and run with it. Nairee became so confident with Shemmy's abilities she left the actual casting to her. This gave her time to get into character without having to rush directly from the balloon. Shemmy was so adept at her newly learned spell, she adapted it to work on living objects as well. Malcolm and I got to be her test subjects.

At nine forty-five, as scheduled, groups A and F were outside the Westend sewer overflow preparing to board our inflatable chariot to the castle. This same debris chute introduced Billiam to Shemmy, and so it would do the same for his reintroduction to his beloved Micah.

"The five of us won't be too much for the balloon?" Zan asked Billiam but stared at Malcolm.

"It can hold three tons. We are definitely fine. Leke will carry Malcolm down the rope to save time, if that's fine with him. She can also hold three tons, I believe," Billiam replied with a grin. Malcolm just shrugged. He was used to such inconveniences and judgments based upon his size. I nodded, though me carrying three tons was a slight exaggeration.

We piled into the balloon, and Billiam barely waited for Shemmy to finish the cloaking. As soon as she had a leg in the basket, he struck up the flame. She fell into me, looking like a strange doppelgänger in her white top and black slacks. Nairee and Jessica had forced her to dress like a Logos. The outfit was a far cry from the low-cut patchwork dress of animal skins we all met her in. We rushed up into the air and off to meet with Nairee and Pierre, who had just reached the castle gates.

The cardinal was the highest-ranking religious leader within Casperland, and thusly did his best to stay true to a pious, devout appearance. One thing he found impossible to humble was his obsessive thirst for expensive wines from across the globe. Having a wine vendor with an order set up, even one that was not formally scheduled, would not raise suspicion from anyone at the castle. To them, it was either an impulsive decision from the cardinal or a surprise that would delight him.

Nairee and Pierre were relieved by how easily they made their way in. They fit the part well, Nairee's exotic looks giving promise for a new foreign wine. After breezing through the front gates, they walked leisurely through the entry garden. They arrived at the door, and Pierre unhitched the wine cart from the donkey who would be sitting the rest of this mission out. The lack of wine not only made for a brilliant way to incapacitate anyone who saw them on their way through the castle, it also made the cart very light and easy to navigate. As soon as they approached, the large door opened, and Marla's round, happy face burst through.

"Aye, you are from the Chateau du Gamoline, 'den? Oi, master will be so excited. He's sure ta be the first in ta capital to get his hands on dis stuff," said the girl cheerfully, leading them in.

The castle was a masterpiece of white marble, dotted with furniture and doors of the richest carved oak. The royal family, the Helvendeeres, had been patrons of the arts their entire long reign. The fruits of their patronage culminated in the castle, showing the long history of Casperland from room to room.

As they passed through the spacious hallway, Nairee and Pierre looked upon the swirl of ivory and gilded wood fondly. This palatial home to kings had played a hugely important part in their lives. Amidst their reminiscing, Nairee engaged in small talk with Marla about grapes and soil quality until they made it into the wine cellar. Once inside the dark, cooled room, Marla locked the door behind them.

"All right, are you ready, miss?" Pierre asked kindly, wiping his glasses on his shirt. He was a thin, sort of frail man of forty-eight years. He was average height with pale, wrinkled skin and a full beard. He looked more like a bookworm than a warrior, which was a bit true. His focus was strategy and explosives, though he was an impressive swordsman in his own right. He was quick and easily underestimated, a fearlessly loyal knight all his life.

She nodded, and they all began piling the gas-filled bottles into their arms. Marla led them slowly through the back exit into the kitchen. They climbed out of the darkness of the cellar and were dazzled all over again with the glittering marble of the ground floor.

As they turned past the kitchen, a flash of bloodred caught the corner of Nairee's eye. Their stomachs dropped to the floor, and the three of them ceased breathing.

"Marla! There you are, you tart! I've had a truly pleasureless morning, dear. You have some time to make up for," called a rich voice from within the kitchen. Cardinal Aldrious's young-looking face watched on calmly from above the crimson robe. "You brought me presents and visitors, hmm? That's a bit peculiar." He cocked his head to the side, waiting to hear what she could come up with.

"Cardinal! I thought you would be at parliament today!" she gasped out, starting to feel faint. Nairee and Pierre were around the corner, trying to stay out of his view although they knew he was aware of their, or at least someone's, presence.

"You thought I was gone, so you'd run around carrying bottles of my wine and strutting merchants through the royal palace? What a silly bird you are. You know how I loathe political charades. It means nothing, so I used a double. I will get my way whether I am there or not. Oh Spirit, those aren't chardonnay, are they? You know I prefer reds," he chided, his words smooth and melodic coming out of his refined mouth. They were somehow terrifying without being so at all.

He walked over to her and reached to grab a bottle. Rage spread over his face, at first from the emptiness and secondly from the gleam of Pierre's glasses as he rounded the corner. After slamming one of his bottles down, he used that newly empty hand to grab the cardinal as he fell.

It was extremely difficult for the couple to not dispose of the tyrant right then, in his vulnerable state, but they knew they should follow the plan. This man and his corruption of the former king were the only reasons they could find for the ruin that had fallen over the kingdom they loved so dearly. To not punish him was the hardest decision they could make, but it was probably safer. There was no telling what the Mortanion Brotherhood would do should Aldrious be murdered.

Marla's joyful face had turned completely sour, and it looked like she was going to be ill. "Girl, change of plans, yes?" Nairee instructed, grabbing her shoulders and waking her up from her shock. "All right, you stay here. I know how to get to the prince's room. You need to throw down a bottle as soon as you see him move even an inch, ya understand? Take all my bottles. When you drop your last, you run as fast as you can out of this castle. I'll be taking your sewer key now. You just run and don't look back for nothing."

Marla was shaking, but she nodded at Nairee, who embraced her before following her husband. They continued their trek through to the hallway of the royal bed quarters.

The first guards came from a room on the left, surely wondering why the cardinal hadn't returned from the kitchen yet. Pierre dropped a bottle, though they both got their pistols ready. Sparing casualties was a luxury they could no longer afford.

They quietly passed by seven or so rooms before Pierre recognized the prince's door. It was made of fine mahogany, with gold flecks embedded in the ivy carved all through it. Nairee shot the lock, and they rushed in, ready for the onslaught of guards that must have heard it.

Micah's crystal tomb was prominently displayed in the middle of the room, only a few paces away from his real bed. It was illuminated by the large bay windows behind it, which would be their exit route to the courtyard. As soon as Nairee reached the coffin, a group of guards rushed them.

Pierre dropped his next-to-last bottle down hard at the same time Nairee smashed open the prince's coffin with the butt of her gun; the accidental synchronization making for one less noise. She flung open the lid, and Pierre made his way over. The frozen gas spilled out, nipping at the duo's fingertips before dissipating. He slipped one arm under the prince's neck and the other under his knees whilst she shot between the eyes of a guard in the doorway.

After breaking down the windows with a kick, Nairee jumped out first. Three servant girls hanging laundry screamed upon seeing her. Two guards heard this and ran from the other side of the courtyard. She grabbed one of the small bombs from the satchel on her husband's hip, lit it quickly, and tossed it in the prince's room. It exploded with a deafening rumble, crashing down bits of the wall all around their exit. This bought them time from the old pursuers to deal with the new ones. She chucked the last bottle hard into the middle of the courtyard, and the gas seeped out, knocking down both servants and guards.

"Up here," I called from a few paces above and in front of where they stood. "Shemmy cloaked us and the rope too. Malcolm is behind you." Nairee felt a hand grab her and could see his round body, clouded almost completely by the spell. "Can you make me out? I had her not cloak my ring. Give me the prince quick."

Indeed there was a silver band floating in front of Pierre's face. "That is amazing and lucky!" whispered Pierre, as he hoisted up Micah. My vaguely visible hand reached under the prince's armpit, pulling him up close to me on the rope. "The bloody cardinal is here. Marla has been keeping him asleep, but I don't know for how much longer." Pierre's distinguished and perpetually calm face was nothing of the sort at this moment. His rage was real and his genuine fear apparent.

I made my way up the rope as quickly as I could with one arm. I saw Pierre throw his satchel of bombs to Malcolm. More painfully loud booms echoed through my eardrums as gunshots went off around me. Zan, Billiam, and Nairee were picking off the guards that rushed the courtyard from all sides.

"We are running ahead, meet you two in the sewers! We are not so inconspicuous," called Nairee, running and shooting ahead of her at the same time, Pierre following close behind. The two elders looked shaken but determined. I was worried but confident in them, mostly because I hadn't seen the cardinal myself yet.

"There is a lot of trouble," I gasped out as I finally reached the top of the rope. Zan and Billiam each grabbed one of the prince's shoulders, gently bringing him into the basket. "Get the hell out of here, now!" I yelled and cut the rope before even jumping. I would waste no time on that, and was able to absorb most of the fall by rolling into a bush.

"Give me back my lamb, you bloody specters!" roared the cardinal as he emerged from Micah's burning room, completely unharmed. He was an attractive man who never seemed to age. His face was sculpted, his hair smooth and shining like onyx. As angry as he was, a small smile never left the corners of his lips. He was holding Marla's head in his hand and threw it up into the sky, to where he saw the prince disappear.

Much to Billiam's surprise, Shemmy reached out and grabbed it. "Bite that focker!" she growled, drawing a hex on the head before handing it to Zan. "Throw it back at 'is face!"

Zan obeyed, and Marla's head connected with Aldrious's chin, chomping down hard. It caused a small geyser of blood to spurt out above his strong jaw.

All that could be heard was a thundering, unearthly voice booming from the cardinal. "Die! Die! Die! Defy me and perish!" As he screamed this, he raised him arms to the air, ignoring the head still chewing up his face. He snapped back his wrists, breaking the bones and ripping his flesh. Blood poured out from the new holes and following it, seeped out two growing forms. The bloody figures flew up, contorting until it was clear what they really were. Two reapers lunged up from out of his hands and were barreling toward the balloon.

The crew in the air had already begun flying away and now had a reaper on either side. It was obvious the creatures could not see them but could either smell or hear them. They snapped and snarled ever closer to the basket.

Zan stood at the edge, examining the beast. "It's a spell," he explained calmly. "I can see the energy's epicenter, and if I break it, the spell will disperse." He grabbed his sword and thrust forward, hard. To Shemmy and Billiam, it looked like he was aiming below the wing on the right reaper, not even at the actual creature. Regardless of how it appeared, the reaper evaporated into charcoal dust before their eyes.

As the passengers looked on mystified at the disappearance of the right reaper, the left slashed at the balloon with its talons. Zan ran and thrust again, annihilating the spell though it had already done its damage. The balloon had barely reached outside the castle and there was now a large tear in its fabric. Billiam handed the prince, whom he had been cradling, over to Shemmy. He stood up in the basket, grabbed his handkerchief out of his pocket, and held it over the hole.

"Shemmy, can you enchant the air behind this cloth to hold it steady to the balloon?" he gasped out to her as the vessel bowed around, heading downward.

"I fink so!" she squeaked, lifting her hand to draw the hex. The balloon leveled out and moved forward. Billiam fanned its flame before slumping back down, both relieved and exhausted.

On the ground, I had drawn my sword to defend against any of the cardinal's underlings who might see me.

Aldrious was still screaming demonically, and he then suddenly turned toward Malcolm. "I smell you, piggy!" he hissed, pulling the chewing head off of his chin. Blood squirted out rapidly, which he pointed at my partner, covering him and clearly showing his location.

Malcolm threw one of the small bombs directly at the cardinal's face. My bloody friend turned tail to run the moment he threw it, though Aldrious imploded it before it could impact. He seemed to be able to negate its power and was unscathed. He ran after Malcolm, so I swung my great sword into the cardinal's arm as he reached for him. His wrists had somehow already been repaired, yet I made his right forearm thud against the ground. He used this opportunity to point the flowing blood at me, ruining my invisibility as well. Undeterred, I swung again and struck his chest. He fell over, allowing Malcolm and I to escape toward the slave tunnels.

I wanted to see what became of Aldrious. A regular human would be quite dead simply from the gash to the chest, let alone all the previous blood loss, but it was quite apparent the cardinal was no ordinary man. My desire to survive won over my curiosity, so we ran, hurling bombs behind us and shooting all foes in front of us.

Malcolm had much more stamina than you would expect of someone of his stature and kept pace with me as we made our way though the tunnels. We passed at least three-dozen disposed-of guards before making it to the entrance.

It was a drop down straight into the drink, which appeared to be about a twelve-foot fall. Malcolm hesitated, so I grabbed him and dunked him down the hole like a play ball. The huge splash of sewage blew all the way up to me. I grabbed the lip of the entrance and swung myself onto the dry edge. Nairee and Pierre were there and already helping Malcolm out of the filthy water. I looked up as I heard plate gauntlets scratching against the stone tunnel. Pierre lit a piece of dynamite, handed it to me, and I set it easily right at the entrance

I'd just swung from. With that we started running as fast as we could along the sewer ledge.

We reached sunlight at the end of the tunnel and were greeted by the torrent of waste that followed us from the blast. We heard giggling yards ahead as we shook off the filthy water that drenched us. It was no use; we were soaked to the bone, but at least we were all safe. Katrina ran over to us, smiling until her mental counting reached only four.

"Marla's sacrifice is why we are here, and why the prince made it out. The revolution would be impossible without that slave girl, so don't you be frowning, child," explained Nairee to her daughter, resisting the urge to embrace her. There was no need for us all to be soaked in filth.

While we walked over to the boats, Malcolm and I regained most of our visibility, revealing our clothing stained by the cardinal's blood.

"Are you hurt?" asked Pierre, taking in the gruesome mess.

"We are fine. The cardinal just wanted to take a look over us so badly, he donated a pint or two on us," I joked grimly, though it was actually quite accurate.

The initial deluge washed most of the blood on our skin away; however, I had a patch of it stuck at the base of my neck. I was eager to study it, and I thought perhaps it would turn to ash or never dry as I had heard happens to blood magic spells. There was nothing of note; it was dark red and crumbled off me as I rubbed it with a dry finger. Pushing away my slight disappointment, I joined the others cleaning up in the river. It was also compromised by the sewage flood but still cleaner than us.

We then said our short good-byes and readied ourselves to begin our respective quests. Katrina gave her parents an extended embrace and each a kiss on the cheek before joining Malcolm and I in the canoe.

I pushed hard against the shore with one of the oars to propel us toward the other side of the large and angry River Marken. Across its length were the forests of western Casperland, known as the Lostwood. It would be a long journey through it to Alafor, but at least it would be dry. We could spy our destination, the western shore of the voracious stream, when we lost sight of the skipper manned by Pierre and Nairee. They were carried swiftly south and out of our hands.

I sat in the middle of the canoe, with Katrina in front and Malcolm behind. I decided I'd do all the rowing myself, as I had reserves of energy left and would rather not have to work in teams for everything. The water was cold, splashing up as it fought against us. This river used to be a pristine blue flow of crystalline water. It was once full of life, but years of sewage and runoff from the corpses in Peace Valley had wreaked their havoc. Any fish that could be caught would be inedible; bears and foxes had not been seen alongside it in decades. The color of the raging rapid was a deep, dark olive with its spray a dingy brown.

We crossed the noxious river in a half hour's time. We unpacked the few bags from the canoe before abandoning it. Malcolm and I took time to get out of our soiled and soaking clothes, and then we were ready to commence.

Our walk to Alafor would take approximately eight days. The last ten miles of our journey were to be spent scaling the mountain range of Alstair, before we could emerge in the icy kingdom of Alafor.

I had brought much of my savings in the hopes that somewhere in this wilderness a horse or two could be purchased. There would be one ghost of a town we would be passing through called Pottleton, which I had a strange sense of hope for. I made sure to include it in our route. I was desperate to get us to Alafor as fast as possible, as it would be ten days at the soonest that the prince's group could get there. Two days did not feel like nearly enough time to make friends, let alone assess the level of safety for Micah.

As soon as we were dry and ready, I started off without a word. My companions followed suit, and silence became the fourth member of our team. It was apparent Katrina was still not herself and was looking as dour and serious as the two of us. I knew I would have to do my best to cheer her up before we got to Alafor; she was supposed to be the charming one, after all. I decided to leave that for later. I hadn't the patience for human emotions on the first day.

CHAPTER 5

May 4-6th, 989

THE BALLOON floated on valiantly, high above the wastes, with its handkerchief bandage working just fine. Billiam and Shemmy had switched back positions, and he was now cradling Micah while seated on the floor of the basket, and she was the "pilot." Piloting the balloon consisted of occasionally yanking on one or the other of the two pulleys, making sure the balloon was headed in about the right direction. She also kept a watch on the flame. Zan had his eyes behind them, scanning the sky toward the castle to be ready for any more flying interlopers.

Billiam sat cross-legged in a corner of the basket, the prince's head in his lap. He brushed Micah's chin-length hair off his skin to take in the view of the face he'd been removed from for years. As he looked over the prince's lovely visage, he noticed a scar starting at his collarbone and disappearing beneath his light blue silken blouse.

"That was not there before," whispered Billiam in a trembling voice.

He opened the prince's shirt to inspect him, prompting Shemmy to stoop down and gawk as well. Zan realized he had lost them both and turned from his lookout position to take over as pilot. Farther down Micah's smooth, pale chest was a veritable graveyard of scars, burns, and bites.

"Cardinal musta been punishing him, I reckon," Shemmy mused and pointed to one of the marks, a round pink mound above Micah's belly button. "He smokes cigars, eh?"

"I suppose he must, or at least when torturing the prince. Oh Micah, I am so sorry." Billiam clutched the prince closer to him, kissing the corpse on the top of its head. He rolled up both sleeves of Micah's top to reveal four-inch vertical and gruesome gashes on each arm. "Spirit, that bastard could have killed you.... Well, I mean... sooner." He got choked up as he rolled the sleeves back down.

Shemmy grabbed his hand before he could finish covering the horrible wounds. "Now, those ain't from the cardinal. Those be from Micah," she told him sadly.

"What are you implying? The prince would never be so weak."

"'Ey, I dun fink he be weak at all. I fink he was being smart, or at least trying to be. I mean, he was sure to have figgered wot the cardinal planned, and how he wos keeping him alive until his twentieth and such. He was juss tryin' to thwart Aldrious in his own way, prolly."

"I bet you are right, Shemmy," he agreed, buttoning up Micah's shirt. As he got to the bottom button, he coyly lifted his trousers and slipped his hand in and out quickly.

"Bloody hell, Billiam. What are you doing?" Zan grunted out from above them. Billiam had almost forgotten he was there.

His face grew hot with embarrassment as he stammered out, "Um, since I was inspecting him... and the parts down there, well, they're important to me.... Just wanted to make sure they were intact, is all. It feels like everything is in good condition."

Shemmy giggled and looked over Micah for herself, though only with her eyes. "He really is quite a pretty thing, isn't he? If ya had'nae juss grabbed at 'is privates, I'd ask if yer sure he's a boy."

Although dead, Micah had been very well preserved and did not look much different than he had when he was alive. He was a petite young man, less than an inch taller than Shemmy, with a slender, waiflike build. His skin was the fairest alabaster I'd ever seen. If you didn't know better, you'd think it had never been touched by sunlight. It was perfectly smooth and milky, or at least had been before the cardinal sadistically decorated his midsection. His hair was fine and silken, the lightest of yellow strands falling all around his regal face. His eyes were large with extravagantly long, dark lashes that added to his feminine appearance. Had he been alive, surely his dark blue eyes would be sparkling and his smile beaming. This was how I always remembered the happy young prince.

"I bathed him and dressed him most of our childhood. I assure you he is very much a male," replied Billiam, proud of his beautiful sleeping prince. "It's funny you should say that, though, for many people could not believe he was. He was only six when royals within our kingdom and also other nations started contacting the king and queen. They all wanted to secure the hand of the royal family's youngest daughter for their offspring or for themselves. Tales of his beauty spread fast and wildly, yet somehow his sex never seemed to register with those who heard of him. Paintings of Micah, commissioned by the queen, became mass-produced, adding to the hysteria and desperation for all to make him their bride first. There were many humiliated dukes and barons who immediately rescinded their offer for his hand when they were informed, again, of his sex."

"You gotta be kiddin' me? Those daft bastards!" Shemmy cried gleefully, snorting as she laughed.

"Oh that's not the end of it. One of his suitors was a prince from Alafor. Homosexuality is completely normal in their society, as all love is celebrated. He was so pursuant that he came here to Drummond to ask for Micah's hand himself, since the royal couple refused to entertain the idea. Micah was ten at the time; I had to keep him hidden in his room because Prince Gabriel refused to leave without him. I remember Micah telling his parents that he was not opposed to being a man's bride. He got quite a lecturing for that comment from King Quincey. After catching a glimpse of the wrinkled and desperate Gabriel, he conceded that he was not the man he'd like, anyways. Gabriel was eventually arrested for lechery and slated for execution, but the Alafor parlayed his release to them, ensuring his complete banishment from all Casperland. All the noise of that made the people of the globe concede he was surely a boy, albeit ever so lovely, and the requests for him to marry noblemen ceased."

"Oh I remember that tosser," interjected Zan, smiling for the first time that day. "He was so crazy it took your father and four other knights to hold him back without seriously hurting him. I think he ended up getting assassinated anyhow, but I'm glad they didn't execute him for being such a pervert. You know Micah'd think it was his fault."

They were enjoying the last bit of their flight together, feeling relaxed and laughing. Shemmy looked over the basket and saw them drawing near her home. "Down, down, less go down! I see my shack coming up! I miss my Gam, I do!"

"Your gam?" asked Zan, with exaggerated enthusiasm. He obeyed her and started cutting down the flame. They wafted down slowly before getting caught suddenly by a pine. The balloon thrashed about, ultimately deflating around the spindly branches. "Oops. I hope you know this is my first time in a hot-air balloon too!" he said, smiling his big phony grin, as he squashed the flame out entirely.

Zan jumped out of the basket and reached up to catch Shemmy, who followed him, shrieking excitedly. Billiam seemed to be the only one who thought about their precious deceased cargo. Carrying Micah against his stomach, he stepped as carefully as possible down the branches. When he neared the ground, he reluctantly passed the prince to Zan, and hopped to the dirt. "Excellent landing, my friend," he joked with a loud scoff.

Shemmy had already started off toward her shack, forcing Billiam to chase after her. "Shemmy, we shouldn't go to your house. We don't want to take any unnecessary risks. The cart is up ahead this way."

"But my Gam! He can carry the prince, and he makes for a brilliant distraction should we find ourselves some trouble," she rebutted.

Sensing Zan's hopeless confusion, Billiam turned to him to explain, "Gam is her corpse carriage. It has human legs and follows her around like a puppy." Returning to Shemmy, he scolded, "And it can't come. We don't need the attention associated with such a wonder." He mussed up her hair and put his arm around her, directing her away from the path to her hovel.

"Fiiiine," she hissed at Billiam and skipped along beside him, as Zan continued carrying Micah. He looked like a rag doll, limp and small in the giant arms of my brother. They reached their destination within twenty minutes of brisk walking.

The carriage was thankfully there, just as it was supposed to be. Billiam was hoping the appearance of the cardinal was the only surprise they were to have for the day, and so far it was. The shabby-looking cart was basically just a wooden slat pallet on four crude wheels, with a small fence all around it for keeping the items inside. There was a pile of dusty quilts and a half-dozen bags of flour, which were there to serve as the perceived cargo. He spied the sort of pathetic but suitable pair of horses beside it. They had been tied to a tree by one of our allies and were mindlessly chomping on foliage as they awaited the band of heroes. Only one horse was needed to pull Micah in the cart, so the other was to carry the lady of the troupe.

Billiam sought to get them focused, calling in a stern but cheerful voice, "All right, team, the walk to Failingveil will be less than three days. We will start out immediately and rest tonight and tomorrow night when the sun sets. We should reach the wood by noon of the third day. The entrance can move, but Zan will be able to track it. Shemmy, how do you think the prince's body will hold up for three days, thawed?"

"Um, well the reanimation ritual should take care o' most the damage, but there's no way to tell how much decay it can undo and how much it cannae." She scratched her head, looking over the cart.

"Should we soak the quilts so you can keep them frozen over him?"

"No, no, I ain't wanting to waterlog the boy, nor frostbite 'im. I'm finking... we should have him on the bottom, wrapped in a dry quilt, and spill the flour around him, as a barrier wif a frozen blanket or two on top. That should keep the moisture away, I fink. Not gonna be all too convincing there be nothing hidden in the cart that way, though.... Stick out like a quilt-covered sore thumb, we will."

"Hmm.... Well, we're an extremely rare breed just being outside the gates. That and us being a faelock, a halflock, and a banished witch, I don't see how any amount of caution could make us anything but suspicious. We should put the prince's health and freshness first," decided Billiam, already unpacking the cart with Zan rushing to assist.

"I dinnae know you was a halflock, Billiam. No wonder you make me look like such a shrimp."

"You are a shrimp anyways, Shemmy." Zan stuck his tongue out at her as he said it, a behavior he adopted from the twins. He was off toward the stream nearby with two quilts to soak before she could raspberry back. Billiam was busy swaddling Micah, so she helped herself to one of the carrots intended for the horses.

"Yes, my mother was a faelock and a knight in the Order. She was killed in battle when I was two," Billiam explained while hoisting the bundled prince into the far corner of the cart.

"Sorry to hear it. I thought your kind, or well your faelock half, s'all dying out because so many of you be queers. I am meeting quite a few o' yous, I reckon. I 'spose yer all pretty fruity, though," she teased while she finished her carrot, top and all, a sight that turned his stomach.

"That is a common and offensive stereotype, Shemmy," Zan lectured upon his return, tossing the soaked quilts on top of her head. Shemmy was not present when I taught the lesson of mating practices among faelocks to Katrina, so forgive the redundancy. "We are not all 'queers,' as you say. In fact, that is hardly the rule and despite what Billiam thinks, is not true for myself." Billiam hid his snickering while covering Micah with a ripped bag of flour, as my brother continued. "We are simply far more driven by feelings of loyalty and respect which grow into lust, instead of the immediacy of desire that occurs in humans. Since our attraction is not dependent on the wish to procreate like other animals, we are not a growing population. In fact, it's sort of our duty, or responsibility at least, to try to breed so our species does not die out completely, like the ogres," he explained and self-consciously looked over at Billiam for approval. He didn't get any, or any shred of attention from him whatsoever.

"Right, thanks for learning me dat." Shemmy stood up from the pile of dirt she'd been resting on and chucked one of the quilts back at Zan, causing some backsplash on his spectacles. "I need ya to hold that out, lengthwise, so I can enchant it. A frozen balled-up quilt shaped like ma face will'nae do us much good."

Zan wiped his glasses on his shirt, while holding the blanket out awkwardly with one hand, as if it were a soiled hanky. She glared at him, so he showed his fake grin and straightened up, holding it like he knew she really wanted.

She drew her hex, freezing the quilt almost completely, so it was stiff but still slightly pliable. She made sure to freeze the water droplets on his fingers as well, causing a biting pain and a small yelp.

"Oi, clumsy me!" she called to him, snickering as he shook the cold off his hand and walked the quilt to Billiam. Once again catching the wet quilt with his face, Shemmy and my brother repeated this exchange almost exactly with the second one.

After getting Micah's travel situation ready, Billiam and Zan moved onto preparing the horses. They piled the remaining quilts and the other flour bags around Micah in the least conspicuous way possible, but it did look like a very strange cart to trek through the woods. Billiam was about to announce their departure, when like a shot, Shemmy dashed into the forest.

"Shemmy, where are you going?" Billiam called after her.

"I hafta make a wee, and I dun want either of you fellas peeking!" she shouted, disappearing from their sight.

"You don't have to run too far! Neither of us are going to have any interest in seeing—"

Before he could finish, Zan let out an irritated scoff.

Unable to control his laughter, Billiam shouted, "Never mind, Shemmy, Zan very much wants to see. Keep running!"

A full eight minutes passed before Shemmy returned. "I don't think that was for a wee," Billiam teased when she returned, but he had been genuinely worried and was planning her rescue.

"Aye, dun go sticking yer nose in my business. It's quite a walk back thatta ways anyhow, and we should get going already!"

Zan sensed Billiam's irritation and knew that he was about to start up bickering with her, so he intervened. He grabbed Billiam's shoulders and spun him around toward the cart, as easily as if he were a top. Billiam tried to slap his hands off, but Zan had already stepped toward Shemmy. He grabbed her by the collar with one hand and set her atop the cartless horse. "Let's go, children."

With that, they commenced through the woods of central Casperland. They made little to no stops, aside from water for the horses and a handful of "wee breaks" as Shemmy referred to them. Thankfully none of these were as long as her first, and they made over a third of the distance by the time night fell.

As the sun became serious about setting, Zan and Billiam were deciding on the best place for their rest. My brother pointed out a clearing to their right and started over to it when Billiam, without thinking, held his hand out against his chest to stop him. His heart beat rapidly, but he obeyed the shushing motion Billiam gave him.

"What are you two feeling on each other for? Not that I mind but—"

"Shh! Shut it, Shemmy. Something is following us!" Billiam hissed out in the loudest whisper she had ever heard.

"Oi, you finally noticed den?"

"Shemmy, what did you do?" asked Zan, grabbing Billiam's hand off his chest and releasing it gently. Billiam's skin crawled, but he quickly regained his composure. It was his carelessness that caused that physical interaction anyhow.

"Oh, it's just Gam. I wanted some other clothes and such, so I packed him up real quick before we left. See! He's a sneaky bastard, won't hurt none of yer plans. C'mon ova now, Gam. Ya dun need to walk so far behind anymore," she called, writing a hex over her shoulder.

Within seconds the hulking carriage came over to them and sat itself down in the clearing. Billiam shuddered at the sight; he was still scarred from his abduction/rescue. Zan went right over to it, stroking its muscular, hairy man-legs in wonderment. This sight truly disturbed Billiam, so he got down to the business of bringing the cart over and out of sight from the path. He unhitched the horse as loudly as possible to drown out the others' conversation of reanimated corpse contraptions.

"Zan, stop that and get branches for the fire," he shouted coldly, sounding like his exhausted mother. Continuing his lecture, "Shemmy, you are in trouble, but I won't punish you until we are back in Drummond. There is a bucket in the saddlebag of the horse you rode on. Go and fetch some water please. There should be a stream to our left, I think. I am going to check the prince for moisture."

"Sure, that's what ye be checkin' for. We was there in the balloon, you know," Shemmy taunted and breezily avoided the rock Billiam chucked at her. She did a clumsy curtsy, called out "Aye-aye, cap'n," and ran off before he had a chance to reload.

They slept fairly well through the night, considering they had only two quilts not wrapped over Micah, no pillows, and it was brisk out. Billiam slept under the cart, feeling it was the closest place for protecting the prince. Shemmy wrapped herself in a quilt and slept inside Gam, with her dirty feet sticking out. My brother leaned against a tree, watching quietly. Whether he slept or not, no one could be sure.

The next leg was much the same and too mundane really for me to hash out in detail. They walked. There were woods. Shemmy pissed a lot. Zan chattered about inanely; Billiam ignored him. Shemmy enchanted a dead rabbit to dance in front of her as they walked until its legs broke, a sight which resulted in Billiam immediately vomiting.

THEY MADE a camp at nightfall, with only a measly two-hour journey left until they reached the faerie woods. It pained Billiam to have to stop when the destination was so close, but there was naught they could do in pitch-black. They had a meager meal of squirrel and more of the horses' carrots, and then they slept much as they did the night before. Billiam tossed and turned more this night, causing him to be most of Zan's focus as he performed his watch.

Billiam rose the same time the sun did. He was so excited, he perked up immediately, forgetting he was lying under a cart. Crawling out, he rubbed the bump on his head but was undeterred and ready to get their journey restarted.

Zan had fallen asleep and slumped into a squatting position. He was facing the cart, but his long neck was totally bent over, his blue hair almost brushing the ground. Billiam walked over to him and grabbed his shoulders, straightening him up against the trunk. Zan opened one eye and smiled at him, the first sincere grin Billiam had seen him make in years.

"Good morning, love," mumbled Zan sleepily, before falling back into his dream.

Disturbed by the affectionate words, Billiam turned away and decided he best wake his other companion instead. He grabbed a fallen tree limb as he walked over to Shemmy in her pram. He scratched the branches noisily against the top of the carriage, causing her to squeal and fall out, scared half to death.

"You arse!" she yelled up at him while lying on the ground.

"C'mon, get up, get up!" he pleaded, bouncing around like an excited child during a festival. "Today you bring him back! Today I get my prince back! We must be off as soon as we can! I am unable to wait any longer!" His eyes were glittering as he pulled Shemmy off the ground, grabbing her close and surprising her with an embrace. "Oh I'm so excited! Thank you in advance, my angel," he whispered. He gave her a kiss on the side of her head before setting her down.

Shemmy blushed and smiled. "Oh fine, I'll get up. Yer acting far too adorable at the moment to be mad at ya."

He grinned and started grabbing the things that had fallen out with her, shoving them back into Gam's belly. "Will you be a darling and go wake up Zan? He was being sort of sweet, and it disgusted me."

"Oi, well, I dun s'pose he'd be sweet to me, so I'll be awlright." She was a bit confused but obediently walked toward my brother, who was sitting straight up yet snoring loud like thunder. She reached her arm out and thonked down her fist forcefully on the top of his skull. She heard his jaw clap together, and he shook his head before looking up at her with shock and rage.

"Wakey, wakey, sleepy bones! Today be the prince's new birfday!" she sang, offering her hand to help him up. He swatted it away and instead strained pathetically to get his long, stiff body off the dirt.

"Right, I suppose Billiam has been patient enough the last few years that I can forgive the lack of sleep and rude awakening." He smiled over at Billiam, and it was mostly genuine, but a sharp pain stabbed into his heart. It was no surprise really that Billiam refused to acknowledge his sentiment.

The final leg of their journey to Failingveil was approaching the northern border of Casperland. Here the woods were thick, and the sky was filtered through pine needles, making it always seem later than it was. Contrary to Casperland's midland, where Drummond lives, this northern edge was consistently overcast. Gray clouds filled the sky, and although the air still hung around thick, it was dry and cold.

After an hour's walk, they reached the base of Mt. Kimper. It was a third of the way up this tree-studded rock face that the elusive Failingveil lay. As the rest of their journey would be an incline, they were forced to park the cart and to put Gam to sleep. A small wooded glen, ten paces or so away, provided a safe place to leave the vehicles. Billiam eagerly unpacked Micah from the cart; the flour seemed to be a bit gummy, but the quilt and the prince were bone-dry and freezing cold. He could smell some death on him as he pulled him near, but he knew that it would soon leave.

The trio began climbing the mountain, and their ascent was swift. Shemmy giggled as she jumped up on rocks, slipping in the dirt and tearing onto branches. It wasn't long before Billiam was struggling to get up the cliff while holding Micah's corpse tight against his body.

If he were alive, carrying his small frame would be no problem for Billiam, but the lifeless boy could not grab him back.

They had less than a half mile left to go, albeit entirely uphill, when Billiam stopped. He sat on the dirt and laid Micah along his lap. Catching his breath, he touched Micah's hair, hoping the feel of it would return his energy.

Zan knelt down, placing his hand on top of Billiam's, which was still on Micah's head. "Let me carry him from here, yes?"

"I need you to be able to fight, if any faeries are about. I can't have you weighed down by him."

"You know he will not slow me as he does you. Please, let me help you," he said while lovingly stroking his hand across Billiam's face.

"Don't touch me!" Billiam screamed, slapping Zan's hand away. "I will rest here. You go off and find the door. Don't come back until it's open, and we will go through together."

Zan jumped back, utterly crushed. He did not fight him but simply obeyed, walking away from the two of them and up the cliff.

Shemmy was shocked by the outburst and walked over to Billiam. "What's going on, then, Dandy? Is ya cryin'? Zan was really bein' kind to ya just now. I dunno why yer actin' so upset."

"You have no idea what that man is being, so butt out, Shemmy," he muttered but would not look at her.

"Aye, I suppose I don't. Tell me."

"About what's going on? What is going on... perhaps he is disgusting me with his kindness. I know what he is, and I know what we were, so I can't stand how he acts like everything is fine and he is just helping me out. He should never presume to touch me like that, even if it is simply genial. I doubt he is capable of geniality with me, anyhow." Billiam's face hardened, and his eyes watered while he gave his vague explanation.

"Oi, Billiam, now ain't the time for this. Let's cheer up and get your prince back, awlright?"

"This is the only time I have left to feel my hatred, before Micah will be here. I will not allow him to see the evil and pain which that man is!" he shouted and pointed angrily to where they had seen Zan disappear.

"'Ey, juss relax, hmm? We can make him tell e'eryone how much he fancies ya as soon as we get back. No need ta spout about hate and evil. We still gotta work togetha." She desperately wanted him to feel better. All she could glean so far was that Billiam was being quite dramatic, not something she expected from him.

"Shemmy, he is a liar. He always lies. I do not care what he tells others, because chances are he will be lying." He seemed calmer, but tears were pouring down his cheeks. "I just cannot abide having been put through what he did to me because of his 'love,' while he doesn't even have the balls to acknowledge any of it!"

"Well, what is it, then? Let it out, ya need to obviously. No sense in you clamming up and bein' a liar too."

He had not had a friend to talk with in a long time. He and I spoke little about our emotions, as I could sense them anyways. I probably respected his privacy more than I should have. He was tired of holding in this poisonous rage and considered laying it out for Shemmy. "You want me to talk about it? Will that really help?"

"It helps to hack up the food yer chokin' on, does it not? Same wif feelings, mate. Just spew 'um out while we got some privacy," she said sweetly as she kneeled in front of him, holding his hands over Micah's body.

Billiam ran his fingers through his own head of dark curly hair and pondered for a moment. His crying had ceased, and it seemed he was gaining some calm as he arranged the words in his head. "Okay... well the beginning wasn't so terrible. It was manipulative, but still mutually beneficial. After being banished from the castle, I was just a frustrated and confused teen. I confided in Zan about my sexuality and love for Micah. He concocted the brilliant idea that I ought to 'practice' for when I had Micah back, offering up himself as the test subject, of course. I realized it wasn't really practice; it was just fucking. It was not for Micah; it was for me and it was for Zan. Neither of us wanted to admit what we were doing, but he took it further and would berate me in front of others, completely pushing me away. My love was away from me physically, and the man I had physically would give me no comfort. He used me. Yes I got something from it, I will not deny that, but he took advantage."

Shemmy squeezed Billiam's hand, sensing that was not nearly the bad part. She forced herself to not envision the acts he just described, a near impossible feat for her, and tried to simply be there with him instead.

"The day we found out Micah had died... a year ago now... I was completely destroyed. I came to him for comfort. I knew not what had happened to his body nor that our comrades were already planning his resurrection. He went so far as to tell me his body had been destroyed. He let me give up all hope and seized the opportunity to make me his. I did not care any longer; I gave in to him and let him fuck me for the first time. He ravaged me, but something went wrong, something neither of us had intended. I lay there, bleeding out, and he refused to get me help, fearing someone would find out about his perversion. He would have let me die there in his arms sooner than have anyone know how he felt for me. Had Leke not sensed my anguish and come to my rescue, I would have perished. As she carried me, bleeding and sobbing, I learned of how Micah could be brought back. I let his evilness in me for *nothing*! He dashed my hope so he could have me and would do nothing to help his broken plaything."

Shemmy hugged Billiam tight, burying his face into her hair. It was at that moment Zan reappeared from the woods, a big fake grin plastered on the monster's face. She was up and running before Billiam could try to stop her. Her palm slapped hard and loud against Zan's cheek, sending an echoing clap down the cliffside.

"You fockin' raped him, you stupid bastard!"

He knew immediately what she referred to and what they must have been talking about since Billiam sent him off. He felt overwhelmed, so he just replied coldly, "Technically, no. He did consent."

"Yeah, cos you lied to him! You broke his fuckin' heart! I am sure he did'nae consent to bleedin' to death." She shook his shoulders, smacking his head against the tree behind him. "No wonder he is so pissed you won't admit nuffin'! Your shame nearly killed him!" She was disgusted at herself for thinking Billiam was being dramatic and for partially taking Zan's side. My brother just slid down to the ground, burying his face in his knees and wishing he could disappear completely.

Billiam stood up and actually did feel relieved. He had never talked about it. He and I scarcely mentioned it since that night. He had been letting it fester. As embarrassing and ill planned as this confession had been, he was happy he got to let it out before Micah was alive. He had no desire to bring this darkness and pain with him into his new life with the prince.

"All right, Shemmy. You can stop, we have a prince to revive," he called and even helped Zan up. He was shocked to see Billiam touch him without looking immediately revolted for the first time in a year.

"Wait, what? Juss like that, yer all fine now? Now I'm not fine! What the bloody 'ell!" Shemmy stamped her feet, overwhelmed by the emotions Billiam's story made her feel.

"I really do feel better. I didn't realize speaking about it could possibly help so much. I do not want to make Micah wait longer. Thank you for being my friend, Shemmy. You know the rest of the way?" he asked Zan, unwilling to make eye contact, no matter how healing the conversation had been.

"Actually, the entrance is closer than we expected," he answered, staring at his shoes. He pointed to a boulder jutting out from some trees, about twenty yards above them. "I see it right over there."

Billiam picked up Micah, his energy mostly restored by the rest. They silently walked up toward where Zan had pointed. Shemmy had not stopped frowning and could hardly stand her proximity to a man who would hurt her new friend so.

The door was not yet open, so Zan explained, "I wasn't sure how long it would stay open. I wanted to wait until we were all here."

He stood in a strange position, bending both knees but with one pointed in, and holding up his blade to his nose. He flicked the fingers on his opposite hand and thrust his blade outward, faster than the other two could see. His blade was down by the time they caught up, and they no longer saw a boulder. A valance of ivy was there in its stead, with a warm scent beckoning them into the forest walkway.

"I cannae even believe this shite," grumbled Shemmy, who had her feet dug deep in the ground, her teeth clenched tight with anger. Billiam grabbed her, and they followed Zan into the newly formed entrance, to enter a realm the likes of which none of them had ever experienced.

CHAPTER 6

May 6th, 989

ALL BLOOD was cleaned, all fires put out, and all other calamities resolved at Castle Helvendeere during the three days it took our heroes to get to Failingveil. News of the siege spread like pox through the streets of Drummond, though no concrete details were made public knowledge. All a given dimwit in the alleys of Westend might have known was this: someone broke into the castle, over fifty guards and monks were killed, and two reapers were seen shooting up from directly above the palace.

That last bit was most shocking, the unbelievable news getting the townspeople all uppity. Reapers had never been seen inside the city walls. In fact, when the Mortanion monks were brought in by the late King Quincey II to serve as advisors, strict restrictions were put on the use of the beasts. They were to only serve as defense against invasions and never to be allowed in proximity of civilians. Such an affront to the late king must've been a move of dire necessity from the cardinal—at least that was all the citizens could hope.

The twin spells released by Aldrious had caused widespread paranoia and a few conspiracy theories as well. For the most part, the simple folk of Drummond had to assume there had been an attack by a foreign agent. To doubt the cardinal or to think of domestic terror in any way was far too threatening to their ignorant status quo. One part they couldn't ignore, however, was that for all anyone knew, the reapers were truly creatures. In that case, why did the cardinal have them in the castle? How long had Aldrious been defiling the wishes of their late king by hiding those beasts of death in his home?

The parliament was desperately trying to retain peace and hoping to hold counsel with the cardinal. He had completely ignored them, relaying the sentiment that they could do whatever they bloody well pleased. Aldrious cared not about settling anyone's unease, aside from his own. The most vital piece of information, all that could undo him, was soon to be acquired. When he could become absolutely sure that no one in Casperland knew of the prince's abduction, besides his own brothers, Aldrious could regain composure. As long as the hope of their sleeping prince being alive was still present, the people could remain putty in his elegant hands.

The monks had been executing a thorough investigation since the moment the prince floated out of the cardinal's sight. All slaves and guards who witnessed the events were added to the pile of bodies we had created with our escape. The brothers found no whisper, no errant suspicion of anything pertaining to the golden boy of the Helvendeere family. They tread a fine line, needing to know as much about Micah as possible, while not encouraging the townspeople to put much thought into him. It was vital to their continued power that the citizens were content with their comatose prince, with no ideas of him currently being anything more or less. The monks conceded all worry was aimed at the eastern nation of Knox and returned to Aldrious, concerned for the growing fear he created with his counterattack.

Aldrious sat at the head of the royal dining table, having a spot of lunch, when Bishop Erek returned with his report. Erek turned green as he spied the cardinal's dining companion. On the plate at the seat next to his sat Marla's head, standing by the stump of her neck. Her eyes were still wide, and the tongue was wagging manically, not caring that Aldrious had ripped her lower jaw clean off.

Noticing his subordinate's change in color, Aldrious indulged him with an explanation. "I am not one to throw away a gift. I've grown fond of this grotesque gesture those twats threw at me. Also, she had been my favorite lay as of late. Not a memory I'd like to forget until I find a new one," he informed him, his thin lips curling a wicked smile around the sausage he had snapped between his teeth.

Erek cleared his throat and attempted to also clear his mind of any judgment he may have for his brother. *Surely someone so high in the brotherhood could sense a disloyal notion*, Erek thought to himself. *He is pure and chosen. I am unclean filth. My eyes deceive me. I know no true good, so this indulgence of a whore's head could very well be it.*

Bishop Erek was quite devout in the teachings and, unlike most ranking brothers, was actually born in Casperland. The church claimed its start and its home in the neutral nation of Enox, neighbor and last ally to the fearsome Knox. Naturally almost all of the brethren, Aldrious included, hailed from Enox as well. Erek had returned from his seminary studies there two years ago, feeling destined to give all his life and light to the salvation of his homeland. "Are you ready for the briefing, sir?"

"No, I'd rather you dance a bloody waltz with me first, you daft fool. Of course I want to know what you've dug up. Spit out your blatherings and then leave my lady and me be!" Aldrious seethed with anger, yet his voice was smooth and sweet like a hymn. The rage faded quickly; he laughed and smiled while throwing pieces of his toast against the waggling tongue of his disembodied lady friend.

"Right, sorry for my foolishness. Of all 3,748 citizens residing in the southwestern borough who were intervie—"

"Oh goodness me, are you truly going to be that drab? I suggest you come sit with us, in case you put yourself to sleep. Neither of us shall bite you, at least not anymore," Aldrious interrupted and waved his hand luxuriously, motioning to the seat beside Marla's head. His green eyes gleamed with the light of Aegis, somehow negating his abhorrent behavior, and did well to convince Erek to come over to his superior.

"Would you like the gist instead, brother?" His stomach turned and twisted when he heard those words spill from his mouth. It was common for all members of the order to be referred to as brother, aside from the archbishop who could only be addressed as father. Despite this being an appropriate way to address the cardinal, he somehow felt he was lacking respect and could expect punishment from him. To his surprise, Aldrious just nodded as he loudly sucked the pulp from a slice of grapefruit.

"No one has any notion of the prince other than the fact that he is here, asleep but well. There is absolutely no suspicion amongst the people of domestic involvement nor could we hear a murmur regarding the Logos. Should they be the culprits, their numbers are undoubtedly few."

"Right, nothing to fret over, then. You lot will bring back my lamb, as unscathed as possible, and we will all be right as rain again! Do you doubt me, Erek?"

The question rang through Erek's ears ominously, as he was sure that no emotion had been allowed to creep across his face. "No, I am simply troubled by the sentiment of the people. They are the ones who seem to be doubting you, brother."

"If you are troubled, dear brother, then you too have doubt," replied the cardinal, smiling pleasantly as opposed to deviously this time. Erek would never see this smile drop completely. Aldrious sat back in his chair, apparently done picking through his meal, and stretched his arms up in the air. "You still have your cherry, don't you, Bishop? It's funny how never having a bone goes hand in hand with having no backbone."

"If you are asking if I am still chaste, I am indeed. I, of course, took the vow of abstinence," Erek replied meekly, trying and failing to fight the blush that crept across his gentle face.

"I took that vow too! There was also that vow to never lie, to never take a life, to never drink vine on the holy day, and to never disobey my father. I am proud to say I have not upheld a single one of those, a load of rot they are. Moving on, brother, I'd like you to get it very clear—I care not what the scrambling masses of idiots out there *think*. It is meaningless. I simply needed you all to find out what they *know*. Surely, they still believe reapers are beasts of flesh and bone, and that the damn cardinal has soiled King Quincey's underpants. I defecate all over the memory of that sod every chance I get, so they are right, and it doesn't bloody matter. Are we clear, dear brother?"

"Crystal clear, sir. Perchance, had you questions for me?" Erek breathed deep and kept his mind clear. *This is the will of Aegis; I needn't understand. Praise be to the cardinal*, he repeated over and again, pushing away all misgivings. His brow ceased its furrowing under his light curly hair, and his pale eyes gained peace.

"I see you've caught on?"

Erek was startled. Had he been right that the cardinal was reading his thoughts? Was the power of Aegis truly so strong to break the mortal coil and infiltrate the inner sanctum of a man's mind?

"That I prefer to take the lead, dear brother," Aldrious elaborated, delighted by how much anguish he was causing the bishop.

"Yes, sadly I find myself ill-equipped to anticipate your needs at the moment," Erek responded, inhaling deeply and taking in the dining room at last. His lack of control of the situation actually felt a bit liberating. It did not matter what he said or how he said it; he was sure he would not please the cardinal, and there was no telling what his punishment for that might be.

This hopelessness freed him to appreciate his surroundings. Although he had been staying in the royal castle for the last year, he spent about 85 percent of his time between the cathedral and library. To witness this splendor, to sit where all of his nation's kings had sat, was a wonderful gift, even if it was to be spent with a severed head and a madman.

The walls were the same crystalline white marble as the rest of the castle, but in this dining hall genuine sapphires were dotted throughout them. The gleam of the chandeliers shone against each gem, creating a dancing blue sparkle wherever you looked. The floors were coated in a plush navy carpet that looked more like the coat of a great beast than any sort of synthetic fiber. Amongst the shining stones, the walls also housed portraits of all the past kings, who looked upon Erek kindly. Although he was not yet officially crowned, Prince Micah's portrait was hung behind the head of the table, the same image that inspired his menagerie of proposals as a boy.

Erek was lost in gazing upon the beautiful prince's face when Aldrious finally spoke again. "So that's what you like, Bishop? No wonder you are so strict to your vows. I myself have always thought the teachings and rules of MortiAegis are more for the people, not for the brotherhood. We enforce them to keep the masses in check, but once you have earned your stripes as we have, brother, they can tend to be optional. However, that 'man shall not fornicate with man' rule, can't say I mind following that. Whatever, each pleasure is a person's own, is it not?" Aldrious mused. He could toy with Erek's mind all day, had he wanted. Manipulation of minds was by far and away his chief hobby.

"Sir, I never really gave it a thought either way. I am a humble man and never considered my vows anything but a solemn promise.

I am, perhaps, not intelligent enough to see the true intentions of our teachings," Erek replied honestly, feeling unruffled, much to Aldrious's chagrin. Instead, he continued to stare at the portrait and into his prince's innocent eyes, feeling for the first time that his devotion had perhaps been misplaced.

"I admire your purity, Erek. I always thought the devout were terribly boring and simply fooling themselves, but you are mildly interesting. Did any of you louts interview the DuBois family?"

"Naturally our investigation of Westend was thorough, as it is the believed hub of Logos sympathizers. As such, we spent a good deal of time with the patron family of that quarter. Nothing that seemed of note to us was gathered, but I have procured the transcripts for you and can read them."

Aldrious waved his hand dismissively. "No, that would be dreadful! All I really need to know is the last time they saw their daughter."

"We interviewed five of their daughters; however, the eldest is currently residing in a sanatorium to treat her fits of psychosis," Erek informed plainly, before being startled by a chicken bone flying at his face.

"What do I care of those cows? I meant the one of the family name. Do you know nothing, brother? Chammerline the XII is the only one of that rabble who I dare let cross my mind. What have they said of their dirty witch-whore daughter?"

Erek felt the fear return to him, clenching his gut in a vise. "Right, I'm sorry, brother. So stupid of me," he said, feeling the desire to flagellate himself further but resisting it. "They haven't seen her since her banishment. The lady DuBois fell into a state of maudlin when her name was mentioned, wishing to not be reminded of the family heir's fall from grace. The eldest son, Connor, said he learned she had recently raised a corpse, which if true, would be the first successful resurrection in 428 years. He said the living corpse hadn't fared well but that her success was still a miracle, albeit a heresy. Other than whispers of her accomplishments as an enchanter, none of them have seen or heard from Chammerline. No hint of deception was recognized in our interviews regarding her."

Aldrious's eyes lit up, and his smile regained a large portion of its luster. "So she really did do it? I heard whispers, but if peons like

Connor know, then there must be real truth to it." He clapped loudly while getting up from his chair. He grabbed Marla's head and held it an inch from Erek's face. Its wiggling tongue grazed the young bishop's nose; he did his best not to flinch.

"That settles it, brother. I had little doubt that my dear cousin was the only one who could enchant this head so quickly and so strongly, but if she can truly reanimate, that would give her reason to take my lamb, would it not? You should look this over, Erek. As grotesque as it is, it is a brilliant display of Chammerline's handiwork. This spell is over seventy-two hours old, and the enchantress could be halfway across the country, yet it still just chomps along with desperation. I really wish you were not such a plebeian and could appreciate her genius."

Aldrious dropped the head, forcing Erek to catch it or have it land on his lap. He was puzzled and entranced by the once beautiful girl's hungry eyes staring desperately back into his own. "Well, I suppose she could intend to revive the prince, but her other attempt was not really a success. I hear it had full motor and involuntary functions restored, but it had no consciousness. What good would having the prince in that state do?"

The cardinal placed his hand firmly on Erek's shoulder, digging his long-nailed fingers into the flesh through the bishop's burgundy robe. A twinge of pain passed over Erek's face, but Aldrious was impressed by how little response he got from the innocent monk. "You should not speak of things you know so little about. Enchanting is something all the globe's children were forced into ignorance of by our predecessors, so I blame you not for your naivety. Do well to understand, brother: there are many ways in which a thing can be done. My cousin did it wrong once, but this does not mean she is not aware of how to do it right. I am surprised she could be bought, though. There is no way she could care enough about politics for this to be her idea."

"For as many ways as there are to do things, there are just as many ways to get a person to do them." Erek set the head back on the table before turning to the cardinal. Much to his surprise, Aldrious looked quite impressed with his apt response. "It is none of my business, but is Chammerline the witch, who you yourself excommunicated, truly your cousin?"

"Oh, thank Aegis, my pious brother finally shows some humanity and reveals his curiosity. She is indeed my cousin, but I do not believe she knows this. That is a perk of being a member of clergy; my family name never need be revealed unless I choose to. Those predecessors I referred to, the cause of our globe's ignorance, were really five people of five families. You have heard tell of the Families Five, yes?"

"I heard of the legend. The five families birthed of the Startspring and sent across the globe to reign over their territories. It is in direct conflict with the teachings of MortiAegis, however, so I never indulged it much."

"Yes, indeed it is. However, it is the real truth," Aldrious whispered hotly.

Those words made Erek feel as though the wind was knocked right out of him. He was aware the cardinal's behavior could be considered quite heretical, but what he was saying now was absolute blasphemy.

Sensing his growing uneasiness, Aldrious chose to explain. "I know this is true, no matter how shocking it sounds, brother. I know, because DuBois is the central family, descendants of sister Chammerline, and my family, the Dalgarie, is the family of the east, descendant of brother Arrikos. Any member of the Families could be my distant relative, but I am aware that Chammerline and I have a direct bloodline through the current lady DuBois. Knowing this does you no good, though, dear brother. It is a secret, and I fear your curiosity has cost your life, as I indulged it. It still feels so good to give in and learn some dirty laundry, does it not?"

Erek felt a wash of acceptance. These names he had never heard, this threat to his life, somehow it made more sense to him than any of his interactions with the cardinal had so far. Erek turned to Aldrious and gave him a smile, the first and only the cardinal was to see. "I understand, my brother. Thank you. Was there anything else you needed from me?"

"No, thank you for the company, dear bishop. You truly are a rare breed; such purity is hardly ever allowed to flourish. Do forgive me for snuffing it out." Erek's smile grew as Aldrious leaned over his face, leaving a heartfelt kiss on the young man's head. He plunged his dagger into his brother's heart before removing his lips. He felt Erek clutch him and grow weak.

"I hope…. Micah…." That was all Erek could last say. If Aldrious was truly able to read the bishop's mind, then he is the only one who knows what the end of that statement was to be. I have thought it over numerous times. It could simply be that he wished Micah would return to the cardinal and in his control. Perhaps Aldrious was right about Erek's carnal feelings toward the prince, and this was some sort of confession, but I find that to be a stretch. I might be an idealist, but I feel this strong and convicted man realized, in his last breaths, where real hope for the globe truly lay. Regardless, the bishop bled out and was added to the pyre that was still burning with our victims from the siege.

WESTEND IS the poorest borough of Drummond, and thusly holds the most resentment for the richly attired and well fed Mortanion monks. Thanks to this contempt, the villagers uttered not a word of their suspicions regarding the patrons of the Philosopher's Rest. Conversely, there were quite a group of them staying about the tavern in the days since the prince's rescue. They were eager to get the monks out and away when they came hounding.

"Ya fink the tossahs all done wif their questions, na?" muttered the old drunk, Maggie, from her seat at the window.

"I surely hope so. They do foul up the place, don't they?" Jessica called over, smiling while she put away some freshly cleaned pint glasses.

Her heart felt like it had been smashing against her rib cage the last few days and was soon to break it down. The questioning was heavily dedicated to Micah, the kingdom Knox, and a revolution. Only once did they ask her about Logos, and it was a simple inquiry of whether or not she knew any members. They either feigned or were ignorant to the fact of who her parents are. The worst and most surprising were the few questions about Shemmy. Adding to her nerves, they had deception specialists with them. These were a strange sect of the Mortanion order who could read intent, marking all lies with a single graze of their finger in their self-recording transcripts. Jess had no trouble fibbing, but she wasn't sure how to deceive fellows of this ilk.

"Bah, f'you ask meh, we otta be ta ones interrogatin' dem. Keepin' dem fings in our lord's 'ome," Maggie cried and spat on the ground.

"I second that, Maggie. However, please keep your spit in your mouth or a glass, no matter how right you are," she instructed with a sigh, walking over with a mop. Alex had relocated to the safe house with Ackerman, so Jess and Roland were now the only ones responsible for the inn's upkeep.

Roland saw to it to hire a cook swiftly but was dallying in finding a maid. Most residents who would be interested in the position were likely to be females, a weakness for him. He became unbearably bashful around young ladies and failed to convey the kind of message an employer should. In spite of this fact, he still took it upon himself to go out and find one before Jess could object. This stuck her with watching the bar and dealing with the interrogators.

Jess wiped up the spit and other spills from Maggie and then scooped up her four empty glasses. As she walked them back to the bar, she was startled by the door swinging open loudly, crashing against the wall. One of the glasses narrowly escaped her grasp and did its own crashing against the floor.

"I found one!" screamed Roland as he ran over to the thoroughly frustrated Jess.

She shoved the mop against his chest without even turning to look at him. Continuing toward the bar she growled, "Clean up your mess! What are you babbling about?"

"Oh, come now, Jess! Do be happy! I found us a maid, quite cheap too!"

"Oh my goodness, Roland, don't be saying that." She finally turned and saw him smiling, next to a very tall and beautiful woman, who was the one actually cleaning up the broken glass. "I am sorry for my partner's disgusting lack of manners, dear. I am Jessica, de facto manager of this inn," she said as she skipped over to them. She was quite surprised to see such a pretty woman. She thought for sure Roland would be bringing in a great-grandmother or someone equally diminished.

"Oh, hullo, Miss! Such a delight to meet you! I am ever so pleased to be joining your team. My name is Loretta." Loretta's voice was deep, with feminine airs dressed atop it. Jess was now aware why Roland could speak to her. Her frame was large and long, similar to Billiam's, with strong hands. A peek of Loretta's Adam's apple could be spied above the collar of her gown, yet none of the masculinity of her body was present on her face. It was made up immaculately, with soft features and full lips. Jessica was actually a bit envious of her mature, ladylike visage.

"Oi, well, he was having trouble finding work, ya know, being a he as a maid. He started dressing as a lass but was still not able to find employ, so his price is way more than right." Roland beamed, feeling he had struck gold.

"He is mostly right, Miss," Loretta explained. "Although, forgive a bit of blasphemy, but I think Aegis makes a mistake from time to time too. I might be one of those, as I have always felt far more comfortable in the role of maiden than any other. That, and to be female is more befitting to achieving my life dream."

"What's that?" asked Jess.

"To clean the world! I want to make it all sparkling clean! I love being a maid, a wizard of the household, transforming her realm into pristine beauty. The housekeepers and cleaners I saw have always transfixed me, and I knew then it was my destiny. I shall be the best maid Drummond has ever seen!"

Jessica laughed happily, not at Loretta's expense. "I have never heard of such a dream, but I am quite glad we will be the ones to benefit from it. So you are, from now on, our maid and are a lady of our house. Roland and I will do our best to address you as such, ma'am." She smacked Roland in the gut, causing him to groan before nodding in agreement.

"Oh, thank you, Miss. No one has ever treated me with such immediate kindness and understanding!" She grabbed Jess and embraced her hard, lifting her tiny body off the ground. Loretta was quite strong and had the hug lasted any longer, little Jessica may have been out of oxygen. "I can't believe a couple so young as yourselves are runnin' an inn. That is wonderful. Kudos to you both!" Roland got the enthusiastic hug this time, and although not pulled off the ground, he was left equally breathless.

"We are quite amazing, ain't we, honey?" Roland grinned like an idiot while attempting to put his arm around Jessica.

"Yuck!" shouted Jess, pushing him off before he could fully grab her. "We are most certainly not a couple."

She stuck her tongue out at Roland, who just shrugged, as if to say, *"It was worth a shot."*

"My parents and uncle own this inn. The former are on a pilgrimage, and the latter has fallen ill, so this buffoon and I are watching it in their stead."

Loretta squealed cutely before exclaiming with a wink, "Oh good, then I still have a shot with you!"

Roland blushed and hid his eyes behind his golden hair. "Oi, I'm flattered, Loretta, but I'm still gonna wait for Jess here to change her mind."

"No, not you! I meant Jess! I only love adorable things, like her. Just because I wear a dress doesn't mean you should take me for something that I'm not."

"Oh, well Jessica has a girlfriend."

"What!" Jess shouted, shocked and embarrassed. "Leke and I are not like that... not officially or anything."

"That's wonderful! I wasn't expecting you to actually fancy lasses! It's my lucky day!"

"No, that is not it at all. I very much like men and manliness," she explained bashfully. "To me, to be a man is to be strong, honest, determined, and brave. Of everyone I've met, besides maybe the captain, Leke is by far the manliest, regardless of her sex. She is the only lass I have ever fancied. Sorry, Loretta." I must say I do not mind being called manly at all, if those are the associated attributes. Honestly, due to my size and strength being a faelock, I never paid attention to my gender nor did anyone else really.

Roland looked terribly confused before mumbling out, "Billiam is the other manliest? I s'pose he's strong and a leader and such... but the way he cares about his shoes is just—"

"No! Not Billiam, you dunce, I was referring to Ackerman before he fell ill." Jess was growing quite tired of these two and their interrogation.

"Well, I am all those things! Just you wait and see, Miss Jessica. If not my masculinity, my ability to make everything sparkle shall enchant you! Please let me start at once!" With that Loretta was off with the mop, skipping and humming in a manner that was anything but manly.

"You are minding the bar now. I have a headache the size of the palace from all your foolishness. Leave me outta your nonsense next time, 'kay?" Jessica was fuming and could be a bit scary when she was angry. She hated to be embarrassed and hated discussing us. I thought it had to do with my sex, but when I asked her, she revealed it was because she feared she would fall for me more than I for her. Keeping me a secret also kept me more distant. As cold as it may be to admit it, she was quite right.

"Oh c'mon, Jess! I was just teasing you. I'm sorry. I will mind the bar, but I don't want you storming off. I'll pour us some drinks, and you can tell me 'bout the monks and such." Roland had grown up with the twins, and they were the only people who resembled a family for him. Although he did hold a small torch for her, more than anything Jessica was his dear friend and sister.

Before she could form a retort, the door swung wide open, and with it went the breath of every person in the tavern. Standing there in the opening was none other than Cardinal Aldrious. He held his hand out as a bit of a salutation, each finger cloaked by a ring of gleaming emerald, which created a lovely contrast against his crimson robe. He was smiling wide, seeming truly pleased to be there.

"Yes, my dear, I too insist you drink and talk with us!" He was laughing softly and melodically as he walked over to my two comrades, who were both frozen in fear. No one had expected Aldrious to catch on so soon, and moreover, to actually come to the inn himself.

"Afta'noon, Cardinal. What can I be getting for you?" Jess squeaked out. Her body and voice were both quivering uncontrollably.

He smiled deviously and licked his lips as he looked her over. "I have so many ways I'd love to answer that! First, some privacy, hmm?" He held up his arm and drew a crude circle around the three of them. "Right, that's better. Everyone shall still hear us talking, but it will be benign drivel. You will probably both compliment my attire a few times, and I am sure to drone on about the weather. We will keep all the juicy bits to ourselves!" He seemed downright giddy and grabbed one of each of their hands, letting his nails dig into their skin. "To answer your question, Jessica Mantine, daughter of Pierre and Nairee Mantine, I wouldn't mind you getting on your knees. How's that for a start?"

Roland grew enraged and threw down the cardinal's hand. "Don't you speak to her like that!"

"No, you don't speak, boy!" Aldrious shouted, drawing one of his nails against Roland's mouth slowly. As he did, his lips fused together. His eyes bugged out in panic, and he started to thrash about. "Now, now, if I were you, I wouldn't do that. You are limited to only breathing in and out your nose, and since I take you for being much the mouth breather, Roland Dallow, I would save your energy."

Roland ceased his desperation and closed his eyes hard before reaching for Jessica's other hand. It was terribly clammy, and she was barely able to grip him at all. He looked over to her, and it seemed she was breathing even less than him. Her eyes remained transfixed on the cardinal's. *What is he doing to her? What is he doing here!* Roland thought, trying hard to not let anger or anxiety overtake him.

"I agree; however, I could have been lacking some tact. We ought get down to business first. You see, dear girl, your lovely parents paid me a visit a few days back. I have a feeling they didn't expect me to be present. They must've remembered how much I love surprises! Despite that, they were terrible guests. They angered me so awfully, I was forced to rip off my lover's head and heave it at their accomplices as they made off with my lamb. I really am quite sore about losing my Marla. I think the least you could do is take her place. What do you say?"

Roland gestured wildly before getting slapped across the face by the cardinal. After, Aldrious grinned and cocked his head to the side innocently.

"I must run this inn, sire," said Jess in a robotic voice, unblinking and unflinching.

"Right, right. Well that isn't all I'd like to speak to you about," he said, finally motioning that the two should sit with him at a table. Before Jess could drop into her own chair, he forced her into his lap. "I had a lovely afternoon, chatting with one of my bishops about the events of three days ago. He enlightened me to an exciting fact before I stabbed him to death. This tidbit is that the enchantress Chammerline DuBois has successfully resurrected a human being. This convinced me so vehemently that the ones who attacked me must be the stupid Knights of Logos, who think they can revive their prince and retake the realm. I was already quite certain it was you lot by spying Pierre and Nairee, but with what I learned today, I know why they would dare come against me so directly! It also let me know exactly whom I need to have my people search for. It is quite obvious that pitiful faggot, Billiam Grimhart, is with his stupid prince now and must also be with my cousin Chammerline. Knowing who to kill makes it just so much easier to kill them!"

"She goes by Shemmy." Roland was shocked to hear that was Jess's only response. He could tell she was in some sort of trance, but why was that of all things what she managed to say?

Aldrious peered over Roland and saw Loretta watching them quite relentlessly. "Right… I think I remember that nickname! Well, I should make this quick, as I feel that lass over there may be on to me. She is quite a beauty, hmm? If it doesn't work out with Jessica, you will introduce me, won't you, Roland?"

Roland slammed his fist against the table, prompting a loud, gleeful laugh from the cardinal.

"Oh, I love the spirit on you rebels, so much fun to toy with. I must say, though, I think she looks slightly like my brother. How wonderfully bizarre!" He set Jess into her own chair as if she were a porcelain doll before continuing to yammer, "My monks do not know about you all and your inn. I scrambled upon it after killing my bishop and deciding I ought skim through his transcripts after all. They mentioned this place and the young caramel-skinned beauty running it. I knew it was either one of Nairee's twins or at the least, a suitable conquest. Now that I am here, it reeks of Ackerman and the Logos tradition. I was hoping to reach out and see how ragtag a group

I am really up against. It goes without saying that I am quite pleased with how pathetic you are."

Roland's face fell down toward his chest. A tear fell from Jessica's eye as she managed to mumble out one word: "Over?"

"Not yet, dear girl. I am letting you two be for now. My monks needn't know a thing yet, and I'd like to see if anyone gets back to you before I get to them. I hope you are aware that this means neither of you are allowed to leave Drummond, understood?" He waited for them both to nod before he continued. "So you keep up your charade, and I'll keep up mine! When I do get to Billiam or your parents, I'll kill you two quickly as well. A small thank-you, as I'll hope you get to join them in heaven, no matter how little I believe in that place."

Aldrious looked over to see Loretta approaching at last. "Our time is up, but one more thing, Jessica. I'd like to invite you to stay in my palace with me anytime you'd like. A man is not strength and honesty, as you seem to think. A man is power, and I have enough to indulge you for a lifetime. Surely, you know that your current knight will never love you. If she admired or respected you enough to fall for you, she would never let you leave her sight. Faelocks are quite easy to read on matters of the heart, which is not always pleasant. I don't plan on admiring or respecting you one bit, but I have gallons of love for you."

"To what do we owe such an honor, Your Eminence?" asked Loretta sternly, with a smile and a curtsy. As soon as she spoke, the bubble of quiet seemed to be broken, and Roland's lips parted.

"Just wanted to see an old friend!" replied the cardinal as he got up and headed to the door. Strangely, he was quite terrified of Loretta, and not because of her manly frame. "I'll see you two beauties, and you, Roland, another day."

With that, the door shut behind him and normalcy fell over the tavern. Oddly, not a single one of the townspeople were speaking of the holy man who had just been in their midst. It felt as though the three of them were the only ones who didn't immediately forget about him as soon as he left.

Jessica slumped forward and laid her face on the table, the strange grasp finally lifted off of her. "What in the bloody hell are we going to do?" she cried, before exhaustion took over. She fell into a nap, right there in the dining hall with Loretta petting the poor girl's hair.

"Do you know him? He seemed quite startled," Roland gasped out, filling his mouth greedily with gulps of air. "He said you look like his brother."

Loretta smiled and held her head to the side in thought. "Hmm, no, I don't think I have ever met that pervert before. But if he did say I look like his brother, that is quite an honor. Arrikos the XXI of the famous Dalgarie family is rumored to be just as lovely as Prince Micah and far less frail."

Roland was terribly confused and studied her for a moment. "That makes it sound like you know quite a bit about him." Curious, but not curious enough to press it any further, he got himself up and went straight to the bar. He knew that he needed two things immediately: a drink and a plan.

CHAPTER 7

May 6th, 989

THE FAERIE wood of Failingveil was the largest that humans had discovered and the only one in the continent of Centra, where Casperland and Alafor resided. Despite being the largest, it was scarcely the size of the royal palace.

The entrance had manifested from rocks and skimpy pines, yet the trees within it were thick and lush. They looked akin to birch trees, with their pale, slender limbs stretching up and intertwining to create a faux ceiling. Their leaves were an unearthly glowing aquamarine with fluorescent pink stems. The ground was the softest dirt their feet had ever touched; it felt like cushiony clay between Shemmy's bare toes. The grains of it were every color you could think of, but when it was all lying together on the ground, it looked like commonplace brown earth.

The wood was dark, but everything seemed to glow from within. The pathway through the trees was barely two feet wide. Billiam had to prop Micah over his shoulder like a piggyback ride to avoid scratching the prince on any surrounding branches. They walked single file, feeling as though they were in a hallway, as opposed to any sort of woods. They could see no faeries, and all they could hear was a steady breeze, melodically rustling the walls of foliage. The smell of the forest consisted of wet moss, honeysuckle, and something metallic, maybe blood. That odor was thick and could be tasted as they drew their breaths.

After a few minutes of walking, they reached a clearing where the path opened up immensely. In this area, the trees were mixed. Some were the bright birches, but farther in there were other trees that were large and dense, like oaks. Their trunks shone a jet-black and looked smooth like glass. They were studded with tiny yellow leaves, making them look bare even when fully bloomed. A bevy of elms joined the mix as well, elegant trees with common brown trunks but full of purple blooms and orange leaves. Some pale grass grew on one side of the clearing, which showed them in what direction they could expect the spring.

Following the patches of minty blades, they were at the bubbling pool within minutes. The earth around it was damp, thus darker than it was in the rest of the wood. The moisture made it easier to see its true rainbow of colors. Zan looked around fervently to see if there were any natives present, but as far as he could tell, they were still alone.

"Okay, we'll start with jump-startin' the brain and the heart. We should have him layin' in front of the pool to begin wif. Once I have those started, we'll strip him and carry him into the pool with us, so I can revive him piece by piece," Shemmy explained, looking a bit exhausted by having to do so. She knelt on the ground and tapped rapidly where she wanted him.

Billiam joined her on the ground and laid the prince between them. As he unbuttoned the prince's shirt, he asked her, "Why is this part out of the pool?"

She groaned a bit, not feeling terribly capable of teaching this novice. She understood how vital this was to him, so she indulged his curiosity. "These two organs be the most important. We dun want the energy to overflow 'um or for it to be flowin' to the wrong place. I have more control up here, well more precision, as to the exact amount of blessin' I put into each stitch. The other reason bein', we know right away whether it has worked. Before I begin enchantin' every damn finger and toe, I'd like to know it's worth the effort."

Billiam's face twisted into a frown, but he conceded she was right. He sensed her stress and decided he needn't know anything else; rather he need only assist her in anyway possible. He looked over to Zan, to make sure he was ready to ward any faeries off. My brother had his back to them and his blade already drawn in one hand, his pistol out in the other. He was hunched slightly and highly alert. There was no reason to check on him further.

"The needles please," Shemmy commanded, holding her hand straight out. She looked more serious than he had yet seen her; the wild accent dropped completely from her voice. He pulled the needles from his waistband and placed them in her dirty hands. She began rubbing them together and twisting them along her fingertips.

"I will do the brain first. His eyes will snap open, but no one will quite be home yet as no oxygen will be supplied. When you see his eyes open, begin mouth-to-mouth resuscitation. It is supposed to be most effective when the first breath comes from the person's true love. I doubt that's a fact your research dug up for you, but we are lucky enough to have you here, regardless. As you breathe into him, I will be waking the heart. When you feel him take your breath, you can part, and we will be in business."

Billiam nodded, feeling as though his own heart and brain were about to burst. His anticipation was burning through his stomach as he sat in the moist earth next to Micah. He thought not even for a second about the mud caking all over his trousers, a first for our fastidious hero.

Shemmy crawled on her hands and knees over to the prince's head at the edge of the pool. She dipped one needle into the transparent pinkish water and scooped some into her hand as well. She dripped the water along Micah's face in a hexagonal shape before swinging the dry needle in the same pattern. Billiam looked on horrified as it appeared Shemmy poked the wet needle right through the prince's forehead, yet there was no real wound or actual puncturing. The needle glided through him like air and also through the earth, from which Shemmy retrieved it. She alternated dry and wet needles for about eight strange stitches through Micah's face. She splashed water on his eyes, which shot wide open.

Billiam wished to stare into those sparkling sapphires, but he followed orders. He pressed his lips against Micah's, which felt cold and stiff, nothing like what he had dreamed. The smell of death filled his nose, but he tried not to think of it as he poured his breath down the prince's throat. Shemmy was sitting on Micah's lap, stitching, and swinging her arms around wildly but with an intricate pattern. She splashed the lightly fizzing water onto Micah's chest, wiping it across the length of his heart, before sending both needles within him. They floated through him and the ground, then back to Shemmy's hands. She stood up before kneeling at the pool, throwing even more of the blessed liquid onto both their mouths.

Billiam was quite startled when Micah first breathed in. He was actually pulling away Billiam's own air, and Billiam felt for a second as though he would suffocate. The feeling passed, and Micah blinked at him. Billiam pulled away only slightly, as the prince let out a small cough.

"Billiam…," Micah whispered, "oh Billiam, I thought I'd die before I'd ever get to kiss you!" His voice was weak, and he coughed again, but a smile grew on his face.

"You did, my prince!" Billiam exclaimed without thinking. He planted another quick kiss on Micah's lips and jumped up to help Shemmy remove his shoes and other clothing.

"What?" Terror filled the prince's eyes as the strange woman pulled off his underpants, and he began trying to kick her away.

"Do not move, Micah. I have not revived all of you yet. You are stiff, and you could tear yourself. Let's get him in the pool, Billiam," Shemmy explained, but it offered the frightened prince no reassurance. He tried to swing his hand at her but felt little response from his body. He then screamed, as the result of his movement was his wrist snapping back the wrong way.

"I told you so," chided Shemmy as she jumped in the sparkling water, which covered her up to her bosom. Billiam followed her, dragging the terrified prince in by his armpits. Shemmy put her hand on his face and looked into his eyes sweetly. "Please, let me help you. I promise this is only for your own good."

"I know Billiam wouldn't let you hurt me, so I won't move anymore," he said softly. He was extremely disoriented by all of this but reassured by the strong, familiar presence holding him from behind. "Was I really dead, my love?"

"Yes you were, Micah. You left me a year ago," Billiam answered, gingerly lifting up his right arm as Shemmy swished in the water around it. Micah looked on in wonder as the needles disappeared into his arm and reappeared back into that woman's hands.

Shemmy was diving down in the water to start on his feet when the shots began sounding. "They have finally found us," Zan called behind himself. He must've been terribly bored. He was shooting them down with deadly accuracy before they got anywhere near, but Billiam could see their numbers were strong.

The faeries were incredibly quick and looked to be simply a foot long or smaller orbs of light. My brother could make out the limbs and snaring teeth, but from the view of the pool it seemed Zan was surrounded with little stars. Their wings made a light humming sound as they circled about his head, ducking in and out of the trees. As soon as one fell, two more came forward from the depths of the forest, yet they luckily seemed entirely distracted by my brother. He was doing his best to keep his energy level as high as possible, as faeries focus on such things.

"You keep them away from us, no matter what!" Shemmy shouted, diving back down to work on his knees. Billiam held Micah tighter, feeling as though that would somehow keep him safer.

Shemmy dove back up and sent the needles in through Micah's stomach. She paused when she saw his eyes grow really wide and frightened. "Something's poking me!" he gasped.

Billiam's face fell and went pale. "That's just me, Prince. I missed you quite a lot," he admitted bashfully, backing up a bit so he was once again just holding him by the armpits. Shemmy giggled loudly and summoned the needles back out.

Micah's face turned bright red as he laughed with her. "Oh, okay. Nothing too scary, I suppose." His words were followed by a loud squeal, the situation growing ever more awkward by the second. Shemmy was now down at his groin, passing the needles throughout his hindquarters. It goes without saying those parts needed to be revived as well, but she probably should have warned him first.

Most of this process was the same as it was with that man she had resurrected ten months prior. She had used her fingers and lit incense sticks instead of the needles, and there was no faerie pool; despite those differences, the general principle of reconnecting energy within the tissues carried through. Shemmy was far more skilled at enchanting than even she herself knew and was able to instinctively adapt to her situation now, one with the right tools and a conscious patient. She still did not necessarily understand everything she was doing, but she was definitely doing it right. The prince's body began to respond, enliven, and even smell better with every pass through.

As Shemmy popped up again for air, she looked over to see Zan had been pushed a few feet back. His arms and chest had received some good slashes, and bloodstains were dotting his white shirt all over. He had switched to his blade; the pistol lay discarded on the ground. Shemmy turned back toward her patient. She had only the fingers and back left before she had to complete the final step, the soulstitch. "Spin 'im please!" she shouted, finally feeling confident enough to allow her accent to peek back through.

Billiam spun him swiftly, switching which armpit either hand held. Facing Micah, he saw almost all life had returned to him at last. He couldn't help the tears growing in his eyes, prompting a little frown from the prince. "I am just so happy to see you!" Billiam exclaimed, causing Micah to cry from joy as well.

They all heard a thundering crash as a branch from one of those oak-like trees fell on top of Zan's head. He grabbed it and swung it angrily around him, knocking at least a dozen faeries to the ground. "How much longer?" He grunted loudly, wiping the blood from his brow.

"Juss the soulstitch! Back towards me!" Shemmy shouted to Billiam. He spun the prince fast, making him dizzy.

Shemmy stared deep in Micah's eyes, making him a bit uncomfortable, not that any of this had been comfortable. With a needle in either hand, she stuck one at the base of his throat and the other above his belly button. They looked like they were going through him, but all he could feel was a warm buzz where she had sent them. He looked down, amazed as they zigged and zagged through his chest all on their own. Shemmy intently watched them, wiggling her fingers rhythmically. Micah could hear her muttering what sounded like counting.

She was mumbling the number twenty-four when Zan was flung by a group of faeries against her. He didn't fall into the pool, but he did knock her to the side of the pond, breaking her concentration. Drops of his blood fell in the water, floating around Micah until they dispersed. Zan shot up immediately, releasing an invisible burst of energy that sent the group of faeries flying back away from the clearing. He drew his sword and destroyed as many as possible before they became mobile once again.

Shemmy had to collect herself quickly. She needed to stitch the length of the soul twenty-seven times before it could be fully grounded to his body. She had finished the twenty-fourth, though the last go of the stitch went a little wonky. She did not want to repeat it, for if she over grounded him she could be cutting years off his life. She quickly went through twenty-five to twenty-seven, and then dunked Micah's head under the water. As she pulled him back up, she squealed, "Go, go, go!"

Billiam grabbed the still weakened prince and jumped out of the four and a half feet of water like it was nothing.

"Just run!" screamed Zan as he released more energy toward the faeries, suspending all of them for those few moments. Billiam hurled himself and the prince through the narrow path of woods, his sword drawn. Faeries surrounded them, but none moved toward him.

Zan took a step back and pulled Shemmy out of the pool by her elbow. He shoved her under his arm like a sack of potatoes and chased after Billiam. The faeries' movement restored as soon as their sprint started.

"Time fer reinforcements!" Zan heard Shemmy shout. He was holding her backwards, so when he looked down to the voice, he saw only her rump.

She was spinning her needles and chanting something. Within a few seconds, all the faeries he had killed rose. They were releasing magic from their tiny corpses, electrocuting the living ones.

Upon catching up to Billiam, my brother saw they were cornered right before the entrance by a duo of faeries. They were trying to carve up Billiam and had struck his cheek. Zan easily stabbed the tiny beasts into one of the birches behind them.

"Shall we?" he shouted, pushing Billiam and Micah out of the woods. They all scrambled downhill, and Zan put Shemmy down finally. She was still commanding her dead faeries, as they had angered the live ones enough to drag them out of their home.

Billiam kept running down the cliffside, clutching Micah against his chest. It was difficult for him to just run when he heard Shemmy and Zan fighting behind him, though he knew he needed to protect the prince at all costs. His feet were slipping around in the dirt, and he could hear Micah breathing fast with panic.

Running down the rock face was worlds quicker, especially as Micah could now hold on weakly, making it a mere fraction of what their grueling ascent had been. Flat ground was only a few paces ahead, and he leapt to it, hoping that would spell safety. Before running over to the cart and Gam, he turned to see Shemmy cackling as she dived off the incline with Zan following at a relaxed pace.

"I think they gave up. They looked really pissed and terrified to see their kin being turned into marionettes by this one," my brother explained, brimming with pride over Shemmy's ingenuity. He pulled off his bloodstained and ripped shirt and placed his sword back in its hilt. He knelt down at Billiam's feet before looking up at Micah and proclaiming dramatically, "Welcome back, Your Highness." Zan wanted to spit on the prince; instead he sniveled.

Micah smiled wide, though seeing a disturbed look on Billiam's face cut his delight at the display short. "Thank you for your bravery, Sir Zan of Ellekós. And who might my savior be?" he asked, straining to look over at Shemmy as Billiam followed her and Zan to the cart.

"Prince, may I have the pleasure of introducing Miss Chammerline Dubois XII, or Shemmy, if you don't want her to pinch you," Billiam informed him, while he dug through a saddlebag with the arm not entirely supporting Micah. He grabbed out a toothbrush and some peppermint soap. It had been at least a year since the prince's mouth had been cleaned; the two of them would be requiring it both sanitary and pleasant.

Shemmy grinned to him from ear to ear, offering up a painfully awkward curtsy. "A pleasure to meet ya, Yer 'Ighness!"

Micah was immediately filled with happiness by the fun he saw in her. "No, no, that won't do. You are the reason I am alive. I will not have you address me with such pomp; call me Micah. I am now in debt to all of you, but especially you, Shemmy. You are a miracle worker!" He was smiling wide, letting foamy bubbles fall from his lips as Billiam brushed his teeth quickly. Once he was finished, Micah spat to the side. It was not the most regal behavior, but at least that vital bit of hygiene was taken care of.

"Oi, I guess that juss makes you my little miracle, then, dunnit! Should we dress 'im or you wanna stay in yer birfday suit, Micah? It is yer new birfday, after all!" Shemmy cheered and tickled the bottom of Micah's bare foot.

Billiam finally set Micah down and breezily caught a blanket Zan threw at him without looking. Micah was in awe at the dexterity and grinned as Billiam wrapped him up. He felt cold, but it was a distant chill, as if he were far colder than what he could actually feel. His body, though revived, felt so frail and tired that he began to sway under the weight of the quilt. Billiam grabbed him tight once again, but allowed his feet to stay on the ground this time.

Zan watched on as the three of them chatted, laughing like idiots. He decided he ought to actually get to work, as no one was interested in socializing with him. He also didn't want to look upon the prince in his "birthday suit" any longer than he had to, even if he was now mostly covered. He changed into a clean shirt, swept out all the flour from the cart, and grabbed the damp quilts that had been thawing on a tree branch. He folded them before setting them down on the cart. All the while he was swallowing down a lump in his throat as large as one of the stupid horses that were watching him.

Feeling slightly less angry after distracting himself with chores, Zan could address them all once again. "We were not able to procure any of your clothes, Prince, but we brought you some from another knight in our order, Roland. He is the only one close to you in size, although they'll still be a bit big," he called over, displaying an outfit he had grabbed from one of their bags. A plain, rough-looking white button-up shirt and some far too loose black denim trousers stared ominously at the prince from my brother's hand. Zan was exuding a forced enthusiasm, sure his humanity and generosity would please the prince.

He was wrong. Micah frowned so fiercely his distaste was practically audible. "I don't think those are near my size, whatsoever," he said as politely as he could muster. "Shemmy looks to be about the same size as me, though! What do you have, love?"

Although Micah was male, he never paid it much mind when it came to clothing or behavior. This was definitely his mother's influence, who had fawned over him constantly and always encouraged him toward things "girly" or "pretty." I suppose he was like myself in that way, only opposite.

She ran over to Gam and started pulling out all the strange clothing she packed from her hovel, spilling it onto the ground. "These are all my own creations!" she exclaimed. There were two patchwork dark leather dresses, much like the one she wore when Billiam met her, with strategically placed cutouts. Some tartan skirts, silky harem pants, and cotton tunics of varying colors and states of soiled were also strewn about her feet.

Among them was an odd crocheted one-piece, comprised of short shorts at the end and thin straps at the top. The hole-filled fabric would cover one's entire midsection, although vaguely. As Shemmy grabbed that up, Micah responded, "I suppose I could wear that to bed," with a loud snicker. Billiam cocked his head to the side, unsure if he liked the thought of that or not, prompting a loud groan from Zan.

Shemmy sensed Micah was none too impressed with her handmade fashions, so she got up and walked to her horse. "I also have the clothes Nairee and Jess made me get. They may be more to yer tastes, Micah." She reached into the saddlebag packed for her and grabbed out a stack of clothing. There was another boring white button-up, although it looked to be better fitting. Underneath that, there was a silken long-sleeve blouse of ivory with a lace collar beautifully embroidered around the front. She held a fine pair of black woolen slacks at the bottom of the pile.

"We have a winner!" exclaimed Micah as he waddled slowly in his blanket over to Shemmy.

She was both surprised and delighted when Micah grabbed the silk top instead of the plain, more conventional shirt. He held it up, marveling at the tailoring, checking the chest area. There didn't seem to be much room for bosoms, as Shemmy was not all that well-endowed, thus it wouldn't fit the prince too loosely. He held the trousers against himself and saw they would land right at his ankles. Despite them being near the same height, it appeared Micah was leggier.

He leaned over to Shemmy and asked, "Is it all right if I have Billiam make these into short pants for me? I think they will be much more flattering that way."

"O'course! I was'nae plannin' on ever wearing 'um anyhow." She threw the pants at Billiam, who caught them easily. He was at work on them within seconds, slicing with his dagger right above where he expected the prince's knee to land. Shemmy noticed Micah was hardly able to clutch his new top and the blanket at the same time.

He seemed to be wobbling a bit as well. "Would ya like me to help ya wif getting into that?"

Micah smiled, and his face glowed with warmth. "Thank you so much, Shemmy. You are far too kind. However, I had been quite accustomed to being dressed by Billiam, so I'd prefer that, if he does not mind." He looked bashfully over to Billiam and then back again, trying hard to not let the pretty blouse fall through his uncooperative fingers.

"It would be my pleasure—rather my honor, to assist you, my prince," Billiam cheered as he ran over to him. He held the newly short pants in his hand as he scooped him up, quilt and all. Micah giggled while they disappeared behind the trees for his dressing.

About seven minutes of silence passed before Zan broke it, sighing loudly and beginning to pace. "I wonder if Billiam will free me to leave now that I've completed my defense in the faerie woods. It's not as if I'm wanted here by anyone." The horse-sized lump in his throat had not minimized. The more he thought of being there amongst Billiam's absolute joy, the more he wished he could just choke on it.

"Aye, I dun like ya; however, I'm sure Billiam wants as many guardians for his prince as he can muster, even if they are you. Also, as excited as I may be to have this free show, I'm sure afta a while Imma wanna have a fourth wheel around, no matter who it be. How badly is it killin' ya, seeing 'um back togever?"

"I am just fine. Why wouldn't I be?" He answered with a ridiculously huge smile, mostly because he wanted to make his cheeks hurt. He wanted to feel something other than the consuming pain in his chest. Why had he let Billiam make him come? Why was he fighting to save the prince? He hated the prince; he had stolen away his only precious thing. Did he really care about saving his nation? He wasn't even sure anymore. He cared about fitting in, and that was why he fought. He fought because it would please Billiam. He felt so pathetic.

"You feel so fine, ya wanna run off into the woods all on yer own? That makes not a lick o' sense!" She was giggling at him when her eyes suddenly bugged out. A funny thought popped in her head and she blurted, "How long have they been gone?"

"I'd say we are nearing the ten-minute mark."

"Well, thass more than enough time to dress him, aye?" With that she ran off into the section of woods where she had seen the men disappear. As soon she spied the outline of Billiam's back with a flash of Micah's golden hair in front of it, she shrieked, "Stop, stop! You cannae yet!"

They turned toward her, confused and laughing. When she arrived where they were, she was panting and fell to her knees. She looked up at them, more specifically at both of their trousers, and sighed. "Oh thank Spirit. Then what the bloody hell is taking so long?"

Micah gave a short spin before exhausting himself and leaning against a tree. Billiam grinned at Shemmy and held his thread and needle below his face, forming a second smile. "What do you think, Shemmy?"

She looked over the prince, amazed at Billiam's handiwork. He had taken in the silk blouse beautifully, leaving no trace that it was intended to encase a woman's chest. The former trousers he not only cut but also hemmed and cuffed attractively above Micah's kneecaps. There was even a pair of black, soft-looking tights emerging from under the short pants. "Where did those come from? That's my tunic sleeves, ain't it?" Shemmy accused, pointing at the prince's cloth-clad ankles.

"Well, as much as I am an enthusiast of always looking one's best, I must also look after Micah's health. In order for me to feel comfortable with him wearing short pants in this climate, I needed to cover his legs with something, no?" He smirked at her, both sneaky and sincere, somehow.

"Bah, fine. He looks so adorable; I forgive you! But doncha dare touch my fings again, Billiam, or I'll put you back in Gam!" Shemmy ran over to the prince and squeezed him. She looked him over from head to toe, making plenty of ogling noises. "How did ya do all this so fast?"

"We all have our talents, enchantress. Tailoring is arguably my greatest skill. Moving away from that, why did you run out here so fervently? What, pray tell, did you think I was doing?"

"Oh, right! This be important! From all my research, I gathered it takes a whole two moons fer the body to be fully restored. That means you should'nae walk much, no eatin' hard foods, no doin' anyfing strenuous. So please, Billiam, for his safety alone, don't ya go stickin' it in him for at least forty-eight hours, ya hear? And dat goes for his mouf too, and I mean it!" she instructed, quite adamantly with no trace of the humor that usually hid in her voice. Micah gasped and tried to hide his large smile behind his fingers.

"Oh, Shemmy, you are shameless," Billiam responded with an exhausted sigh.

He was getting ready to lecture her on rudeness, when Micah interjected with a small, sweet voice, "Forty-eight hours from now or from when I was first revived?" He felt terribly embarrassed and refused to make eye contact with either of them.

"Oi, you little tart! I love it! I'd say you've been alive about an hour now, so we can make it forty-seven hours. You want it the very first second you can, doncha?" she asked him, giggling more as Micah's blush grew a shade redder by the second. Billiam tried not to laugh with her, as he was both surprised and excited at what the prince's inquiry had been.

Micah was mortified and pushed her slightly, but he could not force the grin from his face. "What kind of tramp do you take me for? I simply wanted to know, um… so I'd know when I could expect to… have to fight him off?" That was probably not supposed to be a question, but that's definitely how it sounded. "Has it really only been an hour? I suppose I am not used to time passing. It feels like half a day. I wouldn't have even bothered asking…." Micah trailed off and hid his face in his hands.

Billiam fought away his own laughter and finally intervened between Micah and his new fan. He picked the prince up and cradled him in his arms. He then turned to Shemmy and said, "Right, I will obey your rules and keep my hands and the rest of me to myself, hmm?" He smirked, and she nodded with approval. He pulled Micah's head close to his own and gave him a kiss on top of it, feeling the strands of silk between his lips. "And you, my Prince, are free to try to fight me. I can't say I'd mind you playing a little hard to get."

Micah smiled and snuggled into Billiam's shoulder, feeling quite comfortable getting carried around by this point. He looked over it to Shemmy, who was practically drooling and had remained motionless. "We should probably get back to Zan before he runs after us screaming too!"

This woke her up, and she followed them as they walked back to their cart and comrade. "I have another fing to get clear, too! The resuscitation and any kisses to the head or hands does'nae count as the one kiss I get to see!"

Micah looked curiously up at Billiam.

"Sorry, Prince, that was part of the agreement for her assisting in your rescue. She vulgarly asked to witness much more, but I negotiated her down. Do forgive me," he explained, though Micah looked none too offended.

Contrarily, he got quite excited. "Billiam could kiss me right now, if you'd like, Shemmy?"

"That does not sound like a boy who will be fighting me off."

Shemmy had another laughing fit and was grinning like a buffoon but shocked them with her response. "No, no, no. That will'nae do. I want it to be natural, and passionate, and such. That, and you could be finking 'bout me when you do it!"

"No offense, Shemmy, but I don't know how much passion we will be able to feel if we are thinking of you. It would definitely not feel natural," Micah retorted.

They were almost in sight of the clearing when Billiam stopped suddenly. "This looks like the perfect spot."

He set Micah down on his feet, facing him. Kneeling slightly, he lifted up the prince's chin and pressed his lips firmly against his. Micah's knees gave out a bit as Billiam slid his tongue into his mouth, touching against his teeth playfully. He clutched the prince, once again carrying him; he had gone all limp. The kiss they had been waiting for, for what seemed like their whole lifetimes, lasted only a few moments, though the passion in it was as large as that wait.

"I'm sorry, my Prince. I myself couldn't resist any longer. Also, better to do it with one onlooker as opposed to two."

Micah pressed his head against Billiam's chest, feeling his newly awakened heart could burst with happiness. "I am glad you couldn't! I doubt I will be playing hard to get anymore, not even remotely."

"That was perfect!" Shemmy cried, falling into the boys and hugging them both. "I ain't gonna promise that I'll stop peekin', though!"

"I would expect nothing less from you, my dear!" Billiam held Micah's waist and walked him the few paces back over to their clearing. Shemmy bounded past them, humming happily as she reached my thoroughly distraught brother.

Zan's heart was full of Billiam's happy emotion colliding with his own feelings of despair. At the moment, it made him feel better, but he knew when Billiam's joy leveled out he would feel all the worse for it. He had been fighting in his thoughts on whether or not to ask Billiam if he could take his leave. He knew for the sake of the plan and the prince's safety he should stay but felt Billiam's disdain might allow for his dismissal anyhow. Being around the lovesick couple was making him feel like he could die. Despite that, the thought of not being with him and Micah having Billiam all to himself filled my brother with a rage and jealousy worse than any other. In the end, it was clear he would feel awful either way, so bringing it to everyone's attention would just make the situation worse.

Biting his tongue, he allowed his friendly façade to wash over him and grinned nauseatingly at them. "Welcome back! That's a lovely outfit, Micah. Kudos to the tailor!" His exaggeration of happiness was too much even for him this time.

"Stop bein' a creep!" Shemmy shouted and reached up to flick my brother's head, but it impacted well below his chin. "I guess ye'll be stayin' our fourth wheel, then, hmm?"

"I will be miserable either way, and I hear it loves company, so why not?" he sang in his fake voice, but was speaking the ever elusive truth.

A pang of pity hit Billiam in his gut. He pushed it away as quickly as he could; he knew Zan deserved not a single ounce of it from him, not ever. They had wasted enough time, and there was only a good five or so hours left of daylight, so he turned his thoughts to something actually important. "Right, then, my Prince, how would you like to travel: by cart, by horse, or by your lover?"

Micah felt warm all over, even though only a fraction of feeling had returned to his body. He had always thought of Billiam as his lover, his one and only, but it was never so much as whispered. To hear him finally say it would make him weak in the knees even if it wasn't his first day alive. "I suppose I should give my man-beast a break. I'll want you to have plenty of energy in forty-seven hours' time. I shall resume my ride in the cart, as I gather that's how my journey has been spent thus far."

Billiam helped him into the cart, while Zan reattached the puny horse. Micah sat up against the wall of the cart and crossed his legs. Billiam laid one of the dry quilts across his body and unfolded the moist ones alongside him so they could continue drying in the space he did not occupy.

Amidst gathering any of their belongings strewn about by Shemmy, my brother let his curiosity get the best of him. "What happens in forty-seven hours?" He grimaced before he even heard the answer.

"Oh Spirit, I cannae wait! It's gonna be sublime!" Shemmy responded, swaying with her arms held against her chest.

"Shemmy! You aren't allowed to watch, and you know it!" Micah cried out to her. Billiam was already leading the horse and cart ahead, ready to leave the other two behind.

"I needn't know, you are quite right, Billiam," Zan shouted to him, defeated. He grabbed Shemmy's collar again and hoisted her atop her horse. When he gave the beast a smack, it ran up to and past Billiam, with its rider shrieking all the way.

Their trek began again, a trio no longer, but now a slightly disharmonious quartet. The corpse carriage did its best to catch up, as its mistress was slow to enchant due to her unexpected departure. The slapping of Gam's feet along the soft dirt gave a delightful rhythm to the start of their seven-day journey.

CHAPTER 8

May 6th, 989

OUR THIRD day of travel officially brought us over the border of Casperland and into the nation of Alafor. It brought us also to unending chill and a constantly howling wind. I walked a few paces ahead of my colleagues at all times. This was to act as guard and also to allow my legspan the freedom it required.

It was already midday, and as I surveyed the path ahead, a loud, uncontrollable laugh began falling out of my mouth. I clasped my hands over it, trying to muffle the outburst. It was no use; the joy and laughter would not cease spilling out of me. Overcome, I fell to my knees.

Katrina sprinted up to me, concerned by the noises she had heard. She was shocked to see me fallen to the ground, chuckling joyfully, but with a grimace etched into my face. "Micah is alive!" I managed to squeal out to her, surprised by the high-pitched and feminine sound of my own voice. Billiam had overtaken my emotions and hijacked my monotone sensibilities.

"Oh! That's so wonderful! Malcolm, Malcolm! The prince has been raised! Such a glorious day!" Kat cried out as happy tears formed in her eyes, feeling the hope we had all held on to for so long was no longer a dream. Our prince was truly alive, and if things kept going to plan, reality would be a happier place for us all to dwell in.

"Right, yell that louder, hmm? Maybe scream out Helvendeere a few times too," responded Malcolm dryly, as he passed the happy girl without even a glance. He knelt down to me, and I saw he too was a grinning fool. He looked me over, shaking his head, unable to keep a loud guffaw of his own from coming out. "How unbecoming of my stoic warrior. We really need to find some sort of emotional filter for you. That Billiam is ridiculously sensitive for a man." Strangely enough, there was not even a trace of malice in his voice, and his smile stood strong on his face as he grabbed my arms to pull me up.

My face was hurting from the smiling forced upon it, and my chest felt warmth unlike any my own feelings had yet produced. I managed to stop the laughter but only tentatively. I feared speaking, for it could come flooding back out. I simply nodded to him and shrugged, ashamed of such a display, yet still possessing enough of my own happiness to not fight it much. I walked over to Katrina and gave her a strong embrace, as I could tell she was a bit hurt by Malcolm's scolding.

"Sorry for yelling, I have not been this excited in ages. No matter what battles my heart was feeling before, I know the road ahead can only lead to a brighter future," Kat said softly and smiled, sharing her sentimental notions even though she knew the two of us were anything but. "Since you are such a giddy little girl, I am assuming the prince was revived without issue?"

I don't think I had ever been called a little girl before this instance. I felt for a second she couldn't even be speaking to me, and I glanced over at Malcolm, who had finally given in to hysteria. Exhausted and bashful, I looked to the sky while holding tightly on to my chest. "All I can feel from Billiam is pure bliss. There is no error in this feeling at all; he is euphoric. I am positive Shemmy pulled it off perfectly, and also fairly certain they've made it out of the wood safely. As emotional as Billiam is, he is adept at keeping it at bay when it would put him or his people in danger."

"Right, thanks for the good news, and good show, Leke. We should be continuing, though, should we not?" Malcolm inquired, almost fully returned to his usual, emotionless state, minus the smile that still hung in the corners of his mouth.

"Yes!" I exclaimed, surprising myself with such exuberance. My emotions were still flooded, so I took care to speak calmly and like myself. I cleared my throat before continuing, hoping to hack up the cheer from my voice as well. "If we are swift, we can get to Pottleton in about two hours. We will have ample time to look around before sunset."

"Ample time to look at what?" Malcolm scoffed.

Katrina joined him in doubting me, as she asked, "Why do you care to go there, Leke? It was burnt out and abandoned a year before Casper. It was the test site for those awful missiles, right? It can't be much more than ash and ghosts now."

"I know all that. I just truly would like to speed up our journey. I'd like for us to be fully secure having the prince in the City of Alafor, and there is no way I could feel that way with just a day or two. I cannot explain why, but I have an extremely strong feeling we can find something to aide our journey there. It is a hunch I have carried since before we invaded the castle, and I cannot seem to shake it. I have never been wrong about a feeling like this. Besides, it is hardly out of the way. Less than a mile off our current path is a worthy sacrifice even if I am wrong, as we might find actual shelter for the night." I explained to them my sentiments as best I could, though I knew there was no concrete evidence I could possibly offer to back up my conviction.

"I trust you, Leke!" Katrina told me, nodding as she began to walk ahead. "Let's see what it's got for us, yes?" With that, it was settled. Malcolm and I followed her in silence.

The entrance to Pottleton lay down a heavily wooded cobblestone path. It was the only road that was not comprised of dirt and gravel we had seen since our journey began. Pottleton used to be a thriving community and was almost a perfect midpoint of the continent of Centra. It resides in Alafor country but was always a neutral township. The destruction of Pottleton and Knox's later attempt on one of Alafor's largest cities, the City of Wings, were what drove Alafor to seek alliance with Casperland. That, of course, did not fare well following Micah's descent into illness. Despite that, the Caspers and the Alafor never officially engaged in any war, and we had little to worry for personally as we crossed into our neighboring nation.

The trees encompassing us were large pines, though they were nearly naked. We had not reached the permafrost that covered most of Alafor, but the sharp cold had obviously done its part to inhibit the vegetation. The path widened to a decrepit steel gate, with a fallen, scantily clad tree on one side of it. Past the fence were a few visible structures, the skeleton of a city.

I walked in front, stepping through the threshold of the shabby gate and into full view of the remains of Pottleton. Although I was the one with the strong suspicion, I was still shocked to see a veritable crowd of people. In the middle of the town there was now a huge field with all sorts of folks hard at work tending to crops. The field of dark, bushy leaves was somehow thriving despite the winter surrounding it. To the right of it was a factory line of more faceless peasants flipping switches, filling bottles, and creating Aegis knows what. At the start of the line were two horses, walking endlessly in a wheel, as a power source of sorts.

Malcolm and Katrina caught up with me, joining in my mystified gaze before this awestruck moment was cut short. I sensed an incoming threat and swiftly picked up a cohort in either hand. I held them above my head and jumped atop the feeble fence behind me. As soon as my landing was stuck, at least a dozen arrows flew through the space we had left. They darted by fast before falling to the cobblestone yards behind us.

I teetered upon the frail bars, unable to gain any balance as there was no way to evenly distribute the weight difference of Katrina and Malcolm. Standing on one foot, the other leg kicked behind me, I was able to tuck Katrina neatly under my arm. Keeping myself completely alert and focused on where the attack flew from, I held Malcolm by his round forearm, tossing him as lightly as possible to the ground behind the gate. He grunted as he fell and rolled to his side, producing a succession of loud thuds.

"Stay quiet and lay flat," I hissed.

Able to gain balance at last, with both feet planted on steel, I spun so my side holding Katrina was facing Malcolm's spot on the ground. I guarded her with my body while keeping my eyes fixed on my target. I saw a gleam of reflected light on metal, glowing on the roof of the tallest building left standing. As soon as it flashed, so danced forward another dozen lead-tipped arrows. With no worry of my companions being struck, I was able to jump over the projectiles easily. I was disturbed by their accuracy but glad to now be assured of their reload time.

"I see where you are shooting from, you bastard. You have no chance of hitting me, so come down and face me like a man.

If not, I shall go up there, and you won't be keen on it," I yelled calmly but sternly.

"Bugger off, you sonofabitch!" a ragged and angry man's voice called from my right, much to my surprise. It seemed to come from the nearest small shack, but it was completely dark inside. I had no hope of seeing the speaker from where I stood. Before I could make my way toward it, the third barrage shot out to me, from its same place atop the tall building. I jumped and dodged them again, landing on the ground and wasting no time running to the shack.

I made my way over to the voice, keeping Katrina as parallel to my body as possible, and was able to spare a look at all those workers in the city center. There was no change; their toil continued on with no notice given to the commotion caused by us outsiders. It seemed as if nothing existed beyond their labor, quite a rare and unbelievable work ethic, I thought.

I heard Katrina whimper a bit, as she panted from under my arm. "Sorry, I feel much safer with you here than the ground. I promise to protect you," I explained, ducking behind the shack's wall just in time to avoid the fourth barrage.

The dozen arrows struck the wooden wall loudly, half sticking into it and the other half falling to the ground. When they went quiet, Katrina was able to respond, "I understand, and I thank you. I simply have to urinate, badly," she whispered and wriggled a bit, before going quiet and bracing herself.

I took that as my permission to proceed, and I kicked down the old scorched door in front of me. It fell like a domino and crashed on to the soft dirt of the shack. I found the room lit by a candle, with a tiny old codger crouched under a desk. He had his hand on a lever, though upon seeing me, let go of it.

"Bah, no use now," he growled, pushing the panel with various switches and buttons off his lap and onto the ground angrily. "Why the fock you here, ya monster?"

"I seek transport." I set Katrina down and looked over the wretch of a man. "She seeks a toilet or chamber pot."

"Fock off, ya faelock bastard. I hate you freaks!"

"You can go outside, Katrina, but stay right against the wall." She looked embarrassed and none too thrilled about the suggested facilities yet nodded and headed outside. "Well, I don't hate you, but at this rate I'm sure I will in no time." I borrowed one of the phony smiles my brother crafted and showed it menacingly to the man on the ground.

"Feh, what of it. I have no transport for ya anyhow. Kill me or leave me be."

"Did you do all of this? Are you commanding those people? I assume they are enchanted, made to toil without end on whatever they might be doing."

"I ain't no 'chanter. I have no clue o' their purpose; I'm just here to watch o'er this place." The man was huddling into himself farther, trembling like a damn kitten.

"I don't have intention of harming you, unless you give me reason. You are obviously not a match for me in any way, so I see little chance of you giving me reason. Please come out from there and behave like a man." I sighed loudly and was relieved to see Katrina come back into the shack.

The wrinkled prune crawled out slowly, also seeming to gain relief at the presence of the sweet young woman. As soon as he was fully standing, I began to question him. "You do not know their purpose, but do you know who your employers are?"

"Rich folk in robes."

"Monks?"

"Nah, least I dun think so. They are juss nobles as far as I know."

"Do you know from where they hail? How often are they here? Also, how long have you stood watch?" I was already tired of the back and forth, so I gave my succession of questions, ready to allow time for him to answer them all.

"They come from the south, prolly Drummond. They come only every few months and collect the flowers. They suck up whatever is created and stored in that vat at the factory. They do some upkeep on their spells, and then they run off again. I lived 'ere in Pottleton ma whole life. I was'nae the only survivor, but ma wife and I was the only ones that stayed. I knew nuffin' of the world outside, and I'm too damn old to learn nuffin' new. I dunno how long it'd been, but I'd wager it was at least a few years afta the bombing that them fancy folks came here. They set up my home wif real furniture and brought plenty of food. They said they'd pay me to let them use the land here and to defend this place. I did'nae mind defendin' it. It's my home. I did'nae 'spect them to go raisin' all the corpses, but what could I do? My wife was gone; I had nuffin' else. They rigged up that arrow hurler, and I juss piddle about 'ere. You are the first I've used it on, though."

"Strange," I said, while shaking my head and trying to process his explanation. "I saw some horses running a wheel at that factory. Are they dead and enchanted as well?"

"We're the only livin' fings here, monster."

"When were your employers last here?"

"I telled ya I dun pay attention to time, did I not?" He was frustrated and seemed to be growing tired. He slid back down to sit on the earth again as he thought. "I fink, however, can'nae be more than a fortnight since I saw 'um last."

"Oh excellent! From what you recall, it sounds as though the spell lasts at least a month. Should we take those dead horses, the spell will surely last us the rest of the trek to the capital."

"What? You want us to ride dead horses?" Katrina gasped out loudly. I was a little confused, as she knew my whole reason for the detour had been transport all along.

"Yes, why not? They are enchanted to walk, and they'll surely move faster than you or Malcolm. I don't see the problem."

"The problem is they ain't yer's to take! I will'nae allow it!" the codger screamed, getting back up. "You touch any of them fings, those black-robed nobles is sure ta kill me."

"I thought we already established you are no match for me, and thus I need no permission from you."

"Leke, we don't even know if they'll obey us!" cried Katrina, obviously not sold on riding a corpse.

"You're right, Kat, but I suppose that's something we can find out after we take them."

"No, you cannae have them. They'll kill me, ya monster. Don'cha understand?"

"Well, yes, but I will also kill you if you stand in my way, so it doesn't much matter."

"Leke!" shouted out Katrina.

I turned to her and whispered as calmly as I could into her ear, "Katrina, I am aware this is unpleasant, but you really need to toughen up. We cannot spare everyone, and sacrifices will need to be made on our journey. I do not want you to lose that big heart of yours, but you cannot stand in my way of getting us to our goal, understood?"

She gulped down hard and squeezed her eyes closed. "You are right. I am sorry. I am not used to life in the fray. Do continue."

"Thank you, Miss," I breathed out to her, before turning back to the man. "Right, well I think I might have misled you a bit. I said I'd kill you if you stand in our way, but that's not the truth. You see, as curious as I am about your nobles and whatever this place is, what their goals are... I cannot risk our mission to find out. You are a spineless wretch who spilled his guts to me, someone he claims to hate. How much will you tell your employers? How quickly would they seek us out? I even mentioned our destination. You must realize there is no way I am leaving you alive, whether I take the horses or not."

A small groan escaped Katrina, but she obediently uttered no contest.

"You trash, I hate you!" The stupid man began pushing himself from his desk, attempting to run, I suppose. Instead of getting anywhere, he merely fell into my hands as I outstretched them.

"Oh, you fool, why in the world do you cling to life so desperately? You said yourself, you lost your town and everyone in it, you lost your wife, you sit here alone day in and day out babysitting corpses for money. What use do you have for money? What could you buy, and who would you buy it from? You need nothing, you have nothing. To be honest, sir, you really are nothing. Please, let me put a stop to your futility, hmm? I'd prefer you could see it as the gift it is, as I am not nearly the monster you think I am."

I held his shoulders while he wriggled around, his eyes growing large when he looked up at mine. They filled completely with tears before he became hysterical, screaming, "No! No! I don't want to die! No!"

"Go outside, Kat," I instructed, and held tighter on to the man as he fought. I heard her walk a few steps away from the shack before I proceeded.

He was still so frantic, I didn't want to bother trying to remove my sword from my back, so I simply transferred my right hand to his neck quicker than he could perceive. As soon as he did notice, his fight stopped. Fear still filled his eyes, but luckily his hope had faded. I barely squeezed and his life was gone. I find it rather frightening, actually, how frail human necks are. Such an important piece of their anatomy really ought to have more protection. They do not, and thus his windpipe and spine crumbled to pieces with the closing of my hand.

I had a habit that was a bit superstitious and based on something my mother told me many times. She said that if you kill a person, never let them see you leave. I didn't know what it meant; she didn't explain herself often, yet I took this phrase to heart. I would smash the face of any of my victims with my boot before departing, as long as I had the time. With Katrina outside, I was able to avert the codger's eyes with my heel.

I was impressed when I walked out. I expected Kat to be crying or at least distraught, but instead she was drawing patterns in the dirt with the toe of her shoe. I found myself feeling the need to behave like my brother and give her a fake smile and feed her some reassuring drivel. Why she produced this desire in us, I do not know, but I fought it and refused to condescend to her so. Rather, I just nodded as I walked past her and over to Malcolm. She understood my gesture and followed me silently.

As we reached the gate, I saw my comrade was still laying belly up on the ground like a beached whale. "You can get up now. Surely you noticed there haven't been any shots for a while now."

Malcolm rolled around from side to side a couple times, finally getting enough momentum to pick himself up. "Well, sure I did, but that doesn't mean it's clear. It could have meant you were killed. So?"

"All the people you see here are the dead ones. The arrows were shot remotely by the guardian of this property, an old and now deceased man who was in that shed. Some group has enchanted the former villagers here to continually grow a flower and produce some type of liquid at the factory. Lucky for us, they use two enchanted horses to power it. Each of you shall ride one, and I can sprint alongside. The spell is presumed to last at least another month, so as long as we can get them to obey commands, we shall be shaving days off of our journey."

I began walking over to the makeshift factory without awaiting any response. I would've hated to have to hear another petty complaint about the steeds being dead. Passing the field, I watched the corpses hard at work. The flowers the old man had referred to were like none I had ever seen. They were huge: each leaf surrounding them was about a foot in length. In the center was a giant bud, all of them brick red, verging on black. None of them were bloomed yet, and even if they had been, there was no hope of them being familiar to me. From our distance yards away, I could still make out their scent; it was sweet but musky, dark even. The workers had no reaction to us, which was to be expected but still felt terribly strange.

As we reached the giant wheel the horses were trudging along, Malcolm finally broke his silence. "You think Shemmy is behind any of this?"

I stuck my hand out in front of one of the horses and yelled, "Halt!" To my surprise, it really did, and thankfully still seemed responsive. "Well, the thought crossed my mind, but I really don't see how she'd keep such a thing up. All we researched on her saw her completely isolated and always near Drummond."

"Of course Shemmy wouldn't do this! What are you thinking?" Katrina yelled to me, pulling on my sleeve. "She is our friend, and she is on our side. She wants to help the prince and she has!"

"Stupid girl, you just met her. This here has nothing to do with the prince. She is being paid for her services, and even though the payment is ridiculous and paltry, she is still a hired hand. She is not our friend, and she is only tentatively an ally." Malcolm shook his head mockingly at her.

"That is absurd! You met her; she is genuine and kind. All of this stinks of evil and horror!" Katrina was really wishing to be far away from Malcolm, as she detested him more and more with each word he spoke. She was growing less fond of me by the minute as well.

I placed my hand on her shoulder and knelt to look her in the eye. "I have no reason for it, but I also trust Shemmy. I think it is because of how taken with her Billiam is, and there is no one I have ever trusted more than him. Regardless of the way I feel about her, she is the only person known to us to have such a strong grasp of enchanting. It seems as though these corpses have only their bodies animate, not their minds, and thus resemble the first man she resurrected. Perhaps she helped to get this started or taught her talents to those nobles. If she did, it was most likely out of curiosity and love for her craft. That is much the reason she joined us, as far as I can tell." She finally returned my gaze and her fondness of me stopped dropping, or at least I hoped it had.

"Yes, that makes sense. There is no way she could be back to redo the spell. You mentioned a timeline for it, right? We will save any judgment for when we can speak to her," Malcolm chimed in, most likely just to avoid any further outbursts from Kat.

I halted the second horse and unhitched them both from their wheel. I broke the front bow of it off easily and tossed it to the side with a crunching thud. "Are you ready, Katrina?"

She swallowed hard and tried to erase the look of disgust from her face with little success. Before she could answer me, a sudden absence of noise caught her attention. My second halting was apparently far more effective, for all the farm work ceased as well.

"Th-they are looking over this way, aren't they?"

I turned to the field and found at least fifty pairs of open but lifeless eyes staring toward us. "As long as they just stand there, it's of no matter," I muttered.

I then hoisted her atop the right steed and helped Malcolm up onto the left. I was actually glad his horse was dead so I needn't worry about the effect carrying his weight would have on a living creature. There were reins left around the horses' necks, so I grabbed one with each hand. This would work out for me to travel between them, guiding the horses along, as I had no idea the range of the spell or how well the horses would walk on their own.

"Ya!" I shouted, slapping the horses' rears. Unfortunately, my great luck had come to an end, for there was no response whatsoever.

"Perhaps we need a spell or to draw a hex?" Kat asked while doing her best to stare down at the horse and not at the immobile horde behind her.

"It responded to verbal commands before."

"Well I don't care how we get out of here; I just want to get the hell away. Either get these things walking or I'll be, Leke," Malcolm grunted. He was adjusting himself to dismount but part of the saddle had caught on to his trousers. "Won't you bloody let go!" he screamed.

Upon hearing his plea, the horses started to trot at an agonizingly slow pace.

"Oh, of course," Katrina giggled out. "Go!"

The second utterance of the magic word had the steeds at a steady pace but also started the shuffling of dead feet behind us. Instead of tending to their plants, they seemed to be joining us on our journey to the capital city.

"No not you guys!" she cried while waving frantically behind her.

I held the reins tight and readied myself to sprint before shouting out, "Go, go, go!"

While the horses were practically stampeding, I was merely jogging. I was wishing that extra "go" might give them unnatural speed, but I unfortunately did not get to enjoy that run I was prepping for. We were still moving far faster than any dead legs could move at least.

"I was really hoping to get off this damn thing, not save the day," Malcolm mumbled while finally turning his head forward. He had had his neck turned nearly backward for about two miles. "We have lost them at least. When do you suppose they'll give up?"

"If they simply keep walking forward, they'll end up in Bain Lake by tomorrow. It should be all slush at this time of year, so they'll be undead popsicles on their way out," Katrina mused.

"We'll be getting to City of Alafor days ahead of schedule. That's all that matters," I commented plainly. I suppose I should've cared more. Any carnage wreaked by them would be all my fault, but I was focused single-mindedly on my goal. That, and they seemed weak. I would not fear them simply because they were dead as my human companions did.

All in all, I felt my hunch paid off. Our journey was hastened substantially, and Katrina and Malcolm were far too worried to chatter in the least.

CHAPTER 9

May 7-8th, 989

WHEN CONNOR DuBois was summoned to the castle, it was to be handled quite civilly; however, Connor and civility are not two things that usually coexist. He punched out the monk who spoke to him in his shop and ended up getting apprehended by the bevy of royal guards that had been there to chaperone. Despite it not going to plan, Aldrious's wish was granted, and his eldest cousin was presented before him. I highly doubt there would have been any way for the cardinal to speak with him without his being arrested and held by force.

"Hello, cousin!" Aldrious shouted joyfully, clacking his long nails together as he approached the gigantic man and the two crown guards that held him.

"Da fuck, Aldy? Ya ain't no cousin o' mine no more. Yer Aegis's little faggot now. That hogwash ain't bound to me by blood, dammit!" Connor growled through his long, frizzy beard.

"Excuse me, Connor, but I am well aware half of your siblings are flaming homosexuals, the rest just raving loons, so what gives you the right to judge my blood? Anyhow, I might look nice, but you know the two of us have always held the same interests. Despite my vows, a pair of perky tits and a tight, wet cunt are the things I worship above all else." Aldrious showed a brief grin to the mortified monks lining the wall beside him before waving them all off.

He heard no feet moving and thus turned again, this time with a stern glare. They were pale and terrified yet managed to blather out, "Yes, Your Eminence," in unison. The half-dozen of them scooted out, shutting the doors and leaving the cousins and the two elite guards alone in the large dining room.

"Aye, so you be a heretical and horny slave o' the church. Fuck if I care. I ain't talkin' to you 'bout jack shite, so go ahead and kill me now!"

"Dear Connor, stop being so defensive. I simply sent my brother to ask you for assistance. I need your help. I care not for your life."

"Why the bloody hell should I help you?"

"Well I would pay you handsomely, but your family is wealthier than the rest of Drummond combined. I was hoping some terms could be reached regardless, perhaps involving the safety of your sister."

"Shemmy? Ain't ya done enough to her? If ya be threatenin' her instead o' me, yer a bigger pansy arse than I expected."

"I am quite sure I said the word *safety* and nothing malicious whatsoever. If you can help me, we should be able to get her back here swiftly, and I will pardon her and lift her excommunication. Please, look at this. You will see her face but do note it says alive and unharmed," Aldrious explained while holding a freshly inked scroll in front of his face. "I need mercenaries, bounty hunters, and I am sure you know plenty. Something much more precious than your sister was taken from me; however, the same people that took my lamb are also using Chammerline. They are the ones endangering her by dragging her into their fool crusade."

Connor took turns scrutinizing the piece of parchment and sending Aldrious death stares. "You'd really let her come back?" he asked, his anger subsiding slightly.

Connor was a veritable mountain of a man. He was large, both broad and tall, and covered in orange hair and grease from head to toe. He was nicknamed the Yeti of Westend and definitely looked the part. Despite his imposing appearance and brash demeanor, he was quite sweet and held a mile-wide soft spot for his little sister.

"Of course. It's not as if I wished to banish her in the first place. If I am to stay in rank with the brotherhood, I must at least look the part. You know witchcraft is actually a capital offense, do you not?"

"Oh, so's now you paid her a kindness, is it?" Connor scoffed, blowing through his mustache enough that Aldrious could spy a full grin. "What do I do, just give this out to me mates or what? And I get me sis back?"

Aldrious peered around the room. It was still just his cousin, the two guards, and himself, yet his anxiety reached deep into his chest. He was not used to needing caution, or to having to care what others think or feel. He knew this was all our fault; however, he was beginning to accept his attack on us did not help his case at all. "Let him go and off with you," he grunted to the guards.

Those crown guards were servants to the royal family and its representative alone. They had no attachment to parliament, the church, nor were they ever involved with the Logos. Aldrious had always implicitly trusted their neutrality, but he would take no more chances. He could sense the dogs of the government salivating at the sight of a knife in his back; it would only take the slightest twist for them to have their meal at last. The guards let go of the muscly arms and bowed to the cardinal before taking their leave. Connor was still bound, but it probably was not for long.

In fact, as soon as the doors were shut, Connor puffed out his chest. With a loud groan he moved his shoulders up and then out, breaking the chain that held the cuffs in half. He laughed menacingly to Aldrious who was just clapping, amused by the show.

"How much trouble you in, cousin?"

"Oh, I am your cousin after all? That's a relief. I have a feeling I might be neck-deep in shit any minute now, but currently I'd say it's only around my knees. How about a drink?" Aldrious called over, making his way to a cabinet near the table's head. He grabbed a bottle of zinfandel from within and two glasses from the top of it.

"Now I understand why you had me brought here and not the throne room; however, ya know I don't drink juice," Connor grumbled. He walked to the cabinet and looked through it himself. In a back corner was a small crystal flask filled with a brown liquid. It was brandy. Not that he really cared what it was, it just needed to be stronger than wine. He knocked off the decorative topper, letting it fall to the ground. He then plopped himself down into the head seat before lifting his dirty boots up and onto to the five-hundred-year-old hand-carved table of kings.

"Okay, now I may wipe my ass all over this castle, but I would never do that. Feet off, and I'll do my best to keep my mouth shut about any other impoliteness," Aldrious implored him and must have appeared truly distressed, as Connor obeyed instantly. With that taken care of, he felt calm enough to continue. "You own a printing press, correct? You have your own shop where you mass produce pornographic images, is what I was told."

"Ya, I gots my business. I fucking love it. You a customer, Cardinal?"

"No, not yet at least. I didn't know about it until just yesterday. I'm quite excited to see your work, but for now I'd like to employ you in printing that mundane scroll I showed you." Aldrious looked through his glass to Connor as he swirled it. It felt strange to be sitting anywhere but at the head. He hadn't realized how accustomed he had become to being the Lord of Casperland. It made the nervous pain in his stomach cut deeper.

"You cannae use the press here?"

"My brothers are not the ones in charge of it. There are scholars from the old rule that still take care of that machine. It would not be wise for me to use them or to go booting them out, for that matter. That scroll implies the prince is missing, and should parliament get wind of it, my head will be as well."

"Implies, does it? Seemed to me it *said* the prince was missing and *implied* he was deceased. Him and Shemmy be the only ones you want unhurt? So I can get the brutal fucks involved, I suppose."

"I just need them back and soon. Whatever must be done is fine. You will do it?"

"Aye, but you will afta come get 'um from my shop tomorrow. I ain't coming back here. You also gotta make a minimum fifty-note purchase, not counting the cost o' these bounties. I'm supposin' you need me to distribute some too? Ya prolly don't get them holy hands dirty wif the underworld in yer position," Connor replied, calm and concerned. Despite his gruffness, he was always fond of Aldrious when they were young. He couldn't help seeing him as that little brat once again given how desperately worried he was.

"Sounds fair. I thank you, cousin. Have you a radio at your shop? I need to make a call to a lady friend; my previous chat got interrupted. It appears I can't do anything alone here lately, except for speak with you, strangely enough."

"I dun have one, cannae mooch off me for that," Connor answered, disturbed by how his cousin's face fell. "Control slips that fast, does it? Ya should'nae have gotten greedy. Ya shoulda just kept the brat unda yer thumb, not yer boot."

Aldrious lost it completely upon hearing that and was bawling into his robe sleeve. "If only it could have been so simple," he responded after a moment. "What time should I expect you to be done?"

Connor pushed out his chair and drank the last drips of brandy, standing up before answering, "Whenever I bloody well feel like. Ya best come over after nightfall. Dun want any o' my regulars seeing your pious arse. Cover that blasted red up too, and for Aegis's sake cut yer fingernails. That's more than just faggy; it's creepy."

Aldrious's mood improved immediately from the insult. He picked his head up to grin at Connor and held up his hand, prepping a thumbnail within it. "That is my own choice, not the church's nor the brotherhood's. These nails are intentionally unsettling, cousin," he informed him coyly, while digging a long gash through his palm. The blood did not spill; instead it formed into a three-inch arrowhead hanging out of the cut. He dropped his hand suddenly, prompting the small blade to fly out and crash through the empty brandy bottle before landing at Connor's feet.

Connor was quite startled by this; however, he did not show it. He just coughed loudly and reached for the door handle. He decided to ignore the show of power and called out, "Can I see my own way out, or am I gonna get chained up again?"

"You should be fine. I am going to sit here and drink the rest of the wine in that cabinet, thusly, I am far too busy to see you out," Aldrious mumbled. His head was on the table with the wine glass in his bloody hand.

"Aye, there was what, twelve bottles in there? That should chase away a good chunk o' misery and a good chunk o' yer liver. Tomorrow, then, cousin, and ya best be alone," Connor called out, but he was already halfway down the hall. He wanted no business with the royal family and even less to do with the MortiAegis church. His cousin had drug him deep within the affairs of both.

"I am sure I will be, completely….," Aldrious mumbled into his robe, and mostly to himself.

Apparently Aldrious needed much less poison than he thought. After finishing that first bottle he had fallen into a deep sleep, face to table with his back fully craned.

"Pitiful," boomed an all too familiar, condescending but refined voice.

It half woke Aldrious, but it did not provide him with any sense of where he was or what was happening. He sat straight up, though drool had attached his sleeve to his mouth, leaving one hand hanging limp below his chin. "Good evening…," he muttered, blinking a few times before recognizing my mother and continuing, "Senator Ellekós. To what do I owe the historic pleasure?"

He was undoubtedly referring to my mother's age; she was eighty-five years old at this time. My birth was considered somewhat of a miracle, as she was sixty when I was conceived. Having done it once, my brother coming two years later felt old hat to her.

"You have been avoiding us, Aldrious. Is vine really the reason for it?" she berated him, gaining a few laughs from the other two senators beside her, Misters Allen and Kinsmith.

Since Casperland's conversion forty years ago under the rule of Quincey II, the nation had become practically theocratic, leaving the parliament with very little real power. My mother, despite her advanced age, was never a member of the senate in its glory days. She was still living in Casper then and felt little duty to the kingdom or crown. The legal body was made up of ten elected officials known as the senate, and a prime minister chosen by that ten. It seemed that when we stole the prince, he was not the only thing to be awoken; the parliament was emerging from their decades-long nap at last.

"What time is it?" was all Aldrious mumbled out, after which he proceeded to remove his sleeve and wrist from his face. It was quite stuck and pulled at his stubble as he removed it, akin to ripping a bandage.

"Four in the afternoon, it's a little early, is it not?" Senator Allen answered, scrunching his pudgy face in disapproval.

Aldrious had not slept at all since the prince's extraction five days prior, so he was relieved to learn he slumbered so well. "The opposite, actually. Apparently, one bottle gave me twenty-two hours of straight sleep. That is fabulous; however, I am late on drowning my anxiety for this new day." He was on his way to uncorking the bottle he had ready from the night prior when my mother struck her walking stick hard on the table, right beside his hand. He jumped, dropping the corkscrew onto the cobalt carpet below him.

"Where is Prince Micah?" she growled to him.

"In his room, asleep like a baby!" Aldrious answered happily, grinning wide. He wanted to run out of there so badly that he instinctively readied his nail in his palm.

"Try again. We went there first," Senator Kinsmith informed him with a feigned confidence. He was the youngest of the current lineup of senators, only thirty years old, a few years younger than even Aldrious. He was quite nervous and shuffled about on his feet. My mother found him disgusting.

"Oh? Ask your progeny, then, Estrix. They will know better than I," Aldrious taunted her, revealing none of the anxiety that was boiling him alive.

My mother sighed and moved her cane from the table to just below his chin. She stared coldly in his eyes before hissing out to him, "My child is the reason I insisted I be present while we sought your counsel. That radio call you made yesterday morning, whom did you speak to? Who on earth are you selling my daughter to? Whether she has the prince or not, you do not have dominion over the fate of her!"

"You eavesdropping hag!" Aldrious shouted playfully, leaning into the tip of her cane so that it jabbed into the soft skin of his neck. Giving her an equally unflinching gaze, he continued, "I mentioned both your children. I wasn't sure which one was the apple of my friend's eye, so I just said either could be in her territory. You heard that, of course, but still no thought for poor Zan. I don't even have a bounty out for him. I guess he isn't important to either of us."

"Zan is weak willed, not so much as my firstborn, but nonetheless of no concern to me. You are a disgrace and very much of my concern; you have no right to continue as ruler of the realm. Your replacement, the Bishop Carol of the Southern Quarter Church, is already in the throne room. He can conduct his business without needing to be inebriated, unlike you, you weak fool. You will call off your bounty, radio your whore, and abandon your title immediately!"

"No, no, and fine," replied Aldrious calmly, unpinning his cardinal's signet. He swatted Estrix's cane from his neck and stood up all too quickly. The blood rushing to his head caused him to stumble and allowed my mother to grab his right hand, pulling the thumb from his palm.

"It is over, Aldrious. You shall make a mockery of this nation no longer. You will correct your mistakes, or I shall eviscerate you myself. Enox officials are on their way, but if Leke is unsafe, they will find no shred of you."

Her two fellow senators looked a bit shocked to see this elder acting so aggressively, but my mother was faelock through and through. She had become hunched with age, barely reaching to seven foot four. Her dark purple hair had faded to a lavender-gray, and her skin was completely yellowed by that point, but her strength would never be diminished.

Aldrious, however, had his own substantial power. He saw little more than a very tall old bird trying to poof out her feathers. He clenched his fingers around the hand holding his, slicing into Estrix's paper skin easily. She did not scream, did not panic; she just looked at him with seething rage. He held up both their hands and shook them wildly, creating a veritable tornado of tiny shards of hardened blood. He let them loose throughout the room, terrifying and blinding the three senators enough that he could run out the door.

It just so happened that a shard pierced Senator Allen's aorta, giving Aldrious an ample supply of crimson. My mother was able to grab his ankle before he could flee completely; however, it was at the cost of her hand. He had created a circle of blades around himself out of Allen's blood, one of which deftly took care of her attempt.

Despite dismembering my mother, he was not interested in a fight or with further sullying the palace. The more removed from his seat of power he became, the greater his respect for it grew. It was peculiar, but it seemed his humanity returned with each ounce of control lost; in that vein it made some sense.

As he moved through the halls he passed five guards, all of whom ignored him walking past. He was half-awake, covered in blood, and surrounded by seven levitating onyx blades. It's unlikely many would want to interrupt such a man without orders.

Some such orders must have finally been given by the time he neared the royal bedchambers, his residence since the demise of the king and queen. Most members of the Mortanion Brotherhood possessed the art of blood magic, so this fight he walked into would be much less pleasant for him. Aldrious had an innate talent for it, one passed through his family line, but not such a great gift to be able to take on the two-dozen young monks who stood in front of him.

"Yes, yes, the guest of honor has arrived. What are we planning, where are the festivities to be held? Such a privilege, all this attention just for me!" he taunted coyly, though he released his control on Allen's blood. The circle of blades fell but turned to ash before they could impact with the marble floor.

"Dear brother, you have made quite a mess, haven't you? You planned on leaving it all for me? That is rather unfair; however, if you tell us where the prince is and whether or not he is alive, I'll happily clean it up myself," Bishop Carol chided as he positioned himself in the middle of his row of young monks. He was a weak and tiny man, middle-aged and clad in burgundy. He stuck out horribly amongst the predominantly teenaged monks who were all dressed in brick red with their blood swords drawn.

"Dead, stolen by the Logos, headed to Khur," Aldrious gasped out quickly before running himself into Carol as fast as he could. Just as he suspected, at least four blades pierced through his flesh and deep into his abdomen. He fell to the floor, prompting the others to stand down. Although it brought him within inches of his life and he was on the verge of shock, the ruse worked perfectly.

Lying on the floor beside Carol's sandaled feet, he drew the energy from all the blood he spilt. A single reaper started to grow behind them, but the monks were preoccupied with mocking the dying cardinal. As soon as his spell was at full strength he lifted his hand up, the first and last clue they were to have of Aldrious's scheme. The reaper knocked Carol clear over as it grasped its master's wrist within its talon. It flew up, straight through the glass ceiling. Shards from the blue lotus design of the stained window rained down all over his brethren.

He was riding high above the castle, barely awake as he whispered to the beast pathetically, "Hold me tight...." He needn't give it verbal commands; it was a manifestation of his own consciousness and could interpret them, yet it still felt comforting to ask.

Aldrious was, frankly, rather fucked at this point. Wherever he went there would be trouble, as this hated creature was his only transport. It held him up to its chest with both talons, supporting his jagged torso. He was busy coercing his blood to repair itself and fuse his flesh, while the creature flew as high as possible toward Westend.

After ten minutes of flying up and west, all the holes in his flesh were sealed, although the muscles were sliced apart beneath them. The organs were mostly spared, but he was still sending energy to his spleen and right kidney when his flight needed to be over. He swatted out his hand, breaking the spell's epicenter and starting his plummeting descent toward the roof of Connor's print shop.

The only reason he survived such a stupid stunt was that he landed in the compost pile of the florist next door. Instead of dying, he broke three ribs, both ankles, his left wrist, and ripped open one of the stab wounds. The noise was sufficient in prompting Connor to run out of his shop at full speed. He lifted his stinking, bleeding cousin up and into his shop before anyone else could figure out what had happened. The residents of Westend would have been highly amused to know Aldrious the Wicked fell from the sky into a pile of rotting waste in their own backyard, but it sadly remained secret.

"So this be what neck-deep looks like, Aldy?" Connor asked kindly. He held the awful mess in his arms like a child before setting him in one of the large sinks in the back of his shop.

Aldrious tried to create a witty response but instead just coughed up more blood, pissed himself, and passed out in the metal tub.

It was completely dark out when he woke again. The shop was lit only with candles, and they were all surrounding Connor at his press. Aldrious had been sleeping on a ratty tartan couch in the dormitory part of the building. He craned his neck to see the large sinks used for equipment, and now cardinal washing, across the room from him.

He wanted to get up but knew it was not going to happen. His entire body was on fire with pain; his skin was covered in a sticky sweat, and he was trembling from to toe to chin. The nap was necessary, but it prevented him from encouraging his body to heal itself, and it grew to be as damaged as an average human's would be.

He fidgeted his fingers under the fur he had been covered with, using more than just his mind this time to rebuild his body. It would still likely be an hour or so before he could walk.

He didn't have long to ponder getting up before his youngest cousin bounded through the room holding a candle. Annalise DuBois sat herself on the edge of the couch, barely fitting her small body next to him. "Dun go movin' now, idiot," she scolded him, before turning to pour some water into his open mouth.

"I bet you are little Annalise! Don't tell me you speak like that too? I do not understand. You are all educated and wealthy, not a herd of bloody yokels. It gives me a headache," Aldrious whispered to her after gulping the cold liquid down. It felt as if it were extinguishing the sparks of agony as it passed through him. He was thankful to not be drinking wine for the first time in years.

"We speaks like our people. We ain't no ninnies o' the church or the crown," yelled Connor from the other room.

"Oh, I can speak properly if you'd like, cousin. When I am with my siblings, they drag me along with that nonsense. It has been ages, Aldrious; I could barely speak in any form when I last saw you. I have grown quite a bit since my diaper days, I am sure you can tell." Annalise spoke kindly, with some soft laughter.

Aldrious barely knew her, but he could tell she took after the mother of the current brood. In that family, one looked completely like one parent or the other. The father's half, like Connor and Aldrious's favorite cousin, Lucille, were all tall and broad, with pale skin and fiery orange hair. The other half of them looked more like the mother, thus more Dalgarie, with tan skin and petite bodies. Shemmy and Annalise were definitely of the maternal side. Annalise had her dark brown hair cut quite short around her ears and had perfectly smooth skin besides a large scar under her left eye. She was quite beautiful, prettier than Shemmy, but that could have just been due to the lack of dirt and eight-year age difference.

"You have grown gorgeously. I do so like tomboys," Aldrious whispered with a grin. He was desperately trying to remove one of his hands from under the fur so he might touch her soft skin; however, it was to no avail. She jumped away from him and across the room at first notice of his blanketed movements.

"You're as awful as my brother said, then? I will be off now. If you are well enough to flirt with your baby cousin, you need no nurse," she shouted and grimaced as she made her way into the front of the shop. "My lady is probably worried sick. I'm gonna get outta here, brother. Yer patient is awake; smack him for me when he's well enough. Taking one of these too, you hadn't shown me the new one yet," she yelled to her brother, tucking one of the naughty magazines under her arm.

"The fuck he do?" Connor grunted, but allowed her to leave without answering. Instead he walked into the room with Aldrious, holding a large piece of parchment against his chest. "Get my little sister out of yer sick mind and treat your loins to thoughts of this beaut!" He was guffawing as he drew closer, allowing the reproduced image of a three-breasted woman to become visible to his cousin.

"Wait, is she real?" That sight was encouragement enough to move. Aldrious drew his hand from the blanket and grazed a fingernail against the central nipple.

"Aye, I have the real photograph somewhere in here. She was some mutant from Khur, a bloody gorgeous one. I hear she has since passed. Had I believed in Aegis, I woulda cursed him after hearing the awful news."

Aldrious frowned and dropped his hand to hang beside the couch. "He's real…. He is a greedy, evil asshole who cares nothing for this planet or his children, but he exists," he muttered bitterly, shutting his eyes.

"No wonder you got along with him for so long. Movin' on, yer bounty posters are done, distributed 'um myself and gave Annalise one. My money is on her winnin', as long as her missus lets her off leash." Connor had rolled up Triple Tit and grabbed the stack of parchment from under his arm. He placed it atop Aldrious's chest before turning back to his workroom. "Another fing I want ya to see," he called back.

"I probably don't need these copies anymore. I am a fugitive myself. Perhaps I will drop one in the castle gates so Carol knows why mercenaries are bringing him bodies. I am sorry to have wasted your time, to make you do so much for me…." Aldrious trailed off, trying to think of that poster and distract himself from his pain and misery.

"Does'nae matter, the papers and whatnot. You juss best make sure Shemmy gets her place back, no matter what state you be in. I dun care who you gotta speak to, be it parliament, the dead prince, or even bloody Aegis for that matter. That little bitch sister o' mine is gonna change the world; she's a damn miracle. I cannae abide her talent being wasted in the woods no longer."

Connor had returned with a two-foot-tall leather folder under his broad arm. He swung his empty hand out, knocking the bounties off Aldrious's chest and replacing them with the bundle. He opened it up, showing the cardinal a menagerie of written accounts, drawings, and even photographs of Shemmy's achievements in enchanting. Most of it was regarding the first man she revived.

"She really is your favorite sister, hmm? I always preferred Lucille." Aldrious was laughing but curious enough to begin digging through the file. The first photograph was a bit blurry, but what it contained was astonishing. Shemmy was being cradled in the arms of a man whose head was obviously sewn back on. She was laughing, and it was clear the dead man alone was supporting her.

"You only like her cos she's a slut. The two o' you could'nae have been in double digits when ya started fuckin'."

"We weren't," Aldrious replied with a wicked grin while looking at the before picture. It showed Shemmy with the man while he was still alive, shaking hands happily in front of the rest of her group.

"Bloody disgustin'," chuckled Connor, kneeling beside the couch to look over the file as well. "Members o' her enchanting clan gave me this stuff. They knew how I like to keep tabs. See that sod, his name was Reginald Erewald, a rich prat from south Drummond. Joined their troupe, was obsessed wif the dead. He volunteered himself, was damn near giddy to get his head sawed off." He picked up the last of the photographs and held it out. Reginald was lying on the ground, his head on a rock and his neck out. Shemmy had the ax propped over her shoulder. You could see every single tooth in that man's head as he smiled wide for the camera.

"Her clan, they fink he is still alive. They left him in the wastes. Shemmy could'nae bear to keep him. They say she felt like she failed o' whatever, could'nae be reminded o' the pain she caused him. Nobody else wanted to take care of that thing, but I'd assume his body still needed nutrients after bein' raised. He likely starved to death ages ago, but they are even more taken wif Shemmy than I am. They think she can make immortals, create true wonder. What you fink, cousin? She gonna do this to yer prince?"

"Not that, I hope," Aldrious answered with a groan. He was reading through the records regarding all of Reginald's postmortem bodily functions and could not bear to think of the heir to the throne going through such humiliation. "I doubt the Logos would do this if they weren't damn near positive the prince could rule. I am guessing they found a way for her to do it right."

"Real second life? If anyone could do it, it's her. Below all that shite on Reginald, there are accounts on how she manipulates nature, growin' crops, dammin' rivers, catchin' fire and freezin' water. She's got enchanted companions she made who have been animate since her banishment—that's six damn years. That level o' ability is unheard of, even for a central heir."

"I knew she was skilled, but not this much so. Perhaps he is in better hands with her." Aldrious was crying but did his best to hide it from Connor.

"Dun be a stupid arse. You got stabbed what, five times, fell from the bloody sky, and lost your title. You deserve to cry your prissy eyes bone-dry. Juss not on my Shemmy file!" He scooped up the bundle, letting it disappear under his arm and stomach-length beard. As he smiled with pride over his sister, Aldrious could see through his yeti appearance to recognize his gentle, happy cousin. It felt nice to know the bonds of their blood were strong, even with years, nations, and beliefs separating them.

"Thank you, Connor. You are as a kind as you are gigantic," Aldrious murmured and began to doze off.

"I ain't that kind," Connor shouted, smacking his cousin's forehead with his backhand. "You better be stayin' awake so you can heal yerself and get the fuck out. Annalise and I tortured ourselves by washin' yer sorry arse and dyin' yer robe black wif ink before we dressed you. As soon as you can stand, I want ya out. I dun care where ya go, as long as you still see to it Shemmy gets back here."

"Right, stupid me," Aldrious mumbled, sitting up quickly. He wobbled a bit but still somehow got up on his feet. He would take generosity, but this irritable mercy he did not want. "Have you some coin so I can visit a brothel? That'll heal me faster than your cheap couch."

Connor handed him a few notes from his pocket but also one of his explicit magazines. "In case you cannae get it up in your shit-kicked state."

Aldrious grinned, tucking both precious gifts into his robe. "Thank you so much, cousin. I shall hopefully be seeing you all soon and in better condition. I hope to be dressed in men's clothes by then, no more glorified nightgowns."

"Aye, and Shemmy will be back, yes? I have your word, do I not?" Connor queried seriously. He then led Aldrious to the back door.

"I swear it, cousin, my word is yours," he responded with a grim nod. *My word is slanderous shit, however. I doubt I can do a thing for anyone anymore*, he thought, aching horribly as he trudged.

He knew not where to go, what to do. He had always known what to do before. He knew the key to stopping the havoc wreaked by the MortiAegis church and the brotherhood was from within, so he joined them. He could sense their weak point was Casperland and wormed his way in wonderfully. Back then he had ideals, he had his sense of vengeance, and he was on his way. He was well learnt in prophecy, and he thought he could ease the globe's troubles himself. He was always ridiculously idealistic, he realized now. It was not until Micah fell ill and he became supreme ruler that he lost sight of his nobler goals completely. He wished his idealism could return to him now, to guide him again. Until it returned, he would simply march north and find a suitable alley to peruse his pornography.

CHAPTER 10

May 8th, 989

BILLIAM AND Micah's first two nights together found them sleeping in each other's arms, wrapped in quilts atop the hard wooden cart. The smell of death was far gone from Micah; instead his skin emanated a familiar powder-soft scent that Billiam found incredibly comforting. They did their best to sleep as platonically as possible, attempting to have no temptation to break Shemmy's rule.

She helped them with this by parking Gam right next to the cart and facing them as she slept. Without fail, every time anything more than a kiss began to brew, Shemmy would giggle loudly no matter how deep in slumber she had seemed.

They awoke about forty hours after Micah's resurrection to a light flurry of snowflakes. They landed on the exposed skin of the young men's faces, creating tiny puddles as they melted. The cold air threatened the puddle, forcing it to freeze back up, the frost then biting at their cheeks. These nips of pain were what first drew Billiam from his slumber, but it was the unending trembling from his prince that snapped him into full consciousness.

Micah had taken to Roland's large shirt after all, wearing it as his nightdress. It barely covered him up yet still managed to obscure the important parts. They were a day past crossing Alafor's national border, not the most forgiving climate for sleeping outdoors, especially when pant-less. Goose flesh covered him from the tops of his feet up to the nape of his neck, prickling right below his ears.

Billiam pulled him tight, wrapped around him from behind, and put his cheek to his prince's. The sound of Micah's teeth chattering was almost to a deafening level but worth it if some warmth could pass through him. "Perhaps we should get up, Prince? You will be warmer if you move about."

"I'm not cold," Micah whispered out. His mouth vibrated so rapidly his tongue could hardly keep up. "Just hold me."

"We need to get shelter and warmer clothes for you. I am so sorry. We rushed into this without truly readying ourselves for this frigid land. We had an opportunity and seized it. I blame myself for the recklessness." Billiam positioned himself so he might cover as much of the prince with his body as possible, while still holding himself up.

Shemmy's snickering started as soon as Billiam was on top. "As nice a view as dat is, there be more effective ways to warm 'im up than body heat," she called to them and jumped out of Gam, landing with a light thud on her naked dirty feet. The cold did not affect her whatsoever. She climbed into the cart and crawled on top of both pairs of legs, grinning foolishly. "I can enchant anyfing of nature that has'nae a will o' its own, obviously the dead, and water, and plants, and so on. Billiam, you yerself wos the one that made me realize I can 'chant the very air floatin' around us. I can make it so the air dat surrounds the prince and yerself is met wif an energy to make it all toasty! Awlready dunnit to mahself!"

"Shemmy, you are brilliant!" Billiam exclaimed, happily kissing the prince's icy cheek. "Please do it! You will be our savior once again!"

"I'm not cold," Micah repeated, the words distorted by his shivers. He was showing his stubborn side for the first time to Shemmy. She had actually been quite impressed with how easygoing the heir to throne had been. Seeing his foolish pride come through made the boy fit the name at last.

"Dun worry, love, you could be as warm as the sun and yer man there would still be pressin' his body on ya." As she said that, Micah smiled at her meekly, giving her all the permission she needed.

Shemmy drew her enchanting needles from a slit in her dress. She held them, one floating straight up at the end of a finger on either hand. When she snapped her fingers, the needles danced and swirled out, one encircling each man. They spiraled around them and through the cart swiftly at least five times before shooting back to her and falling in her lap. "Better?"

Color returned to Micah's face at once, and the constant tapping noise from his jaw ceased. He stretched, pushing Billiam off him finally, though just enough so he might sit up. Sheepishly, he murmured to

Shemmy, "Oh, I guess I was a little cold. Right, thank you." He flipped his hair a bit, trying to seem aloof. He was ashamed that he had acted so obstinately yet continued in that vein regardless.

"Yes, halfway to hypothermia is only a bit cold," Billiam teased, pinching the prince's cheek. He was delighted to feel how quickly it had warmed and also enjoyed the comforting warmth around his own body. He pulled the quilt off himself but left Micah partially covered, not wanting to give Shemmy a free show. "How long does this last, dear?"

"I haven't the foggiest! Hopefully it'll still be workin' in eight hours' time!" she chirped, wriggling herself backward to get off the cart. Her hand grabbed into the quilt, pulling it off with her, undoubtedly by accident.

Micah shrieked, realizing his makeshift nightshirt had curled up around his waist as he slept. Shemmy cackled and kneeled at the end of the cart, leaving only her eyes visible as she peeped.

"I may be warm, but I should probably cover up a bit more than this, Billiam," Micah gasped out. His face was entirely pink as he grasped at the ends of Roland's shirt, trying to force the fabric to be longer than it was.

"Just because you help us and do something nice doesn't mean you earn a reward, pervert!" Billiam kicked his long leg out, his bare heel bonking against Shemmy's forehead. He did not kick her hard but combined with her strange squatting position, it was enough to throw her onto her back. "I'll take you to get dressed now, Micah."

Micah climbed onto Billiam's back, using his legs and only one arm to hang on while they crawled out of the cart. He kept the other hand planted on his blouse and backside, blowing a raspberry at Shemmy as they passed her dazed position on the ground.

Billiam slept shirtless and in his trousers, so to dress himself required only that he retrieve his cleanest shirt from his saddlebag. Although he had taken efforts to wash his and the prince's clothes in a stream the day before, he was still pining for his freshly laundered clothes delivered to his room, like at the lodge. He could do also for his coat. Having been so overwrought with excitement took quite a toll on his appearance. His face was the one lovely thing he felt he had worn since having his prince back, and even it was in need of some upkeep.

Micah had just the one outfit that he wanted to wear, so Billiam grabbed it from the tree it had been hanging on. The pretty blouse was bone-dry, but his socks and short pants were still a bit moist. He grimaced at them as he picked them up.

"Billiam, it's fine! I will stay warm regardless," Micah assured his lover cheerfully as they made their way to a suitable dressing area.

Over in the cover of woods, Billiam quickly and carefully got the prince's blouse and trousers on him. After, he knelt down to slide a stocking up Micah's thin leg and looked up at him, a bit concerned.

"What's wrong, love?" Micah implored.

He shook his head and began rolling the second sock up the second leg. "Well, I'm just worried about keeping you safe. I wanted to be with you as soon as our time limit is up, but I must insist we wait until nightfall. It would be much too dangerous for me to put you in such a vulnerable position in the light of day. There could be any number of headhunters about by now. I have been dreading having to make you wait."

"Oh, Billiam! Don't be so silly! You are my protector, my knight. I trust you always put my well-being first, even if it means my every whim is not indulged. I wish to no longer be the spoiled brat you coddled our past life together. I'd like to be a man now, worthy of your love and devotion." Micah grabbed Billiam's hands off his legs and pulled him up from his kneeling position, placing them around his waist. He smiled sweetly, setting Billiam's mind mostly at ease, though he sensed a last trace of anxiety. "What else, dear?"

"Well, Prince, you *are* worthy of my love and devotion, you alone. You are the only one I ever have or ever will give my love to. However… you are not the only one I have given my body. I am so sorry, Micah." He shoved his head down between Micah's chin and shoulder before continuing. "I feel as though I betrayed you, but I swear you were always the one in my heart. Also, I have become a much greater lover than I was when I first started. I am confident I can now give you only the supreme pleasure befitting my beautiful prince." Feeling slightly relieved after his confession, he was able to appreciate the smooth neck where his head was laying, kissing the length of it.

Micah giggled and held him tight. "Billiam, you are too cute! I never expected you to be chaste; in fact I'd probably be a bit disappointed if you were. You were always the older one, the one to teach and to lead me. You know how I spent hundreds of days asleep on end, no? I dreamt all the time. I had dreams where you'd go after your conquests, and, as if seeing it through a crystal ball, I would get to watch you. At the end, you would return to me and tell me all the ways they could never compare to me before it was my turn. Those were my favorite dreams!" He looked as if he had fallen back into one of them, his eyes glazing over as he bit his lip lightly.

"I can't say I expected such a naughty reaction, but I am quite relieved. Thank you, Micah, for your understanding. Now that I have you back, I swear you are the only one who will be in my thoughts, in my heart, and in my hands. I am all yours forever more, and I will have you be all mine."

"Good, for if any other man were to touch or be touched by you, I would have him executed in a second!" he sang out, his eyes sparkling but his smile wicked. Billiam was grateful he had entirely meant his promise, for he knew the prince was not at all bluffing.

After taking the opportunity to thank Micah for his understanding with more than just words, Billiam scooped up his prince and set off to rejoin the others. He was quite recovered and could walk easily; however, they had both grown fond of Billiam's habit of carting him about.

"Hello, lovebirds! I was gettin' ready to run afta ya screamin' again," Shemmy joked with a happy face, though her voice sounded strained and exhausted. She was jumping in front of Zan and stretching desperately, grabbing toward her needles, which he held in the air about three feet above her.

"Frankly, I was surprised we didn't see you," Billiam shot back with a wink, before reaching up and grabbing the needles out of Zan's hand. "Might I ask what you two are doing?"

"She was trying to enchant me. I declined politely, yet she kept trying anyways, so I stopped her. She is pretty relentless," answered my brother with a dramatic sigh.

"What, was she just trying to warm you? She already enchanted Micah and me. It's quite nice actually." Billiam smiled and messed up Shemmy's hair playfully, before surprising them both by sliding the needles into his waistband for the first time since the prince's rebirth.

"What?" Shemmy cried out angrily, flailing her arms around Billiam. "I thought you said you like it, Dandy?"

"I do, and I am extremely grateful that the prince is much healthier and safer because of it. That doesn't mean you should have free rein to enchant people against their will. So, Zan, would you like to be warmed?"

"I'm actually not very cold at all. My skin is tougher than all of yours, thanks to the ogres. I'd rather not have unnecessary things practiced on me."

"Right, that makes sense. Shemmy, will you obey his wishes?" He looked down at her, and she ceased her desperate attempts to get her hands in his pants. She nodded and feigned a convincingly innocent look up at him. "Okay, then you can have these back. Just ask first from now on, or I'll put Zan in charge of holding them."

"Wonderful idea!" my brother exclaimed with an exaggerated excitement, but he meant it. He wasn't sure why, but he didn't really trust the practice of enchanting. He was actually feeling quite cold, as we faelocks don't have much more natural defense against temperature than humans do. He is a wonderful liar and wanted Shemmy to have no idea of his aversion to her craft.

"Hell no, that giant would break 'um by accident within seconds!" she yelled, then looked over Zan for a moment. He was grinning, and it seemed to be genuine. Since learning Billiam's secret she, like Billiam and myself, tried to always interpret whether he was being honest or not. Gazing at him, she found herself noticing he was actually quite handsome behind his imposing size and those dorky spectacles. His lavender eyes began to have a bedroom effect on her, forcing her gaze downward until Billiam's hand on her shoulder stopped her ogling.

"Are you all right, Shemmy?" asked Billiam with a confused smile. "Let's get going, if you are. Seems you all got everything ready as we dressed."

"Bugger off, I'm fine!" she shouted before running off to Gam.

Billiam was shocked by her demeanor but felt it best to leave her be. They got in their usual travel positions and headed off at once.

Night fell fifty-one and a half hours after Micah's resurrection. Shemmy had a pocket watch and had screamed out every hour since the forty-eighth passed. Billiam scolded her each time, yet she continued anyway, squealing "But ya can now!" after each admonishment. She didn't know and wouldn't have cared that the two men had already agreed to wait for the cover of night.

They decided to set camp a half mile off the path, under the shadow of a small cliff. They were well into Alafor now, but thankfully still on the east side and not yet buried in snow and frost. Zan started a fire and tied up the horses. Billiam grabbed a few quilts and made a torch from a fallen branch before climbing up the rocks without a word.

"Where are you going?" Micah shouted after him.

"Must set the mood, dearest."

In a few minutes he returned and was promptly ambushed by Shemmy. "Why you goin' up there? Ain't we gonna have dinner and camp together? I dun fink I can climb that cliff."

"That is precisely why the prince and I will be staying up there tonight. I can only speak for myself, but I do not mind skipping our paltry dinner. I have no hunger for food currently."

"I don't either!" cried Micah, jumping into Billiam's arms. He was forced to drop his torch momentarily, to avoid singeing him. He positioned Micah on his back quickly and leaned down to grab it before it extinguished.

"No fair!" Shemmy stuck out her tongue and flopped down to the ground angrily. "What are we supposed ta do?"

Billiam was already halfway up the cliff, Micah holding the torch to light his way, when he responded, "Eat dinner, talk to each other, sleep, and mind your own business. Any of those things will do, I'd say."

When they reached the top of the cliff, Micah was delighted to see a fire was already struck up. Next to it lay a quilt on the ground, with two more tied up to a tree above it, forming a makeshift tent. "Never had I imagined I would be taking you in a place so lacking in ambience and privacy, my prince, but I had to put some effort in," Billiam whispered over his shoulder as he set him down.

Micah skipped over to the bedroom Billiam had created for them, his body feeling electrified with excitement. He was a bit shocked to feel himself growing nervous as well. This was what he had wanted for so long, and he knew it would be happening this night, and yet the butterflies still raged within his torso. "It is lovely! You never cease to impress me, Billiam. I could never dream of being so capable."

He laid most of his body on the quilt, propping himself up with one elbow. He wanted to appear sexy, a temptress of sorts, but he felt totally unsure of how to do so. Thoughts raced through his head manically, like *Should I just strip now? Do I say come hither? What if I danced? What the hell am I doing?* He cocked his head to the side, trying to clear his mind of the silliness running through it. Micah kept his eye contact, full of lust, but fear veiled his face.

Billiam could see Micah's anxiety growing, so he broke the short silence and spoke earnestly, "Prince, I have sworn my life to you and given you my loyalty since before you could even speak. I intend to follow you and do whatever I can for you the rest of my days. You know I will always obey you and stand by your side, yes?"

"Of course, Billiam. You have never shown me anything but loyalty and love." Micah sat up, still nervous but realizing his attempt at seduction was quite unnecessary.

"Good. For I have thought long about what it would be like when we could truly be together, body and soul. I'd like, rather, I *require* that when it is just us intimately that you be the one to obey me. I would have you submit to me completely, understood, Micah?"

Micah was relieved that he needn't figure any of this out for himself. "Yes, of course, Billiam. I always assumed that you would, well… be the one more in charge?"

"So I have total control of you? Nod for me, Micah."

Micah nodded, locking his eyes within Billiam's. He had not expected such a dominant demeanor from his lover, but it was quite thrilling.

"Good boy," said Billiam, finally joining him on the quilt though not sitting. He hoisted Micah up to his feet suddenly and held his waist tight. "I shall be taking this slow tonight, as it is your first," Billiam spoke into his ear. The words were hot and tickled down his neck. "Do not mistake this for me being gentle; I simply do not want to damage you. I will never hurt you in a way you won't like, but I also intend to never be gentle with you. That is not how I want you; my desire for you is savage and absolute."

Micah nodded without being instructed, desperately wanting to kiss him but knowing to let his lover lead. Billiam's face bore a total joy, which warmed Micah's heart. He could not be more thrilled with how this was finally playing out.

"I am glad you understand so well. You have no idea how very much this pleases me, but I will show you, soon enough." He gave him a long, hard kiss, sucking away his air. He then shocked Micah by abruptly pushing his shoulders, dropping him down onto his knees. Billiam grabbed his chin, forcing his gaze up. "Now, I need to hear you beg me for my cock."

Micah's eyes grew huge, and his face turned red. He had no idea what to say. He opened his mouth, but no words came out. He simply looked up at Billiam and trembled.

"Now, now, Micah. I didn't ask you to be shy, did I? I told you to beg me to fuck you." Billiam looked at him sternly, grabbing a handful of Micah's silky hair and tugging lightly. No matter how rough he was being, Micah could see the love in his face clearly.

"Billiam, please! I want you inside me. Fuck me now!" he called out in a loud, desperate cry. Micah could not believe what was coming out of his mouth, never even having uttered such words, but still he felt terribly excited by them. He knew he meant it and even more vulgar things that he was still too innocent to think of.

"Much better!" Billiam smiled and loosened his grip on Micah's scalp. "Now, why don't you swallow my sword for a bit, and I will see to it that I give you every inch of what you crave, no matter how slowly I might need to go." As if a switch were flicked, Billiam became erect and dropped his pants.

Micah looked at the sword, as Billiam had put it, and understood why he was insistent on how slow he would need to go. Micah did not feel intimidated, however, and still wanted every bit of it. He looked up at Billiam and sweetly said to him, "Yes, master."

"Master? I do like the sound of that." Billiam laughed softly, grabbing the back of his head. He wanted to be strong, to dominate him; however, as Micah's warm mouth encircled him, he grew more content than he had ever felt.

MY BROTHER woke suddenly in his sleeping spot, near the now barely smoldering fire pit. He sat up then looked down, disgusted by a mess he had made all over himself. He knew this was Billiam's fault, and he was furious. He got up from the earth and saw Shemmy was nowhere to be found. He could faintly hear rushing water north of him, probably on the other side of their cliff.

He followed the babbling noise, thankful for the nearly full moon lighting his way. Within minutes he saw the stream. He had to head to the east a bit to get over to it, and upon seeing a faint light ahead of him, realized he was now parallel to Billiam's camp. He could clearly see the two naked men lying together motionless on a quilt ahead of him. He didn't want to be so close, but he conceded they were not in any state to pay attention to him.

Zan stepped into the freezing cold water, which went up only to his knees. He removed his pants and scrubbed them vigorously against themselves. He splashed up onto his lap to clean himself too, feeling it could possibly be at the cost of frostbite. He was fiercely regretting not allowing Shemmy to enchant him. Once he felt completely free of stickiness, he got out of the stream. He was about to start back to his camp when a familiar giggle stopped him right in his tracks.

"Oi, I know yous have history, but I thought you'd be far too stubborn to be peepin'!" Shemmy whispered from a nearby bush. "I fink they are at a stoppin' point, though, sadly. Wow, you really were into it, eh? Yer all soaked and pantless! I'm impressed!" She smiled at him mischievously, apparently forgetting where his face was.

Zan obscured himself slightly with a tree, fearing the men might wake. "It's not like that," he explained angrily. "My bond with Billiam forces me to experience many of his feelings. I was awoken by an uninvited emission, and I came out here to wash myself up. It was obviously because of his pleasure. I'll have you know I stopped having anything that juvenile happen to me ages ago." He adjusted his spectacles and shrugged. He was ready to start off again when they were both startled by voices from Billiam's campfire.

"Shh!" Shemmy whispered and motioned for him to join her, stooping behind the bush. Zan hated himself for it but obeyed anyway, dropping the wet pants and crawling over to her. They both leaned over a fallen tree in front of them and tried hard to listen.

"Thank you so much, Prince, for allowing me that," Billiam whispered to Micah, who he was embracing from behind as they lay. He gave soft kisses along his thin neck. These were gentle and loving, not the domineering, devouring ones he had given him the hours prior.

Micah nuzzled happily into him. "So I am prince, now? I guess that means I am in charge again," he teased, giggling quietly.

"Hmm, yes I suppose you are, for the next ten minutes at least." He joined him in laughing, holding him tight. Billiam had never been so happy, never in his life, never in his dreams. "I did not hurt you, right? I was not too forceful?"

Micah turned his head to steal one of the kisses intended for his neck. "No, it was wonderful! I am so thankful you had experience. I can't imagine getting stabbed with such a great sword if you didn't know what you were doing." He enjoyed having some power back and teasing Billiam. He wiggled his hips, pressing against his lap and feeling some of his energy had been restored. "I never expected you to dominate me so, but I refuse to have it be any other way, now."

Billiam squeezed him tight, burying his face into Micah's shoulders. "I am so pleased to hear you say that. I was terribly worried I'd scare you off. I loved having complete control of you, and I did not want to have to give that up."

"No, you can't give it up! Even if I am not in power in the privacy of our bed, I am the prince, and I forbid you to give up any control of me," he contradicted himself playfully as he turned around and looked into Billiam's handsome, beaming face. "I have always been treated like such an entitled doll. Everyone was always indulging me, fawning over me, acting as though I could break at any moment. I am not complaining; I realize what a fortunate child I had been. Regardless of that, it is exhilarating to finally be the one to beg. Aldrious is the only other person to not treat me like a precious thing, torturing and humiliating me. I will admit, through the pain I did derive a bit of excitement, as it was the only time I was allowed to feel anything. Unlike him, however, I know you dominate me with the intention of allowing me absolute pleasure. I am happy to feel like your dog, and I cannot wait to obey your commands, for I know I will be reaping all the benefits."

"Is that so?" Billiam queried, all his virility and energy now restored. "Then be a good boy and roll over. I have a bone to give you."

"That was definitely not ten minutes!" Micah laughed but obeyed, turning around and eagerly propping himself on all fours.

"Holy hell, can you believe 'e said that? A bone to give you? I never 'spected Billiam to be such a kink!" Shemmy gasped out quietly, shimmying to get her body up against the fallen tree. She hugged it awkwardly while shoving one of her hands up her dress.

Zan shook his head and explained, "Billiam is quite fond of feeling in control. That and puns." He was ashamed but also could not look away. Knowing Shemmy was preoccupied, he allowed his hand to travel south on himself. Although he was excited by what he watched, bitter jealousy was corroding his heart. He would ignore and suppress it for now.

Micah braced himself, expecting his lover to join him little by little as he had the first time. Instead, Billiam slid into him hard and at once, with none of the carefulness he showed before. The prince could not stop the loud moan from escaping his mouth. He was forceful and Micah thought it was going to hurt, but instead his whole body felt alive with pleasure.

"I don't think I told you to dirty your paws," Billiam whispered into his ear. He grabbed Micah's chest and pulled him up, releasing his grip on the dirt. He was then holding them both up with his strength alone. "Hold on to yourself instead," he commanded, as he moved Micah's hand where he wanted it.

Micah did as he said, but felt himself quickly giving in, as it felt far too good. "Billiam, if I do this, I won't be able to…."

"You don't need to. I can last for us both. Obey me, boy, and give into pleasure as many times as you can. The more you do, the greater mine will be, so be quiet!" He grunted, clawing into Micah's chest.

"Yes, master!" the prince cried, to which Billiam grabbed hard on to his mouth. In truth, he loved getting called such in that moment.

"I 'ave never seen such a position in person before!" Shemmy whispered. She was still trying and failing to derive some pleasure from bumping against her hand and the tree trunk in front of her.

"He definitely couldn't have picked me up like that, though I wish…," Zan said, biting his lip, feeling he could not just sit there and watch. His passion for Billiam was boiling up, and he knew he would need a release. "Shemmy, what do you say we help each other out?" he asked, ashamed and unsure of how he felt about it himself but unable to think of any other option. "I'll try that position on you, so we can both still watch."

"Oh Spirit, I dun even like ya, but that sounds fockin' amazing," she whispered, backing up and pulling up her dress while never removing her eyes from the show.

Zan emulated Billiam, starting with Shemmy on all fours before grabbing one of her breasts to pull her against him. He wasn't as familiar with being the one behind as Billiam was, and fell out of her for a second. He grew anxious and pulled away a bit.

"It felt wonderful. I'll try and hold myself out a bit more, yes? Please try again." She looked back at him, her face passionate and suddenly becoming beautiful to him.

As he pulled her back onto himself slowly, he tried once again to hoist her up, this time sliding his hand under her dress. He was able to hold her up easily, and rock himself back and forth as they watched. As she dropped her hand to play with herself like Micah, he batted it away, doing it himself. He felt as though he wanted to give her pleasure alone, not knowing if it was because of what they watched or a real desire for Shemmy.

Eventually, both couples ended up satisfying their carnal urges at about the same time. Zan held Shemmy against him, even though they were both through. He liked having her, more than as just something to be in as he watched Billiam.

Perhaps it was because she despised him; was that what was missing with Katrina? He had thought that he was like Billiam and was an outsider twice, being both a faelock and a queer. He pursued Katrina as he had to try to stop himself from being the latter. He was always able to perform with her but never felt real passion or an unflinching lust as he had with Billiam and now Shemmy. Her body, her parts so feminine, were just as exciting to him as Billiam's had been. Was he really not queer? If not, what was he? These were the things racing in his head, besides continued desire for Shemmy.

He began kissing the nape of her neck, and she submitted to him until she remembered all at once who he was. She jumped off him and crawled on her knees a few paces away. "Thanks for that! I've never watched something so excitin' while 'avin' my own poundin'. I'll prolly barely be able to walk tomorrow, seein' as I forgot about you bein' a faelock. Hell, I forgot even who you were or where I was, it was so sublime. Don'cha be getting no ideas about dis happenin' a'gin. I still find you vile, but… can you carry me back? I'm really sleepy." She got herself in a seated position, and with a stupid grin, was transformed back into the same, ridiculous Shemmy she was to Zan before passion engulfed him.

He began to feel the embarrassment she felt, and obliged her by carrying her above his shoulder. He almost forgot his pants, but turned back a few steps to retrieve them. They walked around the creek and downhill to their camp in silence. He set her in Gam before falling onto his quilt.

CHAPTER 11

May 9th, 989

THE NEXT day all four of them slept like the dead, recovering from their indulgences. They were unconscious almost until noon, feeling as hungover as one would with ale. Their awakening was sudden and not to Shemmy's laughter or to nipping cold, but to the snapping of twigs beneath feet. Billiam shot up but was immediately grabbed at the shoulders by a strange woman, who was kneeling on the quilts with them.

"'Ello, handsome!" the young lady said to him cheerfully, climbing on top of his chest. He looked away from her and over to Micah, furious to see yet another strange girl sitting atop him. She was trying to press her lips against his face while he squirmed underneath her.

Billiam was enraged at the sight of anyone besides himself touching the prince. He threw the girl off of him and over into a tree yards away, before grabbing the one on top of Micah and heaving her just as far. "Don't you touch him, whore. He is mine!" he screamed to her as she fell hard onto the cold dirt.

He was able to pull Micah close to him before the cocking of a pistol behind his head rendered him motionless. "Aye, don'cha be pushin' the boss like that, poof!" a gruff voice called to him from behind said pistol. "Let's bring these nudists over to the others, aye, Bea?"

"Wow, he's as strong as he is good-lookin'!" Bea cheered as she ran over to the second girl Billiam pushed, helping her to her feet. They were laughing and did not seem too hurt. "I agree, Rudy, let's get 'um all rounded up."

The man with the pistol, apparently named Rudy, handed Billiam one of the quilts to cover with before tying it around him with rope. The two harlots were at work, grabbing the screaming and squealing prince from the makeshift bed. He thankfully had managed to get his nightshirt on before falling deep into sleep hours before. One of the girls held his arms as the other buttoned up his blouse. They tied up his wrists, and each grabbed an arm, easily lifting the young man off the ground.

The gunman decided against carrying the quilted hero. Instead he jammed the pistol in the small of Billiam's back, forcing him to waddle around the creek and down to the camp. He was grateful that the girls carrying Micah were in front of him and he could keep watch.

Finally awake enough to take in the scene of the camp around him, he was also able to appreciate the severity of the situation. Shemmy had been pulled out of Gam and was tied to a tree, guarded by an enormous hairy man. There was a short, grim man holding one side of Zan and a taller, weasely one on the other. Counting the gunman behind him, that put their numbers at six.

Rudy shoved Billiam down hard onto the cart. His head bashed a bit against the wooden floor, but he was grabbed up by his hair within seconds of the impact. The man yanked him into a seated position and returned the gun to behind his head. The girls gently set Micah down on the edge of the cart beside him. They took the opportunity to tie up his ankles, giggling and marveling at his smooth, almost hairless legs.

"Found these two cuties up the cliff! Thanks for the hint, giant! Ya just could'nae stop starin' up there like a lost pup! I was'nae expectin' something so intimate, but what a nice surprise!" called out Bea, as she put herself in the middle of everyone, throwing a smile and wink over to Zan. His face fell as he locked eyes with Billiam, showing a silent apology.

"These are the right ones, ain't they, sis?" asked Micah's girl.

The two ladies couldn't have been much older than the prince. They were dirty, but had rather fashionable, striped dresses on under tattered denim jackets. Bea was blonde with a blue-and-orange frock, while her sister had fiery red hair, and her dress bore purple stripes. They were cute and enthusiastic and would've reminded Billiam of Jess, had they not been kidnappers.

"Ya, well three of 'um are," replied Bea, while staring at a tattered scroll with images and words scrawled across it. "Dat girl and the little one you was sittin' on is the ones we are supposed to bring in alive. Though it says to 'bring him back alive if he is alive, if you find him dead, please bring the body.' Innit that weird?" She scrunched her face and laughed.

"Okay, well wot about the looker and the giant?"

"We do have a faelock on dis list, but it's a lady. That giant we can let go," she called over to the men holding Zan, making a shooing motion with her arms.

"What, you really want us to free him, boss?" grunted the short one.

"Ya, we dun need him. I'd say kill him, but I doubt any of us can. That there is a pureblood if I've ever seen one."

With that, the two men let go of my brother. He gave a huge, phony grin and acted quite grateful. "Oh thank you so much, Miss! Your generosity is matched only by your beauty." She seemed to buy his act and grinned happily as a blush crept across her freckled face. "I suppose I'll be taking my leave, then, just a hired hand after all. I am glad you were able to take my cue and apprehend those deviants." Billiam looked on in shock as Zan walked off calmly, disappearing into the woods.

"Oi, dammit. My man is the one we're supposed to bring back dead. That is a shame. I was thinkin' of keepin' you myself after gettin' yer bounty. I guess that's of no use anyhow, as yer obviously queer for the runt."

"He prolly just has'nae found the right girl yet!" Shemmy chimed in, throwing a wink to Billiam.

"She might be right." Billiam was smiling at Bea mischievously, realizing Shemmy could be on to a way to save his skin.

"Oh, no fair!" squealed her sister. "I'm Felicia, and I am younger but more experienced! I must be the right girl!"

"Shut it, Fel. They're prolly juss tryin' to trick us. I am obviously the better woman, anyways. Can't you see my sexy figure?" Bea spun around and fluttered her eyelashes at Billiam.

Micah had grown quite weary of these buffoonish temptresses. He also was not keen at all on being referred to as a runt by commoners. Such insults had never been allowed to reach him in all his life.

"Is this your first kidnapping?" asked Micah sweetly from his seat on the cart. He was trying not to stare at the man holding a gun to his lover's head but snuck a glance every chance he could to make sure that Rudy's demeanor hadn't wavered.

"What of it?" replied the boss defensively.

"Well this is not at all my first time being kidnapped." He smiled and sounded truly pleasant as he explained, "You seem to be bungling it up quite a bit!"

"You stupid brat!" she screamed at him. "Otto, tie him up better, will ya! He deserves to be hog-tied!"

The shorty ran into the cart and yanked Micah to his feet, viciously spiraling a large cord over his midsection. Micah did not fight. In fact, he simply continued laughing as Otto was tying the final knot on his chest. "Oh you really are daft. Don't you know your knots? A toddler could undo this!" Otto carried the hog-tied prince under his arm and joined the sisters, dropping him at their feet with a thud. Micah kept on cackling as Otto positioned his shoe gruesomely across the side of his face.

"Micah, be quiet!" Billiam yelled. Rudy reacted by smacking the back of his head with the butt of the pistol.

"Micah! Omigoodness, is that Prince Micah? All right, Bea, you can have the sexy one. Imma be a princess instead!" Felicia skipped over to Micah and Otto, and knelt down to kiss all over his face once again.

Shemmy sensed Billiam's misstep, and while the girls were fawning over the prince, she awakened Gam. Her fingers were free at her sides and she was able to draw a hex encouraging the pram to run over to Micah. She was hoping it'd be able to scoop the prince up and run off with him.

The bear of a man who had tied up Shemmy ran after Gam with his sword. "Wot the bloody 'ell is that thing?" Without waiting for an answer, he sliced diagonally through the carriage, cutting through the entire top and slicing its left legs in half.

"Noooo!" Shemmy let out a bloodcurdling scream as Gam toppled over. The right legs were still enchanted and kicking at the air furiously. All Shemmy could see was red as rage encompassed her. Not sure of what she was even enchanting, she began waving her fingers beside herself while she wailed.

Billiam looked on in horror as a huge pine tree near the prince was completely uprooted. It became suspended in the air and then hurled toward Micah, the captors, and Gam's attacker. "Shemmy, no!" he screamed, certain he was about to lose his prince yet again.

To his profound relief, the tree made no impact. Zan had returned in the nick of time and was holding the giant tree above his head. He reached out his other hand, grabbing the prince away from the captors, who were frozen in shock. He set the prince close behind him, before swinging the tree all around his front. With it, he knocked down five of the six criminals. He dropped it to his left on top of the man who killed Gam, squashing him to death.

"Shemmy, I know how important Gam is to you, but no one can be more important than the prince, to any of us," he explained, smiling menacingly. He drew his pistol and shot the terrified gunman in the forehead.

"I knew there could be no such fing as a faelock hired hand!" shouted Otto from his splayed position on the ground. "Goddammit, Bea, you idiot!" He probably would have continued yelling; however, my brother cut it short. He took a small step forward, plunging his blade between the short man's eyes as if his head were made of cheese.

"Oh shite!" screamed Felicia. She was trying to crawl away on her hands and knees from him when the blade went through her back. She moved no longer.

The weasely one who held Zan earlier had been trying to wriggle away too, but stopped all movement when he saw Zan's gaze land on him. "I'm sorry… I'm so sorry!" he cried, wetting himself as he begged.

"I'm sorry too," said my brother with an evil grin, lying with his words, not his face. With a swift jump to his left, he plunged his blade deep into the scrawny man's gut. He left the blade there and turned toward the prince, though he kept an eye fixed on Bea at all times.

Using his hands alone, he tore the ropes in half as if they were tissue paper. The freed prince hugged his rescuer tight, his head only reaching halfway up my brother's chest. "Oh thank goodness, Zan! I thought I'd die before I was a week old!" he whispered sweetly, planting a small kiss on Zan's stomach. "Might I borrow your blade?"

"Of course, Prince," said my brother, whilst messing up his golden hair playfully. Somehow, rescuing Micah all on his own had lifted some of the animosity he held for him. He grabbed the small switchblade from his pocket and handed it to him.

Micah bounded toward the cart, his porcelain legs carrying him gracefully to his man. The foolish kidnappers had only managed to tie a single rope around Billiam's body. Micah sliced it and beamed with pride at finally being the hero.

Billiam kissed him, hugging him tight. He let the world around him disappear, being only with Micah, until a loud groan from Bea made it all come back.

"You really was foolin' me, ya damn fag!" she shouted, unable to move from her spot on the ground. The tree had impacted against her legs, and both of them were contorted horribly under the rest of her body.

Micah lifted his nightdress without turning around, giving the girl full view of his backside. Once he heard her sounds of disgust, he was sure his point had gotten across and covered himself back up.

He then jumped from the side of the cart, over to Shemmy. Her whole torso was tied up, and her face was against the ropes. She would not look at Micah as he skipped over to free her. Tears were rolling down her face, clearing away the dirt and making it appear striped. "I am so sorry for your loss," whispered the prince sincerely into her ear as he began sawing at the ropes with the pathetic blade.

"No!" she screamed, lifting her head finally. Her eyes were huge and cloaked in pain. "I am sorry! I was so stupid. Oh, Micah, I never… I would never mean to hurt you… I just met you, but you are precious to me. I brought you back, and I feel a responsibility for you. I daresay I love you. I can't believe I almost…." She trailed off as she began to bawl loudly.

Micah had finished cutting through a few turns of the rope and was able to unwrap the rest with his hands. As soon as he freed her, he fell against her and wrapped his arms around her. He placed his cheek against hers and sat in her lap. "I love you too, Shemmy," he whispered, looking up at her like the innocent child he still was in many ways. "I forgive you!"

"Yay! Happy ending!" cheered my brother phonily, dancing a strange jig in front of the former boss. "Well, I suppose not for you, aye, beautiful?" He kneeled down to her, digging a knee into one of her broken legs. She screamed in agony so he grabbed her face, roughly covering her mouth. "Now, be a good girl and explain yourself, and I just might make this quick."

It was clear to Billiam how much Zan was truly enjoying this carnage. It made him feel ill, and he wished there was a way to intervene, but the information did need to be gathered. It was better to let Zan do it than have to interact with the tramp any more than he already had.

"Wos a bounty," she murmured and pointed over to the now torn scroll she had been clutching before. It was halfway between my brother and where Micah sat on Shemmy's lap.

Micah shot up and ran over to it. "I'll get it!" he cried, not seeming at all disturbed by the destruction around him nor the continued torture Zan performed. "Here you are, sir!" he chirped, handing the ripped but mostly all-there scroll to my brother.

"A royal decree, hmm? From someone who is not at all royal, how pretentious," my brother mused. He looked over it and saw crude drawings of his comrades, with descriptions and directions as to how to handle each one underneath them. He saw my face there, Pierre and Nairee, Ackerman, Malcolm, and, of course, his three companions. He was relieved to not see the faces of the twins on there, nor Roland's nor his own. "Confidential," he read, "to be seen only by select mercenaries, redistribution of this decree punishable by death. Hmm, you broke that rule, didn't you, Bea?"

"I'm sorry, I did'nae know it was the prince. Says that you all attacked the palace. How was I to know His Majesty would be in on it? Please, I am no threat to you anymore." Tears fell down the boss's face, her sorrow making it even clearer how young she was.

"Sorry, babe. A royal decree is no joke." Zan looked in her eyes kindly, although the kindness was faked. He snapped her neck between his hands, almost taking her whole head off. He then picked himself off her thoroughly crumpled body and walked over to the cart. He was folding and packing up the quilts into a saddlebag, as if nothing had happened.

"Is it time to ditch the cart, you think?" Billiam asked him calmly, as he finished dressing himself. He didn't want to acknowledge any of the horror and would much rather keep things with Zan strictly business.

"I'd say so. We will undoubtedly be dealing with feet of ice and snow by the end of tomorrow. This thing will just be a nuisance. You should get the prince dressed, should you not?"

"Right." Billiam nodded and walked to his prince, who had his arms up, ready to be carted off. Shamelessly, Billiam slid his hand up Micah's gown as he carried him off, getting in a loud slap on his backside.

"I'm sure you had full view of that impact, Shemmy," said Zan with a laugh. "I am surprised you are not drooling and fawning like a fool."

Shemmy had not left her spot on the ground and had been staring only at her Gam. She had stopped the enchantment so the right legs no longer tried to walk. Even without its pitiful attempt to continue obeying her, she couldn't bear seeing her favorite creation in such a state. Zan snapped her out of her misery slightly, and she mumbled out, "Dammit, I missed something?" Although she was curious, she was, for once, not feeling randy in the least.

"Unfortunately, I'm sure there will be many repeat performances," he responded, shaking his head as he made his way over to her. He reached down to grab her and she allowed him to pull her up. He used a bit too much strength, and she crashed into his strong chest. He surprised her with an embrace and even more shocking, bent down to lay a kiss on her cheek. It was uncomfortably close to her lips, and sufficient in restoring her to a fraction of her regular raunchiness.

"I too am sorry for your loss, Shemmy. Gam was really quite neat," he whispered and was not lying.

Shemmy studied him as she pulled away. "Yer an odd duck, Zan. You seemed downright delighted butcherin' them sods. I was surprised ya dinnae dance upon their corpses when you was done. I appreciate ya savin' us, and helpin' the prince, though. Spirit, am I glad yer on our side! Deadly, you are! However, I juss cannae put my finger on ya…. Are ya really an obedient soldier, or are ya juss a sadist? Ya juss cannae make yerself be a good, obedient, li'l faelock, right? So why pretend? I feel like I cannae expect nothin from ya. It's like two Zans in one ginormous package."

Zan grinned from ear to ear, and it actually was quite genuine. He had been in battle many times of course, but this was the most humans he had cut down at once. He was a little shocked and disturbed by how well it suited him but decided he didn't care enough to let himself get preoccupied over it. As for her inquiry, he was strangely honest with her. "I think I am all of that, Shemmy. I do like to cause harm, and I do love to lie and ravage. And yet, I feel terrible guilt, so much so I break my back to do good to make up for it. I feel I've made up for myself pretty well, most of the time."

Shemmy stared at him, dumbstruck, as he kept grinning. He was really quite happy. She didn't know happiness could make her feel so uneasy. "Whatever makes ya feel like ya ain't shite, I guess!"

CHAPTER 12

May 9th, 989

BILLIAM AND Micah took the long way around the creek to return to their camp from the last night to retrieve their clothes. Billiam set him down atop the quilt on which he had experienced ecstasy mere hours earlier. Staring at his fragile prince there now, he felt his resolve cracking.

Micah was concerned as he saw the tears welling up in Billiam's eyes. Before he could inquire, Billiam embraced him so tight he could hardly breathe. "Oh, Micah, I am so sorry. I cannot lose you again. We are lucky they were so stupid. Had they been any more competent, you and Shemmy would be gone and I would be a corpse. I was too greedy…." He trailed off as he fell to his knees, clutching Micah's legs desperately.

Micah realized he was not nearly as shaken as he probably should have been. His three days alive thus far still felt like a dream, and the four years prior to his death, he was only allowed to experience reality when the cardinal wanted. He had become so detached, everything was simply passing him by. The idea of being with Billiam again had been the only thing keeping him human. Seeing him in this state allowed Micah's own emotions to surface, although he was not ready for that, not at all.

His crying sounded like a child, a loud wail escaping his mouth before he fell completely to the ground. The tears wouldn't stop. The sounds wouldn't stop. He couldn't grab Billiam as he wanted and tell him it would be okay. He rolled onto his back and pulled his legs to his chest. The feelings of his four-year suffering were coming out; they refused to be stored in his frail body any longer.

His mother's and father's faces flashed through his mind, covered in blood and missing their eyes, just as he had last seen them. Billiam passed by too, getting wrenched from his arms and thrown away from him. Aldrious was towering over him, calling him worm, burning his flesh and cackling. *When will this stop? Will this ever stop?* thought Micah as the torrent of repressed feelings ravaged his reborn mind.

He found suddenly he could not thrash. A groan of pain tried to emerge, but he could make no sound. Billiam's lips covered his own, and his body pinned down each of Micah's limbs. His eyes were loving and concerned. He was not trying to force himself on the prince, as his position suggested; rather he simply wanted to interrupt his fit. He knew of no better way to accomplish it.

Billiam felt Micah growing slightly calmer, tears still spilling from his eyes, yet his attempts to flail had ceased. Billiam kept his lips pressed hard against Micah's mouth, not wanting to ever hear such a heart-wrenching wail escape him again. To his delight, instead of a cry, he kissed him back. Billiam relaxed, feeling he could let him go at last, and laid his head down on the prince's chest. It was still heaving hard, struggling to keep up with the pain forced through his heart.

Micah reached up his now freed arms to hug the man lying on top of him. Billiam was exhausted and overwhelmed by his own distress, having dropped all his weight onto him. Although he was heavy, it still felt nice to know he was a comfort. The prince reached his hand into his short, thick hair and whispered, "You can't worry so much. Look what happens when you cry. I become an utter mess," he teased him. Although many of his emotions poured out of him, he returned to the desire to hide them away. "I... I hadn't been able to feel in so long... aside from missing you, hoping to see you, hoping my pain would end... I was totally empty. It might take me a while, Billiam."

Billiam lifted his head from its nuzzling position, to see Micah did look better. Too much better, he thought. "A while for what, my prince?"

"To be myself again. Not to be carelessly happy as before, but to be the real me and to feel more than longing and anger. You help me. Shemmy helps me. However, I know this darkness is still raging inside me. Please, forgive me for it until you've helped me chase it away completely," he answered, kissing the top of Billiam's head before squirming in pain.

"Oh! I'm so sorry!" Billiam finally realized he was squashing the poor prince and hoisted himself to his knees. He was still sitting above him, though now supporting himself. Micah smiled as he knelt up on his elbows, the physical distress disappearing from his face.

"Not just for squishing you," explained Billiam bashfully. "I am sorry I didn't recognize you were struggling. I was just so happy to have you back, I couldn't see past that. I have been able to live freely the last five years; the only thing missing was you. I didn't fully realize how hard it would be for you to be missing everything—I should have! I will give you all my time and all my patience. I must say you have seemed happy. Were you not?"

"Of course, Billiam, do not fret! I just meant that I might not always handle emotions or situations the way I ought to. Earlier, I should have been terrified; instead I was only angry and excited. Zan was crushing people to death, and even that made me a little happy. That is not right, that is not who I am. It is the distorted me, created by Aldrious. I do not want to be that for you or for myself." Micah shook his head and sat up completely. He held Billiam tight before continuing. "All I have been, all I have felt with you is completely genuine. It is all I have ever wanted; you make me so blissfully happy. I too have been greedy. You cannot hold responsibility for all of this. Besides, I am the prince, am I not? You are all my charges. Should anything happen to you, it is on me, alone."

Tears welled in Billiam's eyes again. He was so proud of Micah for his resolve, and quite impressed by his level of introspection. I suppose he ought to know himself quite well after going through four years of isolation. We had all assumed he was completely out while comatose, but he was actually quite conscious the entire time. He was simply held motionless by a spell put on him by the cardinal. He could do only two things on his own, and those were sleep and think.

Billiam choked his feelings down, not wanting to burden the prince any further. "Not you alone. You shall never be alone again." He kissed the prince hard, wanting to somehow pass his love and strength directly into him. Parting, he stood up and pulled Micah to his feet.

He was off grabbing their things: his outfit from the day prior, the quilt tent he made, and finally Micah's clothing. Billiam was dressing him as Micah spoke. "We should all sleep together from now on, until we reach the City of Alafor. If there are any inns along the way, let us stop there for the night. If we haven't an inn, we should not indulge ourselves, okay, my love?"

Billiam looked up at him from his kneeling, short-buttoning position, conceded he was quite right, and nodded obediently.

"We shall leave the cart behind now, and Shemmy and I can each ride a horse. You and Zan should be just as quick as us on foot. Should we have Zan map out our camps before we reach them? This way we can know if we will have shelter and properly decide on the most secure location, if we won't."

"Yes, of course. He should be quite adept at that," Billiam replied. He had never seen the prince act so mature. In fact, he had never seen him act in a leadership role at all. He was excited to see it, even if it meant he was to relinquish his control a bit. Micah was the real master after all, and Billiam was grateful that he was going to have a true king to serve.

"Can I get some new clothes too, when we find a town? I need some color!" He wiggled his hips and giggled at the thought. The stoic leader melted away completely as he reached up his arms childishly to be carried.

He was all dressed now, so Billiam obliged. He held him tightly, delighted by every side of his prince that he was shown. He had known Micah all his life, and yet in these three days he had found a thousand new reasons to love him.

Billiam decided he ought not waste any more time and threw Micah from his front to his back. He climbed them down carefully, setting the prince down once they hit ground. He tried his best to shove his things into the saddlebag, yet it was a very tight fit. Their storage was immensely diminished with the cart left behind. His shirt was bulging out of the side, but he conceded defeat and left it as it was. As he turned away, he caught a glimpse of Shemmy. She still looked thoroughly crushed, though distant and no longer crying.

He placed his hand on Shemmy's shoulder, a bit of encouragement for the poor girl. He was the only one who had not yet offered his condolences, but for the sake of moving things along, he decided he would leave it with just that touch for now.

She surprised him by clutching against his body with both arms and both legs before he could walk away. "My Gam!" she wailed as she hung off of him. Tears fell out of her eyes as she rubbed the snot running from her nose onto Billiam's shirt.

He stared down in disgust but didn't interrupt her. He simply patted her head and told her, "I'm sorry, Shemmy. I love you, dear. We'll make you a new one, yes?" She smiled up at him, her face covered in dried boogers. It was a bit stomach turning, but seeing the light back in her eyes also warmed his heart. With that, Billiam and the two horseback riders were ready to continue on with their trek.

"I'll do a little clean up, hmm? Go ahead, and I'll catch up in a bit." Zan smiled and waved them off exuberantly.

To begin, he grabbed his blade from where it still rested in the scrawny man's chest. He proceeded to turn the entire cart into splinters and sawdust with it. He gathered these flecks of cheap wood and sprinkled them all over his collection of corpses as if it were confetti. He went to decorate Gam as well, but first leaned into the carriage. It seemed Shemmy had begun keeping most of her belongings in the saddlebag, but what he did see in its belly were a crude rag doll, one of her dirty tunics, and a vial of dark liquid. He collected the items and shoved them into his pockets.

He then threw the sawdust atop Gam and struck a match against the side of his leg. He looked down at the dancing little flame in his hand and whispered to it, "Please destroy the bodies, but do hold yourself back from creating a forest fire, yes?" With that, he dropped the match down and jogged off to catch up with the others.

Zan caught up to them in about ten minutes, smelling of smoke, with a happy look on his face. His mood was better than it had been in ages; he had never known six human lives were all it took to feel so content. He strolled at a relaxed pace next to the speed-walking Billiam and the two trotting horses.

"Zan, please get out your map and study it. I'd like to plan out how long we travel each day and where we will camp. I would like also to stay in as many inns as possible," instructed Micah, smiling from atop his horse.

"Right, I will do that, Prince. Though, as far as security and such, we might be safer simply picking more discreet locations outside and staying together. Inns mean people, and people mean a chance to be recognized," my brother explained with a feigned kindness. He pulled the map from his back pocket and held it in front of his face as he walked.

"Yes, well, safety is important. When there is no inn, we shall all stay together. However, I would dearly love some privacy. I have only had my first taste. You wouldn't truly want to deprive me, would you, Zan? I mean you of all people should understand, as you have had the pleasure of being his as well." The prince was grinning wickedly and looked over to Zan, startled to see just how disturbed a look grew on his face. Micah meant only to tease, not do whatever it seemed he had done.

"You told him?" screamed out my brother as he angrily shoved Billiam's shoulder. Shemmy and Micah stopped their horses, realizing a scuffle could be breaking out. It was best they sort it out at once.

Billiam looked just as shocked as Zan and stared at my brother with no trace of anger. "No, I didn't tell him!" he shouted desperately, and then looked over to Micah, sincere and ashamed. "I wanted to tell you. I want you to know everything. I was afraid of causing unnecessary tension, so I had decided to wait until we were safe in Alafor."

Micah was struck by that. He realized that truly no one had told him. How, then, did he know? It was as if he remembered it, not that he was told. Instead, he saw clearly an image of Billiam taking Zan, like he was taken the night before. The prince looked at his lover sweetly, before explaining, "Billiam, I am not upset. I know I am the only one you love. I was just teasing. It's so strange…. You really didn't tell me, did you? You just let me know, vaguely, what an experienced man I was to have! I wonder how it is I know? I certainly do know, and it was quite a number of times, wasn't it?" He felt a little bad embarrassing Billiam further, but he found his bashful squirming adorable.

"Zan, when ya got yerself thrown into me, when I was 'chantin' the prince, did ya fall in the water?" Shemmy asked nervously.

Zan was very irritated, especially now that it seemed she was insinuating some fault of his own. "No, all I hit was you. I most certainly did not wish for it." He adjusted his glasses, and then glared at Billiam. To his surprise, he looked sorry for the position my brother was now in.

"Some drops of blood fell in, Shemmy. I remember watching them dissipate into the pretty pink water," Micah said innocently, as if it were the first fond memory of his new life.

"Oi. Dammit. Contaminated ya, he did."

"Excuse me, I am not infectious! I am the reason you lot are alive now, am I not?" Zan shouted at her, defensive and enraged. He couldn't hide his emotions in the least at the moment.

"Aye, sorry, Zan. Dinnae mean on purpose or nuffin'. Anyone's blood woulda dunnit. What that means, though, is erm… 'e can access your memories. I 'ad read as much, and I fink that's all it should affect." She shrugged, acting as innocently as possible as she said it, although she knew full well how damaging those memories would be.

"What the hell?" Zan screamed, punching a nearby pine so hard the thing cracked and leaned to its side.

"Oh, well that's bizarre. That's all I've remembered so far, anyhow. Did something really embarrassing happen? Is that why you are so worked up? What did you do, Billiam?" the prince teased. He was blissfully unaware of what would soon be dug up and displayed across the canvas of his mind.

"Let's just get going. I suppose you'll know whatever it is that's upsetting him soon enough. Our first time was much more embarrassing for me than it was for him, so I highly doubt it's that." Billiam did his best to redirect the conversation and make light of it at his own expense. He struggled with whether he should just tell him and get it over with but decided against it. The prince was already quite emotionally unstable. The longer it took him to remember, the stronger he might become, Billiam conceded.

Micah began giggling uncontrollably. He must have triggered Zan to remember, causing a chain reaction, or he just thought of it on his own. Billiam wished desperately to know how this recollection process was to manifest.

"Oh, poor Billiam!" Micah was barely able to cry out amidst gleeful laughter. He fought it enough to get his horse trotting again.

Billiam and Shemmy followed him, though my brother hung back once again. "I will work on this a bit and then catch up. We should be able to stay in an inn tomorrow night, Your Highness!" Zan yelled, waving the map at them.

"Yay!" My brother heard the prince cheer as they got farther from his line of sight. He could make out Shemmy pestering Micah about his newest memory, but it seemed he was still unable to form words about it. Billiam was mortified but happy that the prince was pleased.

Zan could barely breathe as he stood in shock, desperately trying to look at the map. He could hardly decipher it; either his hands or his brain were shaking fiercely, and he couldn't tell which. He was firmly aware that when Micah learned what he had done to Billiam, he would want his head at once.

My brother thought again of what Shemmy asked him. Was he a loyal knight, who would submit to death at his king's hands? Was he a ravenous psychopath, caring only of meeting his own needs? He could see being both wasn't an option for much longer. He was far too involved with what others would think of his actions, when he should have thought of how they made him feel. Had he thought of that, he may have finally seen he was neither of those things and never needed to be anyhow.

He hurriedly fumbled through his jacket pockets and produced a blank scroll. He kneeled to the ground and began scrawling directions. He wrote out their entire path to Alafor, with all the suggested spots to camp. He wrote out inns and names of terms that might help throughout their journey. He would hand Billiam this scroll and run. He didn't know where he could possibly go, but he couldn't stay with Micah. Fighting him off would be no problem, but my brother did not think he could bring himself to do it. He knew any punishment was deserved, but he also wanted to put that off for as long as possible.

Zan finished his scroll and shoved it into his pocket. He gulped hard as he walked in their direction, feeling as though he could very well be taking his final steps.

CHAPTER 13

May 9th, 989

MY BROTHER procrastinated his journey to the others with painstakingly slow steps at first but ended up sprinting after them. He realized the sooner he got to them, the sooner he could slip Billiam the scroll. He would then distract them somehow, before turning tail and fleeing like a coward. He thought up excuses while running through the pale green pines, his feet staining the recently fallen snow he crunched atop. His only idea of where he wanted to go was somewhere warm. That would have to do for the moment, he decided amidst his panic.

It felt like it took ages to catch up, though it was only a few minutes before they were in his sights. He jogged up to them enthusiastically, but he felt his heart stop upon seeing Micah.

He had forced everyone to halt. "Hello, Zan. Please light a match and take it to that scroll in your pocket," said the prince calmly, his gaze burning through my brother.

"What?" asked Zan, feigning the utmost innocence. Could Micah learn even his new memories? Or could Micah just read his mind? He was desperate to know what this connection with the prince truly was and sever it immediately.

"I said in so many words, destroy that good-bye letter you wrote us. I am your king, Zan. You cannot desert me simply because you feel uncomfortable."

"Right, yes, Your Highness." Zan bowed slightly before grabbing out the scroll he had written so thoughtfully. He watched it become ash in his hand.

"Good. When we reach the camp you picked for us, you will tell me why you were going to flee. If I remember before that, so be it, but you will tell me yourself, regardless. If you dare attempt to insult me again, to deceive or betray me, I will shake the world so I can see you die. I will make Shemmy pull up every tree in the forest, I will have Billiam cut off your miserable head, and I will trample your fucking body with my horse. Are we clear?" Micah sounded just as calm as when he started, but his face was distorted by a dark rage. This was not at all the prince my brother and I knew when we were children.

"I panicked. I honestly thought my absence would be better for everyone. You are right, though. You are the one who should decide my judgment. I know what that will be, however. You will be killing me tonight, Prince." Zan cleared his throat and adjusted his glasses, allowing himself to be emotionless, forcing nothing.

He looked over to Billiam and Shemmy, who were both awestruck and horrified. Neither of them could do a thing anymore, nor could my brother. He would simply have to follow Micah until the little lord's anger reached its zenith, having Billiam execute him. Zan knew this was the only way this could play out and did his best to begin accepting it.

"I will make my own decisions. Let's be off."

With that, my brother's interruption of their travel ceased, and they continued on. Shemmy grew discontent after a while, tiring of the scenery, a monotonous sheet of white-covered green and gray. "All we fockin' do is walk. Walk through some woods, walk up a bloody mountain, and walk in the damn snow. Then we eat scraps and sleep on the dirt. I am bored! How much longer?"

"Four nights, five days left if we waste no time. It may be five nights should any situation arise, like today," my brother grumbled, his eyes never leaving the ground. He was able to force a phony smile, although he felt as if his organs were getting pickled inside his body.

"We shall pick up the pace tomorrow, no more mistakes and no more attempted betrayals," Micah said with a snicker. He was slightly disappointed that he'd not remembered anything yet. He wanted to be a step ahead of his treasonous charge.

Turning to Shemmy, he smiled and sang to her sweetly, "Shemmy, we will play tonight. I know quite a few riddles, and we can make up stories too. You can even braid my hair, if you want!"

"Yes! Dat sounds marvelous, my lil cream puff!" Shemmy smiled big and felt quite comforted.

Ever since she was a child, she had held a strong connection to the dead. She embraced her family's legacy as enchanters and was secretly tutored in it from the age of five. The love she felt for the things she enchanted, the life she gave to discarded waste, was a truer, more legitimate love than she could ever feel for the living. Having resurrected Micah, she felt a strangely maternal bond for him. He was her crowning achievement, so sweet and beautiful. Unlike her other creations, he was able to actually love her back. She felt a deep happiness when she saw how much he wanted her to feel better, to enjoy being with him.

"Please keep braids to a minimum, and no matted dreads like yours," Billiam joked, though he reached a hand up to hold some of the golden strands before they could be compromised. He was terrified to let her touch Micah's sacred head but loved to see them both smiling once again.

The rest of their day's trek was over hard-packed snow. Shemmy had enchanted around the horses so the poor things were not freezing. Their hooves slipped in the icy parts, threatening the beasts' knees and ankles, yet they continued along admirably. The clomping sound they made as their hard feet fell through the snow, clapping against stone, reverberated with the painful drumming of Zan's heart.

They reached the point where they'd need to leave the main road, the beginning of the hidden trail to a cluster of caves. Zan was sure a suitable camping spot could be found up the steep, rocky path. Shemmy and Micah were forced to dismount, leading the weary horses amidst the frost-covered spiny trees. It took them about twenty minutes of perilous hiking until the trail evened out. There they found a small patch of soft earth, clear of snow, with a shallow cave behind it.

"This should be far enough out. We will have a fire lit here until we retire and then I will snuff it out completely. You should all fit in that cave fine, and I'll tie the horses a few yards away," Zan informed them with a strange enthusiasm, feigning human so desperately. It should have been clear to him by now how pointless this was, but it was a habit he couldn't quit. He grabbed the horses' reins, dropped the saddlebags on the ground, and headed out to tie them up without another word.

Billiam began snapping all the dry branches he could find and collected them under his arm. He headed to the middle of the dirt patch, set down his bunch of twigs, and grabbed his matchbook from his pocket. He was growing their small fire as Shemmy and Micah started unpacking the saddlebags. They were all startled by a loud booming sound, followed by a fat goose that fell from the sky and landed at Billiam's feet.

Zan appeared from around the side of the cave, slipping his pistol into its holster. "I wanted something other than squirrel for my last meal."

"I'll get her ready!" Shemmy ran over, excited to have real food, no matter how depressing Zan's reason was. Billiam backed away from the flame, allowing her to take over. He had no desire to see her rip the poor bird apart, but he handed her his dagger before walking to the prince.

Micah had been leaning against a tree, desperately trying to recollect something, anything. The stress was collecting in his brow, crumpling his small, lovely face. Billiam grabbed both of his shoulders eagerly and pulled him into his chest. He wrapped his arms around him, feeling worlds better with Micah's warm breath covering his heart. "The goose will be on the flame soon. We should have plenty of time to talk while it roasts. I love you, Micah, and I stand with you, no matter what."

Micah returned his squeeze, placing a soft kiss on his chest. "Thank you, Billiam. I love you more than I can say. I am so lucky our fathers picked you as my page."

"I highly doubt this is what they expected of our relationship, but I couldn't agree more." He gave a short laugh before grabbing Micah's chin. Billiam slipped his tongue along the inside of his top lip, before pulling away from the half kiss slowly. This was a devilish temptation, awakening Micah from his anxiety completely, leaving him unable to resist following his lover. Unfortunately, he led him only to the fire. He sat on the earth and tapped on his lap, motioning for the prince to take his seat.

Micah shook his head and clenched his fists. He had let this brew for long enough. "Zan Ellekós, speak your piece now. I assure you, you very much do not want to lie to me or waste my time. Tell me what is so awful in your memories that you would betray your own king?"

Zan had just finished positioning the goose over the fire, using his blade as a spit. This was undoubtedly going to weaken the sword, but that didn't matter. He was sure he would not need it after tonight. Getting up from the fowl, he collected himself a bit. He wasn't sure where to start, so he just blurted out, "I put Billiam in grave danger and refused to get him aid...."

"I said don't waste my time. I didn't say be a vague twit!" Micah was growing impatient. He saw a flash of memory: Billiam was crying, saying his name over and over, curled on a stone floor.

My brother took in a deep breath. He looked at Micah, locking those burning sapphire spheres in his sights. He would do this, thorough, like a man, and hopefully get in a swing of his own. Micah would hear the truth and feel pain at his hands, punishment for winning Billiam's love.

"After we were removed from the castle, Billiam told me of his attraction to men and how he felt for you. I had loved him for ages, never acting upon it, so I took this opportunity to use you to my advantage. I told him if he made love to me, it would be better for you when you were together again. Those are, no doubt, the memories you had, and it went on for almost four years. It was quite a bit of practice for you, not that I was the only one." He was smiling one of his grandiose forced smiles, yet it was actually genuine. He had always enjoyed twisting the knife, though rarely allowed himself to do so.

Billiam's eyes bulged as he sighed, not believing Zan would drag him through the mud, even now. He didn't have to defend himself, however, as Micah jumped in. "Billiam is not on trial, you are. Do not tell me things I already know." Micah placed his hand lovingly on one of Billiam's broad shoulders. This showed his solidarity to him but was more so to prove his ownership.

"Fine, if you insist I will skip to the good bit?" He bared his teeth menacingly at the prince, who simply nodded and grinned back, looking equally deranged. "Well, the day you died was the last day of our affair. We had heard of your death from friends still in the castle. I was ordered by my sister to see if I could gather any information on you and the state of your body, if you could be salvaged. There was no way I could get anywhere near your home, and even if I could, I didn't want you restored. I wanted you dead and gone at last. I had thought to myself, if you were, he could be mine. I made the decision I would return and tell Billiam alone your body had been burnt up. If it were true, there would be no harm. If it wasn't, I knew that he would be mine for at least until he found out. Viscerally, this brief hope of having him made me willing to say anything. So, I did."

Zan paused but kept his eyes locked only on Micah's. Billiam had gone a bit pale, staring motionless into the flames while holding Micah's hand on his shoulder, dearly. Shemmy came over to sit with her friend, leaning her dirty head of hair on his other shoulder, staring over the roasting goose with him. The succulent smell had begun dancing up each of their noses.

"When I returned, Billiam was a pathetic wreck. I brought him to my parents' home, up to our tower for some privacy. I told him my lie and let him cling to me, leeching comfort from me. Since I was giving him my sympathy, I thought I was entitled to kiss him, but he pushed me away. I feared for a bit my plan had backfired. I suppose it was quite presumptuous. Yet to my surprise, he turned to me, a pathetic and hollow shell, to say, 'I suppose it is just to be us now, Zan. Will you still be ashamed of me if I am actually yours?' or some such thing. I lied to him that I would be proud to be with him, that I could be his strength; he needn't be anyone's any longer, et cetera. It was sufficient in breaking his defenses, and he kissed me on the mouth for the first time in ages before giving up." My brother's face lit up, against his will, as he remembered a kindness shown to him by Billiam.

"He murmured pathetically that he would be mine, so I ceased my nurturing demeanor. I thought of nothing but ravaging him, having him finally, and that is what I did. I forced myself, all at once and with quick succession. I must've ruptured an artery, deep inside him. He was screaming and grew faint below me, so I made myself stop. I lay there with him on the ground, beautiful and broken, as he begged me to get him help. I didn't want anyone to know of what I was, what I had done."

Zan's gaze finally fell upon Billiam briefly, though it was not returned. "So I told you, Billiam, that maybe you were supposed to be with Micah after all. This brought a smile to your face as you lay in my arms. That, Prince, is the reason I wanted to flee." My brother exhaled loud, a bit disturbed by the amount of detail he put into his account. That disturbance was short-lived, however. A feeling of vindication grew in his dark heart when he saw Micah's face contort with rage.

"Yes, that is why…." The prince had his eyes closed, watching the unfortunate scene in his mind. "Your sister felt his pain and ran to your location, where Billiam lay bleeding out. Leke screamed at you while she grabbed him off the floor; she slapped your face as you finally shed a few tears. She was holding Billiam and carrying him away from you, when you heard him tell her to stop, that he wanted to be with me. It was at this time you both learned how much better she was at procuring information. She implored Billiam to hang on, as hope remained. I could still be saved." Micah finished the awful story and wrapped himself behind Billiam momentarily. He kissed his head and held his body tight before walking over to my brother, strangely content.

"I wonder…," Micah began coyly, walking small circles around Zan as he looked him over, "who remembers it better? Do you know, Zan, how close he was to death?"

Zan stared straight ahead, avoiding Billiam at all costs and giving up trying to lock eyes with the rotating prince. "No, how could I know that? I am not a medic."

"That's funny, because I know!" The prince gained a strange enthusiasm, stopping his movement. He reached out his pale hand and smacked his palm hard onto Zan's sternum. My brother did not flinch, but could not bring himself to look down at him. "I can remember the beats of his heart, the way they slowed…. If your sister had been only a few minutes later, his light would have been snuffed out. You do know that he had to have a transfusion; quite a risky operation with the lack of skilled hands in Westend. You truly could not make yourself get him help?" Micah looked up into Zan's distant purple eyes and saw what he thought was a flicker of emotion before they closed hard.

"I want to be human. I hate being different. I hate myself. Even if I had been the one Billiam loved all along, I don't think I could've ever been open about it. I hate the stares that stalk me wherever I go, the whispers and cursing. I could see those amplified a hundredfold with a man on my arm. I could not make myself compromise my need for normalcy, even to save him." Tears fell slowly, but his face remained calm. My brother had been warring with himself his whole life. The real him and the him he thought he should be were constantly tearing each other apart, and they took Billiam as their casualty.

"I see," Micah exclaimed, releasing his hand from my brother's chest and reaching down to grab his groin instead, clenching it tight. Zan's eyes bulged, and he could barely breathe as he locked eyes with the tiny prince once again. "I know you remember this, but I doubt Billiam ever knew." Micah stretched up his other arm, barely reaching my brother's face to push it to look over at Billiam. "You saw the blood, saw the crimson silk trickle out before Billiam screamed from the real damage. You didn't care. I know also, as he wailed and began to lose his life, you spilled inside him. You were slow to let go for this very reason; for it was the singular best feeling you had felt then and even since. You let Billiam believe it was a failed effort all around, unwilling to share that you reached the purest bliss in his destruction."

Billiam shot up as the prince finished this revelation. Zan watched on in horror as he began to retch, over at the side of their camp. He could not contain his disgust and hate, as it poured out with the rest of his stomach's contents. Knowing the worst moment of his life was the best feeling of his tormentor's made every cell in his body want to purge with him.

Micah tightened his grip, making my brother's knees buckle. He shrunk slightly as a pathetic yelp fell from his mouth. The prince's face was no longer contorted. He looked up to Zan, as sweet and lovely as ever while he continued. "I'd like to perform a test, Zan. I want to see if I can know with certainty when you are telling a lie. Give me three truths and one fabrication, mixed all about. I am sure it will be difficult for you to be honest three times, but do give it your best!" Micah smiled, his eyes sparkling up at Zan, piercing a real fear through his heart. Earlier, Zan had assumed he would be killed quickly, but he could now tell the prince had gone quite mad. There was no telling when his terror would be over.

"All right...." Zan's voice was finally wavering, his vindictive confidence from before replaced with genuine panic. Even so, he was unable to fully humble himself. "I am allergic to shellfish. I once saw your mother naked. I raped Billiam. I enjoy embroidery." He looked Micah hard in the eyes, waiting to see what the results would be. He was being stupid, egging on the prince in this way.

Micah grinned gleefully, letting go of Zan's crotch at last and grabbing one of his large hands. He looked over it, stroking the long fingers lovingly, almost erotically. He stopped at the middle finger and held it tight in his hand, while his face showed a burning lust. Zan was confused and scared, but his body was reacting to the prince's seduction without his permission. Micah lifted the finger to his lips and began to suck it until he finally saw real desire cross my brother's face. He stopped, smiled around it, and pulled the finger from his mouth. "You tried to trick me, Zan. You really still think that halfhearted consent makes you exempt from your monstrosity? Pathetic!" In an instant, Micah snapped the entire finger off of my brother's hand.

It looked as if Micah were breaking a wishbone. It sounded similar as well, but with more of the cracking crunch of a snapped twig. Ripping off a human's finger so quickly and cleanly is a difficult but not impossible task for other humans. However, the idea of a weakling nineteen-year-old boy ripping off a pureblooded faelock warrior's finger as if it were the petal from a flower, now that is downright peculiar. I suppose human emotions are a force of nature in themselves. From my experience feeling them, I have seen the immeasurable amounts of energy they can produce.

Billiam was back at the fire, his head in Shemmy's lap. The two of them hardly breathed and made no sound. Nothing seemed real; there was no way they had actually just seen that. My brother followed suit, silently looking past his bloody stump into Micah's twisted face.

"Your lie was, of course, saying you raped Billiam, for in your deranged heart you believe you did not. Also, I saw my mother naked hundreds of times, and so did everyone in the palace. She was not a very modest queen, so don't think you are so special." He giggled deviously, dropping Zan's hand to his side. Blood dripped from it rapidly and formed red, muddy puddles around him. Micah held the finger he acquired in front of their faces, looking over it a bit before turning to throw it at Shemmy. "Have you a use for this, my dear?"

Shemmy reached up from her spot, not sure at all what she could do with a single finger, but catching it exuberantly regardless. She grabbed it and tucked it away, wanting it out of Billiam's sight and mind as soon as possible. "Thanks, Prince!" she called before running her fingers through Billiam's hair. She did her best to comfort him as he remained in his state of shock.

Zan had pain written on his face but continued his desperate attempt at stoicism, raising no contest with Micah. "All right, Zan. You will indeed be executed. Such treasonous rumors spread about the prince are enough for that alone; however, an attack on the king's future husband will be the reason our people will see you burn. Still, I would prefer for you to die at our home, not here in the middle of nowhere. I will give you a chance to have that. Would you like it, Zan?"

"Yes, Your Highness."

"Good! These are the rules; they are simple. Lie to me and I get a finger. Run out of fingers, end of the road. Do you agree to my terms?"

Zan nodded silently. This would be best, a chance to say good-bye to everyone before his ultimate humiliation. He thought it would probably be better, but he supposed if he changed his mind, he could always just lie and get it over with.

"Excellent choice, Zan Ellekós. I also get a finger anytime you make any sort of advance or even dare touch my Billiam. He is *mine*, you understand? The fact you could hurt him so and you are allowed to keep taking breaths is a testament to my incredible mercy. Still... I'd like to ask you something that is troubling me. If you had a chance to ravage Billiam again, with no way you would be caught by me or anyone else, would you take it?"

My brother swallowed hard. He knew he needed to tell the truth, but he couldn't. He was too vile, he hated himself too much, and he could not bear Billiam despising him even more. He would not admit this. There was always a chance Micah was not as good a lie detector as he thought. "No, he is yours. I will not hurt him."

"That's what I expected, you disgusting monster!" Micah shouted and ripped the pinky off the already damaged hand. Zan screamed and fell to the ground, the pain and shock finally setting in. The wishbone was broken again, the snapping twig ringing through all their ears.

"You will never get to touch even a hair on his head, ever again! I wish to rip out your eyes so you cannot even see his beauty, but you will be of no use to me blind." Micah was shaking while standing over his victim. Zan looked pathetically small in front of the prince, his rage making him tower despite his tiny frame.

Micah threw the finger over his shoulder, and Shemmy caught it easily. She then whispered in Billiam's ear, "This is pretty freaky an' all, but it is a little romantic, innit?"

Billiam looked into her face and surprised her with a real smile. "Can you believe how much he loves me? He called me his future husband! It is quite disturbing the way he is doing it, but he is avenging me. He is being so strong!"

He melted in her lap like a lovesick puppy as he continued watching the angry prince. Shemmy giggled, feeling excited but conflicted. She was happy my brother was to pay, but she was not glad she was having to witness so much of it.

Zan reached up with his good hand to plead with Micah. He swatted it down with a look of disgust before screaming in his pitiful face, "Do not presume to touch me! Do not presume to touch any of us! You are a knight no longer; you are not a member of our group. You are my property, understood? You are now my slave until we return home and you earn your sentence."

"Yes, Your Highness." No longer feeling entitled to gaze upon the prince, Zan kept his face down, imploring, "I know I do not deserve to ask this... I feel it is justice that I don't... but if you'd like me to serve you, Prince, could you please cauterize the wounds? I might bleed out or become ill if you do not."

"That would be quite fitting, hmm? Shemmy, could you take care of that?" he asked sweetly, walking away from my brother at last.

Micah felt himself growing weak as he skipped over to Billiam. By the time he was within arm's reach, he felt his eyes closing on their own. When they opened, he was laying on the ground with his head in Billiam's lap. It felt as if his eyes closed for only a second, yet that wouldn't have been nearly enough time for the scene to change so much. He saw Shemmy wrapping up Zan's hand from the corner of his eye, before getting lost in the sweet face floating above him.

"Hi, Billiam," he whispered meekly with a cute smile.

"Hello, Prince!" He grinned so happily, Micah thought for a moment he had dreamt up the whole gruesome scene he had just produced.

That could not be right, though; he just saw Shemmy treating the wounds. *Was Billiam really not terrified by what I did?* thought the prince with a troubled look on his face.

Seeing his worry, Billiam leaned down to kiss away all the furrows in his brow. "You overexerted yourself, Micah. You must've been running on pure nerve and then used it all up!"

Micah could not understand how he was being so cheerful, so kind. "You... you are not scared of me?"

"Prince, no one has ever stood up for me like that. I have never been avenged... until now, of course. It was frightening to see you be so violent, but I know exactly your feelings. Had the tables been turned, I doubt I could've shown that much restraint. I must say, no matter how bloody, that was the most romantic display I have ever seen! I cannot wait to be your husband!" He gave the prince an upside-down kiss, feeling as though Micah had sucked the darkness and pain he had held in the last year right out of him. He wished so hard it hurt that he could do the same. He wanted the prince to have nothing but light and beauty filling his heart as he had in their past life.

"Is that why you are taking me to Alafor? We are able to be married there, are we not?" Micah grinned and started to wiggle about in his lap.

"We are going to Alafor to form an alliance. Why would we need to marry there? You are the rightful king and will be sitting on your throne soon enough. There is not a soul who will be able to stop me from marrying you in our home."

"Yes, yes! You are right! I wouldn't have nearly enough time to plan this way, and I never dreamed we would elope.... It will be so lovely! Wait... you are proposing to me, aren't you, Billiam?" Micah grew embarrassed, a blush crossing over his nose to reach both cheeks. He realized it was merely an assumption at this point, and he was getting very much ahead of himself.

Billiam lifted Micah off his lap, helping him to sit beside him. He turned to him and grabbed both of his prince's hands into his own. He gave him a look so heartfelt it made Micah feel as though his legs were softening butter. "Micah Helvendeere, King of Casperland, will you be my bride?" There was a huge grin present as he said the last part. He meant it all but couldn't resist bringing up that memory.

"Oh Spirit! You remember that?" squealed the mortified prince.

Billiam shook his head and became serious again, asking earnestly, "Micah, will you please make me the happiest man to ever live and take my hand in marriage?"

"Yes!" he screamed joyfully, throwing his arms around Billiam's neck, landing against him with a good deal of force. "You have always been the only man whose bride I wished to be!"

As soon as he heard his own volume, he grew bashful and scanned the camp. He heard Shemmy laughing but saw that she was content sitting at the fire, picking at the flaming goose with her fingers. It was not ready and hadn't been the half minute before, but that would not stop her persistent examinations. He saw Zan slumped in front of the cave where he, and now Shemmy, had left him. His head was down; he would not be caring about Micah's exclamation.

"Thank you!" Billiam cheered. "I cannot wait to consummate our engagement tomorrow!"

"I thought the only thing that got 'consummated' was a marriage?"

Billiam grinned wickedly and explained to his amused prince, "That would be rather boring, now wouldn't it? The way I see it, we've already consummated your rebirth. Tomorrow, it shall be for our engagement. The time after we can consummate you turning a week old or some such thing."

"All right, all right, we can consummate our engagement, but after that let's just fuck, yes?" Micah laughed as he said it, even more when he saw Billiam's ecstatic expression at his vulgarity. He leaned in for more kisses and affection, before pulling away slightly. "Billiam, might I ask you something?"

"Yes you may, Prince, but the answer will be no. I will not break your rule of indulging without an inn." He grinned triumphantly before getting his nipple twisted hard by Micah, knocking the smirk right off.

"I'm being serious, you lech!" He sounded irritated but looked both flattered and highly entertained. "I wanted to ask... why is it that you brought Zan with you? How can you even stomach looking at him?"

Billiam leaned back, sighing while he caressed Micah's hair, gaining encouragement from the touch of it, as he now had a habit of doing. "I cannot stomach it. You'll notice I barely ever do. I have had to live with the bastard, pretending we are fine to benefit the others and the Order, for the last year. I suppose I became accustomed to stifling my feelings, ignoring his presence. That, and he avoided me quite completely, rather kind of him. I am glad he is not a human, never feeling he ought make amends nor repay me for his injustice. I never had to deal with his snivelings nor be tempted into forgiving him. Since we were able to be so distant living in the same home, I felt we could do the same as we traveled. I needed a faelock with us, so I brought him."

"But why didn't you bring Leke? Couldn't you have been free of squelching your feelings and avoiding his gaze for this journey?"

"I trust Leke more. I needed her to be on her own team, to lead in my stead if need be."

"But why?" the prince cried. He was feeling ill from his own actions, and he hated this situation he had made even more grotesque.

"Micah, I was afraid that if we did not succeed, and you remained dead, that I would take my own life. Honestly, I know I would've. I had written a course of action for Leke should you and I be out of the picture. There was no way I would trust Zan with something so important or with feelings so vulnerable."

Micah nodded, understanding at last. "We are blessed things turned out so well! I should not dwell on one noxious beast. You and I are what's important. Our friends, the Logos, the people of Casperland, they are all so important. Forgive me my preoccupation, my love, and thank you so much for your sacrifice!" He fell again into his lover's arms. Billiam embraced him hard, never wanting to let go, ever again.

Unfortunately, that hug did not last for eternity, as Shemmy broke it up with two flaming hot goose legs. "Suppa time, my sweeties!" She handed one to each man, then grabbed a breast out of the dress pocket she had shoved it in. Billiam really wished he hadn't seen that.

"Thank you, Shemmy!" cheered Micah as he took a large bite, so happy to have some real meat for the first time in his new life. Chewing quick, hoping to speak with his mouth mostly empty, he asked, "Shemmy, will you see to it that Zan eats? He may need your help, due to the shock and all. I know he wanted goose for his last meal, and as much as I'd like to be cruel and make him wait, I am far too happy for that now. Billiam and I are engaged!" Micah surprised Billiam with a sloppy, greasy kiss as he attempted to swallow down his own mouthful. This should have disgusted him, but he conceded anything Micah did would be lovable, especially when it involved his mouth.

"Congrats, Mr. an' Missus Dandy! I 'ope to be one o' yer bridesmaids, love!" she chirped, pinching Micah's cheek before frowning. "Why I gotta feed 'im?"

"Would you really like me to say?" He had a mischievous sparkle in his eye and spoke to Shemmy while looking over to Billiam.

"Right, nope. I'll be off ta nurse duty, then," she replied reluctantly, with the giant hunk of goose meat hanging out of her mouth. She trudged to the fire to grab some of it for Zan before walking to him. Micah watched on amused as she started smacking him in the mouth with the floppy chunks of food.

"What was that about?" Billiam queried, licking the grease from his fingers, a habit he was ashamed to have adopted on the road.

Micah smiled and grabbed Billiam's hand to lick his last finger for him. This should have, again, turned his delicate stomach, but instead did much the opposite. "I thought it was a hollow threat, but apparently Zan also has a memory of Shemmy, one that she doesn't want known."

Both their faces grew sour as they joined in a collective "Ewwww," followed by uproarious laughter. It was hard to believe such a tumultuous a day was ending with glee and high spirits.

My brother couldn't believe it either. The giggling pained him, while the meat in his mouth turned to mush. He had been chewing that same piece for longer than he cared to know. He wanted to not eat it; he was avoiding swallowing it. He could not bear the idea of sustaining his own life. Shemmy had apparently grown tired of waiting and smashed another chunk between Zan's lips, caring not if he ever swallowed.

He began to masticate this flesh into oblivion along with the piece from before as he made a list in his head. He was thinking of his most amusing lies—he needed only eight and the energy to yell them. The latter he was nowhere near to possessing yet. With that, he would suffer no longer. Who did he care to say good-bye to anyway? It would not matter to his corpse, either way, and he doubted it would matter to the living much more.

CHAPTER 14

May 9th, 989

OUR SIXTH day of travel was coming to a close, and the sun had ceased its work, but we continued trekking. We were crossing through the outlying area of City of Alafor, which was kind enough to be lit with gas lamps every quarter mile. It was a great relief to not have to stop when we were so close. We walked along the salted stone tiles, taking in the frosted wonderland about us. The lamps caused each crystal of water to glitter up at us as we passed, momentarily ceasing our resentment at the bitter cold.

I could see the large filigree gate of the city in distance. It looked to be a half mile ahead, at the end of this enormous snowfield, which would be a grand park during the four frostless months. Some other travelers passed by us as we walked, although they ended up running. I had forgotten how vile the beasts my comrades were riding on truly were. We quickly parked them off the path, behind one of the frozen elms. I halted them, not knowing how to truly break the enchantment. With that, we could continue on foot. The second group that passed us was only gawking because of my size. I was used to that and definitely preferred it to sending potential allies screaming.

Alafor's capital was not sealed off from outsiders like Drummond; they were actually known to be quite welcoming. I wasn't sure just how welcoming they'd be with darkness encircling, but I was hopeful we could be in without issue. We were all missing civilization differently and had our cravings of what to get out of Alafor. I was thirsting for a soft pillow and some warm milk and dearly hoped no guards or bureaucracy would stand in my way.

Walking through the gates was a breeze. The guards waved us in happily, encouraging us to get warm at once. We were bundled as much as we could be while traveling but looked quite bare compared to the locals.

Entering the City of Alafor felt like falling into a dream, like visiting another planet. The whole city was on the side of a mountain, cutting through it and climbing up it. We could see each intricate layer of life on top of life, businesses and homes pushing one another up. There was a glass dome around the city that also found its end in the mountain's side. It kept the contents about fifteen degrees warmer and stopped the snowfall from wreaking constant havoc. I was amazed to see a cluster of moondrop flowers growing beside a shop front, taunting the winter with their happy, yellow petals.

We walked through the crowded streets, enjoying the warmer climate and genial atmosphere. There were many quaint shops and food vendors, tempting us with the smell of toasted nuts and other goodies. I had studied the city quite a bit before our venture, so I knew to lead us through the city proper into the northernmost part. That quarter surrounded the castle's front and was known as the Goddess Gardens. It housed only the most affluent of families and poshest boutiques. There was only one inn there, and although quite pricey, it would keep us as close to those we needed to meet as possible. I was not sure how easy it would be to seek royal counsel but knew that was something best saved for daylight hours anyhow.

As underdressed as we felt entering the city, it was a hundredfold stepping within the richness of the Gardens. All the citizens about were covered head to foot in silks, diamonds, and furs. I do mean and, not or—they wore all three, all of them did. I was surprised to see the fur, as the Alafor were predominately vegetarian. Their national religion Spathalíeism condemned the killing of animals for frivolous reasons, yet I could not understand at all how food was frivolous and furs were not. (I learnt later that these furs were humanely trimmed from living Ekkits, a mammal native only to Alafor that is large and deer-shaped yet soft with a rabbit-like face.) Waltzing past these opulent nobles unbathed and in our dirty clothes should have been mortifying, yet we were too dazzled to notice.

Here in the Gardens, the land spread out, not upward. The castle had its front to us, its heavily guarded marble gates sitting right next to a quaint florist's shop. The back of the castle had a private port, and all in between was a flat and sprawling open layout studded with beautiful courtyards. We couldn't see any of that yet, though. We could just stare in wonder at the beautiful people, the sparkling tile below our feet, and the elegant buildings. Each of us had spent time either being or just being amongst the wealthy in Drummond, but it was nothing compared to the refinement we saw around us.

All of us, even Malcolm, were quite struck. We knew how advanced the Alafor were in terms of architecture and industry yet were not prepared for true wonder. As I gazed upon the beauty, my eyes landed on something beautiful I had seen before. Malcolm noticed where my gaze sat and knew immediately we had trouble.

She looked the same as she did that bloody day outside of Casper. Her black hair was long, silky, and wrapped around the curves of her body as if it were sculpted. I was thrilled and horrified at the same time to see a far more becoming outfit encasing her this time, not the dirty lab coat she wore before. It was a short, elegant sheet of white velvet. No, not velvet, it must have been a liquid poured over her that somehow clung on. I know if I were dripped on her, I too would have clung that desperately. I saw in front of me Camilla Dalgarie, chief researcher of Knox's military sciences department. She was wife to Arrikos the XXI, heir of Enox's noblest family, and the woman I had fallen in love with six years ago.

Camilla was standing in front of the inn, our destination. I think Malcolm was trying to pull me. I did not move. Katrina was screaming something at me. I heard nothing. Police? Were there police? I suppose there must have been; there was a cuff around my wrist. I could not see them. I could not feel them as they tried and failed to get me off my feet. I saw her smooth skin, a polished mahogany escaping from the white snow that was lucky enough to caress it. I saw her almond eyes, finally reaching mine, the black marbles within them looking endless, inviting. Her lips, wrapped in burgundy, finally opened. Would she smile? No.... She didn't smile, did she? She shouted. More police. "That's them, that's them." I think I heard that. A bag on my head, there was a bag on my head? I could not see her; she was gone.

"I love you!" I stupidly cried. This was the last thing I remember.

If being a faelock were a qualitative trait, I would say I am quite good at it. My brother, on the other hand—I would rate him less than mediocre. Firstly, as far as physical strength and speed, I am the best I have seen. I say this in earnest, not as an exaggeration or to pat my own back, but as a simple fact. My brother is strong but lacks precision and patience. His stamina is much higher than humans, about equal to Billiam's, but only half my level.

As a second faelock quality, I offer up logical and rational thought. I excel at balancing my thoughts and feelings with the emotions of others and against the situation at hand. My brother is a bungling mess. I also have an extremely enhanced third-eye sense, a rare trait among faelocks. This gives fruit to those gut feelings I have and also allows me to step past the realm of empathy, perceiving all sorts of information through any number of boundaries.

That third eye plays into my excellence with the next faelock trait I will discuss. Faelocks are extremely valued for their connectivity, with a great importance put on how well they can sense others. Being strong and beastly is all well and good, but the ability to know when an ally is in danger is invaluable. All faelocks carry blood-bonds with their family members, sensing when they are in physical distress. We do not have to be burdened by their emotions. My brother is quite out of touch with his true faelock self and can barely feel even these blood-bonds. The only thing he had sensed was when our father died a decade back. Other than my own death, I doubt he could feel a thing from me. As far as the emotional bonds with humans, he told me the only one he had was with Billiam. As for me, I am highly in tune with my blood-bonds and carry unshakeable emotional bonds with both Billiam and Ackerman. I have strong bonds with Jessica and her mother and slightly weaker but still essential connections to Micah, Pierre, and Katrina. I probably had one with Malcolm, but he had next to no feelings, so I was unable to test it. This is quite a lot of bonds, and I always thought that showed I was a damn good faelock.

The fourth quality I have to grade myself on, sadly, is the one I fail at miserably. That is the ridiculous subject of love. I am faelock; I am not a base creature who is slave to the bondage of flesh. I am supposed to fall for mind, fall for inspiration, fall for altruism, fall for bravery. Did I? No. Did my brother? Yes. He wouldn't accept it, but he did. He never won; he was never better. How, then, did I become the superficial one?

I awoke, standing tall on my knees. There were manacles on my wrists. My right—I saw Malcolm, also on his knees. I looked away; he was very angry. My left—Katrina was there, seated with legs crossed, her eyes were closed. I doomed us. This was my fault. I heard a voice, high-pitched but elegant.

"These are the ones?" I looked up and saw the queens. Angry. Hate me. Messed up. Stupid. My brain smacked these words back and forth like a racquetball. As far as I can remember, we were in a large open room, set down on a wooden floor. The queens were seated a few yards ahead of us, but I could not focus on them. Bare legs descending velveteen steps beside where they sat, that was all I saw.

I heard heaven; I heard the love of Aegis personified singing to me. I don't believe in Aegis. "Yes, these are the ones my brother-in-law told me to expect." Please, keep talking. Why did she stop?

"You look distressed," the other queen spoke. Was that the younger one? It didn't matter, for Camilla opened her mouth again.

"Oh, it's nothing important. He told me a faelock would be here, and there is, but it is not my knight. A handsome faelock knight saved me years ago even though I was an enemy. I wanted so much to see him again."

"It was I!" No, stop, shut up. Why? Why was I acting so stupid? Pain, back of my head, the hilt of a sword. Was she looking at me? She was. She was studying me; she was coming close…. She was laughing.

Her laughter, it sounded cruel, but she kept walking over. Did I get hit more? I don't know. Were the queens still there? Were Malcolm and Katrina? I don't know. She was almost here. Round face, dark, beautiful eyes, rouge on her cheeks. Could I smell her yet? Yes, it was rose water. Yes, I smelled mint and a hint of clove. Camilla, speak, I need to hear you.

"You… you are my knight, aren't you? And you love me? How long did you know me, pureblooded faelock? It couldn't have been longer than five minutes. How strange…." She was above me; her long raven hair was within inches. Please… please lean down just a bit more.

This was when I should have spoken, commanded that we be freed, pleaded with the queens. What the hell was happening to us? Why didn't I care? I was being a godawful faelock. "We fall for whom we admire, those who amaze us…." How did I say that? So many words, they made sense, but those were not the right words. Those words did not matter.

"Yes, but I was barely conscious when you saved me, knight. How could I garner such admiration so fast to gain the lasting, unshakable love of a faelock?"

Do not ask me this. So stupid. Don't tell her. No. "Your body, it was the most immaculate thing I'd ever seen. Your face was true beauty, the likes of nothing else. I was amazed with the way you were shaped, the impossibly perfect human form. I could not help but admire and love you, even if it was only your outside; that is how beautiful you are." Ridiculous. Idiot. Why? Malcolm, I knew he was laughing; why couldn't I hear it? He was much too angry.

I saw it! She blushed; she was flattered; I made her happy. "Adorable!" Speak more Camilla, your sound… "Oh I was so looking forward to meeting my knight, and you are truly such a white knight, so chivalrous and sweet. Why did you have to go and be a woman? I was in a tizzy, thinking I'd get to experience making love to a pureblood, to see how true those rumors are. Aegis, why do you trick me so often when it comes to love?"

Crushing defeat, I was done. Let me disappear; take me away.

"That is not important. We do not care about this, and you are wasting our time," lectured the older queen with shorter time as monarch, Mayleil. I needed to show respect. Instead, I was crying. I was impossible. I fell down to my knees, disgraced.

"Right, sorry, so unprofessional." Camilla laughed and swished her hair around her body. Thankfully, I could see it no longer. "This is part of the group that invaded the castle, attacking the cardinal, abducting and killing the prince. There is no doubt a plot to get to his sister, Margaret, as she is now the only heir. It is such a shame. Micah was nearly twenty and coronated at long last."

Alark was the younger queen and the one to my left. She was elected queen at age five, a strong and remarkable woman. She was bound to her spouse Mayleil for life. She spoke calmly. "We shall question them ourselves, as they are current prisoners of Alafor, not of Knox nor of the MortiAegis Church. I thank you, for your warnings and your support. Feel free to leave now." She was abrupt; I was lifted to my feet.

An Alafor guard, not the military police like before, was holding me. Cold hands were touching cold metal touching my wrists. My face was up; I could see her. Camilla was angry, not with me, with the queens. They were rude, but why? Why was she there? Why did Knox care? Why did they know what we did?

I was pushed along; Malcolm was beside me, a row of guards behind us. Alark appeared in front of us. Her face was kind; she wanted to help. Did she not believe Camilla? "This woman, let her go. I sense she has shed no blood; she was not in that palace. She will stay with us, and we will question her ourselves." Mayleil agreed. She was holding Katrina's arm. Kat smiled at them; she was such a good girl, they were right.

They started to walk off, and I was screaming. I wasn't screaming anything moronic like before, I was wailing in pain. I thrashed out my arm, and the guards threw me down violently. I was getting used to this pathetic position on my knees.

Katrina ran to me, and I saw Malcolm in the corner of my eye as I watched her. He hated me so much right then. I hated me too. "Leke! What has happened?" The queens were beside her and looked concerned. Alark was holding out her hand, bidding the guards to go easy on me for a bit.

My hand was seething in pain, crunching, ripping pain. Or was it a stabbing, cutting pain? "It is Zan," I yelped. Something had happened. Didn't he know I had plenty of my own problems? Was he still unable to take care of himself? I wasn't really one to talk in this instance, but I was quite angry with him regardless.

"Is he okay?" The queens were holding Katrina's shoulders as she cried. I found myself actually wanting to be in a cell, away from this, from her tears. I wanted to be away from Camilla, or closer. I wanted to be anywhere but where I was.

"He—" Again, it crushed and it cut, and my hand spasmed. The guards allowed me my fit this time, screaming in pain. I flailed but I hit nothing. I was a harmless fool. "His hand, something is happening to it. He lost fingers? I don't know, Katrina. I am sorry."

She fell apart, and the queens were done indulging me. They began to walk her away, and I was picked back up. Malcolm was finally laughing before he was hit to shut up. I was one of many who disliked my brother; this laugh was for him. I was not yet forgiven enough to have him mocking me.

We had been in the throne room, but I saw nothing but flashes of faces and Camilla. I took in none of its splendor, and all I saw getting pushed to the dungeon were stone walls. It must have been the servants' tunnels.

I thought hard as I walked to my imprisonment. Camilla, she was an officer of Knox. She was married into the most affluent family of Enox, yet they had no real power there. The church was the only one who ruled in that country. She said her brother-in-law informed her of us, someone in Enox? Why would they care about Casperland? Why would they know anything? No, this brother-in-law must've been in Drummond. He must be in the Mortanion Brotherhood, the only ones bound to either Enox or Knox. What was Aldrious's surname? I could not remember; I could not remember if I ever knew. They knew we would come here, yet they say we killed the prince. Was Knox going to attack Casperland, to ally with Alafor? Were we to be responsible for its destruction?

This was too much; I needed answers. I hoped she would be gone. I needed my head clear to deal with this. I could not be a babbling fool, for it was on me to undo this damage.

Two cells stood in front of us, solid walls, not bars. The steel doors were swung wide open. They pushed Malcolm into the first cell. He fell hard on the ground. They did not take the shackles from his hands; he would have a lot of trouble getting up. For my turn, they pushed me in gently before slamming my giant door behind me. Whether it was mercy or fear that made them polite, I couldn't tell you.

I sat on the stone slab I assumed was my bed. There was a crude chamber pot in the far corner, near a bucket of water that looked quite clean. They were actually decent to their prisoners here and there was a small lamp lit on the wall. They did not intend for us to rot in darkness, as Casperland did for its captives.

I swiveled my body around on the hard surface so I could swing my feet up to join me. The six days of walking had been quite tiresome. I was thinking of Katrina. I hoped she was all right. I couldn't bear to think of what her reaction was to my foolish display. I felt a bit of relief, at least, knowing it was her and not Jessica who was with us. If my situation had been any more ridiculous and embarrassing, I would have been smashing my head against the stone wall I leaned on.

My thoughts turned again to war, what moves to make, how to contact the prince. I thought, perhaps if I hurt myself badly enough, Zan might realize this was not a safe place for the prince. I chased that thought away quickly, remembering again what a horrible faelock my brother was. I conceded that if they killed me, he could at least get the message that way.

I don't know how much time passed before a clanging at my door disturbed my pondering. I'd guess a few hours; it would be the dead of night, if so. I thought it was my turn for interrogation, but I was wrong. The person struggled at the door for at least a minute before it swung open. The smell came first, clove, mint, and rose. Camilla stood in the shadow of that large door. There was another strong smell with her, the fermented musk of wine.

"'Ello, my knight!" she said cheerfully, still holding a bottle of red and clutching it against her chest. She was wiggling her hips a bit, I think trying to entice me.

"You are intoxicated," I said plainly but was unable to stop the smile forming on my lips.

"Well you are incarcerated!" This retort made her laugh so frivolously she stepped from the door, allowing it to close hard and trap her inside my cell.

Something about her being so drunk allowed my mind to not act like it was too. Feeling sane in her presence was a miracle in itself. "You know there is no handle in here? We are both incarcerated now."

"I can think of worse places to be, worse company," she replied as she looked around my cell. She must have seen every stone in it at least three times. She had studied the walls over and over to avoid looking at me.

"Am I that awful to look at?" I could not stop staring at her, like I did each time she was in front of me. I was the one who was rude, behaving like an ill-mannered lech. I began to look over the stones too. Perhaps that was the right way to behave.

"You are not. You are carved of marble, a sculpture of pure muscle, agile and thin. Your armor before, it obscured your breasts...." She was looking at me finally, trying to match the me now to the me then.

"I don't have much of them, anyways. My friend Billiam calls them mosquito bites. You must have been staring quite hard to notice."

"Cheeky! I like it! You can finally speak to me? You aren't going to clamor and cry?" She teased me, but it didn't seem cruel. Her shapely legs, two smooth, golden pillars dancing across each other, began to move toward me. She wobbled a bit.

"Have you a key for these? Or are you here to punish the murderer of Prince Micah?" I asked, displaying my manacled wrists. She was still so far away. Why would they make this cell a mile wide?

"How could I do that? I am not in Drummond," she sang playfully, setting her bottle by the chamber pot before skipping over to me. The cell was tiny again. She had some strange type of blade in her hand; it turned molten with the push of a button. She cut my cuffs easily and grabbed them off, throwing them to the ground.

"So you know of your own lies?" With my arms now free, I turned, setting my feet down on the ground and my back against the wall. She took this as an invitation to lay her head in my lap, as she got up on the slab with me.

I looked down at her, a goddess of pure beauty, grinning up at me like a foolish child. "I have known a lot of things, for a long time." She became briefly serious before she touched the cuffs on the ground, giggling. "I guess I could've left those on. Are you a kinky sort, my knight?" She hiccupped. It was cute and proof she really was human. In all my memories, she seemed ethereal, untouchable. She was solid, she was warm, and she was gassy. This delighted me. I don't know why.

"No, not particularly, and you seem in no condition to be handling a captive anyways," I answered and let out a small laugh. Why was she here? Why would she say a thing like that to me? "I am terribly sorry I disappointed you so, not being a man and all. I did not expect to see you again after you found out. Why did you come?"

She looked up at me, and her eyes were so happy. Her cheeks were even pinker than usual, the wine's fault. Some of her lipstick had come off, and I was able to see the soft mauve color they really were. She smiled; I got to see her whole smile. Every tooth made of smooth pearl; another hiccup fell from under them. So perfect, yet she was so human. "You told me you loved me. I wanted to hear that again." She was nuzzling into my lap, her warm breath reaching everywhere.

"Why? Your husband Arrikos, cannot he tell you that?" I had given in; my hand finally went through her hair. I dropped my other hand on her stomach, feeling that dress. I learned it really was velvet, not a liquid that refused to fall.

She was frowning, but she was still lovely. Did I hurt her? Could she even be hurt? "I do not see my husband. We are married for political reasons alone. I suppose there was lust at some point, but never love. Actually, I don't think we ever really liked each other. He has a weak mind. The Dalgarie are terribly inbred. He left to live a new life, I think about three years ago. He had a dream to fulfill or some rot. I still do not understand why he stole so many of my gowns." Her chin began to tremble, and she was growing quite upset. I had a feeling it was for her gowns, not her husband.

"So you want to hear of my love because you cannot have his?"

"No." She reached up, grazing my cheek. Her skin, was this the first time I felt it? It was, other than her lips on the battlefield. It was soft like a peach, smooth like glass. Was such a thing even possible? "I meant it when I said I had looked forward to meeting you. Yes, I thought you were a man, and that is what I was prepared for. No matter what you are, you are the knight I see when I fall asleep. Every night since the day you saved me, I see you kiss me once again as I drift off. I cannot simply turn that image off because of your anatomy. That is not how it is working, at least.

"The test fire that day, it was my fault it went so wrong. It was supposed to blow up you knights, but instead I blew up my own damn base. It was lucky I was flung so many yards away. If I were not that far from the others, you wouldn't have found me, saved me. I still… I want to know why."

"I thought I already told you?" My hand was at the back of her head now. I was on a mission to touch each strand of hair, each of them precious, each of them Camilla's.

"What, because I am beautiful? You like my shape?" She shouted, though quietly, snorting out a laugh. "You really saved me for such a reason, putting your existence and the lives of your allies in danger?"

"I am probably the first faelock in all the world to fall in love at first sight, and that is only because it was you I saw. The reason, it sounds stupid and pointless, but the feelings I felt when I saw you were not lust. They were created by your physique, but they were still pure love. I could not leave you. I needed you to be safe."

She pulled down my head at last. My lips finally pressed against hers. They were pillows. No, they were softer than pillows. She tasted like plums. That's it—her lips must've been plums, so sweet and juicy.

Inches away, she looked up at me and whispered, "I do not know you; you came out of nowhere. I had always been fascinated by your kind.... You appeared out of my childhood dreams. I always knew a human man would never love me like a faelock. Perhaps that's why I cared so little that I was marrying for power. I didn't think I could have the love of a faelock—a love that is earned by only one and cannot be broken; the love so fierce it has both caused and ended wars. I don't care the reason for why I earned it. It is something far too precious to ever reject. Please, just tell me again."

"I love you, Camilla. I loved you when we first met, and I will love you forever, you alone." I kissed her this time, reveling in more plums, more sweetness. I wanted to stay here forever; I wanted her to stay here. I wanted us to be lying, I wanted to hold her close. This was what my heart screamed, and my body began to obey, shifting so that we both could lie. She was in front of me; we barely fit on the hard stone bench. I was forced to hold her closer, and I was grateful to the bench for that. Amazingly, my brain worked still. It won out for a moment, and I asked, "Camilla, is Aldrious your brother-in-law?"

She tried to avoid answering, wanting to join mouths with me again. I lifted up my head and stretched my neck so she had no hope of reaching. She began to suck on that instead, weakening my brain's chances of winning. I pulled my head back down, able to lock with her eyes, keeping my mouth firmly shut. She grimaced slightly, pulling me tight, and finally answering, "Yes. I agreed to do this only because I thought I might see you. We are not close."

"So Knox did not send you?" I rewarded her; I rewarded myself, with a kiss. Her soft hands had found their way under my shirt, but I needed an answer. Had she really fallen for me too? Did she fall for me as superficially as I for her but with my species, not my body? These were not the questions that needed answers, but they were bursting through my chest.

She parted. She would answer me, even if I was giving in. "No, I am a scientist. I would be a silly person to send," she said with a small laugh, scrunching her nose like a rabbit. "Aldrious asked me directly; he informed me his grip was slipping. You know, of course, he wants Casperland for himself. Why else would you fight him? He said you took Micah. I told him Micah is dead and to shut up. He said that the Logos would be in Alafor and that both their faelocks were missing. I happened to be here anyways. I have a lab at Wings; we are doing weapons research there. He baited me to create a charade, to stop you all, work the Alafor into a frenzy. The MortiAegis, Knox, my husband, they do not know about this. Drummond would be gone, Aldrious and all, if they did. I do not think the Alafor are falling for it, not that you helped yourself any." She told me everything I needed to hear, and I did not think she was deceiving me, not that I'd be a good judge at that point.

"Thank Spirit, I feared it was all for nothing. Thank you, Camilla, thank you for being with me." I felt free to enjoy myself at last. That was not all I needed to know, was it? It had to be enough though; I wanted her out of that velvet prison. I needed to see the goddess herself. I pulled it up over her legs, and I was almost to paradise, but I stopped. Was she nervous?

"I have never been with a woman," she whispered shyly, but she looked happy to be with me regardless.

I smiled, my teeth touching against her soft chest, speaking into her heart, "I am not a woman; I am a faelock. I am not human; I am different. I am a love that is pure and just for you, a love you always wanted. Don't worry about anything. Your body will respond to mine, and it will know just what to do." With that, her worry truly vanished. She pulled onto me as desperately as I did her.

Heaven. Nirvana. Enlightenment. These words crashed through my mind as our bodies collided. Love. Happiness. Joy. Peace. We were okay, and I had Camilla. Malcolm was wrong, and I was happy.

Eventually we were interrupted by the sound of crashing metal, and I could feel Katrina was very scared. She had heard screaming, and they thought I was attacked. It was not my voice. I covered Camilla up, that was the first thing that needed to be done. Once no one else could see her, then I could deal with the cacophony of startled voices and shocked faces. I wanted to be greedy, to be the only one to see perfection. She was not really mine, but I needed her to be.

Camilla, I have no idea how we dressed her so quickly, she sat so small in my lap. Her face was hidden in my shoulder, and it was clear she was now the criminal. "Arrest her," shouted Mayleil, or was that Alark? One of them gave a command.

Camilla looked at me and smiled. "Your love for me, it will never stop? It will never transfer to another?"

"Never." I kissed her before they pulled her away from me quickly but also gently. Her small bare feet floated on the dirty ground. She was being dragged away, under arrest, and still looked graceful, as if she was dancing.

She was gone, and I could see the rest of the room. I was not worried for Camilla. The Alafor were an extremely lenient and peaceful nation, and her crime was not violent. Had they believed her, it could've been quite destructive, but they hadn't. I had faith she would be freed; if I didn't there was no way I could've heard a word anyone said.

Katrina's face was bright red, and she was avoiding me. My shirt was still unbuttoned, I realized at last. I turned so I could be modest, once again. I could not believe I was such a lewd sight in front of the royal couple, in front of Katrina. Even more unbelievable was how little I cared.

"Katrina told us the real truth. That woman's story was ridiculous but was sufficient in terrifying us for a spell." Alark spoke sweetly, and her face was so kind. She was two years younger than me, and she was one of the most powerful people in all the globe. "You two really did know each other, then?" She was smirking and quite amused, while hugging Mayleil tight. I felt she might've been a bit inspired by us.

Her wife looked me over and shook her head softly. "You needn't ask. We will be as merciful as possible. Her research troubles us, though. We would like to shut down her lab, while leading Knox to believe all is still functioning properly. Will she cooperate?" Mayleil was calm, not entertained like her wife, but not angry either.

"I do not know her well enough to make such assumptions, but the feeling in my heart leads me to believe she would. I highly doubt she would choose her lab over her own life."

I looked around the cell; it was its original size, not a mile wide or wonderfully close. The queens stood in the open doorway, Kat was halfway between them and me, but I did not see Malcolm. The guards had left as well, so it was just we four women. I knew Malcolm had been angry, simply because I knew him. I could not feel it before, and I could not feel it then either. Was he just disappointed? Could I not feel that emotion? Or did I truly not have a bond with him, my own partner? I felt, once again, like a terrible faelock.

Katrina looked so embarrassed, so overcome, but she was eager to get me back to normal. "You don't have to stay in here anymore. They have rooms for us in their guest wing," she whispered. Both queens were smiling, nodding in agreement. Kat was fighting tears and looked like she could scream at any minute. She didn't. Instead, she spoke quietly. "Have you felt anything else of Zan?" She tried to help me up, but my pants were falling. I buttoned them quick, trying to save her from any more trauma on my account.

"Nothing, he has not received any more pain. Unlike humans, I cannot feel any of his emotions, so that's all I can tell you." Even if I could sense my brother's emotions, I highly doubted they would make any sense whatsoever.

We were walking out of the cell, and I grabbed Camilla's wine. I hated alcohol for myself. I depended on my senses; weakening them seemed imbecilic. As I held it, I was grateful to the wine. It weakened Camilla's control over me, allowed me to be with her, to not be stupid. I held it pressed against my chest as she had.

The queens were walking ahead of us, holding hands. The shape of their arms was mimicked by the cord that hung behind their backs. Alafor was very strict on matters of love and marriage, but not in the same way as the MortiAegists. They valued an unconditional love, a love that can overcome any difficulties, thus they made it permanent. In ancient times, they would attach a rod between the couples' wrists. The only way to get divorced would be to either cut off your own arm, or cut off your spouse's, holding it for the rest of your life.

In the last century, their holy people came up with a new way to cement a marriage. They scientifically created a pseudo spinal cord, a glowing blue wire wrapped in a soft, clear plastic. It attached to each person's real spinal cord, right at the base of the brain. The artificial cords were about eight feet long, so the couple could move about freely. If the cord was severed in the middle, both would be completely paralyzed. If the cord was cut on an end, only the other member would be frozen. This was the new way they dealt with divorce. Whoever was found to be at fault by the tribunal would be the one immobilized. This also explained their unflinching acceptance of homosexuality when no other nation had. They felt if you would go so far as to bind yourself, there was no way your love was anything but true or pure, no matter your anatomy.

I stared in awe at the glowing cord, mystified at what strong faith it would take to attach yourself so. What was the point? Who did that please? Their goddess Spathalí wanted that? I liked the idea of unconditional love, one you cannot give up on, but I wasn't sure this was really what their cords did. It looked to me like a leash.

"Does Jessica know about her?" Katrina was shuffling her feet. She didn't look at me when she spoke.

"I think that only Malcolm, Ackerman, and Zan know about her. They were there. I've barely mentioned our meeting to Billiam."

"When you saved her? An enemy?"

"Yes. Knox troops had revisited outside Casper, checking the long-term results of their blasts. Camilla and her team were there too, wanting to test out even more explosives in the wasteland they had created years prior. We set out to drive off the soldiers and apprehend the creators of destruction."

"But you saved her instead? You ruined the mission?" Her words felt like a knife, but her voice was still so small and sweet.

"We took all of her team but her, all that were alive at least. They had messed the test up; the target was off. She blew up her mobile base instead of our decoy battalion. I found her as we were collecting the other scientists. She was out farther than the others, so I was able to take her near her ship before my comrades could stop me. She woke up as I carried her, told me when to stop so I would not be seen by her men. She thanked me with a kiss, and I ran back to the others. Ackerman greeted me with a black eye. I didn't ruin the mission completely. I just stopped us from attaining the most vital target." I felt ashamed, not only for my actions, but also for how warm my heart felt from talking about it.

We were no longer in the service tunnels; now the walls were a soft purple, a bit like my eyes. The cold gray stone was replaced with a floor of lovely parquet, filled with diamond shapes. Katrina was looking only at it as she walked. "Are you going to tell her?"

"Who? What?" I was oblivious.

The queens stopped. "You two are staying in this room. Malcolm is in his own room across the way," Alark informed us, while pointing over her shoulder. "There are two beds, so you needn't worry. We have little house help lately, so I hope you don't mind bunking together."

"I am just overjoyed to have a bed," I said, exhausted and grateful.

"Good. You are no longer our prisoners, but you are not really guests. We have much to discuss with you tomorrow, and later with Micah." Mayleil bowed slightly, walking her wife away from us with a wave. She seemed quite perceptive, possibly shrewd. She would be the one to get insight from but also the one to keep an eye on.

I followed Katrina into our room. It was opulent and warm; the beds looked incredibly plush and were covered in silken blankets. A large table piled with snacks tempted me from the middle of the room. I wanted to celebrate! We were alive, and things were actually going to be okay! Casperland was not in danger, we had lodging, and I had Camilla! In my heart, everything was perfect. I tried hard to remember it would not be the same for my comrades. I had put them in grave danger. I could have ruined everything. We were lucky and everything worked out, but that did not take away the risk I caused.

Katrina sat on her bed and whispered sadly, "My sister, and about that woman. I am not as stupid is everyone thinks. I realized what was going on with you two."

I was glad to finally know what was wrong with her. I hoped that was all that was making her upset. It was a simple subject and took little apologizing. Had she been hurt by my failing her as a knight and jeopardizing our entire mission, our prince—that would require extensive repentance. It seemed that was a far too rational thing to upset her.

"Kat, I gave your sister no false pretenses. I made sure she always knew I was not in love, that I wouldn't be. I didn't want to be cruel, and I tried to distance myself to avoid her falling for me. She accepted how I felt, so I allowed her close. That is all we had, though. I will tell her. I have no intentions of ever hiding something from her. Camilla… I met her before I knew Jessica and yourself," I explained, hoping we could get to eating and sleeping at last.

"Is that why you couldn't love Jess? You already loved Camilla? I heard her say…. A faelock's love doesn't end, that it cannot be transferred?"

I realized I was wrong. This was not about her sister; this was about my idiot brother. I sighed and grabbed some of the goodies off the table before sitting beside her. I spent the rest of the night listening to her cry over Zan, lying about him. I couldn't wait for his charade to end. Eventually, she let me sleep. I have never slept better.

CHAPTER 15

May 10th, 989

THE PRINCE'S group had been walking through icy slush for six hours, mostly in silence. Billiam and Micah whispered to each other a few times. Shemmy made a lot of strange noises and grumblings. My brother was a walking corpse. There had been no group conversations whatsoever, not since what happened the night before.

They had only two hours until they reached a village with the inn Zan had promised, when Micah broke the silence. He said abruptly, "If you make a wish on it, a radish can transform into a carrot."

"What?" Billiam asked before laughing uncontrollably. Why was that so amusing to him?

"In Alafor, they wash their hands before using the toilet. To do so after is considered rude. To scare off a bear, you should clap your hands loudly four times. Cats can sense when a person will soon be expelling gas."

"Um… did I muss up 'chantin' yer brain, Micah? Yer talkin' like a loon." Shemmy was laughing loudly now too. They kept looking at one another, causing themselves to crack up more each time.

"Billiam doesn't clean behind his ears." Micah was giggling quietly with this one, a smile breaking up his icy expression.

"What? That is vile! I clean every inch of my body. Why in the hell would you say that, Micah?"

"Because I am lying, Billiam," he said sweetly, reaching down from his horse to rub Billiam's arm. This melted his anger, and he could enjoy Micah's peculiarity once again. "I have three more to go."

The prince was staring hard at my brother, but Zan just walked. He could barely breathe. He walked and he ached. He realized his backup plan was no use.

"Shemmy wears underpants," Micah continued, producing loud, immediate snickering from both counterparts. "In Khur, they use elephants to plow their fields. If you eat enough moondrop petals, you can defy gravity for a few moments. Now I'm done! Although Zan, the part about the elephants is actually true. An unlucky guess, I suppose. I remember my father told me of that. Those mountainous beasts fascinated him. I gather it's still a lie, because you thought it was, but I wanted you to know the truth."

"These were Zan's lies? Hmm, everyone knows Shemmy doesn't wear underthings, so I can't really assume anything with that. If only you kept your legs closed when you sat, I could have had fun teasing you," Billiam mused.

"Crossin' 'um is so uncomfortable, though! My thighs get all chafed!" Shemmy was pouting but hysterical. She dearly loved Micah's performance. He had delivered those lies in an impressively deadpan demeanor.

"I can't wait to clap at a bear!" Micah squealed and wiggled on his horse. This was too much for Billiam; it was too cute. He climbed atop the small horse with the prince. That poor beast's life span must've been shortened by a few years, after all that weight. He hugged him tight, and he bit him all over. He was simply being Billiam with his Micah.

"So that won't work, then?" Zan asked, though he knew the answer.

"Of course not. I really wasn't expecting you to give in so quickly, either," Micah explained matter-of-factly, as he was briefly able to part Billiam from his mouth. "Will you ever stop finding ways to disappoint your king?" A cruel laugh, then back to Billiam.

"Once I die," Zan aptly replied with a grim smile. He was thankful for once that he could borrow Billiam's happiness. It kept him from completely falling apart. It allowed him to distract himself, to think of Shemmy's lack of underpants. My brother's response was sufficient in dampening everyone's mood a bit, aside from his own. Thusly, silence overcame the group once more as they finished their trek to the mountainside village of Param.

I am still curious as to why Zan kept following them. He was not bound, and even if he was, he could've broken free. He could have easily destroyed any of them, the only wildcard being Shemmy's enchanting. And yet he followed obediently, truly becoming Micah's slave. Did he think he was being a good man, that submitting to his own humiliation would make them like him again? I agreed with Micah's punishment, so I did not want him to be free, but from an objective stance it made no sense. Did he want to see the rest of us badly enough to sustain this torture? That was highly unlikely. It could have been, of course, that he really wanted to save the kingdom. That would be a decent, good-hearted reason to submit. My brother was neither of those things. All I can think of was that he foolishly could not bear to leave Billiam.

Param hung about in Alafor's gut. It was near the center but still more east if I had to choose a side. It was a snow-covered quaint collection of wooden buildings and tiny shacks.

Upon entering its gates, Billiam jumped off the horse excitedly, grabbing Micah with him. He had caught sight of a tailor. *Some color, some silk for Micah*, he thought. *A coat, a tie, a hat, another tie for me!* He could hardly contain his giddiness, until he realized they were closed for the evening. He then set the prince down, defeated.

"We will have new outfits tomorrow, worry not, my love. It's not as if we will need clothes tonight, anyhow," Micah encouraged him, perking him right back up.

They were in front of the frost-covered but cozy-looking inn when Billiam grew serious. "We shall go in and see about our rooms. There is a stable behind us. Zan, please talk to the stableman about housing our horses and return promptly. On second thought.... Shemmy, go with him." Neither of them was pleased by this, but both silently obeyed, which was a bit odd for Shemmy.

Billiam set his bowler cap atop Micah's head. It was much too big, and his hair looked like golden water spilling from a cauldron. He grinned up at his lover, a silly but very happy sight. It wasn't much of a disguise, but it did make him look slightly less regal. With that, Billiam pushed open the slat door for his prince and himself.

Billiam held his arm tightly against Micah's waist as they walked over to the barkeep. Micah was shocked by it; he knew they were in Alafor, but they were still in the backcountry. Would they really not hate seeing two men entwined as such?

Billiam smiled wide and began to speak charmingly to the grizzled man behind the bar. "'Ello, good sir, and good tidings! My bride and I just married; we are on our way to City of Wings to celebrate. I hear there is no more beautiful a sight, besides my little lady, of course."

Micah gasped and felt his face get hot. *Billiam will pay for this*, he thought, amidst wondering if he still truly passed for female. He was almost nineteen now (subtracting his year of death). Had he really remained so pretty and delicate? He felt he couldn't evaluate that himself but trusted Billiam regardless.

"Congrats, ya happy bastard! Some guys got all the luck, dun they? We got some rooms, sure. Just one, then? Ain't ya freezin, trekkin' yer lady about in short pants in the dead of winter for yer honeymoon? A bit odd...." He scratched his bearded chin and was a little suspicious of them but still quite friendly.

"Oh worry not, we shed a few layers just now. We had worked up quite a sweat, finding a spot of privacy during our travels."

Micah tried his best to keep smiling sweetly, to be a polite, bashful maiden. It was difficult though; Billiam was laying it on quite thick. He had a devilish grin, which the barkeep returned as he eyed the prince up and down. *Yes, he is definitely getting punished*, Micah schemed.

"We actually need two rooms. My sister-in-law and her houseman have come along with us. We needn't anything fancy. The true delight shall be in Wings!" Billiam slapped his hand hard against Micah's rump, making him bulge his eyes and produce a startled squeal. Thankfully, it was an extremely convincing and feminine reaction.

"Aye, thass good. We ain't got nothin' fancy!" the man said with a hearty laugh, his gaze only going to Billiam every few seconds, as it was mostly transfixed on his bride. "Is her sister as lovely as yer gal?"

"No, not at all, sorry."

Micah giggled at Billiam's abrupt response. He wished Shemmy had heard it. Had she been a half minute sooner she could have, as Zan was now looming in the doorway, framing Shemmy in front of him. She was bounding over and luckily saw Micah secretly lift a finger to his lips. "'Ello, loves!" she sang, a safe salutation.

"Oi, dat her?" asked the barkeep. He was done undressing Micah with his eyes and turned the mental striptease to Shemmy. "She's dirty, but I think she's every bit as lovely as her sister. Got some curves too!"

The man chuckled and started yelling to a woman in the kitchen. He was instructing her to get them their rooms and was thankfully distracted as he made his way in there himself.

"Hey, sis, who said I was'nae pretty?" Shemmy growled, smacking Billiam in the gut. She looked over Micah, who was blushing so cutely she just wanted to bite his cheeks off. "What do I call the little lady?"

"Mariah," answered Billiam with a grin.

"That was quick. Have you thought of me as that before?" Micah whispered and threw daggers at Billiam with his eyes.

"Only when we were children. We can discuss that later." Billiam had his arm wrapped around Micah again. The barkeep's wife emerged, so he was unable to contest the touching one bit. It felt nice, but Billiam was still very much in trouble.

She led them up the stairs, silently and unimpressed. There were two rooms open: one was large with two beds and the other smaller with only one. "Newlyweds can have the single room," she grumbled, disappearing down the stairs as soon as her words stopped.

"Nope!" Micah cheered, acknowledging Zan at last, grabbing his arm softly. "You will be our guard, faelock. You can sleep in front of our door. Billiam and I will take the large room. Why not use as many beds as we can? That's only if he earns my forgiveness, of course. Shemmy, you can have the single. Don't let this man in your room. He might take advantage of you too. You are also precious to me."

"Not ta worry, Mariah. If he gets fresh, I'll scratch him up wif his own fingers!" Shemmy was snickering but fled into her room without another word. She seemed a bit more distant, a bit less carefree. It must've been because of Gam, or at least that's all they could think of.

"Zan, if I leave you out here, you will not desert me, correct?"

My brother nodded solemnly. He had given up.

He was being honest, and Micah knew it. He wanted to test him anyhow. "If I tied you to something, would you run?"

"Yes," Zan replied, looking at the ground.

"Right, I trust you. The truth on both accounts. You will be unbound, then." With that, they turned to retire. Micah ran into their large room and grabbed a pillow and quilt from the extra bed.

He shoved them into my brother's hands before slamming the door on him.

Zan sat the pillow on the ground and then himself atop it. He wrapped the quilt around his shoulders, letting his head and back fall against their door. He wept until exhaustion forced him asleep. It was actually only minutes, but it felt endless. He had been holding himself together surprisingly well, and now he no longer had to.

Billiam grabbed the cap off Micah and threw it like a discus onto the first bed. He wanted to grab that beautiful face and force it against his own. He needn't keep starving himself, as they had privacy at last. He could have his fill of Micah. He was already removing his blouse by the time he noticed the incredibly sour face the prince was making. Billiam ceased his fumbling, allowing him to stay dressed for the time being. He smiled meekly and asked, "So you are mad about that, then?"

Micah pouted and crossed his arms over his partially exposed chest. "Do I really still look like a girl?" he shouted, genuinely offended.

Billiam was allowed to hug him, so he reached a hand under the blouse, holding Micah's shoulder. He would get that stupid scrap of fabric off; he was determined. "Not when you are naked, my prince."

"What kind of answer is that?" Micah pulled off Billiam's hand before closing up his shirt and turning his back to him.

"What? I prefer you naked!"

"I prefer you quiet." Micah sat on the bed and held his face in his hands. How could Billiam not realize this was hurtful? It was not that he minded being girly or pretty, but he was a man. He was himself, whom Billiam was supposed to love just as he was. *It was so easy for him to make me into Mariah....* He knew he was being sensitive, but he was hurt. Billiam was just so silly, so sexual. Did he not care about anything else?

"Do you mean that, Micah?" Billiam asked and felt stung. He realized he had gotten carried away, downstairs and up here as well.

"Sometimes... when you are being such a fool."

Billiam finally looked up. He had softened, he was sweet, he understood. That was all Micah wanted, to have Billiam know he was wrong. With that he could forgive him and feel free to tease back.

"I am sorry for getting caught up. I am just having so much fun being with you that I didn't realize I was being ridiculous at your expense. I will try to talk a bit less, Prince. I'll at least choose my words better." Billiam was unaware he was already forgiven. He was paining himself to act as serious and prudent as possible, which Micah found quite amusing.

"I have something you can gag on, and that should keep you quiet," he whispered, grinning and uncrossing his legs.

Billiam looked so ecstatic, he practically floated over to Micah. He couldn't believe the prince talked dirty to him, all on his own and so well. "Where?" asked Billiam coyly. He was already kneeling between Micah's legs. He pulled on his trousers. "Can I have it?"

"Are you going to behave?" Micah was grabbing at Billiam's hair this time, pulling it tight. Billiam was so strong, so capable, but such putty in his hands. "You are in trouble, so you don't get your control of me back until you earn my forgiveness."

Billiam nodded, biting his lip. It took all the self-control he had to not throw the prince down and mount him at once. He was excited to see Micah try to dominate him and couldn't wait to show him how it was truly done afterward.

"BILLIAM, WAIT!"

My brother was awoken suddenly by Micah's shouting. The door that was his headboard flung against him, sending him and his pillow part way down the stairs. He lay on the steps, which were surprisingly comfortable, for a bit before forcing himself up. As he looked up he saw Billiam walking to Shemmy's room, completely naked. *What is going on?* Billiam slammed his fist on Shemmy's door. She opened it just as he saw a flash of the nude prince running after him and in to her room, as well. *Odd*, was all my brother thought as he picked himself up, leaning against the wall next to the door this time. *Back to sleep.* He smiled slightly as he passed out.

"Wot the 'ell? I thought you dinnae like lasses. Is we doin' a three way?" Shemmy asked with a smirk.

"Look at my shoulder!" Billiam shouted, motioning at it manically with his other hand. He was missing a whole chunk of flesh, with blood trickling down his arm before pooling into his elbow.

"Billiam! I am sorry! I got caught up in the moment! Come back to bed with me, and we will switch back positions." Micah was crying and pulling on Billiam's arm from behind him.

"What is wrong with Micah?"

"Looks like 'e was givin', when 'e is made for receivin'. Dat's what's wrong. Question answered." Shemmy was giggling, but grabbed a candle off her desk to come look at the wound. She stuck her finger in it, checking the teeth marks, causing Billiam to groan in agony.

"Goddammit, Shemmy, can't you be more careful?" He winced but did his best to not push her away. The prince was still crying, so Billiam grabbed him under his other arm. He held him tight, wanting him to feel better but couldn't quite look at him yet. "He was on top because I was in trouble. Will you answer my question now?"

"Trouble? Oh, coz o' the newlywed thing?" She wasn't answering, she was laughing. She turned to Micah and began looking at his mouth, but he wouldn't open it. He just kept crying. "Tell me what happened."

Shemmy was wiping alcohol on the wound. Who knows where she had gotten it from? Billiam grit his teeth hard, making himself ignore the stinging pain. "Well, you know what we were doing, I needn't explain that. It was actually pretty amazing. I have never had success being in that position, so I was quite pleased. That is, until he ate a bite of my shoulder. I looked over, and his eyes had turned black. I had to rip him off of me." He continued holding his prince close, for he couldn't let him think he was mad. He wasn't. He just wanted to know what was going on, to know that Micah would be all right.

"I wasn't eating you!" Micah wailed, falling into Billiam's side. He had blood staining down his chin, but he looked so pathetic and innocent.

"Where's da hunk o' shoulder den?" Shemmy was looking at the prince, smiling sweetly.

Micah's lower lip trembled like thunder, a new flood of tears spilling onto his face, onto Billiam, onto the floor. "I did eat it! I'm sorry! Why did I do that?" He was speaking in between loud, hiccupped cries.

Billiam realized how loud they were being, how easily their cover could be blown. He bent down and gave Micah a long kiss, scooping up tears with his fingers. This was the only proven method Billiam had found for calming him.

"Aren't you scared I'm going to eat your face?" It didn't work. With more uncontrollable crying, Micah fell to the ground.

"Eyes was black, you said? All black, o' juss the irises?"

Billiam was down on the ground with Micah, wrapping around him as best he could. "Prince, I am not afraid of you. I wish only to know you are okay." He looked up to Shemmy and answered her plainly, "Completely black. As soon as I got his mouth off and he swallowed, they were back to normal, and the crying started. Did something go wrong in the ritual?"

"Billiam, pull out yer needle and thread. Imma sew that gorge up." Shemmy mouthed out the words "trust me" to him, before kneeling down to them. "Micah, you are fine. That's quite a normal reaction to fockin' somebody. It means yer blood boiled; you were virile! I 'ave bit pieces off many o' my lovers. Billiam juss does'nae know that cos he spends all his time on top an' he ain't a chomper."

The prince looked up finally, still full of tears with his nose running terribly. In a soft, shaking voice, he was able to ask, "You've eaten your lovers too? I don't want to be a chomper!"

"When I was new to it, yes. Learned a bit o' self-control, I did." Shemmy was grinning, being sweet to her boy. She helped him off the ground and offered a hand to Billiam as well. "Just stick to takin' for now, 'til yer an old pro. Scoot on off to yer room; I gotta sew this one up. Dun wanna 'ave you see yer strong, strappin' man wincin' like a babe!" She playfully pushed Micah toward the door. He was dazed, but his crying had slowed almost to a stop.

Billiam scowled. He was not satisfied with this. "No, we aren't switching back yet. I will get fucked even if it kills me!" He was serious and grabbed Micah's shoulders hard, holding him close so he couldn't leave him yet.

"Uh, Billiam, yer the last person in the world who should be sayin' that, wif yer luck," Shemmy snickered but was honestly concerned.

"I know. Shut up, Shemmy! We will do this my way, and I should survive just fine. Micah, go to our room now, lie on your back, and play dead." Micah looked up at him mystified, blinking his now dry eyes a few times before he obeyed, turning again to the door. "If you aren't hard as a rock when I get in there, you will regret it!" He playfully slapped Micah's backside as he was finally allowed to exit.

The prince left them feeling content. Hearing Billiam turn naughty again helped him feel worlds better. He knew that meant he was happy. "Yes, master!" he called and skipped out of the room.

Shemmy was smirking as she heated up Billiam's needle with her candle. She held it in front of her face, waving it around to let it cool enough to house thread. "That's my topman, Billiam. Even when you's takin' it, ya gotta be in charge."

Billiam couldn't help indulging her with a small laugh. It was kind of nice having her be a pervert in instances where such difficulties might arise. He could not think of another friend who would understand his situation. "They say if you want a job done right, you do it yourself, hmm?" His smile turned quickly into a grimace as the needle began to fuse his flesh. "Now tell me what the hell is going on."

"Can ya believe 'e bought my chomper story? I am glad it's so believable I'd cannibalize a lover.... Actually I dunno if glad be the right word." She shook her head as she dabbed the wound with a piece of clean cotton. She needed to get rid of some more of the blood before she could pass through again. "Remember how Zan bonked me, in the pool?"

"Is this also his fault?" Billiam was ready to get up and annihilate my brother as soon as he got his answer. He cared not how sewn up his shoulder was.

"No!" she shouted, flicking his forehead. This forced her patient to calm down, allowing her to continue. "I was doin' the soulstitch when he was thrown into me, which was an accident, you best remember. This be the most vital step in creatin' a true, complete human a'gin. It has to be done twenty-seven times, one for each spiritual energy of nature. I was on my twenty-fourth stitch, and I could'nae quite complete the end 'cos the needles swerved outta place. I also could'nae redo the stitch, or it would overground him. That could shave years, decades off 'is life. I ain't sure which energy the twenty-fourth is, but I plan to find out in Alafor."

"So, you knew all this time that something is wrong with him?"

"No, it's not like that!" She looked quite sincere while dabbing the wound again. "I was'nae sure how messed up it was. This is all completely experimental, ya know? I dinnae think there was anything wrong until last night, when 'e was snappin' off Zan's fingers. Where did 'e get such strength from? 'Is aura was all diff'rent too—an energy that ain't human, well not completely."

"What the hell do you mean not human?"

"Shh, dun freak out. What good is dat gonna do? He seems fine most of the time, yes? He loves you, he is happy? We just must see to it he stays in as good a mood as possible. I dun fink the defective stitch is life-threatenin' anyway, an' I dun fink it affects 'im all the time. It is prolly somethin' 'bout violence that brings it out. The rammin', the bitin', that can all be pretty vicious, no?"

"I suppose…," he mused.

Shemmy was done stitching him up at last. He looked at his wound in a mirror hanging on the wall. He was surprised with how well she had done; how able she was to close the flesh. There really had been quite a chunk missing.

"So he is okay? He is human? He is not going to turn into a flesh-eating zombie? I have no intention of loving him less or turning my back on him, no matter what is wrong with him. I just need to know how to handle him. You think he will be all right as long as I keep him from acting violently, whenever possible?"

Shemmy nodded, gathering her bloody cloths and heating Billiam's needle once again, sanitizing it for him. "You would really still love 'im if he was a zombie? I'm not sure 'ow healthy that is, mate. Never mind that, though. I fink he's doing quite well. Can you imagine what it must be like? Cannae be easy, dying and coming back, and you have to juss be yerself a'gin, juss like that. He ain't, though. He's still Micah, but a new Micah. You and e'eryone else are juss gonna 'ave to accept 'im as he is now. That, and keep 'im either in front o' ya or underneath ya when yer gettin' frisky!" She was smiling, but she seemed not all that excited by what she said, what they did, not like before. She looked concerned, but it was not about Micah. She was very sincere about feeling he was doing well.

"Right, thank you, Shemmy! I should get back to him. I did my best to stay calm, but obviously it was quite a strange situation. I hope I did not offend him. Are you feeling all right?"

"Ya, why?" She scratched her head, getting ready to lie on her bed. It was barely dark out, yet she was thoroughly exhausted.

"You seem preoccupied, that's all. You aren't being as bizarre as I'm accustomed to. I just wanted to be sure you are feeling okay. I care about you, you know?" Billiam smiled, obscuring his nudity slightly as he got ready to leave.

"Aye, love ya too, Dandy!" She smiled and waved as he left, but her head was down. She was ready to sleep. She felt very sick, very desolate. She had not brought enough elixir with her. She could tell this was going to be a big problem.

My brother awoke again after Billiam walked back into his room. It was not he who woke him, however. He felt a twinge in his stomach, a nervous emptiness. He was hungry, but this was not his feeling. It was Shemmy's. Could he really feel her? He had never had an emotional connection to anyone but Billiam. He was surprised one night with her was all it took, when hundreds with Katrina could never bond them.

Zan could hear that Micah was quite preoccupied through the wooden wall, so he decided to take his chances. He strained to get off the ground, as he could only use his left hand to get himself up now. He knocked softly on Shemmy's door yet did not wait for her to respond. He could feel how exhausted she was, and he didn't want to make her get up. "Shemmy, I'm coming in, yes?"

"Feelin' brave, eh?" Shemmy mumbled. She was lying on her bed but above the covers. There was a thin layer of sweat along her face and down her collarbone. Her whole body was shivering lightly.

"No, not brave at all. I could hear them. I think I am quite safe for a while...." He was staring at the ground, walking over to her slowly. She looked really ill, and he wanted to hold her. He didn't know why he felt that way. "I had forgotten to give these to you before. I removed them from Gam for you." He pulled the tunic out of his pants pocket with his good hand, letting it fall on the ground so he could retrieve the vial and doll from his coat pocket.

Shemmy looked up finally and grinned at him, exhaling heavily. Zan felt relief pool in his body, as it swept over her. "You are my fockin' hero, didja know that? Come over here, bring my fings, and gimme a kiss, ya idiot."

Zan took the one and a half steps to reach her and knelt at the side of her bed. He turned to reach for her tunic, but she grabbed his arm while shaking her head. He set the doll and vial on her stomach before positioning his face above hers. She smiled and grabbed the back of his head, smacking him into her mouth. Their teeth bounced against each other before his lips landed comfortably.

"Can you open dat vial for me and put a tiny drop on my tongue? I don' feel like movin'." Her arms and head were both down again, as she stuck out her tongue between her rows of dirty teeth.

My brother grabbed the bottle off her stomach and looked over it a bit before uncorking it. He obeyed her, dripping a small drop onto her tongue. He couldn't help his curiosity as he closed it up, asking, "What is this stuff?"

She had brought her tongue back inside her mouth and was able to sit up slightly. "Well, it's kinda like, the cost for what I can do.... The energy I put out has to be sustained, replaced somehow. That little beauty does the trick, juss fine. Here, put another drop on my tongue and I'll show ya." She stared at him and stuck her tongue out again, this time a bit suggestively.

As soon as the drop of black fluid was on her tongue, she pulled Zan's mouth onto her own. She slid the top of her tongue against the length of his, so that the liquid transferred into his mouth. He thought of how much easier it would've been to drop it on his own tongue, but he still appreciated her kissing him.

"It'll affect you more, an' differently, than it does me. I 'ave a tolerance an' also have depleted energies from 'chantin'. Dunno how elfbloom treats faelocks, but I s'pose we'll find out."

"Elfbloom?" my brother repeated, not knowing if he had really spoken or not as soon as the word left him. It had tasted like dark greens, maybe arugula, and felt like a sticky spot of honey. It was already gone, and his mouth felt numb. His hand wasn't hurting, which made him quite ecstatic. He lifted it up between both their faces and started pinching the finger stumps while giggling.

"Ey, now. This is temporary! It'll juss hurt more later if you muss wif it." Her voice sounded serious, but she had a huge smile on her face. Zan could see she was admiring him and it made his heart feel warm. It was impossible for him to tell if it was her feelings, his own, or the elfbloom, but he wanted it to never stop.

"Shemmy, you are smart and pretty!" My brother was quite intoxicated, but at least he felt no compulsion to lie. He was grinning wide, the first smile that large to ever be genuine. He put his right hand, the incomplete one, between her breasts suddenly. This caused her to gasp and blush a bit, but she saw this was not intended as a grope.

"Shemmy, I can feel your feels now! You are the second person I have ever connected with. I like the way your heart feels." He had his head plopped on her stomach and was giggling softly.

"I dunno if that's cute or worrisome," she responded with a laugh, stretching her upper body and enjoying how repaired it felt. She could not believe Zan had been kind enough to search through Gam, especially not knowing how important that vial was. The tunic didn't matter, and the doll was pure superstition, but with the elfbloom he had saved her life.

"Let's get you back in the hall, yes? We dun wanna give the prince reason to be harmin' ya any more." She picked up his heavy head and swung her legs off the bed to get up. He tried to lean on her as she led him out, a near impossible feat with their height difference. She walked him over to his pillow. He was silent and smiling the whole way. She sat him down and leaned his head back against the wall.

"Thank you, a'gin, Zan. I dun fink I can make myself hate you anymore." She gave him a small kiss and smiled back at him as his smile only grew.

My brother's eyes were closed. He was overwhelmed by the euphoria of the elfbloom, and it was trying to force him back to sleep. Before it could, he whispered, "I love you, Shemmy."

"No ya don'. Yer juss high. Thanks for the thought, though." She heard him laughing a bit as she closed the door behind her. She really hoped he didn't. That was a level of awkward she felt unwilling to deal with.

CHAPTER 16

May 10-11th, 989

THAT NIGHT Billiam passed out before Micah, a surprising first. The prince took the rare opportunity to visit Shemmy briefly and learn what they had spoken of. She, of course, had to inquire about his reversed experience. He then revealed that he knew of her affair with Zan. Although she refused to admit any feelings for my brother, Micah still gave her permission to invite him in if she was so inclined. He was then abruptly retrieved and drug back to bed by his lover.

This prior conversation was obviously unknown to Zan, so it was a bit of a shock when he awoke on Shemmy's floor, beside her bed. She had tucked him in with her rag doll, but he did not remember moving whatsoever. The sun was still waking up itself, so it was only half-light outside. The magic of the elfbloom had all but left his body, and his hand throbbed beside him.

He rolled himself onto his unhurt side and looked over at Shemmy sleeping in her bed. He had no idea what he was doing, why he was feeling the way he did about her. His attraction to Billiam had always made sense. He was strong, intelligent, dedicated, and loyal. Those are all very reasonable traits to admire and would make a natural pairing, as far as faelocks go. Shemmy was crude, criminal, and unpredictable. She obviously had a good heart and was brave enough to help them, but the reason she agreed was mostly self-centered. What Shemmy truly loved was enchanting, something that disturbed him. Was it her passion he admired?

He realized it was pointless to think about it. It didn't matter why. He would not be with her; she would not have him. No one would, and soon he'd be gone. He knew it was only days until he would have to face Katrina, face me, and be unable to lie. Thinking of that forced him to curl in a fetal position. His stomach, his chest, and his hand all ached in tandem.

He hadn't realized he was still staring at Shemmy until she opened her eyes. He had been thinking as he looked, seeing nothing. He shook his head as she saw him, waving his bad hand in front of him apologetically. "Morning. I was simply lost in thought, not ogling. I am sorry."

"Feh, dun care. I dun fink no man's watched me sleep before. I guess still not." She stuck out her tongue at him, smiling dreamily. "You sleep awlright?"

Zan nodded, stretching out his legs and turning onto his back. "How'd I get in here? Won't Micah be upset?"

Shemmy jumped from her bed and skipped over to my brother. She climbed on his lap and sat atop him, digging through his pockets. She was looking for the elfbloom and found it in his pants pocket. He must've mistakenly returned it there in his stupor the night before. She held the vial but left her hand where it was. It was very warm. "I got permission for ya to stay in 'ere as long as ya slept on the ground. Dat's why I'm down here instead of grabbin' you onto my bed."

"What?" My brother blushed, but with our gray skin it wasn't red—it was more of a light blue. He was going to ask what he knew but then realized that was pointless. It was possible Micah knew anything that he himself did. "He hasn't told Billiam, though, right?"

Shemmy smiled before pulling her ragged dress over her head. Her thin body looked smooth and clean in the areas that had been covered, unlike her dirty limbs. She pulled Zan's good hand up and placed it on one of her breasts. It was perky and soft, filling only his palm. "Do you fink you'd be 'ere if 'e did?"

Zan's finger stubs throbbed, but he couldn't resist touching her more. Using his thumb and index finger he grabbed her hip, pulling her harder onto his lap. "I know you no longer hate me, but I didn't think you liked me enough to pay me this much attention."

"I guess I'm desperate," she said with a laugh, surprising him by taking her hand from his pocket and crawling over his body. His neck was between her naked legs as she continued, "You were very nice to me yesterday, quite gentlemanly, I'd say. You wanna be nice to me again?" She did not wait for his answer. His grin was enough.

She needed only to make one step with her knees before her second pair of lips were atop his. She uncorked the elfbloom vial in her hand, placing a drop on her tongue before lifting herself slightly to place a drop on his as well.

Billiam was awake and getting ready at the same time Shemmy was stupidly amusing herself with my brother. Micah lay in bed, exhausted and sore. He had, perhaps, let his lover overdo it when they returned to bed. He was enjoying himself immensely, yet as morning arrived, he wanted to never move again. Every muscle in his legs felt as if they were stretched and overused. Both he and Billiam needed to learn the limits of his body. He wished and acted like he had none, but now he felt like a baby deer that could only wobble, not even dream of walking.

Despite his exhaustion, he knew he had to move. Billiam was dressed and would want to get them all going. Any minute now he would be heading to Shemmy's room, but Micah didn't want to let him know of the mercy he had shown Zan. "Billiam," he called out weakly while trying to sound enthusiastic. "Come kiss me!"

"You are awake, my prince?" He bounced onto the bed and bent over Micah, holding his shoulder to prepare for the kiss. He was horrified to see him wincing in pain at the touch, as it was actually quite gentle. He removed his hand and gave only a light kiss on the prince's forehead instead. "Did I take it too far? You are hurt?"

Micah grinned, and falsely shook his head no, but he hardly moved other than that. "Um… I think so."

"Why didn't you stop me, Micah?" He was so concerned he sounded almost angry. He brushed the hair off his forehead, rubbing his head lovingly. This was the only place he wasn't afraid to touch.

"It didn't hurt then, you silly brute; it felt absolutely wonderful. Why would I stop bliss?" Micah was smiling and tried to kiss his hand as it grazed him. He was glad Billiam was so distracted by his weakened state, as he could sense that Zan and Shemmy were still indisposed. "We'll have to be more careful, I think, my love. That, and you are going to have to wait awhile to play with your toy again."

Billiam knew he was being teased, but he didn't respond with his regular excitement. "I will learn your limits, Prince, so I can give you the pleasure you crave, with no adverse effects," he professed, lying beside him but barely touching.

"Yes, and I'm sure all these muscles I hadn't used before will grow much stronger. However, just for today, can you carry me? I don't feel up to walking or riding horseback."

"You shouldn't travel at all, then. We can stay another night. Spirit, I am so sorry, Micah."

"No! No apologies necessary. I just want to keep moving. I'd rather not have to explain why we are delayed to anyone, either. Let's get me dressed and go see the tailor before we bother with the others."

Hearing that, Billiam lit up like a firecracker; he had quite the weakness for fashion. He carried Micah while dressing him, not wanting his body to have the strain of holding itself up. I highly doubt the prince was quite that damaged, yet that was Billiam's love for him. It was a bit overbearing but endless and kind.

My brother and Shemmy were downstairs at the tavern when the prince and his page returned from their shopping trip. Zan was going on his fourth glass of milk and second bowl of stew. Shemmy was nursing her third ale and picking at bits of her pot pie with her fingers. The barman was laughing and chatting with her, that is, until he caught sight of Micah.

Although Micah was not entirely sold on his passing for a woman, he realized the ruse would have to live on as long as they were in Param. Furthermore, he conceded it was quite an effective disguise. No one was looking for a missing princess as far as they knew.

At the tailor's they had many lovely long gowns, but not many short ones due to the cold. Micah's enchantment kept him warm, and he wanted to have nearly the range of motion of wearing trousers; thus he was against anything floor-length. He located a pretty navy blue silk frock that had a ruffled front and bounced with frills at the tops of his knees. He could see the tailor did not want him going out into the cold in such a delicate dress, but he insisted he really could not stand long gowns. She brought him a nice, long cloak; it was an ivory wool with a silver fur trim. It was long and gaudy, and definitely would dissuade a person from thinking he was cold.

Billiam agreed he would buy his bride the cloak, so the tailor brought out some other knee-length dresses she had for the summer months. Micah got one in pink cotton, tight on the body but with a full skirt so nothing could poke through. The third and final gown was a brilliantly tailored glamorous concoction. It had a black skirt crossed over with violet and emerald ribbons, following up to an intricate corseted chest. It looked like it would have a rough brocade feeling, but it was smooth to the touch. That was his favorite, and of course the one he chose to wear out, along with his coat. The tailor's husband was a cobbler who brought out some lovely black heeled ankle-boots for him. They had real pearls at the lace inserts, rather ridiculous but opulent enough for the prince.

For himself, Billiam grabbed three pairs of woolen slacks, black of course. One pair happened to be Micah's size, yet the tailor didn't mention it. He procured a thick black peacoat so he might fit in with the frigid area as well. He got a few of their finest knit shirts, even getting a pale blue one to break up his entirely monochromatic wardrobe. Micah picked out his ties for him, deciding on a veritable rainbow.

Billiam combed Micah's flaxen hair to the side. He was beaming, his happy face completing the outfit beautifully. The tailor was so taken with the image he created that she donated a beautiful jeweled barrette of her own to his head. She couldn't bear to see the outfit leave without the perfect accessory.

With their trip to the tailor being such a success, it was not a surprise they left the barkeep speechless. Billiam held the prince in his arms, his knees hanging over his elbow and Micah's arm over his injury-free shoulder. His ivory mantle hung down around him, veiling Billiam's body so that it appeared he almost floated. The ribbon-covered skirt peeked through the cloak, leading down to his black tights. The boots hugged his delicate ankles as they swung around the arms that held him. Billiam looked quite dashing too, but he was not awe-inspiring like the lovely ladylike creature he held.

"Aye, now thass an outfit suited to 'oneymooners in Alafor!" the barkeep yelled with a laugh, turning to get his notebook from behind the bar. "I won't mind ya'll leavin' now. Won't have to be fearin' my guests are turned to icicles."

Billiam smiled as he walked over, setting the prince in the seat next to Shemmy. She was petting him, touching every bit of fabric and giggling.

"Yes, thank you, sir. I suppose we were a bit ill-equipped. Shall I settle the tab with you now? Might we also be able to procure as many loaves of bread as you can spare, a few flagons of ale, and any preserved meats you have?" Billiam asked over the bar.

"Oi, I'm sure my wife can put some type o' picnic togetha for yas. Dun think she'll make it cheap, though. She said you folks were loud as all get-out. I dinnae hear a thing. 'Course I was passed out drunk as soon as the sun set." He laughed and grabbed his large belly before walking into the kitchen.

"We are fine on the budget?" Zan asked, glaring at the pearls on Micah's boots.

"Of course. I will use our money from the Order for the inn and foods. The clothing came from my own pocket. I have been saving most of the gold I earned the last five years so that I might spoil my love when *she* was back to me." Billiam held Micah tight while fumbling through his billfold, grabbing the Logos marks from beside his own.

"You are so sweet, Billiam!" Micah sang up to him.

"Oh. I understand. Please forgive any suspicion." Zan looked into his stew, staring hard at it, as if it were communing with him somehow. The stew broke its spell, and he spoke again. "We are getting a late start, so I think I can adjust our path, and we will end up at another small village by nightfall. You can have another inn, Mi.... Mariah?"

"No thank you! I am quite fine; I needn't another inn so soon. You probably ought not plan for one the next night either. After that is hopefully our last night of travel, and I shall likely be craving one, so then is fine." He was leaning completely against Billiam at this point, reaching his arm up to touch his face. He was hoping he had not made him feel guilty again, but it was no use.

Shemmy snorted and smacked Billiam on the arm. The barkeep reappeared with a large basket of supplies and their long paper bill before she could say anything lewd or embarrassing. After settling the tab, which was a rather exhaustive amount, they collected their horses and were off.

"Zan, would you like to ride Micah's horse today?" Billiam asked my brother politely, as they led the two horses past the village exit.

"What? No, I am faster on foot. I am too tall for such a small horse, anyhow. Micah, you don't want to ride it?"

"Who said you could say my name, faelock? I did not correct you at the inn, simply to keep up my guise. That changes nothing when we are on our own. You are beneath us all, you pathetic worm," Micah replied with a scowl, using Aldrious's pet name for him on Zan. "If you must know, I haven't the energy to keep myself on it today. So you will either walk it or ride. I don't give a shit which you choose."

Zan's face fell to his chest as he grabbed the reins of the horse, silently beginning his march. The day had been quite happy so far and had tricked his heart into thinking he was near equal to them once again. He was not; he was the prince's property.

Shemmy was up on her horse, trotting ahead to Zan, who was walking with his neck sunk all the way down. She looked over him to grin at Billiam. "Ya really got 'im that good, didja topman?"

Billiam's heart stopped. *I didn't mean to!* he screamed inside his chest.

Before he could respond to her, the prince interjected from his arms, "Shemmy, I will have none of your perverted nonsense about this. Any injury I suffered is no fault of Billiam's; it is due to my own ignorance. I will not have you make him feel badly or delight in his torment. You will keep your ridiculous mouth shut. Are we perfectly clear?" He glared at her so sternly that she felt genuine fear for a moment.

"Yes, Yer 'Ighness," responded Shemmy, absolutely gobsmacked.

She could not believe he had reprimanded her so, not that she hadn't deserved it. She had thought Billiam was the one with that intensely protective, all-consuming form of love, but she saw she was half mistaken. Micah was just as ferociously and possessively in love with Billiam. It made her feel she ought to tread a bit lighter, as there was no room to cause even the slightest rift between the two. Their loyalty to each other would tear anyone apart if their love was threatened, even her. As extreme as it seemed, she was frankly quite jealous. A love that strong and also fully requited is a rare and wondrous thing.

"Oh good, then we can be pleasant again!" He kissed Billiam's chin and whispered up to him, "I'll love you forever, as always. Please do not fret. You are perfect and have treated me perfectly."

"I'll love you forever, as always, my dearest, sweetest, loveliest thing." Billiam smiled and relaxed, nuzzling Micah's head. Hearing those words made him feel he had the energy to walk them the whole day at last.

I'll love you forever, as always. This was what Billiam's mother, Ella, would say to Ackerman. In fact, it was the first thing she said to him outside of training. Billiam had no memory of his mother; she died when he was just a toddler. Pierre told him of this saying and how his mother and father would speak it to one another before each battle.

Growing up Billiam didn't see his father much, as he spent all his time with the royal family instead. He wanted to hold on to that saying and show his love but didn't feel that strong a love for Ackerman. He began saying it to Micah when they were still quite young. Ackerman first heard his son say this to the prince when he was ten and at first thought he was hearing Ella. He knew at that point who his son was, whom he loved, the man he would be. He always thought Billiam was hardly faelock, as one did not raise him. He was wrong, and though he was a bit shocked his strong son was the way that he was, he accepted him. Seeing Ella in him was the start of him trying to build a relationship at last.

Zan knew the story of those words, and hearing them again brought back his first pangs of jealousy. His heart was aching. He was still affected by the elfbloom from earlier, causing his emotions to be fresher and more present. Although he had developed feelings for Shemmy, Billiam was his first love. He was being further and further removed from him, and he could only watch as he was swept away completely. He began to weep as he walked himself and Micah's horse ahead of everyone. Although losing to Micah at last saddened him, these tears were from bitter frustration. He wanted to lash out at them both. This was an extremely stupid way to feel, thus he walked alone, wishing he actually were.

CHAPTER 17

May 11th, 989

BACK IN Drummond, Loretta had been dusting up a storm in the dining room the whole afternoon. Every time she passed near Jessica at least three sneezes and an equal number of "bless yous" followed. There had been little to no business, and the two of them were the only ones in the giant lonely room. The inn had been so void of life, they even had to put their new chef on indefinite vacation. He didn't seem to mind. He was as bored as the rest of them.

Jess was done trying to busy herself and plopped down in her favorite corner of the bar. She kept a soft, pink pillow on a stool there and was able to lean comfortably, practically out of view of the patrons, had there been any. Nestled below the bar was her secret stash of pulp novels, framed by seldom-used antique tankards. After she dropped hard on the stool, she reached down blindly, feeling the spines of the books.

She decided on the roughest-feeling one. The binding felt cracked, so it must've been old and meant it had been a while since she had read it. Grabbing it out and into the light, she turned it over to see the familiar black leather cover. Emblazoned on it was a crimson illustration of a reaper along with the words, *The Goon's Gal.* It was a ridiculous and tawdry tale of the forbidden romantic journey between a woman, a goon, and his reaper. It was one of her favorites.

The Logos spent all of their study time on informative texts, scientific or historic, with the remainder allotted to classical literature. They all looked down upon the frivolously enjoyable yarns Jess loved so much. That is why they were her dirty secret, though I would let her read them to me. They were entertaining at the least, I'll give them that.

She was ripping through the first chapter when the largest of sneeze attacks ravaged her face and lungs. She coughed so hard she all but fell from her stool, throwing the novel onto the counter.

"Oh I'm sorry, dear! Dinnae see you there!" Loretta's cheerful voice called from above her. She had been standing on a stool, dusting the awning of the bar. She jumped off with a loud thud. Jess was inches away from reclaiming her novel when Loretta swept it from her hands. "Oh so you are a W. H. Twingles fan too, then?" she said with a small laugh, happily handing the book back.

"I'm a what now?" Jess was a bit befuddled. She wanted to hide the book away but instead she looked it over. Under the glorious reaper she saw inscribed W.H. TWINGLES =^-^=.

She reached down to pull up her entire collection, revealing them all to Loretta. She searched through the novels to find over half of the miniature book mountain had the same inscription. Loretta was smiling and looking through them too, and was quite impressed by her assortment.

"Huh? I guess I am. I never paid attention to the author; I would just ask the shopkeep which one was the weirdest or most humorous. What's with the cat face?"

"Oh, that's kind of like his signature. He does quite like cats," Loretta replied, grinning and stacking up the books neatly. She saw Jess was not at all satisfied with her answer. She began scratching her chin in thought. It seemed her five o'clock shadow liked to to come in more around two. Jess knew she would be running to the washroom any moment now to cake up her face with more powder. Said powder came off on her finger as she scratched, but she seemed to not notice. "I suppose since you are a fan, he may not mind me telling you the real reason…."

"Yes, please tell me!"

"Okay, well he is obviously quite an odd guy. How else could he come up with such scenarios? He is a bastard and never met his father. He somehow became thoroughly convinced his father was a stray black tomcat he saw everywhere he turned as a child. Thus he feels he is a cat-man, though he vehemently refuses to show me any of his cattiness."

Jessica's eyes were wide and glassy, as she mused, "Why doesn't he write about that? That would be an amazing story!"

"That's exactly what I asked him! He told me something about the Mortanions finding out and how they'd punish him for being a heretic, some paranoid delusion like that. I think if they found out, they'd barely care enough to call a sanitarium," Loretta informed her with a laugh. She looked in the silver sink of the bar, finally noticing the gaps in her makeup.

"So you really know this Twingles?" Jess asked excitedly. She had been so bored since the cardinal's visit. She had hardly gone out of the lodge, not wanting to catch a glimpse of anything crimson. This provided her with the entertainment she had been craving.

Loretta grabbed a rag, wetting it in the sink and taking it to her face. She wiped off all the powder, all the rouge, while she spoke. "Winston is the first friend I made when I got here to Drummond. I knew no one here, and although I was well-off in my homeland, I had to leave everything behind to escape. I was a penniless man in a dress, so it was quite hard to get anyone to spare kindness. That plump bookworm almost trampled over me as I lay drunk in the alley by his apartment. He lives in Northwest Drummond, not too far from here.

"He thought I was going to get angry and attack him, so he started throwing all his money on me. I gave it back and told him to get me a bath and dinner instead. I had never purchased such things on my own by that point; I was quite hopeless. He was still terrified but took me in anyways. He sensed my harmlessness before long and put me to work numbering pages."

"You had never bought yourself dinner?" Jess asked her with a look of disgust.

"That is really the part you care about? Not that I possibly worked on one of your favorite books?" Loretta tried her best to act upset, but she was excited to be bonding with Jessica. Her face was perfectly clean now, and she was tying up her hair in a tight knot. She truly looked like a man, Jess conceded. "I'm going to go change and wear some man clothes. Winston gets all weird and handsy when I look too pretty."

"Wait what? You are going to go see him now?"

"No!" Loretta shouted as she ascended the stairs. "*We* are going to go see him. Go ahead and call me Ari while I am stuck having to act like a man."

Ari…. Is that really a man's name? I suppose it could be a nickname, Jess thought while conflict raged in her gut. She was so excited to meet this Twingles, but she didn't want to leave. The outside world was a world where she could be preyed upon, she felt. In truth, she was first preyed on in the lodge; it was no safer than outside.

Loretta, or rather Ari, descended the stairs gracefully in a lovely tailcoat, white shirt, and black tie and slacks. "Found these in a third-floor room the other day. They fit me like a glove!" They were Billiam's, and Jess recognized the stunning vision at once. Just the head was different. He wiggled his hips in excitement, but as soon as he dropped Billiam's bowler cap on his head to cover his hair, almost all traces of femininity were erased. "Shall we, dear?"

Jessica was impressed. He was quite dashing and made her heart skip a few beats. She wished for a moment that he could be Ari all the time but felt ashamed. That was rather selfish of her to want to change the real Loretta, the one she was inside.

"I don't want to run into any monks," she said anxiously.

"We won't! We shall have a nice, fun visit. Where's that Roland to watch the bar?" Ari was peering at himself in the sink, adjusting all the little flyaways under his hat.

"Sleeping, right? He got stupid drunk last night. I know how to raise him, though." Jess jumped off her stool and grabbed a broom near the bar before running to the middle of the dining room. She jumped up on one of the large tables and repeatedly bonked the end of the broom against the ceiling.

She was dancing on the table and hitting the floor above her to the beat in her head for three whole minutes before Roland finally emerged. He was pathetically leaning over the railing, barely dressed and quite pale. "What's the big, bloody idea, Jess?" he grunted at her. He had given up going all the way down and sat on the steps.

"We are going out. Mind the bar, will ya?"

"What! You can't go out on your own! Two lasses with the cardinal's nose all up in your business, yer juss askin' for trouble. Where you gotta go, anyhow?"

"Open your eyes, dummy. We ain't two lasses," she cried, jumping off the table and stamping her feet on the floor instead.

Roland looked over the rail, his eyes taking a while to adjust to the sunlight that seeped in all throughout the ground floor. As he peered between the wooden bars, he caught a glimpse of that familiar tail-coated visage. It was incentive enough to get him off his lazy ass, jumping down the stairs two at a time.

"Billiam! You are back? Why are you back so soon?" he yelled, never thinking he would be so happy to see him, as they were not particularly close. The climate had been both tense and horribly boring, so the familiar sight delighted him.

"Billiam?" Ari asked, turning to Roland at last.

Roland was so shocked by the mistaken identity he bashed into an oaken chair. He sat on the floor, cursing himself for being so excitable.

"Quite an uncanny resemblance, especially from behind, huh?" Jess called to him, grabbing at Ari's coat and grinning. This made the wearer blush brightly, and he became Loretta to Roland once again.

"Oi, sorry 'bout that uh… boy Loretta?" He got himself off the ground, rubbing his bumped knee before hobbling to the bar. He buttoned up his shirt and somehow made his undershorts look like decent clothing. "Awlright, go out, then. I ain't up to escortin' you anyhow. Where do you hafta go suddenly?"

"I get to meet W.H. Twingles!" Jess squealed and bounced about.

"Who?"

"That's what I said too! He's an author of a lot of those books I like, and Ari is friends with him. Ari is Loretta's boy name." Jess grabbed his arm, as excited as if it were the first day of spring. She hadn't realized how terribly cooped up she was feeling. "Let's be going now?"

"Of course, my lady." Ari bowed slightly, trying his best to be gentlemanly. It was quite obvious to all of them he was uncomfortable dressed as he was. Loretta was much more lively, much happier than Ari.

The streets were quite packed in the Northwest borough. It was a Saturday, so all the vendors had stalls set up, peddling their garbage. This neighborhood was primarily middle class, merchants and craftspeople who lived happily though not easily. Ari held on to Jess tight, not wanting the tiny lady to be swept away. He scanned the crowd diligently for any flashes of red robes.

They were turning on Twingles's street when an enraged though melodic voice screeched out, "Stop right there, you stupid faggot!" There was clear desperation in the voice—the only reason it was not instantly recognizable.

Ari continued walking. Whatever creature was screaming was surely not aiming it at them.

"I said stop, Billiam!"

Oh, that is who Roland thought I was.... They are screaming at me after all, Ari thought before hiding Jess with his body and turning toward the voice. As soon as his face was turned, he caught the flash of gleaming metal as it flew toward his eyes.

Ari lifted two fingers in front of his nose, catching the blackened throwing knife gracefully. "I think you have me confused with someone else, little brother." Ari was readying himself to throw the blade back; however, it turned to charcoal dust, falling through his fingers. It was another of Aldrious's parlor tricks.

"Oh bloody hell!" Aldrious yelled, ducking in a doorway and pulling the dingy black robe he was wearing over most of his head. He was not hiding from them; he seemed to simply be hiding from the masses. He reached out his hand, bidding them to cease their departure. In a low whisper, he tried to communicate civilly, "So that really was you at the inn, Arrikos? Ugh, I should have known. Now I feel ill."

Ari shocked Jess by walking them closer to the disguised cardinal, yet she found herself trusting his decision anyways. They stood together in the cover of some townsperson's stoop.

"Oh dear, you didn't jerk yourself thinking of me again, did you, Aldy?" Ari was grinning and even pinched his brother's cheek.

"Of course I did. When am I not touching myself thinking about strange women? You need to introduce yourself next time, dammit!"

Jess was amused but also irritated, a bit disgusted, and terribly confused. Why were they being so friendly? Were they truly brothers? Their olive complexion and jet-black hair was the same, but Ari outstood Aldrious by almost a foot. However, after seeing them smile at each other, there was no doubt they were flesh and blood. They had the same mischievous and constant grin, though the brothers used them with very different intents. She was done pondering this; it didn't matter. Aldrious was her sworn enemy, and if Ari were to sympathize with his brother, then he was her enemy too.

Jess had a dagger in the pocket of her dress, just in case something were to be amiss. She secretly slid it into her hand, and then held it to

Aldrious's groin. "I don't care a bit what you think of, but if you move a muscle, you won't have anything to yank on!"

Aldrious went pale and gulped hard. He looked to his brother, but Ari was just grinning. "Right. I deserve that. I treated you without respect, my petite Mantine. I am quite sorry, now that I am finally paying for my actions. Responsibility is such a dirty whore." He was smiling, but he was hardly a shell of the tyrant he was before. "Arrikos, will you listen to me? I haven't much time left until I am apprehended. I have foreseen it, and I am quite sure there will be no change to that. So don't you worry, my ladies, I will be paying the ultimate price for my sins whether you show me mercy or not."

"Would you like to see a piece of cow feces try to spin us a yarn? We can bring him to Winston's if you are so inclined," said Ari, smiling.

Jess held the blade in her shaking hand. She was curious, and she wanted to keep seeing the cardinal in his pathetic state, although she was sure it could very well be at the cost of her own life. She was not with her friend as she thought; she was with the heir of the Dalgarie family, a corrupt and foreign nobleman.

"You will not look at me, and if you touch me I will scream your name as loudly as all get-out into the streets. Do you understand me, you sick fuck?" She jammed the blade into him slightly, scraping him but not breaking the flesh.

It was sufficiently intimidating, forcing a nod as he kept his gaze averted from her.

"Good, let us go." Ari grabbed their hands cheerfully, leading them a few measly paces down the alley before ascending a decrepit-looking steel staircase against the tall building. He tapped lightly on the door, and it swung open.

He led them into the dark room and motioned that they take their seats. That was a rather impossible thing to suggest, as there were no seats. All they could see was a single black cat, licking its back in the corner of the empty room.

"Oh, I get to see your cattiness at last!" Ari squealed, jumping up and down in place.

"No, no you don't," a nasally voice whispered from behind the door. Ari had practically squished Winston against the wall. "Why have you come back, Loretta?"

Jess and Aldrious could hear Winston, they could feel his hot breath, but they saw no one. They watched in wonder as Ari bounded to the middle of the room and sat down, seeming to levitate.

"You really have taken that transparency thing to heart, then, hmm?"

"One can never be too safe, especially when one's only friend brings his archenemy into his home!" The voice was screeching and pushed against Aldrious before it knocked Ari off his floating perch and onto the ground.

The apartment was small, with off-white walls and a dusty wooden floor. A connected kitchen sat in the near corner of the room, though entirely sparse. There was one door ahead of them, presumably the toilet. The furniture Ari floated above, any appliance in the kitchen, any manuscripts, even the host himself, were completely invisible. The smell was musty, a bit decayed, but its source was a mystery.

"He is not your archenemy; he is my kid brother. Also, I am not your only friend; I am your best friend, sweetheart!" Ari replied happily. He was floating once again, trying desperately to get the cat in the corner to visit. "Shut the door, Aldy, and come on over you two. Winston, we originally came because the lass there, my new employer, is an avid fan of your work. My brother happened to accost us as we drew near, and since he promised he'd die soon, I decided not to kill him."

"You are really a fan? You are so pretty, though." The voice was right in Jessica's ear. She had remained standing, but Aldrious tried to sit with Ari. He ended up not finding a chair and fell on the floor instead.

"Yes, I love your books. Especially *The Sailor, the Siren Sang*. That's my all-time favorite." Jess had been excited to meet Winston, but the reality wasn't all that satisfactory, as she couldn't even see him.

"Good taste, girl." The voice chuckled and moved farther away. "Okay, well, she met me. Shouldn't you leave now? I want no trouble."

Ari nodded grimly. "Might you play host to our brief discussion? We shall leave promptly after my brother is done with his pathetic tale."

"Five minutes. I will take off my transparency if you are not done, and I assure you, none of you would like to see the level of filth amongst you." Winston was laughing, as Jess saw the cat curl around his invisible leg.

Aldrious groaned, holding the black robe's sleeve over his mouth. "Right, I will be quick. Do you know that your employer's friends abducted the prince?"

"I do now!" cheered Ari. He was grinning as he placed his hand lovingly on his brother's knee, forcing Aldrious to grimace.

"Yeah, the prince that you killed a year ago!" Jess kicked him in the back, but he did not turn to her.

"That is debatable, but yes, the prince was already dead. Well, I had a hunch they would take him to Alafor. Our cousin has learned the art of resurrection, so the sacrificial lamb of Casperland will need allies. Where better than Alafor?" Aldrious stretched out and scratched his long nails playfully along his brother's arm, wishing he could be stripping off his skin instead. "Well, I contacted your wife. She has a lab out there."

"Do not call her that." Ari threw his brother's hand off of him, turning away in disgust. "Call her Camilla, call her bitch from hell, call her anything but mine."

"Whatever you say. She is the finest piece of tail in the eastern hemisphere; who else but my freaky brother would get her and not appreciate her at all. Regardless, I tried to get her to help me and have the Alafor arrest them. She agreed, but after that I do not know what happened. There have been at least three Knox ships spotted near the eastern harbor, which leads me to believe it didn't go quite as I had planned."

"She fucked you. Why are you surprised?"

"If only that were what she did." His smile barely hung in his mouth. His face was sour and looked aged, not youthful as it always had.

"Okay, so Knox is going to take you and kill you, and I care about this why?"

"I don't give a damn about you or what you care about!" Aldrious shouted, flailing his arm and accidentally smashing it against Winston's table. "Although I perverted Casperland and wanted it all my own, I entirely prefer it to Knox. I do not want to see its essence evaporated by blind and stupid faith. I want to talk to you so Jessica can hear me. If you listen to me carefully, I think you can warn your lover."

"Why the fuck should I trust you? You killed Micah! You just want to kill him again!" Jessica was livid as she yelled to the back of his head.

"I don't expect you to believe me, but I never intentionally hurt the prince, and that is pure truth. I don't like him, but I find him very important and definitely didn't want him dead. I had planned to keep him as my puppet. I wanted power; I needed no crown or throne. That just puts a target on one's head. What I want now, as continued power is out of the question for me, is for sanity to be restored in this realm. I want the brothers and sisters of wicked Aegis to burn to ash, and I feel your little prince might be the very phoenix for the job. What will it hurt, anyhow? All I want you to do is think, to feel. You will likely get a feeling back, and I'm sure that could be a comfort."

"Feh, so Aldy didn't want me all along. First you think I am that Billiam fellow, and then you try to entrance the lady. Such an ungrateful, unfeeling sibling," Ari pouted out.

"I had no idea what or who I was running to or from. I just knew in my gut that I needed to go north, and then I thought I saw the towering dandy. I guess I still sort of did, just not the right one."

"Hey! I'm no dandy!" shouted Ari, causing his brother to become hysterical for a moment.

"Yes, yes whatever, I didn't mean literally. I just meant a tall deviant of some sort." He stopped laughing and clacked his nails together. "Miss Mantine, will you listen? You needn't come closer to me. Simply close your eyes, relax, and picture your faelock. See Leke in your heart and mind."

"Fine, if that means I can be done with this blasted reunion, go ahead." She sat against the door, closed her eyes, and held my memory in the front of her mind.

"Micah is precious. All nations will try to use him. Leke, you alone will save him. Trust the Alafor now. Do not trust anything of them from the past. All right, Jessica, repeat all that in your heart. Feel it deep, try to ache yourself. Think of how she does not love you and never will, as you repeat it." Aldrious grew quiet and was surprised she didn't lash out at him. He continued, "Leke, the Families Five are the answer, and Micah is the cure. Keep him close, form your bond deep and quickly." Aldrious paused again, desperately hoping she was reaching me.

She was actually getting into my heart slightly. I was in the royal reading room studying some maps when my chest throbbed. I suddenly felt a need to switch my research. I lunged toward the most ancient texts, pulling out a heretical piece on the Families Five. I felt Jessica hurting for me, and it made me feel ill. I felt her telling me *Micah* clearly, and the rest was vague whispers of what he spoke.

"Casperland is not the answer. It is in danger. Set your sights to the Startspring. Leke, I am sorry." With that, Aldrious was done. He was completely silent and covered his face.

Jess finished her repetition and was able to make herself hurt enough to force tears from her eyes. These masochistic thoughts made Aldrious's last words clear as day in my heart. They were so plain to me, I wrote them on the ancient book I was reading just as they are written above, with one difference. Instead, it said "Leke, Aldrious is sorry." I ripped the page quickly, disgusted at myself for desecrating such a precious artifact. That didn't stop me from writing down the first part of the message on the back of it. The damage was done, and I thought it better I not forget anything.

In the midst of Aldrious's silence, the door was kicked in. Jess was flung hard to the floor. The cat puffed up huge and jumped out the window, and from the loud thud, I assume Winston followed it. Three shiny Enox soldiers waltzed in, assisted by two monks. "Cardinal Aldrious, you are hereby convicted of high treason and murder of the crowned prince," called one of the monks. The voice was smooth and happy, quite like Aldrious's own.

Jess felt her heart stop. Was this the end for all of them? She was strangely thankful they had run into Aldrious. Were she to die, at least she had passed an important message for the prince. She could be struck down by the enemy a hero, not just the helpless girl they left behind at the bar.

The soldiers paid no attention to Jess, nor Ari. They lifted the fallen cardinal easily off the floor, placing a burlap bag over his face and pushing him toward the door. They seemed to avoid even looking at my comrade and her friend; that is how little they mattered.

The second monk, a bishop, took his turn to mock Aldrious. "We are taking you back to Enox for your execution. The archbishop has been salivating at the idea of hacking off your head for the last decade. I cannot wait to deliver you to him, at last."

"Jessica, Camilla is a traitor; Camilla lied. Traitor! Traitor! Traitor!" Aldrious's screams were muffled from the bag. He was quickly knocked unconscious, silencing the noise for good.

Jess took his cue and threw me her pain once again. Her fear and anxiety amplified the thoughts she passed tenfold. She never knew of Camilla—not even a passing notion did I share with her. Hearing her feel that name into my brain, I knew I had never ceased being a fool. The sanity I thought I regained in her presence was simple manipulation.

As quickly as the commotion appeared, it was gone. They left, truly caring nothing for the other two, Aldrious was their one target. Had they recognized Arrikos, they may have wanted him too, yet he looked quite distant from the opulent nobleman they knew. They heard the scraping metal from the knights in the distance as they descended. Following it was the terror of the townsfolk reacting to the presence of foreign soldiers in their home.

Jessica picked herself up from the floor and dusted herself off. She could see none of the filth on her, but she could feel it. She was ready to lay into Ari, Loretta, Arrikos, whoever the hell that person was. Before she could unleash her rage, she saw he was completely distraught.

Tears were falling down Ari's face, revealing the bits of mascara he hadn't quite gotten off before they were washed away as well. He was heaving, he felt sick, and he could hardly breathe. *This was a terrible idea.... What did I think I could do here, anyways?* he thought, clenching his nails into the palms of his hands.

"Let's go back home, Loretta." Jess held a hand down, ready to get her to her feet and off to the inn. "And I mean Loretta. I do not care much for Ari. Good-bye Winston, wherever you are! Keep up the good work!"

"I... I still have my job?" Loretta sputtered out between loud hiccups.

"Of course, you are the best maid in the world. That, and I can see you have strong hands. I truly need a shoulder rub after today."

She was smiling as they walked, helping Ari to recover slowly from the traumatic reunion. They got themselves out of the Northwest borough within minutes, happily emerging into the familiar slums of Westend.

"I am very sorry for all that. He is a disgusting, vile creature, which is why I didn't say anything before. He brings out my very worst. You must think I am just as awful. I am the inbred loon, Arrikos the XXI, after all."

"Arrikos, I do not know. I may have seen glimpses today, but for the most part I just saw a pair of siblings with a rather bizarre relationship. That does not matter, for it is Loretta I hired. She is my dear friend and definitely no one's brother. Let us leave Ari and Aldy behind in that filthy loft."

Loretta grabbed her hand, stopping her diligent march. Jess turned and was sad to see tears still falling. Before Jess could say anything, she was embraced hard. "You are truly the sweetest creature to walk this globe. Thank you for understanding. You are the only one who does."

Jess stared in her eyes, a man's face but a kind woman's heart glowing back at her. She saw Loretta was desperately debating whether to lay a kiss on her or not. Jess was flattered but simply gave her another hug before pulling her down the road. "I'm starving! Roland is probably asleep at his post. Let's make sure we haven't gotten robbed!"

"Let's!" Loretta cried gleefully, thankful she had crossed no lines.

They made it back to the lodge by nightfall. To their surprise, Roland was not asleep. In fact, he had cooked them dinner. It was burnt and inedible but still quite a kind gesture.

Their night had a genial end; the three friends drank and ate scraps until midnight. I, on the other hand, had horrible chest pains and barely slept. Aldrious was placed in shackles; his neck, arms, and legs were bound to the point that circulation practically ceased. He was snapped back to consciousness each time he dozed off by a studded flail to the face. Loretta, Jessica, and Roland had happy dreams enough to make up for Aldrious's and my lack thereof. Knowing the cardinal got what he deserved allowed them to sleep happily for many moons to follow, even if his good-bye was a bit complicated.

CHAPTER 18

May 13th, 989

"OI, ZAN, you awlright?" Shemmy called to my brother, near the end of their last full day of travel. He had been walking ahead of them all since leaving Param two days earlier. He had barely spoken, and he paid no attention to Shemmy. She forced her horse to catch up to him. She was lonely and quite through giving him his space.

"No, and I don't want to hear any of your stupidity right now." He would not slow nor look at her.

"Geez, who shat in your stew?"

"Did you not hear me? I don't want your obnoxious voice in my ears, dammit!" He reached to shake her but stopped himself. He was not mad at her. He was upset at Micah, at Billiam, and at himself.

This leg of their trek had been nothing but white and gray. The thin, naked trees were thick, and the path was rocky; however, the lack of vegetation made the landscape look blank and endless. The monotony, the cold, the loneliness around him and within him were creating an aching pit in his stomach. He didn't want to speak; he was so empty already. He felt if he let his words, his air out, his body would just collapse. He couldn't tell Shemmy this. These were his real feelings, the ones he thought didn't make sense and couldn't be related to.

"Pfft, dinnae fink you'd had enough 'bloom to be wifdrawlin'…. Seems like it, though, moody for no reason like a damn junky."

"*No reason?*" he asked her pointedly, stopping his march at once and locking his eyes with hers. He had reason, he was empty, and he was going to crumble apart. The only thing he was ever certain he wanted would never be his. Why did he not tell her that? He finally showed her feeling, but he made himself angry when he wasn't. He was heartbroken, which is what he should've shown her. She could have actually helped him with that, I think.

"Aye, I said no bloody reason. Ain't nuffin' changed except you gettin' a scoldin' the other day. Well I got one too, so get over it. Some fockin' warrior you is, hurt by the tantrums of a child." She did not respond well to undue rage and would serve it back to him tenfold.

My brother began laughing, quietly at first, though it grew deranged as Billiam and Micah drew nearer. "Are you both stupid and blind, Shemmy?"

"The fock I am not!"

"Well, then you should see the six-and-a-half-foot reason walking over to us as we speak."

"Oh, that old noise? Is that really why you've been all clammed up? Was'nae you sayin' 'Shemmy I love ya' and 'Shemmy is so smart an' pretty'? What of all that shite, you pathetic arse? You know nothing of love. You know only of lyin' like a brat to get your way." She spat in his face while jumping off her horse.

Their faces were inches apart as they hissed their venom at each other. My brother was perfectly vulnerable and jilted. Shemmy was adequately invested in him and stubborn. From this, their egos created something of a perfect storm as they thrashed against each other. Neither had hated the other nor was even directly angry, but as they spoke a violent rage warred between them.

"What the hell are you two doing?" Billiam called over to them. Micah dismounted and walked over as well, holding his hand.

"Oi, here's the man of the hour. Go ahead, Zan. Tell him how hurt the poor faelock is. So enamored, although you cannae even admit you like cock. Sure that's true fockin' love!"

"Not everyone is as comfortable being a disgusting sexual deviant as you are!"

"Ezzackly my point, Zan! How can you love him if ya find the way you feel about him revoltin'? Give it up, ya self-loathin' piece o' shite! You ain't in love. You deserve not a shred of that man's attention. Yer obsessed, dangerously and *deviantly* obsessed. I dun care what kinda creature you be; love is never sumfin' as ugly as what you have!" She was screaming and belligerent, shaking her arms wildly, and yet she wasn't trying to hurt him.

Zan was biding his energy, desperately trying to not grab his sword. He looked at Billiam instead of Shemmy, something he probably shouldn't have done. "But… I do love you!" he screamed, forcing himself to fall to his knees so he wouldn't run over to him.

Billiam was shocked and terribly confused. There had been no warning of this dispute brewing. There was tension, yes, but no more than usual. He grabbed the prince, holding him closely in front of him. He felt as long as Micah was between them, my brother would do nothing drastic.

"Zan, what has happened? Why are you distraught so suddenly? And Shemmy, why are you in such a fit with him about it?" He spoke earnestly. He was both heartfelt and concerned.

"Please…. Do not speak kindly to me, Billiam. I cannot bear it." Zan was pathetic, crying with his face in the snow.

"Whatever you two are arguing about, any pitiful feelings you think you have for my lover, it does not matter. Zan, just continue walking paces ahead of us. We shan't speak to you, as you are in no state. We must continue, understood?" Micah was commanding, his voice sounding quite masculine despite the lovely pink gown it emerged from. He was ready to resume traveling immediately.

"I dun wanna fockin' see him, make him walk behind us. We can tie his neck to one of the horses," Shemmy grunted out.

"I don't care what either of you want. I care only that we make it to City of Alafor swiftly. Reclaiming Casperland is what matters, not your feelings, not even my own. Stop acting like children and stifle your emotions at once. Zan, can you continue, or must I kill you now?"

"No, I can't." My brother was still forcing his head in the slush, clenching his fists.

"You owe me a finger for that. Now get the hell off the ground!"

"Get me off it, you stupid shit!" Zan rose to his knees, frantically screaming at Micah.

As soon as Billiam heard an insult slung at his prince, he ran to smash his fists against my brother. This is what he wanted, to have Billiam touch him, to be near him. He wanted to make him feel better, give him pleasure, even if it was by letting himself get beaten to a pulp.

He reached up his intact hand, letting his index finger collide with the plummeting fist. The pitiful appendage snapped back, flying toward his face. Billiam was able to reach his jaw, even with the interruption. His brain jostled in his head, like it was vibrating within his skull, but the real feeling was in his heart. It was bursting; he felt so joyous to make Billiam happy.

Zan was brimming with pride as he lifted up his hand to show everyone. The finger was flung against the back of his hand, gruesome and contorted, but still clinging on. "Billiam, will you take it?"

Micah was disgusted. Zan had taken his own game and used it to get close to Billiam, albeit in the most masochistic way imaginable.

"No! My rules, my fingers!" Micah screamed while running the few yards over to them and landing against my brother with all his force. Zan barely moved but was effectively stunned.

"Micah, please, you shouldn't act violently. Let me do this unsavory business," Billiam implored him.

"Billiam, you truly don't get it? He wants you to touch him, to get pleasure from hurting him. He is using me to use you, so please, stop letting him look at you. I appreciate your concern, but I will do this." Micah looked at him sweetly, making a pushing motion to bid him to leave. He then ripped off Zan's broken finger easily, chucking it into the woods.

My brother groaned but stayed transfixed on Billiam. *Do you love when I am punished? You treat me so kindly, Billiam....* Those were some of the sick thoughts in my brother's deranged head. He was always obsessive and pathological, but he was obviously getting much worse. Everything about this journey was driving him to the edge; certainly he would soon fall off it and likely be laughing.

"That was for the lie. You also made Billiam touch you, which went against my second rule. How boring would it be for both rules of the game to have the same prize? I have always loved the color violet!" Micah squealed gleefully as he plunged two fingers into Zan's eye socket, ripping out his lavender-iris clad eyeball. The thing slipped in his fingers, making a deceptively silly sound as blood spurted from my brother's skull.

Zan was cackling and Micah laughed with him. Billiam was, of course, vomiting. Shemmy watched the prince's face closely, but his eyes never turned black. She ran over to him anyway, dragging him to their horses. He thrashed in her arms, getting blood on both of them and throwing the eye down during their struggle. She didn't care about that; she knew they needed to get going, to be away from there. They were quite literally tearing each other apart in the woods for *no reason*.

"Does this make you happy, Billiam? Does my pain please you? I hope it does, your pain pleased me before. I'd like for us to be even." Zan was still laughing; he had lost it. He no longer wanted to die. He felt happy, and this was how he could show his love. He surprised them all by jumping to his feet as if he felt just fine.

"Zan, shut your filthy mouth!" Micah screamed at him, thrashing about as Shemmy held his arms. He had been overcome, but his eyes stayed blue. Was violence not the trigger? She was wracking her brain, amidst kicking herself for making things worse.

As Zan walked over to the horses, he passed by Billiam with a kind smile, his one eye sparkling. It confused him, as he never truly hated Zan, regardless of what they had been through. We had all grown up together, and despite my brother's constant façade, he knew him well. Before the last year, they had been the best of friends. They could never be more than that, but Billiam never expected they would become this. He thought Zan's feelings would fade with the prince brought back; instead they just became desperately distorted.

"I don't think we should stay in an inn as we had planned. I am not something the public should see in this state." Zan was grinning and speaking calmly as he lifted a lit match to his finger stub. It went out. He lit another, and must've held it to his eye socket, though no one dared to look.

"Fine. You two can watch us, then. I don't care anymore," Micah said with an ugly scoff. His hands were finally free, and he grabbed the rope reins off of his horse. Uncurled, it was actually quite a long cord. "Bring me your wrists, Zan."

My brother obeyed and walked over to the prince cheerfully with his arms held out. He saw Micah was none too pleased and spun himself, connecting his wounded hands behind his back. He tied them up quickly with an impressive knot and had enough length to attach it to his horse's bridle.

"Stay behind us, faelock. I have come to agree with Shemmy. Now Billiam, get over here already," Micah commanded, sweet but stern.

Billiam woke from his shock at last and ran over to them, keeping his gaze away from Zan. He grabbed Micah, whispering, "Are you okay, Prince?"

"I will be tomorrow. I need him to at least confess his sins to his fiancée, and then I might cut this short. It is not safe for us to be around him, especially you."

He kissed the prince for reassurance and picked him up, setting him atop his horse. Despite the effort, Billiam felt entirely unsoothed. In all their years together, he had never seen Micah behave violently. The young prince even contested the murder of spiders within the palace, requiring the servants to relocate them instead. Knowing of the defective stitch, seeing the torture he endured at the hand of the cardinal, empathizing with his desire for revenge, all of this had made it possible for Billiam to rationalize Micah's behavior thus far. The escalating brutality and pathetic state of his victim were making it painful to do so. He would mention nothing of these feelings, however. He swore undying loyalty to his king, and madness wouldn't budge that, not yet at least.

"I can take care of myself, Micah. Do not worry," he whispered up.

"Of course, Billiam, but I'd like to care for you too. I can notice things you do not, and you do the same for me. We are partners, and everything we do, we do together. I'll love you forever, as always."

Billiam repeated the phrase, albeit with a heavier heart than usual. They still walked hand in hand the rest of the day's trek.

Shemmy not only refrained from speaking the entire walk, she hadn't even giggled or taken a single wee break. Body slamming, finger ripping, eye gouging, those were all extremely violent acts, and yet he was the prince the whole time. What had triggered the defect before? It didn't seem to be violence, and it couldn't have simply been arousal, or else he would be a black-eyed cannibal half the time he was even near Billiam.

The camp they picked was on a whim, like the ones they had chosen prior to the attempted abduction. No one wanted to speak to Zan to hear his opinion on where to retire. He didn't care; he was blissfully content.

The first thing Micah did was tie my brother to a tree, yards away from where they set camp but within eyesight. He cared little whether he attempted to flee or not. After, he sat with Billiam at the fire he had struck up for them.

Shemmy ruined their silent, cozy snuggling by suddenly commanding, "Micah, I need to examine you." She was already lifting him up by the arm.

"Ack! Fine, but do anything pervy and I might have a child's tantrum."

"Should I supervise?" queried Billiam.

"No, Dandy. I ain't doin' nuffin strange. I just wanna make sure the enchantment is holdin' up fine."

Micah gave him a reassuring wave before disappearing behind a cluster of barren, frosty trees. "What's this all of a sudden?"

"Oi, first, uh…. Micah, I'd apologize 'bout what I said but…."

"There's no point if you aren't sorry," he said dismissively but didn't look particularly offended. He appreciated her honesty; she was shamelessly true to herself, even at the expense of her own king.

"Right, good, you understand." She was grinning as Micah scoffed. Appreciative of it or not, he wasn't really liking it at the moment. "'Kay, let's get started. Can I have you in your skivvies, den?"

"My whats? Are you really examining me? I thought you just wanted to talk about Zan or something."

"Your underfings, love. And a hearty hell no to that! He deserves neither of our attention no more." She was helping Micah to remove his pretty clothes, gingerly placing them on a clean-looking rock nearby. She did not want to see Billiam's reaction should they be ripped or sullied.

"Do you even know how to check the enchantment? I thought this was all experimental?" He grimaced as she traced along his body with her needles.

"I know, but I 'ave to try and see if I can help ya, so I'm winging it. I can check the strength of other revived materials, so why not wif you? Imma make sure that physically yer all recovered, as dat's important; however, what I really wanna check is the repair of your soul. I dun fink I can fix anyfing, but it might help me narrow down the trigger."

"So we've decided it's not violence?" He couldn't help gasping as he saw the needles fly into his chest and sit there, even though he felt nothing but warmth, just like before. Shemmy stared forward hard. He felt as if he were with a physician and she was burning her eyes through his record of health.

"No, cannae be. I suppose that's all you. Yer prolly borrowin' strength from the defect, but other than that, I am quite sure the rage and intent are yers."

Micah's face fell. He was dearly hoping it wasn't all him. Learning of the defect made him feel far less monstrous for his treatment of Zan. He did not regret it; he simply worried for the safety of the soul she was probing. "Thank you for taking care of me, Shemmy. Anything?"

Shemmy didn't look angry at all anymore, not at my brother or anything else. She was concerned and loving once again. "I cannae tell anyfing. T'all seems fine, in the practical sense. I really wanted to 'elp." She pushed her needles in her dress before turning to get Micah's clothes. "I just wan' ya to be yer perfect little self. I'm sorry, Micah."

"Shemmy, you are so kind. I do appreciate it!" Micah reached out to hug her and placed his hand on her waist. "*I have to stop it.*"

That voice was not Micah's. It was deep, it was cold, and it was inhuman. Shemmy thought she had learned nothing from this examination, yet to her surprise, a pair of completely black eyes stared at her. "Who are you, then?"

"There is evil in you. I need to get it out. I must remove the rot. You will understand." The voice was calm, and Micah's face was not moving, yet his hands viciously grabbed at her midsection. The air grew incredibly thick, choking in her throat, as Micah moved faster than she could think.

"Fockin' hell!" She screamed as Micah's fingernails broke her flesh. She grabbed out her needles and parted the snow-covered dirt from below the prince's feet by dashing them across each other in a downward motion. The earth hollowed, piling itself all around him. He thrashed and almost managed to get out, yet Shemmy forced the evicted soil back atop him.

Billiam heard the sounds of struggle and ran over. By the time he arrived, Micah was buried three feet in dirt. His eyes were normal again, and he was terribly frightened. Shemmy dropped to the ground, panting and holding Micah's dress, which had become filthy.

"Why are you buried?" he screamed, while fervently digging up his lover. "What in the world is going on, Shemmy?"

"What did I do? I don't remember! I was about to give her a hug, then I was in the ground!" The crying fit had started up, just like before. Billiam had him pulled up quickly and was brushing off the dirt with his hands.

"You were talkin' ta me. Well I guess it was'nae you, but yeah, the black eyes and such 'appened. It started when ya touched my waist. Yer voice was all diff'rent, scary-like." She was extremely shaken and quite unwilling to get up off the ground.

"What did I say?" Micah implored amongst the tears. He remembered the soft touch of Shemmy's flesh as he hugged her, and holding his hands together, he felt it again. He looked in horror at his short dirty nails, seeing the tiny bits of skin he had ripped from her. From that soft feeling until this moment, the only thing he could recall was the overwhelming smell of moist earth. As his crying fit carried on, he was able to think despite it. He remembered how terribly hungry he was before they came over for his exam; he now felt entirely sated.

"It did'nae make no sense." She shook her head as she allowed Billiam to help her up, handing him the dress, ashamed at its condition. "You said you was gonna stop it, evil an' rot wos in me an' you'd get 'em out. Then you started scratchin' me up."

"What? Why?"

"How the hell should I know?" She watched as Billiam worked quickly, simultaneously dressing the prince and wiping up all tears with his sleeve. *"The rot out... what is rotten...."* She was thinking hard, for that word was resonating with her. Surely she had used it plenty as a euphemism for shit or a term for garbage, but there had to be a deeper meaning.

"So none of it means a thing to you?" Billiam asked, sitting on the stone that had housed Micah's clothes. He held the dressed prince against his lap and stroked his cheek. It looked as if every speck of dirt had been miraculously erased.

"I feel like the term rot, as in someone having it, is something I recall from my childhood. I cannae remember why, though."

"Well, what could be in you that Micah would want to get out?"

"Hey!" objected the prince. "I don't want anything out of her. It wasn't me."

"I know. I'm sorry, Micah. It's a bit of a strange thing to know how to speak about. You haven't anything embedded in you for enchanting, right? Or something from birth due to being the family heir?"

"Nuffin' embedded in me. Where ya get such an idea?" she asked with a laugh.

Billiam grinned at her and ran his finger over his eyebrows.

"Oh, I suppose I'm a bit modified den, ain't I? Never knew you had such wild imaginings 'bout me, Dandy! As far as the DuBois thing, the heir is chosen if you are born wif the sister's shroud, which I was, obviously. But it was an apparition on the face, not inside me, and it was cleaned off afta birth. I do have this stupid doll called Chammerline's soul, supposed to house the first one's in it. I have cut it up before, though. Ain't nuffin but straw and mites inside. Zan's holdin' it anyways, so Bad Micah could'nae have gotten it."

"No! No dolls for Zan! He is but a servant now. Why should he receive niceties from any of us?" Micah shouted childishly. His hands were clenched into fists, enraged that he would leech comfort from his lover so masochistically and still have a bit of Shemmy to hold onto. Little did Micah know my brother didn't even notice he had the doll—he was just used to having it in his pocket.

Shemmy shook her head; she dearly loved her boy, but his spoiled side made her weary. "I will take it back, not to worry, Micah. We should get back to camp anyhow, and I can see if mebbe you do react to the doll. Mebbe yer stitch thought I had it."

"My stitch? Yes, that's a good way to put it. I do not want to be blamed for hurting my dear Shemmy, nor do I want to think of a 'Bad Micah.'" He looked at her longingly, wishing to apologize, to hug her, but he was too afraid.

Billiam picked up on this desire, so he wrapped his arms around the prince from behind. With Micah's arms held to his sides, he felt safe to carry him to Shemmy to give her a kiss on the cheek.

Micah was delighted to be able to do so and giggled as he spoke to them both, "Oh thank you, Billiam! And thank you, Shemmy, for taking care of me even more!"

"O'course, cupcake. Let's go play dollies den, shall we?"

Billiam followed her, enjoying carrying the powerless prince a bit longer. He was squirming and pretending to struggle, adding to his man's delight. His demeanor turned more flirtatious as Zan was in view, thrusting backward and biting his lip. My brother's jealousy was already to a violent level; I do not understand Micah's desire to consistently increase it, yet he did.

"Awlright, Billiam, keep hold of yer captive while we try dis."

"Gladly, my lady," Billiam replied, easily tossing the prince up to cradle him in his arms instead. Micah made sure to loudly kiss his new surroundings as they descended around my brother.

"To what do I owe all this attention?" Zan asked, feeling quite curious. He had untied himself but kept his hands behind his back. Seeing Micah frown, he explained himself genuinely, "It was itchy, and it was inhibiting the clotting of my hands. I have no intention of leaving or harming you. You know I am not lying."

"Fine, give Shemmy her doll back," Micah commanded, disappointed that he was unable to punish Zan for anything.

"You wan' me ta grab it, hence yer hands an' all?" Shemmy asked.

"No, I'm fine." He grimaced as he pulled the doll out of his pocket, at first from the pain and after when he realized he had lied. He got himself off the ground and handed Shemmy the doll before presenting his right hand to Micah. He decided he'd rather lose a third finger than a second.

"This is your one free pass, Zan. You lied to spare strife for the lady, so I don't really want your finger. This will not happen again, understood?" Micah shocked them all by shoving Zan's hand back into him. He smiled, quite impressed with his slave's obedience.

"Since we ain't dismemberin' each other, be we ready to try dis out?"

Billiam nodded to her, so she readied the doll in her hand. My brother looked on in awe, as he had no idea what this was about and knew nothing of either time Micah's eyes turned black.

"Okay, hold him tight, he gets rill strong and rill fast."

She was thinking hard about how to do this. Should she just touch the skin on his arm with it or throw it on his face? She decided to place it in his hand instead. Billiam obliged, letting the prince move his wrist slightly. Shemmy set the doll in his smooth palm, jumping at least three yards back as soon as she let go.

The three of them sat breathless for what felt like an eternity, while Zan began to laugh quietly. It was really strange to see them so terrified of the prince holding a doll. He thought it suited Micah perfectly.

"Nothing is happening, right?" Micah asked, looking up at Billiam who just shook his head.

"Really? Huh. I thought we was getting somewhere, but I guess my Chammerline would'nae have nuffin to do wif the first time." She skipped back to them and grabbed the doll. To be sure, she started touching it all over the prince's body. It was extremely old and dirty, and dampened by my brother's sweat. It was gross enough to make even Micah uncomfortable, who was hardly as fastidious as his betrothed.

"I think it's no use, Shemmy," Billiam informed her sternly, blocking the doll from touching his lips.

She obeyed and went to throw the doll back to Zan, before a glare from Micah stopped her dead in her tracks. "Right, she'll go in a saddlebag, den."

"Um…. Your Highness, do you mind me asking what is going on? I understand if you do not want to indulge me, but this an extremely curious scene I just witnessed," my brother asked, on his way to sit back at his tree.

"Let us go back to the fire to discuss it. It is getting quite dark. You will, of course, still return here to sleep." Micah tugged on Billiam's arm, alerting him he was ready to be set down.

He obliged him and was happily surprised as the prince wrapped his arm around his waist, pushing him ahead. Micah really did want to take care of him, to protect him from Zan.

"Thank you, Your Highness," my brother replied, quite earnestly.

"Spare me your sniveling!" Micah shouted whilst playfully pushing Billiam into the earth as they reached the fire. He curled in his lap while grabbing some bread and ale from their food basket that sat behind them. His hunger had not returned, but he wanted to make sure Billiam ate. The ale would be for them both, as he was feeling quite vexed. "Shemmy, you witnessed the most of it, followed by Billiam. I think you would explain it best."

"Awlright, Micah. I can do that." She was helping herself to some of the jerky and swallowed it down with the prince's ale before continuing. "Well in Param, they was doing naughty stuff, and Micah bit Billiam rill bad."

"Oh, is that when I flew down the stairs? I fell back asleep and forgot to even ask what happened. You bit him?"

"Yes, *I* was fucking *him* and got carried away it seems." Micah gloated as he stared Zan down.

"I think I'd liken that to sitting on a thumbtack," Zan muttered. He was pale white from the injuries, so the prince was unable to tell how much he had gotten to him. He definitely had, as my brother foolishly thought he would be the only one to do that to Billiam, after damaging him so. He wanted to reach out and snap Micah's neck and throw his head into the woods, as he had done earlier to his finger. Instead, he sat motionless, waiting to hear the rest.

"He's not dainty everywhere, a happy surprise even for me. I'd say he's my perfect fit," Billiam defended, beaming with pride and effectively plastering a huge albeit bashful grin on the prince's face.

"Yes, yes, boys. Micah is a man too; we get it. Can I move on, or do ya all gotta whip 'um out and compare notes?" she asked, wanting to sound angry, but knowing Shemmy that wouldn't bother her at all.

Since she heard no objection, she got further along with her account. "Right, well technically, he *ate* a chunk of his shoulder. Billiam said his eyes turned all black, but when his teef was off, he turned to regular, sweet Micah again and could'nae remember none of it. The black eye fing happened again juss now. It was juss me and the prince. I was checkin' on the enchantment. He reached for my waist ta hug me, and then, boom, 'twas Evil Micah. His voice changed, and he clawed at me, sayin' he had to get sumfin' outta me. Billiam's runnin' over afta I buried him seemed to snap him out of it."

"Now it's been upgraded from Bad Micah to Evil Micah? I thought we were calling it the stitch!" Micah objected.

"Well, he does'nae know 'bout the defective stitch. Neva told him."

"It doesn't matter," my brother said calmly. "I know what is inside you, not that I have any idea what the Bad Micah's stitch would want with it."

"What? How would you know? And how do you know you know? Is this your fault?" Micah wailed. He had finished all his ale and fell into Billiam, getting a bit caught up.

"I can feel the blood-bond."

It sounded like something simple, yet it made no sense to either Shemmy or Micah. Billiam clenched Micah extremely tight after he heard Zan's reason. His hand closed hard around the prince's frail wrist, forcing him to yelp. "Billiam, stop! You are hurting me! Are you okay?"

He let go of his wrist and kissed the top of his head before releasing him completely. I guess the kiss was an apology, but his face was full of rage and fear. He knew exactly what a blood-bond was. As a halflock, those were the only ones he felt. He got up abruptly and asked, "So, you have sown your seed then, Zan?" He had his back turned to them all, making Micah extremely concerned. He couldn't bear hearing Billiam sound so cold.

"Well that's a way to put it, I suppose. Shemmy carries my child."

"What? Billiam, I have no idea what he is talkin' 'bout!" She shuffled backward on her butt, feeling that somehow increasing her distance would also increase her innocence.

"The only time it could've happened was when you watched us, no?" Micah asked suddenly, sounding oddly excited.

"Watch? I dinnae watch nuffin!"

"Right, of course you would know if something happened between them. You felt no need to tell me our friend was sleeping with that monster? And watching us?" Billiam's back was still turned. He was enraged at all of them, and he couldn't decide who had angered him the most.

"Shemmy, lying is pointless," Micah berated her before trying to reach out to his angry lover. "Billiam, I am sorry. You can thoroughly punish me later. For now it is extremely important I know the truth. The only time you could have possibly 'sown the seed' was when you were watching us, right?"

"That was the only time I was inside her, yes," Zan answered, amused.

"Oh, but you have been carrying on with him otherwise, Shemmy? I thought you hated him. I thought you were my friend.

I understand being civil, but that doesn't mean you should go and polish his knob!"

"Oi, Billiam, wait, I'm really—"

"Quiet!" the prince screamed, effectively getting Billiam to turn at last as well as commanding the others' attention. "If you two conceived a child at that moment, the only reason you did so was because of what you saw. Had Billiam not been making love to me on that cliff, the child would not exist, right?"

"That is correct," Zan answered calmly. "Why is that so important, Your Highness?"

"Well, perhaps you and Shemmy are my surrogates. I know it doesn't technically work that way, but it is not as if I can create an heir on my own with the person I love. As I see it, the two of you would have never even considered copulating had you not been peeping on us. Thus the child was created from the love between Billiam and I alone."

Billiam looked sick, but he did not give in. He sat back down with the prince and held him close. This talk of surrogacy and an heir made him extremely anxious, but remembering his first time with Micah brought a wave of happiness, whether they had been watched or not.

"Yes, I follow that, Micah. I would not have touched her had we not been in such a situation," conceded Zan.

"Such a situation? You say it like it was an accident. You don't accidentally climb a cliff to watch your former lover fuck, and you don't stumble and drop your dick into his friend." Billiam's regained calm was wavering, so Micah held his hand and fought away the jealousy summoned by the term "former lover."

"It was not premeditated, is all I meant."

"The fuck it was not!"

"No! It really was'nae, dammit!" Shemmy screamed as she crawled up close to the fire again. There were tears stinging in her eyes, and her voice was extremely shaky. "Ya, I was up there watchin' yas. I had been, and I know it ain't right. I never once learnt how to control myself, and I know I can be disgustin'. But I swear to Spirit, to all the energies of the globe, I meant ta juss watch. I am really, really sorry." She choked down more tears as Billiam's face only hardened further.

"You gave me an emission in my sleep. I only went up there to wash in the creek, when Shemmy found me and invited me to watch with her," Zan explained, free of any malice.

"You are so pathetic and revolting, Zan. Do not blame this on me or your species," Billiam fired back.

"We dinnae intend to, though! We were watchin', and it was just so sensual. Yer so masterful, Billiam, we could'nae 'elp it."

"I don't need you to tell me how well I fuck. I have Micah for that. His opinion actually matters." He grabbed the prince and forced him into his lap, but he did not hurt him this time. He needed to hold onto him, to gain sanity from the loving presence. If he did not hug him, he felt he would kill one of them.

Micah looked up to him concerned, whispering softly, "I agree it was a violation. I am sorry I didn't tell you. I should have been upset, but as I remember things instead of being told, I think I am forced to feel the way he did about them."

"No, prince, it's not your fault." He hugged him tighter and wanted them to be alone. He also really wanted this journey to be over; it had become completely overwrought with hormones and lunacy. "How do you even know so soon, Zan? That was what, five days ago?"

"Faelocks and halflocks grow fast I guess. I'm not sure. My blood-bonds are extremely weak, so there was nothing competing with this new presence. I think the spark was lit, meaning the soul created, in Param. That's when I first felt this warmth," Zan answered him, but didn't look up. He felt a peace thinking of that being inside Shemmy, and he didn't want Billiam's hatred for him to break it.

"Well, spark or no, it has'nae a will o' it's own yet. I can stop dis fing, and then Micah should'nae try and rip me open," Shemmy grunted out from her knees, where she had kept her face buried.

"No! Did you not hear me? That child was created out of Billiam's love for me. It is not yours to dispose of! It is my heir! I will not have you kill Ella!" Micah shouted. His cheeks were bright red from the ale, and he swayed a bit as he pouted.

"You really want this, Micah? You want *his child*?" Billiam asked him, both concerned and disturbed.

"No, she isn't his. She is ours. I really, honestly believe that. I felt her presence before, when we were in Param, just like Zan did. That must be when I, you know… but I feel her, and I love her, and I know she is mine. I would have never expected to start a family so soon, and I understand if you are not ready but…."

"I ain't even agreed to let this fing live in me rent free anyhow! Ain't ya forgettin' your stitch wants to tear it apart and destroy it? How are ya gonna be able to raise it?"

"You will find a cure for him. We have nine months, do we not?" Billiam held Micah tight, allowing the prince's joy to pass into his own heart. He did not feel ready to be a father, he did not like the idea of how this child came to be, but he could understand where the prince was coming from. He would need an heir, and as bizarre as this was, it truly was the closest thing to two men conceiving a child on their own. Whether he felt prepared or not, he could and would do anything for Micah.

"I guess I should'nae anyhow. Yer kind is endangered, right?"

"I am not his kind; we are not the same!"

"No, but Ella will be a halflock, just like you." Micah smiled up at him, cutting away a few layers of anger. It warmed Billiam's heart immensely to hear his late mother honored so. "Will you carry my child, Shemmy? I am your king, but I would never dare order you to do something like this."

"You needn't order me. I will do it. I should'nae have let this happen in the first place. I am very sorry, Billiam. I hope I can earn your trust, your forgiveness. I know I owe you at least this much." Shemmy felt extremely guilty. Regret was not something she felt often, but she was not an immoral person. Despite how wild she was, she had her own code for how she lived her life. Betraying her friends was definitely against it.

"If this hadn't happened, we would not have our baby. I will try to let my rage subside, but forgiveness is out of the question. I should have never opened up to you. You gave me your word. You said a kiss and a cat and you would be satisfied. You have no respect for me, for my privacy, for what is sacred to me. I will show you respect because I am a decent man, but I shall never trust you again," Billiam responded coldly, staring her hard in the eyes.

"Billiam, just think of her as a tool for the mission and the carrier of our child, and she will surely cease disappointing you. You said our baby!" Micah chirped up to him.

The prince's words cut like a knife through Shemmy's heart. She was a lovable weirdo no longer; she was now an insidious violator. She hated hurting Micah, making him feel that callously toward her. She still loved him regardless, and he was still her child. She wanted to give him everything, and she would, even if he couldn't love her back.

"Your Majesty, it would be my honor to carry your heir," she said in an oddly elegant voice, getting up to execute a perfect curtsy.

"Thank you, Shemmy. Do take care of yourself, as you hold very precious cargo. Will you tie Zan back up for me?"

"Yes, m'lord."

She walked over to Zan, expecting to have to lift him up. Instead, he got up on his own, walking ahead of her to the tree. "How you want it?" she asked when they arrived, holding the rope.

"What, are we really doing that again?" He laughed as he fell back hard into the tree. He was exhausted and ready to sleep, with or without waking.

"Right, I'll tie yer fockin' neck up, then."

"Whatever you need to do, Shemmy. I can't believe how willing to obey the little shit you are, giving up your body for his whims. You aren't even a citizen of Casperland as of yet. Why do you belittle yourself so?"

She had the cord wrapped three times around his neck, using the last bit on his hands. "I love that boy. I'd wager to say I love him more than Billiam does, least a different kind. I will protect him the rest o' my life and give him any stupid fing he wants because I made him, you hear me?"

"Oh, so the wild witch has become a mama bear, is that it? I suppose I can see that. Now leave me, I am tired." He closed his eye and tried to lean his head over, though he could barely move it an inch.

She kicked him hard in the side, forcing him to scream louder than any of the times his fingers were ripped. "That is for the shit you pulled. You coulda told me yourself. We dinnae hafta get Billiam involved like that, not all of a sudden at least."

"It would be obvious you lied when a halflock popped out of you. It doesn't matter when he learnt of it. I do not feel bad for you, or for him, or for myself. We are all fucked-up, and it doesn't bloody matter." He was both smiling and crying quietly. He felt a mix of every feeling. A bit of bile won out, at last, as he muttered to her, "Billiam was wrong. You have only five months to cure him. That is the average gestation for halflocks. Purebloods gestate for only three, in case you are curious. You will show in a few weeks, most likely."

"Blow it out yer arse!" She smacked his head against the tree and knocked him out cold. There was a possibility he could be concussed, could die, but she doubted he'd give up that easy. She didn't care if he did, anyhow.

Shemmy was walking over to the fire but stopped short. Micah had drunk quite a bit of ale for someone with no experience with the stuff and had fallen asleep in Billiam's lap. She could hear his cute quiet snores and didn't want to disturb him. More so, she did not want to be alone with Billiam. She knew no amount of apologizing would do any good; this would take time.

She was about to sit just where she was, uncomfortable and alone, when he called out to her, "You can come over. I won't yell at you."

She skipped over happily, for she had expected it to be ages before he addressed her. Despite his invitation, he was scowling. "Can you hand me a blanket? I don't want to disturb the prince, but I require some padding."

"Uh-huh," she muttered solemnly, handing him a quilt.

As soon as he grabbed it he turned away from her coldly, erasing her presence from his mind. She recognized this behavior; this was exactly how he had treated Zan when she first met them. *Does he really hate me as much as him?* she thought to herself, distraught.

She grabbed one of the other quilts, then laid herself down a few paces away. She pulled it over her head, trying to force herself asleep. She felt more alone being with them than she had over by the trees.

As she lay there lonely, she felt some solace knowing they would be at the City of Alafor the next day. She would be reunited with those other faces she met and not have to depend on these men for her sole company. She tried to convince herself any friends, any laughter would do. It did not have to be with Billiam. She knew it wasn't true—she grew to love him quickly, yet she was too proud to accept that.

She couldn't sleep, so she thought hard on how to make Malcolm, Kat, and me as enjoyable of companions as Billiam and Micah. Her first hurdle was to remember our names, which was what she mulled over in silence until her brain finally switched off.

CHAPTER 19

May 13th, 989

IT WAS about two hours after sunrise when Micah awoke with his very first hangover. It was not that awful, thankfully, but he felt dizzy as he lifted his upper body from the ground. He instinctively went to pull on his nightshirt to cover up and found he slept fully clothed. He was confused, but seeing the smoldered-out fire pit next to him, it began to make sense.

"Good morning, Micah," Billiam whispered before sitting next to him on the quilt. "Other than you and these blankets, we are all set to go. Zan is tied up to your horse already; however, it seems there was an issue in the middle of the night with Shemmy's. It passed away while we slept, so she is working on reviving it. She is confident she can, but that it will take at least another hour."

Micah leaned into him, craning his neck up to look him over. Billiam's voice sounded distant, and his face showed only distress. He was still extremely upset about the betrayal, whereas Micah was essentially over it. This was not only due to borrowing Zan's feelings, but also to his own lack thereof. His emotions were still clouded and easily repressed, replaced with a pleasant albeit superficial joy. Regardless of why, he felt better and wanted Billiam to do so as well.

Micah crawled over to face him, leaning his back against the stump he sat in front of. "So, basically, you are telling me I have you to myself for the next hour?" he asked coyly, sitting on his lap and going in for a kiss.

Billiam moved his mouth away and frowned, before lecturing, "Micah, not only are we out in the open, it is broad daylight. Besides all that, I am hardly in the mood. We will be in Alafor tonight, as long as that horse is alive. You will have to wait."

Micah shook his head and giggled, wriggling himself closer on Billiam's lap. "You are not in the mood? Does that even happen? I think that might be a sign of the apocalypse."

"You are right, that doesn't sound like me at all. As sure as I am you could coerce me into it, that does not eliminate the danger." Billiam groaned and wanted to remain upset, but Micah's flirtation was making it impossible. He was quite irritated with Shemmy and felt if he were to let go of it and be happy, he would be letting her off easy. In reality, he was just punishing himself by forcing the bitterness.

Micah smiled triumphantly and was finally allowed to kiss him. "Well, right here as we are, I can see all behind you and you can see all behind me. It is not *that* unsafe. I could do what you did to me back in Param. That would work, would it not?"

Billiam was not entirely convinced, yet he did not stop the prince from undoing his pants. "You mean when I rode you?" he asked with a laugh, amused by Micah's ever-decreasing innocence.

"Riding? Is that what it's called? I guess I can see that, but I think you make a better horse than me," Micah whispered, as he pulled up his dress. He found there was benefit to wearing frocks other than just discretion; it seemed to also be rather convenient.

"Micah, you cannot just hop on me. You will hurt yourself. Honestly, we should really just wait" was what Billiam said; however, his actions seemed all for continuing as he reached a hand up Micah's dress.

Pleasure had encouraged Micah to bury his face in Billiam's shoulder, completely dissolving his effectiveness as a lookout. Before he could lift his eyes, a pistol was cocked against his lover's skull once again.

He looked up quickly, and though he was terrified, couldn't help himself from laughing. "What is it about the back of your head that attracts guns in the morning, my love?"

Billiam looked at his prince, not the gunman behind him, and saw he was oddly calm. There was obviously something about the person that put him at ease, so he joked back, "I must have a magnet back there. I'll have to visit a physician in City of Alafor." He began to retrieve his hand and push Micah off his lap, resulting in the gun digging angrily into his scalp.

"I don't want to see that!" grunted out the furious female voice. "Just leave him where he's at. The damn dress covers you all up, thank Spirit. Where is Shemmy?"

Billiam was about to answer honestly as he was mad enough to hand her over. Micah bounced himself up and down a few times, making him groan instead.

He placed his hand over his embarrassed man's mouth and replied, "I haven't the foggiest of whom you are speaking. Just us perverts fucking in the woods. However, outdoors isn't enough for him; he requires cross-dressing as well."

"What the hell," Billiam mumbled angrily through his fingers.

The gunwoman pulled the pistol from his head, shoving it in the prince's face instead. Billiam was finally able to look up at her, quite ready to rip her head off.

She smiled at him, a familiar goofy grin with sparkling sienna eyes. Her short hair was cleaner, but the same shade of blackened brown. There was no mistaking the resemblance, especially when Annalise DuBois spoke with her accent. "How 'bout the truth, now that I have yer precious li'l twink targeted."

"Your sister is over in the woods a good twenty yards. You will find her with two horses and a bound-up faelock. Which one are you?" Billiam asked, smacking the gun off Micah's forehead and hugging him close.

"Not important, but obviously I ain't her enemy. Carry on; you are safe. I have been taking care of all the other mercenaries on my way out here, and this region should be quite clear," she snickered as she continued into the dense albeit naked forest.

Annalise could have found Shemmy on her own, but she couldn't resist tormenting them. She had heard the entire conversation regarding safety and whatnot, hence her picking the exact moment Micah's eyes were averted to run up behind them. Getting to witness the heir to the throne seducing a man while wearing a pink frock was too ridiculous to pass up, even if she was not at all interested in dandies. She was laughing to herself her whole walk over.

"Oi, sis, there is somethin' right up yer pervert alley goin' on o'er there!" she yelled out as soon as Shemmy was in eyesight.

Shemmy had been lying under the late horse, enchanting its midsection, but wriggled out at the sound of the familiar voice. "I've already seen it! Quite delicious, are they not?" she yelled. She was nearly finished, though she wasn't certain how well she had done. She was attempting to give it second life, not just reanimate it, despite her lack of a faerie spring.

"Not my thing at all, you know that, sis. It was hilarious enough to watch for a bit before I interrupted them, but I doubt that I stopped them for long. Are all men just stupid, humping rabbits?"

"Pretty much," Shemmy laughed, holding her sister's ankle fondly before turning her needle back to the beast's heart.

"It was dead?" Annalise queried. She held her bloodstained hand in front of its muzzle, feeling its warm breath collect against her palm.

"Now it's alive!" Shemmy cackled as she got herself up. She was quite positive she had done it, a genuine resurrection; however, not a blessed one. She worried little for the stupid beast's soul, making that of no importance. "So, you got that bounty too, eh, Annalise?"

"Yes, the cardinal himself brought it, printed it at Connor's. He promised something to our brother about lifting your excommunication, but I don't trust that pious asshole with my toilet water, so I came out here after you myself. Besides that, when I saw him it looked as if he was already booted from the castle, not to mention within inches of death. How could he accomplish anything for ya in that state of disgrace?"

"Feh, dun need his pardon, I revived the damn Prince o' Casperland. He gonna take care o' me forever, owes me his life he does," Shemmy bragged, wrapping her arms around her sister's waist while being pushed off by her playfully.

Zan was hysterical, interrupting their reunion and forcing Annalise to finally notice him. "What happened to him being your babe, and you doing anything for him? Now he owes you, he is in your debt? Make up your damn mind, Shemmy. I'd be careful too; he will know anything I hear."

"Oh, so you is one to speak of two faces, eh? I was talkin' shop, idiot. I dun wan my sister to know I am wrapped around his little finger. Which I am, Micah, happily I might add, and I love you, so when you get this memory please hear this part!" She shouted the last bit in Zan's ear, making him wince in pain. She didn't do this to punish my brother; it was simply because she was worried about Micah becoming upset. She could not bear having him angrier with her, especially as she believed Billiam to be a lost cause.

"I have no idea what the hell either of you are speaking of, but I gather it means you will not return with me, sister," Annalise muttered, while looking over Zan in disgust. He was a complete mess.

"No, I am stayin' wif Micah, no matter what. How bad is it? We only had one group of bounty hunters come afta us so far, and they was awful at it."

"I have been dispatching the others as I've made my way up. So you burnt up Beatrix's troupe? Found the charred-up lot o' bastards a few days back. Thank goodness, that slut was an insult to all female mercenaries."

"That freak did all o' it," Shemmy muttered, pointing at Zan. "I thought the blonde looked familiar. She was your little heartbreaker, eh?"

"Heartbreak? Hardly. Pocketbook breaker, yeah that could be, but you can't crush steel!" Annalise yelled, toughening up her pretty face.

Shemmy couldn't help laughing at her cute baby sister's attempt at acting macho. "So we are okay to keep headin' up? You got our backs?"

"Well yeah, I already ran up to Alafor and back this morning. It's totally clear. You know you are only three hours out at your snail's pace, right?"

"The fuck? Zan, you said a whole day. Thass why I wasted time on the horse."

"I lied. I am not excited about getting to Alafor like the rest of you. Who do you think killed the horse?" Zan grunted from his pathetic seat on the ground.

"I am gonna tell the prince, ya know!" she shouted childishly, jumping in front of him.

"You don't need to bother. He will find out anyways. You loved enchanting that thing, so don't feed me your fake anger."

"You are all really weird," Annalise laughed out, slapping her hand onto her hide-covered knees. She was dressed head to toe in dark brown leather that was lined with fur. You could only see the soft tan fluff poking out around her hood. She was quite well dressed for the territory, unlike the rest of them. "I can't believe the Prince of Casperland wears girly dress and gets fucked in the woods. Connor is gonna shit himself when he hears this. It's too good!"

"Noooo! You cannae tell him!" Shemmy shouted, pushing her hands into her sister's face. "The prince needs to to get back on the throne. He cannae do that if he becomes Connor's sideshow centerfold."

Annalise frowned, kicking her boot into the dirty snow angrily. "He'd never have a dick in his centerfold, you know that, but there is no way he would'nae write about it. I cannae tell him at all, can I? I can't tell any of our family, for that matter. I sat through that for nothing!"

"How much did you even see?" Zan asked, both curious and jealous.

"I didn't see anything, but I think I know what was happening, and that is bad enough."

"Aww, my pure little sista, yer so cute!" Shemmy squealed, picking her up although barely, to show her off to Zan. "Isn't she gorgeous? She be scared of cocks, though. Yours would give her a bleedin' heart attack, but can you imagine this li'l bod on ya?"

Shemmy was patting and groping Annalise all over. She was bright red, embarrassed and furious, knocking Shemmy onto the ground as soon as she could.

"She just looks like you, only cleaner. You are both absolutely stunning," Zan answered, smiling at them. He was not lying, although he did find Shemmy more attractive because of his feelings. Annalise was just the younger model, without the passion her sister held that had entranced my brother so.

Shemmy was blushing but also looked nauseated, prompting Annalise to back up from her. "I would offer to escort you all to City of Alafor, but I am getting more creeped out by the second. Just because I am your sister doesn't mean you get to grope on me, Shemmy. Will you ever learn to keep your hands to yourself?"

"Nope!"

"Right, since you can't be trusted to act like an adult, I will be gettin' the bloody hell outta the snow and back home. I need some proof you're okay, though, something to show Connor so he doesn't have a fit."

"I'll sell ya my soul for a big kiss on the lips!" Shemmy yelled gleefully, as she ran over to her horse. She rummaged through the saddlebag lying on the ground beside it.

"What are you on about? How could I buy your soul let alone show such a thing to brother? Furthermore, you dun even like lasses. I can't understand why you act like such a creep towards your own sister."

"It's cos you is my darlin' sis, yer just so cute. You can give the kiss to Zan instead, if yer so opposed. Here's my soul, should keep brover from havin' a meltdown." She held the nasty doll and danced around her sister while dangling it out in front of her.

"I ain't laying lips on either of yas, just give it!"

Annalise was unable to rip it out of Shemmy's constantly flailing grasp until Billiam interrupted. She snatched the soul from her distracted sister when he called over, "Is the blasted thing alive yet?"

"Wha?" Shemmy called to the voice, staring at her now empty hand in defeat. She looked at him before answering and took a moment to appreciate the fact that Micah was not only wearing pants but that also his black dress had become a blouse.

"Yeah, 'tis alive, but what are the two of ya doin' here so soon? Ain't no way yer awlready spent, topman." Shemmy felt very uneasy teasing him with as tense as things were left the night before, yet she still couldn't resist showing off in front of her sister.

Billiam showed none of his usual indulgence of her. He simply gritted his teeth and kicked up the snow as he walked within reach of them. "I'm not sure what Miss DuBois here thinks she witnessed, but if you're all so curious, I had just barely begun using my fingers to tease His Majesty's—"

"Billiam Grimhart!" Micah shouted, blushing enough for both of them and stepping on his foot with the pointy heel of his boot.

He shrugged and shook his head apologetically at the prince before smirking at Shemmy. "I'm sorry, I didn't realize we are allowed intimate details all to ourselves now. I was under the impression everything was to be shared with *your dear sister.* She was obviously fantasizing up her own scenario anyways. I'd rather it at least be accurate."

Shemmy looked like she was going to cry as she began desperately pleading her case, "Hey no, it was'nae like that, just Annalise said you was... I dinnae fink of it on my own, I just—"

"It doesn't matter! Do not embarrass me to get even with her!" Micah whined up to him, tugging on his sleeves angrily but also as if he just wanted attention.

"Right, I suppose you don't deserve that, even if you should've listened to me and waited for City of Alafor," Billiam teased as he ruffled the prince's hair and pulled him close for an embrace.

"You should have listened to yourself!" he rebutted, but was happily hugging him back. Any difficulty between the two of them seemed entirely squashed, unlike the situation with Shemmy.

"All right, if you introduce me to your sister, I shan't try her for treason," Micah commanded with a small grin.

"Dis is my baby sister Annalise. She's been followin' us I guess, takin' care of bounty hunters. She will be headin' home now, though, as long as Yer 'Ighness dun object."

"Woah…. Why are you acting so polite and sheepish? Did you do something really bad, sis? You only act like this when you feel real guilty, like when ya accidentally burnt down that orphanage," Annalise questioned her sister, not acknowledging the prince whatsoever.

Shemmy kicked her hard in the knees, forcing her to bow slightly. "That does'nae matter. Show some bleedin' respect for fuck's sake. This be your king, well, soon to be, and he is showin' ya an undeserved kindness."

Annalise looked bewildered as she scratched her head and studied the completely foreign face her sister was making. She shrugged it off and kneeled in front of the prince, truly looking him over for the first time. She had been ridiculously brazen, threatening a person she was quite sure to be the heir to the throne with a pistol like that. The way he looked, though, so sweet and young, it was impossible for her to take him seriously. The DuBois never held much loyalty to the crown, as they had their own inherent power, so she was not accustomed to showing respect.

She looked into his eyes briefly, thinking, *He is stupid pretty for a boy, like they say*, before lowering her gaze politely. "Your Majesty, please forgive me," she whispered to the royal kneecaps in front of her.

"Forgiveness is not something you ask from the crown; it is something you are either granted or are not. You are lucky he is the most loving and kind king we shall ever have, as there is no doubt you've already received it," Billiam informed her coldly and grabbed her arm, pulling her back up to her feet. "Thank you for protecting His Majesty, but I will take it from here. You are going back to Drummond?"

"Aye," Annalise muttered. She was surprised to see this man smiling at her. She thought he was something fearsome with the way he spoke and how upset her sister was over him. She thought he looked pleasant, and grinned to him while conceding further Shemmy must have truly done something terrible. "You want I should do something for the prince when I get there? I have no loyalty to the church or Aldrious. I only took the bounty to help my sister."

"Do you live in Westend?"

"Nah, I have a loft with my lady friend in Southside, though she prolly kicked me out by now. She does'nae appreciate the mercenary business much. So yeah, guess I'm goin' back home to Westend."

"Perfect. I'd simply like for you to run your mouth," Billiam replied with a wicked laugh before walking over to inspect the horses.

"What does that mean?" Micah asked. He ran up to Annalise and hugged her tight, smashing his face against hers and feeling the soft fur from her hood on his other cheek.

"How are you so warm out here?" she whispered, hugging him back. She could not believe this was the future king, clinging on to her so affectionately. She also could not believe that she did not mind or that holding a young man was making her heart feel so full and happy.

"I want you to get people angry. Bad-mouth the church and the cardinal, tell them he is evil…. Actually, why don't you tell them he killed the prince? Make the people doubt His Majesty is what the church says he is so they begin to crave him. Take it slowly, of course; we don't want a revolution. It will be easier for us to succeed if Drummond is already in disarray. I think that is about all you can do," Billiam explained while stuffing Micah's pink dress inside a saddlebag. He determined he would alter that one later; the first two he had reworked before the prince woke up. It would be unnecessary, and frankly ill-advised, for the prince to cross-dress in Alafor.

"I get it, yeah. Us DuBois can cause a lotta stink, dun worry. I am sorry for the rudeness, Your Maj—"

"No, no! Call me Micah. We are friends now!" Micah cheered, punching Shemmy in the gut with those words. He did not mind her addressing him informally anymore; was she not his friend?

Shemmy grabbed her sister off Micah, feeling overwhelmingly jealous. "Fine, enough, you should get going," she grunted, pushing her sister a few feet away. "Hey, why the fock was Aldrious at Connor's place anyhow?"

Annalise brushed herself off, bowing slightly to Micah. She could not put her finger on the dynamics going on in this group, so she was eager to leave herself. She understood her sister's devotion, though; the prince was extremely adept at endearing people to him without even really trying. Slipping her gloves out of her pockets and back onto her hands, she answered coyly, "You don't know, then?"

"Know what? That bastard brutalized Micah, tortured him, and took his land. He is an evil, twisted creep, and I'm gonna destroy him. That's all I know."

Annalise shook her head and giggled softly. She supposed she wouldn't have recognized him either if Connor hadn't told her. She decided it best not to bring up the truth, as Shemmy was messed up enough already it seemed.

"Aye, I guess they was mates when Connor lived in Enox for a bit, with Ma's family. Does'nae matter, he only entertained him because he mentioned you. It all seems kinda strange, though. From what brother told me, it seemed the cardinal was genuinely concerned about ya, Micah. It was probably an act, but I feel I must ask: you do want to stay out here, right? You don't want me to tell him anything?"

"I will be back in Drummond in no time, with my one and only love over there, who you embarrassed so awfully earlier. He is the only one whose concern I need. I'd ask you to tell the cardinal to eat shit, but I wouldn't want you to get punished. Despite how he may have acted, Aldrious really did kill me. However, unlike what Billiam suggested, I do not think you should mention that. It is uncertain whether my nation would want a former corpse on the throne. Do make them angry, and let them doubt my existence in the palace. That part sounds quite brilliant." Micah grinned over to Billiam while he chatted with her. He didn't seem as taken with her as Shemmy thought; he really was just trying to make her envious.

As much as Micah appreciated her intentions, the mention of Aldrious made him want Annalise out of his sight. "You can go now. I have unsightly business to take care of before we head out. I wouldn't want to sully your impression of me any further."

Micah was snickering as he turned away from her, skipping happily over to Zan. Annalise was curious about my messed-up brother, about what her sister had done, and she had a feeling if she stayed she would soon find out.

Shemmy did not allow her curiosity to win out. She spun her sister around roughly and pushed her into the thicker frozen trees to the south.

"What is he gonna do?" she whispered over her shoulder.

"More o' the same, love," Shemmy answered, leaving a small kiss on Annalise's cheek before turning back around.

Not wanting to chance looking back, Annalise spoke behind her, "Are you sure you are okay? Micah is sweet an' all, but if he can do stuff like that... and his man dun seem to like you none. I dun wanna see ya gettin' yerself killed cos you dinnae know when to stop."

Before Shemmy could answer, they heard a bloodcurdling scream echoing from my brother. She had not heard him make any such sounds of pain yet. It was extremely honest and also terrifying.

"Like you said, sis, I am feelin' guilty. I know what to do, though, and that's redeem myself. I fink I can this time, least wif Micah. That faelock, he fucked up way worse than me, not ta worry. The prince, he *is* very sweet...." She trailed off, followed by the sound of crunching snow letting her sister know she'd be alone soon.

"You did well, Shemmy, I am proud. He is lovely and perfect, a rousing success!" Annalise cheered but ran immediately after. Despite the successful resurrection and the beautiful face that treated her so warmly, she felt nothing but unsettled by her sister's travel companions.

She knew there was no one chasing her, nothing to fear, yet Annalise could not stop running. Really, she was sprinting at top speed, and she could not make herself slow for at least two miles. She was descending one of the small peaks of the Alstair range, so the decline helped; however, it was pure adrenaline that propelled her so quickly.

The sun was quite bright for the region that day, making the snow become slush as she got farther south. A large puddle is what slowed her retreat; she slid through it and fell face-first into a large pine.

She was unsure if it knocked the wind from her or if she was simply gassed out from running so quickly in the frigid cold. She fell onto her back in the mushy frost, trying and failing to inhale for a horrifying minute. As she lay on the ground, she looked up. The sky appeared to be framed completely by the insanely tall, spindly trees all around her.

The skeletal branches were forming a crown around the sun, making her think again of the prince. She stared upon him, and she felt herself love him instantly, not a natural thing for her, and it was actually quite wondrous. Why, then, was she so scared of him?

She was pondering hard on this as she closed her eyes, taking in deep breaths at last. *I hugged you, and I even wanted to stay with you... I care nothing for the crown, for this war, hell even for boys.... Why did you make me feel like that, Prince of Casperland? Did my sister make you like that, or is that your nature? You felt so kind but so powerful.... Will we be okay in your hands?*

She shook her head before forcing herself up, clutching her knees to her chest. This wasn't like her; she was not the introspective sort at all. She was a woman of action, and she needed to keep moving. The intentions of others, the fate of her land, there was never a passing thought she gave to such matters, and it was pointless to start now. Shemmy was alive and well, she had done her duty, and now she could go home. She felt a smile grow on her cheeks as she jumped up, walking at a leisurely pace this time.

Shemmy should've easily reunited with her companions in the time that it took her sister to get her wits together. Regrettably, it was my own actions that were making this difficult for her.

That scream she and Annalise heard was not from torture. The growing madness Billiam saw in his lover was apparently abating, and Micah had no taste for violence. He was still toying with Zan and engaging in conversation over how many lies or deceitful actions he had partaken in so far that morning. It was in the midst of this that Billiam spotted the former residents of Pottleton barreling toward them and screamed bloody murder.

He gained his wits quickly and untied Zan.

Zan in turn grabbed Micah, caring little what consequence that would have and set him within Billiam's arms. "Go, just run. Get him to the capital, that's all that matters," he commanded, doing well to avoid looking at Billiam's face and thus hiding the heartbreak in his eyes.

He turned instead to watch the running mess of undead peasants. There were at least thirty of them left, none of them popsicles, but all covered in snow. They were still merely sprinting forward, but when they bumped into a tree, they corrected their path and kept moving. At the pace they jogged they were less than a minute from being on top of him.

"No, Shemmy is still out there. I will not leave her. We fight together." Billiam set Micah behind him, then grabbed out his dagger. He may have been angry at her betrayal, but he had not at all stopped loving his friend.

"Are you sure they even want to fight? What the hell is happening?" Micah cried as he clutched fearfully to Billiam's shirt. He uttered no further contest, however, and agreed heartily they ought to stay together.

Shemmy was thinking near the same thing as she watched the horde running right in front of her. There were so many she couldn't even see through them to her companions but felt entirely sure they were close ahead.

"Aye, mate, what's the rush?" she called at the decaying man nearest her. His arm was barely attached, and his flesh had turned black as coal from frostbite. Still, Shemmy had actually seen worse in a living bloke, so she figured it was worth a shot.

She got no response. A lady trailed behind him, so Shemmy stuck her bare foot out. The dead woman tripped, fell to her knees hard, then got right back up as if nothing happened.

Shemmy concluded they were mindless and harmless, much as I had, and simply joined ranks. She ran with them, pushed them a bit, and enjoyed the company. She was positive she had reached her living friends when one of the dead ones' heads got sliced right off.

"Shemmy! There you are!" Billiam screamed while pulling her into his arms. "What in Spirit's name is going on?"

"Dunno. They just running!" she chirped and hugged him back.

"No, no they aren't," Zan stammered out.

Shemmy lifted her head from Billiam's shirt to look over. My brother had Micah set on his towering shoulder. Looking lower, right at his feet, knelt one of the dead folk. Behind him sat another, its face at the back of Zan's knees but staring up to Micah. At every side of Zan there was another dead man or woman kneeling beside him but gazing up at the prince.

As soon as they got within proximity, each dead farmer that reached them did the same. The four of them stood there silent as the circle of animate corpses around them grew larger. They were packed tight, now nearly squishing Shemmy and Billiam into Zan.

"Did ya say sumfin', Micah?" Shemmy asked up while getting bumped closer. "This looks like the work of necromancers to me. Them folks be lazy. They use words and spoken spells and such, nothing fancy like weavin' energy or the like."

"No, I don't think so," Micah whispered down. He was doing his best to not make contact with the empty open eyes staring up at him. Each time he did he felt deeply cold, in spite of his warming enchantment.

"You called one disgusting and screamed for it to go away. That's when I picked you up, but they were already kneeling around you by that point," Zan corrected.

"Yes, well they didn't bloody listen to me, now did they?"

"Should we just cut through them and forge on ahead?" Billiam asked. He readied his dagger at the rotting corpse that was uncomfortably close to his right side and making him feel ill.

"They'll keep on following. The one ya decapitated is right behind me. Dunno if the Queens of Alafor will be keen on all these stinky visitors in their capital," Shemmy rebutted.

"We have to do something! I am not sitting on this monster's shoulder in the woods all day!" Micah shouted down. He cared little about Zan at the moment, but he was an easy target. What truly bothered him was that tugging feeling he kept feeling in the pit of his stomach each time a lifeless eye met his. He couldn't place it, besides a feeling akin to the heartache he felt when he was separated from Billiam.

"We gotta stop the spell. Just keep talkin', some command hasta clear 'um off."

Billiam looked all around him. There were at least five rows of kneeling corpses circling them. Beyond them and around them were equally lifeless trees, being tossed about roughly by a growing wind. Forces both unnatural and natural were conspiring against them, for a blizzard was due any minute.

"Stand up!" he shouted. Nothing happened, so he nudged his shoe into Shemmy's foot gently.

"My turn? Bugger off!"

They were only hours separated from us. The promise of revolution that I saw in Prince Micah was so very close. Once he was here, true change could finally start. Unfortunately it seemed that geographical distance was the least of our worries. The fate of our future rested on breaking a spell cast by an unknown enemy, braving the planet's vicious elements, and above all, on the extensiveness of my colleagues' collective vocabulary.

"Go away! Stand yourselves up!" Zan yelled confidently.

"All of that was already said, you ninny!" Micah chided.

In all likelihood, Casperland was doomed.

APPENDIX I

The Birth of MortiAegism

ACCORDING TO the MortiAegis faith, Corseca was originally a lifeless planet with no land on its surface, covered only with a massive ocean. The genesis of life on the planet began when the very Spirit of Existence crashed through its surface, shielded by the God Aegis. Held inside the shield of God, the Spirit fell to the core of the planet. The gorge formed by their descent was never filled; instead it created a star-shaped canyon, known as the Startspring, where the oceans continually spilled.

Trapped inside its shield, the Spirit could create no life, and it lay dormant hundreds of meters underground. Aegis knew the Spirit would dwindle if it were to remain trapped within him. He knew also how desperately it wanted to share its spark of life, so he sacrificed his stone body and stabbed out five large holes within himself. The Spirit extended its fingers through the wounds and up to the surface. Taking the pieces of Aegis up with it, the Spirit placed them around the Startspring, creating five small islands.

The Spirit of Existence used the five islands to create all the different forms of life it could imagine. Firstly, on the northern island, it began creating the sun, moon, and celestial bodies, growing them slowly until they were large enough to fly into space. On the southern island it created natural elements, growing clouds and blowing winds. On that island sands formed all around, fires burned, and rain poured from the new clouds. These creations spread across the planet, the sands building the continents that make up the world today; the fires and winds contorted the shapes of the land, building mountains and carving canyons; the rains filled in bodies of water. On the western island, the Spirit created vegetation. It grew all the grasses, the plants, the trees, the flowers, algae, sea plants, and fungi.

The Spirit was disappointed with the lifelessness of all it had created and thus gave every last bit of effort into the creations on the central island. It started with growing all species of insects to inhabit the dirt and grasses it had created. It filled the skies with birds and the oceans with all manners of aquatic creatures. Returning its focus to land, it created all of Corseca's mammals and reptiles, starting with tiny rodents up to towering elephants and mammoths. The Spirit encouraged its aquatic and avian creations to help the land dwellers so they too could spread across the planet.

After creating those many lives, the Spirit had all but dissipated, sitting within the hollow shell of the God Aegis. It poured its last essence into its shield, bestowing its blessing that Aegis create whatever he wanted with the last eastern island.

A shield with nothing to guard had no purpose, and Aegis yearned for a being worth protecting. It dwelled under the earth, pondering for what could have been centuries, on what the holder of that shield should be. He eventually dreamed up humans and came up with the form he deemed perfect. He released that last bit of Spirit up and onto the eastern island. Mankind was created and flourished on that island, and Aegis loved them dearly.

Just like the elements, the plants, and the animals before them, humans found themselves outgrowing the small island. They began constructing crude vessels and making their way around the globe, with the largest concentration on the eastern continent of Knox, as it was the closest. After approximately two hundred and fifty years, almost all the people had left. Aegis could not bear losing sight of his creation, to not watch over his humans. He could not leave Corseca's core as the God Shield he was, so he sought to change himself into the only being he knew to make. Aegis turned himself into a man, and although he was burnt to dust by the planet's molten core, his soul rose to the top of the Startspring.

Being free of a solid form, Aegis could hold dominion over Corseca and observe all of it. His soul stretched out and covered the world, finally becoming a heavenly shield for his beloved mankind. He found, however, that his creations were not behaving the way he had intended. They were living in wickedness, killing each other and summoning power from sources that were not him.

He discovered also the faeries and the ogres, creatures that were not made by Spirit or by himself, that had somehow manifested on the planet and perverted the lands. Aegis saw the vile truth within these beings and became certain it was they who had corrupted his beautiful creation.

In an effort to intervene, Aegis imbued his spirit within the one human still left on the eastern island. He was a thirteen-year-old boy known only as the prophet, who was blind, deaf, and left behind. He was on the verge of death by starvation, though Aegis merging within his body healed him. It awakened his long-sleeping eyes and ears and gave him knowledge of what Aegis' true will really was. He gave this boy instruction to spread knowledge of God Aegis' existence and to warn of the evil that was the interloping faeries and ogres.

The prophet was seen first by villagers west of the Knox city that is now known as Thornwood. All who witnessed him simply saw a scrawny brown-skinned adolescent boy with clouded eyes walk from the ocean onto the sandy beach. It was the year 252 when the prophet first emerged in Knox, and he would not explain how he arrived there. They didn't know if he could breathe underwater, walk atop it, or if he had been pulled ashore by a dolphin, and they never would. They wanted to know his name, but he didn't have one. They wanted to know his age or anything about him. He didn't know any of those things, but he wouldn't have told them even if he had. He simply walked from the sand and onto the land, toward town. He beckoned them all, "Follow me if you seek truth, should you want deliverance."

The prophet walked to every gathering of people spreading his message. It is thought year one is when Aegis first created man, yet there was no recorded language at that time. By the year 252 there were common spoken tongues as well as the beginnings of written languages. People willingly followed him. They took little convincing, and some of them were educated enough to write their experience down. Many of the believers continued trekking with the prophet, to every stop he made, while others spread the message for the prophet where they lived.

The belief in Aegis spread fast, as well as the adherence to the rules for his people he passed on through the prophet. Aegis' will for his people was simple; he merely wanted them to stay uniquely human. It was those acts, those behaviors inherent within the faeries and ogres that he could not bear to see in his creation. This included but was not limited to a few key laws, such as the condemnation of: any magical practices; violence against mankind (the faeries brutalized each other constantly. Aegis thought humanity would have never hurt one another without this influence); lying with creatures other than one's own species/bestiality (this is also a common faerie behavior); sex without sacred consent and without the intention to reproduce. (This was not from the faeries, but the ogres, with their one sex and fascination with fraternity as well as romance while never repopulating.) That last commandment listed gave fruit to the outlawing of homosexuality, adultery, polygamy, and rape.

The outlining of all Aegis' laws and ideals for his people can be found in the scripture of MortiAegis, as well as some commandments that were said to have been passed down later through divine intervention. These are not important enough to list now, as doling out rules was not the prophet's primary purpose. Aegis wanted the prophet to deliver his promise, and it was that which brought so many eager followers.

When Aegis allowed himself to become mortal, resulting in his corporeal death, he created more than just his own omniscience. His sacrifice created a new plane of existence, a life beyond the current one toiling on within Corseca. This afterlife is where Aegis' mortal body dwelled, and there he could meet with those of his children who were never corrupted by the interlopers. This heaven, as it came to be called, was the reward for living the life Aegis intended for them.

Although the prophet had no name and no blood relation to the mortal Aegis, his followers chose to refer to him as the son of Aegis or Aegison. The prophet and his growing number of followers made it to Frosthorn, the present capital of Knox and largest city on the globe even then, by the year 261. The city was ruled by a tribunal of three, made up of an ogre, a faerie, and a man. Despite the fact the prophet's words condemned two-thirds of the governing body, they were intrigued enough by the scrawny man to invite him to dine with them. The prophet did not eat, however, nor had he during any point of his travel, he simply stared from ogre to faerie the entire long meal.

The ruling ogre was an extremely wise and patient philosopher known as Casperius. He was three hundred twelve years old when he met the prophet. He had many students, who later became the settlers of Casperland. There are differing accounts as to how the silence was broken. According to ancient scholars, Casperius spoke first, informing the prophet, "I know why your God hates us. We are older than him, and we interfere with his claim; however, we do not want it."

This is utter blasphemy to the MortiAegis, and it is their belief that the prophet spoke first. He watched on, disgusted, as the three of them engaged in frivolity, gorging themselves and imbibing wildly. The prophet locked eyes with the human, Callux I, and when he did brought a tear to the man's eye. He set down his food and ale and wept for a consecutive seven days. This man had spent more time with the interlopers than any other, yet he too could be forgiven by Aegis. It was this forgiveness he saw in the prophet and the overwhelming gratitude for God's mercy that produced the weeping.

With his connection to God's child made, the prophet addressed the others at last. He asked them calmly, "How did you come to be here?"

The faerie, named Mecki, ranted and raved, getting belligerent and throwing plates across the table. It howled to the prophet not in words but directly into his mind. It screamed thoughts that they were here first, waiting for the energy to manifest. It continued on that Spirit and Aegis crashed into them, that they were obligated to take the energy Spirit wasted. They were the isolated, malicious consciousness inherent in the planet's core, which seeped out the gift of the unknowing Spirit of Existence. They didn't care that it was not of the Spirit's will that they lived and did not respect the creatures it made for that matter. Mecki just raged and screeched, fighting for its right to exist and destroy as much as it saw fit.

The prophet closed his eyes and simply whispered, "That spark was not yours to take. Return it now." The faerie ceased its movement and fell to the ground, becoming a speck of dirt, the same speck it was before stealing away the gift of life.

Casperius bowed his head to the prophet and whispered, "We knew nothing but desire before; the envy and greed was unintentional. What would Aegis have me do now?"

"Submit" was the only answer given, and it had seemed Casperius did. He stepped down from his position of power, bestowing it all to Callux I, the very first emperor of Knox. The ogre seemed to grow repentant and helped in spreading word of the prophet. He told his brothers to submit, to not fight, that their lives were not truly their own. Despite the devout attitude Casperius showed, he did not follow the prophet. He instead gathered his students and headed south.

Emperor Callux I begged the prophet to stay in the capital; however, he could not. He had more to share, many more ears and hearts to reach. The prophet made his way to the northern part of Knox before heading east to the land that is known now as Enox. In the year 274, he reached a peaceful settlement that was completely untouched by the influence of the interlopers. They had not given into any wickedness of their own accord, proving it really was the outside influence that had corrupted man. These people he found were living exactly how Aegis intended, the sight of which brought the first wave of tears any were to see fall from the prophet. He was so overcome, he could barely convey his message; however, it was obvious they understood. This encampment later became the city of Morte, home to the Temple of MortiAegis.

After spending a day with these people, the prophet was certain he had fulfilled his duty to God Aegis. He took time to speak every single influence he received from Him to the elders, a thing he had never been able to do so thoroughly. It was they who saw the true value in Aegis' death, that it was the sacrifice of His shield body that gave them His watchful eye and the immolation of His mortal self that granted them life eternal. The elders were the ones to begin praising Mortem ec Aegis, which literally meant the death of Aegis. They shortened it to MortiAegis, but the focus of their devotion was solely on this gift, not on the shield, the man, or the ethereal being.

Seeing that His children could truly understand His will and show Him such gratitude, Aegis knew He could allow the prophet's pilgrimage to finally end. It was only a day after arriving in Morte that Aegis conferred with his vessel, letting him know that he could stop. Aegis offered to continue supporting his body so he could live out a life with his brothers and sisters. The prophet had never had to eat, drink, or sleep with the essence of God Aegis dwelling inside him, but if it were to leave, his body would wither.

This was a simple decision for the prophet, as his only family, only home, had ever been Aegis. He wanted to be free of his mortal coil, just as Aegis had become, and to rejoin with him forever. The prophet once again filled Aegis with a pure joy and pride. He rewarded his servant by withdrawing his essence, leaving the body as a withered shell. The prophet was able to say good-bye, and his followers watched as his body dried up completely. It had not been hydrated or fed for twenty-two years; the husk he left clearly showed how powerful the will of Aegis was.

In the time it had taken the prophet to reach Morte, the students of Casperius rallied against this growing faith and defended their teacher. Casperius traveled far south, away from the capital, and truly had planned on submitting. His people, however, did not share his sentiment and would not be that weak. They spoke blasphemously of the life present on Corseca before Aegis, of the natural creation of the ogres and faeries. They fought the followers, rioting and defacing the churches that sprouted to worship the new God Aegis.

The emperor Callux sided with the followers of MortiAegis and began excommunicating all these heretics from the continent, chaining them to doomed rafts. Veritable war broke out between students of Casperius, as well as other nonbelievers, and the children of Aegis. Although the religious side had the backing of the crown, the undeveloped civilization was still too flimsy to hold up against the civil war breaking out all around it.

Casperius could not bear to see all this destruction caused in his name. He brought himself back to the capital, to the feet of Callux I, and laid himself down. He told of how his submission before was halfhearted, that he submitted only his power; he had done nothing with the pride in his heart. He begged the emperor to take his life, to stop all the lives being lost in his name. Callux obeyed the request and embraced his former friend before stabbing the giant's heart. It has been rumored and widely believed that Casperius died at the same moment as the prophet; however, there is no proof of it. It is certain, however, that he also died in the year 274. It is written in the Book of Aegis that it was the prophet's sacrifice of his mortal body that created the miracle of Casperius' submission. It is thought it was the final wish of the prophet that the ogre would do as he should have done all along—stop existing.

Despite Casperius laying down his life, his followers refused to accept MortiAegism as society's new master. The warring continued, but the rebellion got squashed more readily after the death of the symbolic ringleader. A mass exodus of the students of Casperius occurred in 289, when thousands of nonbelievers made their way to Centra, the continent across the Startspring.

In the absence of the dissenters, peace took over Knox, and the children of Aegis were able to worship their God with no contest. Temples sprang up all over Knox and Enox while the people thrived. They succeeded in killing all the ogres remaining in their lands and also in terrifying the faeries into retreat, hiding themselves in desolate woods and never emerging. This fulfilled Aegis' desire, leaving this land completely uncorrupted by the interlopers so that his children could live exactly how he intended.

Despite the lack of outside influence, the residents of Knox and Enox did not behave as they should have. The emperors that succeeded Callux grew more and more tyrannical in hopes of reining in their people, to force them to live in accordance to God's laws. The military grew and grew within Knox, enforcing devotion to MortiAegis as a mandate for all citizens.

Enox remained the home of the holy city where the prophet died, and although they were just as strictly devout as Knox, they did not militarize their faith. They simply organized it, creating the Mortanion Brotherhood in year 332. These monks were charged with keeping people in line with their faith but by offering spiritual guidance, not with threats. They kept charge of the church and were even allowed to help within Knox, which had all but shut itself off. With the influence of the brotherhood, things went smoothly in Enox, and it seemed people were behaving without having to do so at gunpoint.

Alongside the red-robed brothers of the Mortanions, the church also formed the Aegian Sisterhood. Unlike their brothers, the sisters did not go out and spread the word, nor did they maintain the churches. Their sole purpose was to reside in the temple built on the neighboring Lain Island, where they prayed. Every sworn woman of the Sisterhood would spend the day of her vow until her last inside the temple praying only that Aegis' will would be done. They wear all white and are nearly never seen by outsiders or even the brotherhood, as it is considered taboo.

Knox remained completely isolated from all lands, allowing only members of the brotherhood to cross the borders. This was done to keep the land pure from the influence of the interlopers, even after the extinction of the ogres in the year 565. The emperors of Knox sent their officers on missions outward to retrieve resources and to keep tabs on the wickedness of the heretics. Knox became a looming threat, for behind its walls were battalions that could be unleashed without warning. On these scouting missions supposedly sanctioned by Aegis, death followed right behind.

The Mortanions were able to reach outside of Enox, spreading the kinder word of Aegis to those willing to listen in the lands of Casperland, Alafor, and Khur. Despite this gentle approach, the faith did not spread far in these lands due to the evil they saw inflicted in that God's name by Knox.

Things carried on much the same for centuries, until the doubt of humans all over Corseca got smashed in the year 944. After hundreds of attempts, a pilgrimage of monks finally succeeded in entering the Startspring. The expedition was comprised of a bishop named Ashton, three young monks, and two women of the Aegian Sisterhood. This was the first time they ever involved the sisters, also the only recorded time sisters ever left the temple. Their purpose was to pray for Aegis' will and that it hopefully be their mission's success.

Be it the presence of the sisters or not, the mission did succeed. The small dinghy fought its way through the constant storm surrounding the Aegis Isles, and they found calm at the cliffs of the star-shaped waterfall.

At the southwestern point of the Spring they found a dry cliff where they were able to anchor the ship and descend to the pit where all life began. They could not get all the way down, for the rapids and heat from the planet's core would devour them. That did not matter, as they found all they would need only two hundred meters down. Within a cave in the cliffs was an inscription scrawled by the fingers of the Spirit of Existence. The brothers got rubbings of the walls and even obtained photographs, although they were primitive and not well developed. Regardless of the simplicity of it, they still had enough proof of the message to bring it back and translate it.

The group returned with their findings six months after they had departed. Everyone was sure the mission had failed yet again, but to their delight they instead brought with them what is referred to as the Promise of Aegis. After a year of deciphering and studying, the members of the brotherhood came to understand this was a message left by Spirit. It detailed how it bestowed its power to Aegis and granted Him dominion over Corseca. It spoke of the origin of Aegis and Spirit; however, that part was beyond comprehension or translation it seemed. The Spirit then promised it would revive itself one day and rejoin Aegis, but only in the land who proved to be most loved by Him.

Knox knew this had to be them, but they also hungered for the real Promise. They sent their fiercest battleships to go to the exact point the monks had to descend the Startspring. They wanted to rip the cave walls out and study them in their own kingdom; however, none of these expeditions succeeded. Thousands of Knox soldiers died trying to perform a task seven holy people in a crude boat had performed a year prior. Knox gave up trying to get the Promise and instead devoted themselves to an even more extreme religious fervor. They would be the land where Spirit revived; it was the only possibility.

The Mortanions wanted to share this information with all the people of Corseca, as it seemed to be concrete proof at last of God Aegis. They also encouraged scholars of neighboring countries to verify the authenticity of the original rubbings as much as they could. They wanted to share this gift with everyone; it mattered not which land was chosen.

Although it was not the Promise itself, those foreign scholars could not disprove the validity of what they saw. The dim, fuzzy photographs confirmed it to be the genuine article, and a massive conversion spread across the lands of Khur and Casperland. Both those nations were spiritualist or completely neutral, their beliefs ranging from in Spirit alone, nothing, or anywhere in between, which made the transition rather simple. Alafor had their own religion, a conflicting albeit complementary faith known as Spathalíeism. Due to their current faith, even with the discovery of the Promise, MortiAegism held little sway.

The King of Casperland, Quincey Helvendeere II, was so moved by the discovery of the Promise he officially converted his land's national religion to MortiAegism is 949. He sought the help of the brotherhood, opening churches throughout the capital. He went to so far as to appoint a Mortanion Cardinal as his chief advisor, opposed to the scholar knights Logos who had always been right hand to the king in the past.

The sudden shift toward devotion in Casperland terrified the Emperor of Knox, Halix III, into waging war against them. He would not allow another land to gain Spirit's favor. At first, Casperland did nothing but defend themselves, but as the war raged on over decades they fought back. When Halix III was succeeded by his son, Halix IV, the war grew outrageous. He turned his sights to all lands outside of the continent Knox, making enemies of Alafor and Khur as well. His goal was to eliminate all others so that his kingdom would be the only choice.

This war that still rages on is known as the Aegis Conflict. The heaviest number of casualties occurred in the bombings of Pottleton in 975, a neutral township of Alafor, and Casper in 978, the second largest city of Casperland. Knox bombed the City of Wings in 978 as well, a metropolis on Alafor's eastern shore, yet a blizzard dampened its destructiveness. Casperland sent numerous battalions to Knox as counterattack, the most successful of which being the scourge of Thornwood in 980. Knights and monks killed over 70 percent of the hundreds of thousands living there. Thornwood was not a key military target, but it still served as a grave threat to Knox.

There has been no sign of submission on any side in the war. The church refuses to speak on Aegis' behalf, neither condemning nor condoning the war. Despite constant pressure, the Archbishop of the Mortanion Brotherhood also refuses to muse on the chosen land whatsoever.

The neutrality of the church and the complete lack of communication between nations are leading the conflict to seem endless. Faith in MortiAegism seems to still be going strong; however, resentfulness toward the church has also grown as the war rages on. This is especially true in Khur and Casperland, though any voicing of this is a punishable offense.

Another thing of note is the relationship between the MortiAegis faith and faelocks. Despite the fact that the parents of the species are the two condemned interlopers, the spawn themselves are not necessarily hated. This species is believed to have not yet existed at the time of the prophet, so his voice on it is not known, but the church vehemently believes Aegis and the prophet would show these creatures mercy. The reasoning for this is based on intent. The ogres and faeries were intentional in their theft of the spark of life; they themselves craved it and stole it. The faelocks were simply the offspring of thieves; they had no choice in their birth or in not being human.

Although they are not condemned, it is also thought they are not welcome in the kingdom of heaven as they are not Aegis' children. Some more benevolent members of the Mortanion Brotherhood feel that with true faith and devotion to the teachings, even faelocks can join in the afterlife promised. Conversely, there are groups within the church who treat faelocks the same as the other interlopers and disagree with showing acceptance of their kind. This sentiment is almost exclusively found in Knox, where faelocks are treated as subhumans and live very difficult lives.

APPENDIX II

A Brief History of the Casperland Nation

THE CONTINENT of Centra had been inhabited by nomadic tribes since the beginning of recorded history; however, it did not become widely populated until near the year 300. A mass exodus from Knox began a decade after the death of the prophet of Aegis and the subsequent wide spreading of MortiAegism. Heretics, doubters, all those vehement in the continued practice of magic, as well as those who voiced their belief solely in the Spirit of Existence, were sent either west to Centra or east to Khur. Amongst all this forced exile by the church, a group of about two thousand people, spiritualists and students of philosophy, sought freedom from the growing control of MortiAegism.

The group was organized by a young man named Darus Helvendeere. He and many of the other pilgrims had been students of the great philosopher Casperius, an over three-hundred-year-old ogre. It was after the execution of Casperius by the emperor of Knox in 274 that they began planning their relocation. After the teacher's death, his students decided to identify themselves as students of Logos. They were the followers of the logic spoken by Casperius, not sheep led by blind faith in Aegis.

They were some of the best educated people on the globe in those primitive times and were able to discreetly prepare and assemble their five ships, draw up blueprints for their new structures, and come up with detailed plans for their new society. In early winter of the year 289, they sailed south from the Aegis-controlled shores of Knox, hoping to create a home for themselves in the Palelands.

Prior to departing, the students of Logos and the other dissenters had agreed upon emulating Knox and forming a tribunal of sorts. They determined it should be a group of three acting as leader, an ogre and two humans, one Logos and one not. They also decided to later implement an elected governing body to handle most matters. The group took it upon themselves to choose leaders before departing so that order could be managed as quickly as possible in their new home. The Logos overwhelmingly chose the brave and charismatic Darus, as well as highly endorsing Casperius's brother, Drummond, as the ogre party. Drummond was indeed chosen; he and Darus were joined by the leader elect of the outsiders, a sorceress from the southern tip of Knox named Lyllu Misril.

A succession of storms and a strong western current blew them well off course. One ship was lost completely; however, the other four ended their grueling journey in the spring of the year 290, when they finally hit land. Upon disembarking, they thought they actually had reached the Palelands due to the peninsula's similar shape. It was not; instead it was the tail of the large continent Centra. This new nation was named Casperland in honor of their teacher, with the first colony known simply as Casper.

The two human leaders journeyed in the same vessel, whereas Drummond rode in a separate ship designed to transport ogres comfortably. The ship held about twenty ogres as well as a good fifty Logos and other humans. This ship was tragically the one that separated from the group. It not only got blown off course by the typhoon, it is also widely believed that the ship was caught in the swirling storm surrounding the Startspring. Of the few successful ventures to the Aegis Isles, ogre bones were found on the eastern and southern isles. They do not deteriorate the way human bones eventually would, so it is plausible that they could belong to Drummond or his comrades.

Despite Casperland not being the intended destination, they embraced the land they found. They got to work at once on building up structures, the skeleton of what would be their utopian city, but the work did not go easily. In all their planning and the schematics they had drawn up, they planned to rely heavily on ogre strength. With their ogres missing, the work was spread amongst all the humans. No one was exempt from the toil, not even Darus or Lyllu. Luckily, the Logos connected with some of the nomadic natives and were able to get their assistance as well. These natives were never treated as slaves; conversely they were the only workers reimbursed monetarily for their toil. By the year

293, the settlement was mostly complete. All the habitations were constructed; a large common eating hall and bazaar were built, as well as the small but carefully crafted Hall of Logos, the building that would hold the tribunal.

All the time spent leading together brought Lyllu and Darus so close that they eventually fell in love and married. Darus had refused to entertain the idea of electing a third member to the tribunal before their marriage, as he was convinced Drummond would make his way to them eventually. After their matrimony it was clear they were essentially living as monarchs of the thriving society, which disturbed Darus. He did not want to be above his people, he wanted to be amongst them. He finally gave up on Drummond and pushed for a third member to be chosen, yet both the elected parliament and his brothers of Logos objected.

They had come to accept the idea of a monarch as ruler of their land, as it was easy for the people to understand. They determined it would not turn out awful or militaristic as it had in Knox as long as the power did not belong to the king alone. The ruling of Casperland would still be divided by three, but they would be three groups, not three individuals. No laws could be passed without majority vote, and no vote would be more valuable than the others. One vote would be held by the senate, those elected by the people themselves (referred to as the hand vote); the second vote would come from the Logos, the educated scholars who were eternally devoted to their land (the head vote); the third would come from the symbolic leader of Casperland, the king or queen whose blood came from its first leaders, Darus and Lyllu Helvendeere (the heart vote).

Darus himself did not understand this, as he was a student of Logos, nothing more. He felt he should not have a vote separate from theirs. His contemporaries had come up with this monarchy on their own and were quite convinced it would benefit them. They believed that having a party one must be born into—with no possibility of buying membership or entrance to— would eliminate its corruption in ways the senate and even the Logos could be vulnerable to. Despite the fact they wouldn't know the goodness of each monarch to come, it was assured at least they could not be handpicked by any enemy. Darus felt there was merit to their argument, although he believed in the idea of pure democracy and thought it should be given a chance. He was alone in this idealism, and so he submitted to his own coronation.

The nation of Casperland grew to become much what their forefathers had dreamed of; a society focused on logic and scholarly endeavors, not budging on its stance of spiritual neutrality. The city of Casper grew large and industrialized at a rapid pace. The three-vote rule had worked splendidly, and there had been no internal conflict worth mentioning. In the year 410 it was clear the people of Casperland were outgrowing the first settlement, and it was decided that a new colony should be formed.

A group of specialized Logos who were trained in combat, known as knights, scouted out the land heavily. They eventually decided on a plot of land next to a canyon sitting beside the ocean, perfect for a port. The land was quite fertile and mostly vacant and it would offer a much needed contrast from the crowded and industrial Casper. The only peoples living in that region were all of the same family. They were living in squalor, sleeping in crude wooden structures, and hunting for their meals. They seemed to be completely wild, yet they communicated with the knights just fine. They identified themselves as the DuBois, masters of the land on which they stood.

The Logos were expecting some contest from the DuBois in acquiring this land for their new city, but they were surprisingly accommodating. Their demands were simple: that they got to have the largest and fanciest house, people to clean it for them, and to never have their position as wealthiest in town disputed. The knights were shocked such savages knew of things like wealth and status, yet they were willing to indulge them. Casper was to remain home of the King and Queen, so there was no worry in giving the DuBois a grander estate.

The parliament was hesitant to give special treatment to strangers; however, the scouting knights had won over their elders and the current King, Jacob Helvendeere, by convincing them that it was an indisputably perfect location. Not only was the land fertile and quite temperate, the canyon port it sat against could prove invaluable from military and trading standpoints. The agreement with the DuBois got both the head and heart votes, commencing the building of Casperland's second great city. It too came to be named after an ogre, and Drummond was a livable habitation by the year 422.

The city had four distinct quarters originally designed for agricultural purposes. It allowed for a cycle between fallow lands, active crops, and livestock to be moved seasonally, with the eastern quarter surrounding the port. The eastern quarter's focus was and remains fishery and importing. In the center sat what started as a house but eventually became a massive palace.

The Logos had thought the wealth the DuBois had spoken of would have to be provided to them, but they were quite wrong. From whence it came is unknown, yet the DuBois had vast stores of gold and gems. It appeared they simply wanted acknowledgment of their nobility and to finally look the part. The DuBois not only funded the ever increasing palace, but also poured money into building up Drummond. Despite the filth they lived in before, it seemed they were not satisfied with their city being simply a country farm.

Drummond grew to be just as large and industrialized as Casper in less than a century. A Hall of Logos was constructed beside the DuBois Palace, and later a secondary parliamentary house was built in the southern quarter so that all politics of Drummond could be handled from within. All farming was pushed out to a few villages surrounding Drummond; however, they still thrived and provided vital resources deftly to both cities.

The storms raging in the southern ocean of Corseca are constant, making trade to Casper difficult from the other large nations. Despite that, Casper had the distinct advantage of being parallel to the Palelands and landed at the end of a strong western current from that island. The Palelands was one of two places where ogres could still be found and the only where faeries lived amongst other species. The magical wares and advanced medicines that came from them were unlike any others, and the only place with whom they traded was Casper. This made it the wealthiest city on the planet and helped establish trading relationships with many other nations. Those nations would still go through Drummond, but all the goods were thanks to Casper.

Casper's fortune took a drastic turn in 561, though the tragedy was not truly its own. Corseca suffered a ground-shattering quake, the effects of which spread the entire globe, with the epicenter lying under the Palelands. The movement of the plates was so sudden and severe that it triggered the plentiful natural gasses beneath the island to release in excess. Among these were methane and carbon monoxide, deadly substances that spread over the entire land. All creatures present on that island, all the ogres, anything organic was killed off either by firestorms or simply poisoned. The land remains arid and has never recovered. The gas leaks continually, and the island appears to be cloaked in dingy clouds. Ogre bones have been seen via telescope amongst the broken landscape, but any expedition to the Palelands was aborted before docking. The land is so toxic that many travelers fell ill or perished simply from sailing too close.

Casper was affected by the quake some as well; however, it was merely structural damage with no casualties. The true harm was Casper's new obsolescence in trading. Casper was an industrial city and could produce goods but was now devoid of its constant cash flow. Casper's economy became dependent on the success of Drummond. It seemed the rest of the globe was aware of the capital's weakness and almost all diplomatic meetings were henceforth held in Drummond.

It was apparent by the year 600 that Drummond needed to become the new capital, at least in terms of foreign relations. The governing bodies were unsure of whether the royal family needed to be moved until they received an impossibly good offer. The Knights of Logos had met with the patron family DuBois to inquire of their thoughts on moving the capital. They thought they would be met with resistance; instead, the current head, Chammerline VII, was ecstatic. She had long wanted to mingle with the royal family and to have their lineages mix. She offered up DuBois Palace as the new Helvendeere Castle on the condition that her daughter Gertrude would be promised to the next heir, the ten-year-old Prince Quincey I.

Chammerline had the second largest estate in City Drummond constructed within two months, choosing the most industrial quarter. The western edge of town had the easiest land to snatch from its poor owners and also the flimsiest of buildings to knock down, so it was a rather practical decision. It was strange for the richest residents to suddenly be neighbors with the poorest, yet the DuBois seemed to not care about such things.

Although the DuBois had already constructed their new home, the relocation was not yet agreed upon. The vote of three still needed to be held on this sudden move of their nation's seat of power. The hand vote was given easily, as most parliamentary actions were already taking place solely in Drummond, as well as the majority of the senate residing there. The heart vote was no; Queen Lylia Helvendeere was completely against the idea. She hated not only the promise of her son but also the idea of abandoning the land first constructed for the Logos. She felt if the royal family were moved, Casper's decline would be hastened, if not ensured. The head vote took over a year to be given but eventually was a yes. The Logos also hated leaving behind the city their predecessors built with their bare hands, yet that sentimentality was not worth the success of Casperland. If the nation were to truly thrive, adaptation was necessary.

Drummond officially became the capital of Casperland in the spring of 601. By the end of that same year, twelve-year-old Quincey Helvendeere wed the twenty-nine-year-old Gertrude DuBois. For the first time in their shared history, the patron family and the royal family were connected both legally and by blood.

Casperland's economy and foreign relations really did improve with the relocation. Peace was enjoyed throughout the continent of Centra, and a strong bond was formed with the northern neighbors in Alafor. Casperland also became highly involved with Enox and gave much needed aide to the struggling Khur, assuring themselves another ally. Everything appeared to be going well, but there was internal struggle.

Lylia Helvendeere died suddenly in the year 603, resulting in the immediate coronation of Quincey I and his bride. Quincey was only fourteen and easily manipulated by his mature wife. She had already produced him an heir, Jacob, and was pregnant with their daughter, Joan, by the time of their coronation. They would have later another son, Eckhold, who would actually become king.

Queen Gertrude was independently wealthy as a DuBois and wielded all the more power because of it. She resented the three-vote system and the way it removed power from the royal couple, despite the fact that it was the only reason she even became Queen. She secretly began pushing at the parliament, even threatening the removal of DuBois funds. Her goal was to get them to introduce legislature for a fourth vote, one for the King and one for the Queen. She argued that both Lyllu and Darus were the founders of the country. It was not fair the king held all the power. (Her exact words were, "Darus did'nae 'ave more sovereignty tucked away in his sack.") This did not seem to resonate with them, for Lyllu's role as a non-Logos leader was truly given to parliament, but the financial threats did.

In the year 606, Parliament officially introduced a bill to create a fourth vote, titled the home vote but known as the Queen's. It was immediately voted down by the Logos, as it ensured that there would be constant stalemates, and its only real function was to give the crown a second say. Despite all reason, King Quincey I sided with his wife and voted yes, passing the catastrophic law. The Logos were able at least to strategize the solution to tied votes. They decided to arrange impromptu elections by randomly chosen citizens for an impartial fifth voice. Gertrude was certain the DuBois would remain entangled within the royal family and would be able to buy off those voters as well, so she posed no contest.

Queen Gertrude used her new power to begin the spread of MortiAegism throughout Casperland. She had converted along with her father as a child and was ravenously devout. She got nowhere with her more orthodox proposals, such as the genocide of faelocks and homosexuals and the outlawing of prophylactics (the fifth vote always siding with reason despite her bribes), but she did succeed in getting the first churches built. Northern and Southern Quarter temples were constructed and members of the Mortanion Brotherhood became residents of the nation for the first time. Queen Gertrude was quite unpopular for this with most, but she also drew many followers who sought the comfort of religion.

The Queen's ultimate goal was to officially convert the country to MortiAegism. By the time it was introduced as a bill in 616, her husband had perished. He was only twenty-six and died in a hunting accident, though it is widely believed the wound was self-inflicted. Due to his passing, there was no crowned king and also no heart vote. The conversion was thrown out, and many protections were put in place for their spiritual neutrality in this time of three votes.

The Queen, the heir Jacob, and her daughter were all victim to a plague of smallpox that spread through Drummond during the year 620. This resulted in the crown being passed to the five-year-old Eckhold Helvendeere, who was advised by the acting captain of Logos until his eighteenth birthday. With the guidance of the captain and minus the influence of his mother, Eckhold grew up focused on preserving the ideals on which his country was founded. He righted many wrongs brought about by his parents but also kept the relationship they forged with Enox strong. He felt all faiths had a place in Casperland, even MortiAegis, and did much to cement their place within Drummond.

Contrary to what Gertrude had dreamed, another DuBois never married into the royal family. Eckhold was loyal to the Order and married a knight from within it. Queen Stila chose to set aside the home vote, never using it for herself, viewing it as an unfair power. Eckhold still conferred with her on his own votes, but her sacrifice encouraged politics to go much smoother during their reign.

Most Queens to follow put aside the home vote as well, but not Queen Lyllu II, crowned in 810. She was the only Helvendeere heir of her generation and thus felt herself the rightful monarch. She forced her husband to set aside the heart vote in her stead, continuing the peace brought by majority votes. Despite the progressiveness of the first leaders of Casperland, the foundation of their society was still traditionally patriarchal. This led to the monarch always being the first-born male, except in cases such as Lyllu II when there was none. Female citizens would take the family names of their husband; however, with the royal family Helvendeere stayed the last name; all crowned Queens would change their husband's names instead. Equality between the sexes was better in Casperland than it was in most nations but still obviously stilted. Perhaps Gertrude's comment was accurate, at least toward the feelings of the forefathers.

Drummond continued its growth into a grand metropolis, yet Casper was not far behind. It remained the continent's capital for industry and was home to a great many scientific researchers, who founded the Misril Institute. It was also a very popular residence for faelocks, as MortiAegism never took any hold there. Faelocks felt completely free of persecution within the walls of Casper and held many positions of power.

COMMUNITIES:

Only three townships outside of Drummond have remained populated since the bombing of Casper. The first is Codswell, a tiny fisherman's hamlet on the western shore, about parallel to Drummond. The village of Arronvil sits northwest of Drummond and is the chief agricultural site of the nation. All the residents are farmers and have been treated more and more like servants of the state since the bombing of Casper. The last of the villages that are still inhabited is on the northeast side, near the shoreline at the base of Mt. Kimper. Grummlet is a mining town that was also marginalized by Aldrious and Quincey, but the rowdiness of its inhabitants allowed it to retain more of its independence than the other two.

CLIMATE:

Given Corseca's tilted axis, the southern side is always facing the sun, turning somewhat up during winter months. This causes the northern pole to be cold almost all the time and the south always sweltering. Casperland is fairly central, though stretches far enough to have many different climates. The Casper Peninsula is humid and tropical with a three-month rainy season, in sync with the tilted orbit. The middle section where Drummond is located had been historically temperate with a mildly wet spring and cold, rainy winter. The weather changed dramatically as the city grew, though the reason is yet to be understood. Drummond and its outlying areas grew hotter and hotter, becoming near miserable in the last century. Despite the lack of rain, it grew more humid, adding to the unpleasantness.

The western shore is stormy with a very warm first half of the year and a very cold, rainy second half. There were four villages along its side, but only Codswell has survived the last decade's unbearable sanctions on travel and trade. The eastern shore south of Drummond is plagued by storms and is so constantly blasted by wind and waves it cannot be inhabited. The northern part of Casperland is heavily forested and rather cold most of the year: the eastern side of it is drier, getting frost at the border; the western half is more lush and rainy, getting snow the second half of the year.

Demographic:

As is true for many nations on the globe, the appearance of the Casperland population takes most after its family heir. The first Chammerline had pale ivory skin dotted with freckles, fiery red hair, and bright blue eyes. All the family members and nomadic tribes looked as such, though some were blonde or brunette, before the influx of Logos from Knox. Knox being as large as it is and having the largest population in ancient times, the appearance of the pilgrims varied greatly. There were some that carried with them the looks of the southern heir (raven hair, mahogany skin, gray eyes), but there were plenty of varying shades of tan skin and darkness of brown hair and eyes that traveled over. The new residents and old mated, making Casperland even more of a mixed bag in terms of appearance. More than any other nation, it has variety in appearance, and there is no "typical" Casper. The Helvendeere family itself has changed in appearance vastly throughout the centuries, only taking its turn toward pale since the marrying of Gertrude DuBois.

The society started as scholars, magicians, and carpenters but has weeded out the middle group and now plays host to hundreds of professions. South Drummond is famous for clothing designers and haberdashers. The northern quarter has a thriving literary community and a large mercantile industry. The western quarter still has an abundance of factory workers and drunks. Casper was renowned for its chemists and geneticists, but with it gone much of the research was lost as well. Within the two large cities, well-funded educational systems were in place for all children in public schools and also in the Logos Academy for gifted children. Education was affected little by the nation's conversion; however, many families opted to have their children tutored at home or in church schools by the brotherhood instead. This still made for an intellectually thriving society but led one side to be more fervent and biased. In the poorer sides of Drummond, namely Westend and the Northwest, parents forced their children to apprentice or work instead. This led to low attendance and the schools being not as well maintained as the rest of the city. The outlying areas suffered more from the conversion, their tutors being completely replaced by monks. MortiAegism seemed to be the only subject comprehensively covered, along with installing a sense of duty to continue the specific trades that benefit the nation (farming, fishing, etc.). After the bombing of Casper, Drummond grew extremely overcrowded with survivors. This dropped student enrollment, increased unemployment, and desperately increased poverty.

L. ROCKWOOD is survived by his artist wife, Rae, and their three adorable but stupid cats. He is also quite alive however terribly morbid. It is thanks to this macabre fascination (and likely his Scorpio moon) that death and rebirth is the central focus of all his works. L. definitely has a lighter side, usually manifesting in hot pink or glitter, as he is just as obsessed with all things kawaii.

L. is an out and proud pansexual transgender man. He draws from his own experiences, striving to celebrate the various and beautiful ways love and sexuality can manifest through his characters. His time is split between the Central and Lost Coasts of California. He has yet to spot his favorite animal, the unicorn, in his travels, but he will never give up hope.

Also from Dreamspinner Press

WARRIOR PLEDGE
E E MONTGOMERY

www.dreamspinnerpress.com